EXODUS:
GOD OF THE SLAVES

I0564126

KRIS MURRAY

Published by: BibleByte Bookskindle
PO Box 701
Maple Valley, Washington 98038
1.425.413.1185
www.BibleByteBooks.com

Printed in the United States of America

ISBN-13 978-1-937161-25-5 (Print Edition)
ISBN-13 978-1-937161-23-1 (Electronic Edition)

Publisher: Philip Conrod
Editor: Nancy Rouche
Book Cover: Neil Savageau

The people, places, and events depicted are fictitious. No association with any real person, place, or event is intended or should be inferred.

This book expresses the author's views and opinions.

Dedication

I dedicate this book, Exodus: God of the Slaves, to:

My wife and son, whom I love and are an
inspiration to me for all the work in which I endeavor.

And

The God of Abraham, Isaac, and Jacob to whom I
give all the glory for the work I do.

Acknowledgements:

My wife, for helping me make time to write.

My mother, for her encouragement and help to review and edit the book.

Nancy Roche, for editing the book and providing expert feedback to improve it.

Neil Savageau, for the design of the cover art.

"Lord, I have heard of your fame;

I stand in awe of your deeds, Lord.

Repeat them in our day,

    In our time make them known…"

   - Habakuk 3:2 (NIV)

Chapter 1

Drops of water splashed onto Yalu's hands as he plopped down on the fine desert sand. He quickly licked them up so none went to waste. Stretching out his legs, he finally felt relief from the ache in his feet. He lifted the clay jar to his lips and drank. As he lowered it, the warmth from the fire slapped him in the face, but it was a welcome slap and he smiled with satisfaction.

Behind him, the large band of merchants and soldiers in the caravan were unpacking their camels and carts to setup tents and fires for the evening. The caravan leader told Yalu that with over a thousand camels carrying goods for barter, he needs good men like him. The few other individuals and families who bartered into the protection of the caravan setup smaller tents or fur blankets nearby the fire warming Yalu.

Pinpricks of light shone through cuts and holes of the cloak worn by a man with curly gray hair walking toward him from behind the fire. It crackled and sent a shower of sparks into the windy twilight air as he passed by. The sparks ascended into the swirling colors of blue, red, and yellow. Yalu's eyes followed them up until they went out and he noticed a plume of smoke rising from behind a dune.

Yalu frowned when the man passed by a few others warming themselves by the fire and sat next him. He took another drink. "Desert bandits again?" Yalu asked. The man nodded. "Flesh and Fire, Lior! They've been plaguing us the entire trip. Why Set doesn't take them is beyond me."

"And since Set doesn't take them for killing your father, brother, and wife, the job fell on you?" Lior looked down at his friend with concern. He always felt the need to say something to help but it never seemed to come out the way he intended it.

Yalu took a breath as anger swelled up within him. Images of the ruined wagon and the bodies lying on the ground flowed into his mind like the flooding season of the Nile. If it were anyone but Lior he'd have sent him sprawling. He took another drink and calmed himself. "A lot of jobs fall on me lately. Getting vengeance is one I take willingly. Tell me what happened."

Lior gazed toward the rising smoke and shook his head, "Bandits seemed to have just left. A handful of survivors remain. The guard-leader wants his second in command to take some of us and investigate."

Yalu sighed and nodded toward the fire. Lior looked into his face with interest as he waited. Yalu took a final drink and set the clay jar in the sand. Then he got up and, with his aching feet, started off toward the smoke. Lior followed behind.

By the time Yalu and Lior arrived at the burning wreckage, they found two other guards to follow them. A familiar sight of dead laying on the ground and wounded moaning in pain littered the area. Most of the uninjured were tending to them. Then, one of the elders took notice of the four and approached them cautiously.

Stepping forward, Yalu said, "We came with a caravan from Wadi Maghereh and saw the smoke. Bandits?"

The old man looked relieved. He nodded and continued walking up to them. "Yes, they came upon us while we were getting ready to camp for the night. Alas, they killed a good number of our fighting men and stole the young maidens travelling with us, as well as our food and supplies. My name is Aaron, can you help us?"

"We'll see. Finish tending to your dead and come join us across the sand." Yalu pointed back the way they came.

"You said you come from Wadi Maghereh? Do you perchance have a traveler named Moses with you? I must speak with him." He asked.

Lior spoke up, "Indeed we do. He came with his family."

"There will be time to talk later," said Yalu. "Where did the bandits go?"

Aaron motioned with his head to his left, his long gray beard swaying in the wind. Yalu saw a large rocky outcropping not too far away. He touched the bronze shield slung across his back and stroked the hilt of the curve-bladed khopesh next to it.

As he turned and was about to take a step the old man protested. "You're not going after them, are you? There were at least thirty who attacked. What chance would the four of you have against so many?"

Yalu looked at Aaron over his shoulder with an impatient look. Lior took the initiative and talked to the man in a language Yalu didn't understand. Aaron first looked surprised and then nodded at Yalu with admiration.

Yalu took another step when one of the guards spoke up, "Sir, shouldn't we ask the guard-leader first?"

"That's a good idea," Yalu stopped and looked at him. "Why don't you go ask him?"

The man nodded and ran back toward their camp. After watching him for a few moments Yalu turned again toward where the bandits went and continued walking. The remaining guard, who was rather young, stood confused. But Lior chuckled to himself and jogged to follow. The other finally followed suit.

"You know the guard-leader's going to yell at you again," Lior said when he caught up.

"My father always told me to say what is right and do what is right."

"I'm not sure this was what he had in mind."

Yalu didn't reply. He kept his eyes on the ground. There was just enough light to follow the footprints. "By the time we ask him and run back, who knows what will happen to those maidens. The sooner we can rescue them the better."

"Assuming they're still alive."

"Oh, the maidens are still alive. I'm sure of that," Yalu said grimly.

Lior cringed in response. He and the other guard followed Yalu to the rock in silence. Luckily, they saw no signs of watchful eyes. When Yalu scanned the horizon he easily spotted the glow of campfires to the East.

Yalu took a cloth and covered his bronze shield. When the young guard looked at him curiously he said, "Don't want a beam of light to give us away." Lior and the other guard also covered up exposed metal.

Leading them underneath the crest of a sand dune, Yalu saw that the bandits were hiding out among some ruins. He could see broken stone columns and piles of rubble from the last light of the setting sun. They hid behind an exposed rock as Yalu caught sight of a watchman standing between two such columns.

"No doubt all they guard all entrances." Lior scowled as he moved his head to get a better view.

"He's right," the young guard growled. "It would be best if we left without being seen."

"Maybe," Yalu said softly. "And maybe not. Follow me."

When the watchman was looking away, Yalu led them, creeping toward the right side of the ruins where there was another large outcropping of rock. When they made it, Yalu looked back to make sure they weren't spotted and started climbing.

"Where are going? What are doing?" Do you mean to circle the ruins to look for a way in?" The young guard asked while trying to find his footing.

"I'll wager you know something we don't." Lior looked up at Yalu who looked over his shoulder and slyly grinned.

When they reached the top, they saw various shrubs growing that made it easier to hide from any searching eyes. But hiding wasn't Yalu's aim. He went straight to a big flat rock. He started to lift it and after the others helped move it they saw a dark hole underneath.

"How did you know that was there?" The young guard asked in muffled surprise.

Yalu didn't answer. He just climbed down. "Lior, hand me one of your lamps."

Lior did as requested and when Yalu lit it they could see him in the passageway which sloped downward, toward the ruins. Lior lit another lamp and they started down. The tunnel, cut in the rock, snaked back and forth, always going deeper and deeper into the ground. The ceiling was short and they had to hunch over as they walked.

"A couple years ago I was travelling with a caravan. While out scouting I stumbled across this secret passage that goes into the ruins," Yalu explained. "I... spent too much time exploring these tunnels when I needed to be elsewhere."

"Are you here to join the dead?" Said a high-pitched whispery voice.

Yalu stopped in his tracks and whirled around shouting, "I am not!"

Lior and the other guard stared with astonishment into his angry brown eyes. The guard asked quietly, "Not what?"

Yalu stared at the guard intently, making him feel as though he did something wrong. Then he shook himself and looked down, his anger slowly fading. "We're wasting time here. Let's go."

Then Yalu turned and continued down the passage. Lior and the young guard exchanged puzzled glances but quickly followed behind him. They left the winding tunnel behind and continued straight. Here, the passage turned to stone slabs and the ceiling was high enough they could raise their arms and still not touch it.

He led them through several chambers and forks in the tunnel. Finally, they arrived at a dead end. Yalu looked up and the other two looked up with him at an odd-looking square stone on the ceiling.

"Lift me on your shoulders, Lior." Yalu said. "Let's see where we are."

Lior offered his interlocked hands to Yalu who stepped in them to his shoulders. Lior grabbed Yalu's legs to help balance him and the young guard helped by stabilizing Lior's torso. Then, Yalu slowly lifted the square tile up on one side.

Boisterous laughter and shouts filled their ears and dim firelight invaded the dark recesses of the tunnel. Yalu saw numerous campfires, men talking and making merry, as well a number of stockpiled supplies and weapons. But he didn't see what he was looking for, so he lowered the stone square and hopped off Lior's shoulders.

"Not here, let's try a different one." Yalu grabbed the lamp and ran off.

Rushing to catch up, Lior asked, "What's not there? What are we looking for?"

By that time they found themselves in another dead end. Rather than explain himself, Yalu indicated that Lior give him his hands again to get on his shoulders. This time, when he peeked through the crack in the stone he smiled.

After he hopped off Lior's shoulders he said, "Found them! This way."

"You mean the maidens?" the guard asked with surprise. But both he and Lior huffed to keep up with Yalu.

"This should be it," Yalu breathed as they reached one more dead end. When he lifted up the stone he looked up at a shocked young woman. He quickly put a finger to his lips indicating for her to remain silent. However, one of the women gasped when they saw him.

"What's going on?" asked a deep rough voice.

"Rats!" said the young woman. "Mary here saw a rat scurry by and was frightened. If you weren't so messy with your food then there wouldn't be so many pests."

The voice laughed deeply. "We let the pests stay together. And don't worry, your turn will come."

Yalu waited for the woman to look back down at him. He raised the stone higher and motioned for her to come down. She quickly got the attention of the other maidens soon they were sliding down into the tunnel one by one.

Just as the last maiden came down and Yalu was about ready to lower the stone square, it was lifted up and Yalu found himself face to face with one of the bandits.

"Rats for sure!" The man shouted. He swung his sword at Yalu's head who hopped off Lior's shoulders just in time. Then he shouted for help and an alarm raised within the bandit camp.

"Run!" Yalu shouted as he worked his way to the front. "Lior, you two take the rear!"

Lior drew his sword and backed up facing the dead end as first one bandit dropped down, then another, and another. He looked to his side and saw the young guard looking scared. "Don't worry. I've fought many battles with Yalu against bandits like these. He knows what he's doing."

The young guard glanced back and Lior could tell he didn't feel as scared. They kept running behind the maidens, hoping Yalu would lead them the right way.

Yalu ran through the tunnels. He looked back and made sure the maidens following him were keeping up. As he continued running through three-way intersection he nearly jumped out of his skin when a woman appeared in the darkness on the left-hand side.

"Stop running. You belong with us," she said. Her long black hair and the white linen dress Yalu always liked waved as though a draft was drifting through the tunnels. Her skin was the color of ripe barley and her lips like pomegranates.

He stared at her and gaped. He felt a tug at his heart drawing him to her. It compelled him to take a step closer. She looked so real. He know she wasn't, but he badly wanted her to be.

"Why have you stopped? Have you forgotten the way?" The young maiden asked in desperation. When she noticed his pale face she said, "Are you alright?"

Yalu looked at the maiden. From the flickering lamp-light he could see her soft face with dried tears from the suffering inflicted by the bandits earlier. Then he looked back at the woman in the darkness, but she was gone.

"I know the way. Follow me." Yalu continued down the passageway and the maidens followed close behind.

A few more turns of the tunnels and Yalu recognized the final straightaway to get to the exit. Just then he heard a yelp of pain from behind them.

"Take this and lead the others up to the exit." Yalu handed the young maiden his lamp and drew his khopesh and shield. The others passed and he soon saw Lior with sword in one hand while using the other to help the young guard limp back. Blood flowed from a large gash on his thigh.

From the darkness ahead, Yalu heard the sound of metal against metal. Then he heard footsteps. Stepping into the light was man holding a khopesh in each hand. He rubbed them together with a maniacal gleam in his eye. He steadily advanced, as three other men rushed passed him.

When the last maiden passed him, Yalu dashed over to Lior's side. He knocked the first bandit's blade aside with his and bashed him in the face with his shield sending him toppling backward to the ground.

The second and third froze in place as the sound echoed through the tunnels. Yalu wasted no time and after a few slashes the second and third bandits were down as well.

Yalu raised his shield just in time to block two slashes. He readied himself to block even more when a shout echoed in the tunnels. "Don't you know your place?" Another man walked into view.

The man facing Yalu smirked and replied, "Can't you see I'm busy? Lend me your blade and we'll easily strike these dirty dogs down."

As they continued to bicker, Yalu took the opportunity to feint and then knocked the bandit away with his shield. As he turned to run he noticed that Lior and the young guard were able to get away. While running he glanced behind him and was pleasantly surprised to see the two men didn't stop their argument to give chase.

When Yalu caught up to them he saw Lior was helping the young guard. Yalu asked, "Can you walk on your own?"

"I… I don't know." He said between groans of pain.

"Lior, take our weapons." Yalu lifted the man on his shoulders as Lior complied. "We need to leave before they realize where we are."

Yalu ran as fast as he could, making sure not to drop the young guard. Lior followed behind with weapons ready just in case. Soon, they reached the tunnels cut in the rocks and the hard climb up. Yalu's feet ached previously from the day's travels, but now his legs ached as he carried the young guard on his shoulders up the slope.

When they got to the exit, Lior jumped up and helped lift the young guard out of the tunnel. Then Yalu climbed out. From behind the cover of the shrubs they saw dancing shadows among the campfires and heard the shouts of angry bandits.

Lior wrapped a cloth tightly around the young guard's wound and said, "Another victory for bandit-hunter Yalu." Lior looked up and Yalu smiled back at him. "How many have you slain now?"

Yalu shrugged, "I stopped counting a long time ago." He and Lior helped him down the other side of the rock as seven maidens they rescued followed behind.

When they got to the sand below Yalu asked, "Do you think you can walk the rest of the way?"

"Sure, let me give it a-," he didn't make it two steps before he fainted. Luckily for him Yalu and Lior caught him before he hit the ground. So Yalu slung him over his shoulders once again and they walked the long way back to the caravan, out of sight of the nest of angry bandits.

The guard-leader stood next to a campfire with his arms folded watching the approaching group. When they got close enough, the maidens ran forward to meet their friends and family in joyous reunion. Yalu and Lior walked up to him and set the young guard down on the sand, who had regained his consciousness.

"What can I say?" The guard-leader sighed and shook his head. "You should have waited. But you made a good decision and have proven your bravery and strength once again. Go rest for the night. We'll have more words tomorrow as we finish our journey back to the great City of the White Walls."

Stroking the hilt of his worn khopesh behind his back, Yalu scanned the passersby, his eyes darting from one to another. A woman caught his eye. From her perfect black wig to the rings of gold hanging from her ears he guessed she must be very wealthy. A wesekh of beads and precious stones wrapped around her neck with a large jewel in the center.

"No more thieves?" Said an authoritative voice.

Yalu looked at the guard-leader and shook his head.

"Good. Stay watchful with eye of the great god Ptah himself."

Yalu wiped the sweat from his brow with the back of his hand. The armor of leather protected his upper body in battle but also protected him from the sun. He was proud of his effectiveness as a guard in the marketplace and for caravans, watching for thieves and mediating disagreements. But the guard-leader had brought him unwelcome news: an official from the city heard of his exploits and wanted to hire him.

The afternoon dragged on unpleasantly as Yalu worried what kind of work and if he could talk his way back to guarding caravans. He put up his hand to shade his eyes from Ammon-Ra rolling the sun across the goddess of the sky Nut wearing her dress of pure sapphire.

As Yalu finished enjoying the viewing of another young beauty, his eye caught a hurried motion. Turning, he saw a man start, then dash off with an armful of imported wooden planks.

"Thief!" Yalu shouted, following the criminal.

Every trader within earshot panicked for a moment, looking around to take stock of their inventory. The guard-leader, who heard the shout, returned in a moment to see Yalu giving chase.

The thief turned to an alley, but Yalu followed too closely to be lost. The light loincloth and sandals gave the thief an edge as he spryly dodged a ponderous cow, and moved deftly toward the mud and brick houses. Yalu's leather armor, hindered his agility somewhat, but he was determined. His khopesh and shield, both still strapped on his back, clanged loudly at each stride.

He chased relentlessly through the market and into the tighter maze of houses. Yalu closed the lead inexorably, pace by pace, but the thief, hearing the clangs, took a desperate and unexpected turn. Unshaken, Yalu found the thief halted in front of a dead end, who turned to face his pursuer.

Yalu approached calmly. From the side of his loincloth, the thief drew a small bone dagger and pointed it at Yalu. Sweat dropped from the man's face and he panted from the exertion.

"Have mercy!"

"Return what you stole and you might stay in the prison pit for a day or so," Yalu replied, still moving toward him.

"Please… my family must eat."

Yalu drew his sword and strapped on his shield. "You feed your family by stealing. I feed mine by catching thieves."

Intending to startle the thief, Yalu lunged forward and shallowly slashed at him. He slipped to the side, and thrust at Yalu with his dagger. The bronze shield clanged as it blocked the blow. Another swing from Yalu left a wound on the thief's shoulder. The thief yelped and flinched backward.

The two exchanged blows for a short while and the thief desperately threw the stolen planks at Yalu's head. But Yalu blocked them with his shield and rammed it into the thief's forehead. Yalu stabbed the stunned man through the shoulder. He fell to the ground, bleeding and groaning in agony.

Yalu turned from the body of his dying opponent to pick up the stolen wood planks. As he was about to leave the ally to return the stolen planks he glanced over at the thief curled up and clutching his shoulder.

This man is no bandit. Perhaps he really was trying to feed his family, Yalu thought as he watched him. In a bout of pity and guilt Yalu walked over to the man and said, "How about I wrap your wound before you lose too much blood."

As Yalu knelt down to him the thief turned toward him with fire in his eyes and the bone knife in his hand. Yalu caught the man's hand and instinctively stabbed him through the chest.

At first Yalu felt surprised by the man's sudden rage toward him. Then irritation of his offer of mercy being rejected. Not knowing what else to do, Yalu picked up the planks and left him to die alone.

"Do you see what I mean, Kasmut? This soldier is skilled," the guard-leader gestured to Yalu, after examining the returned wood.

He had introduced Kasmut as Yalu's new master. Golden rings sparkled from her ears, nose and toes in the evening sunlight. Her tall figure exuded confidence. After he saw her wesekh he recognized her as the woman who passed by him earlier.

"Yes, I see. He recovered the stolen items. But what became of the thief?"

"Dead," Yalu said bluntly. The official and Kasmut nodded approvingly.

"Yes, he has a keen eye, like the great god himself, fleet of foot, and a skilled fighter." Kasmut strolled around Yalu, examining him, "We may use those talents. Come with me."

"If I may speak my piece," Yalu started politely.

The guard-leader quickly took aside him by the shoulder and whispered in his ear, "The deal was already struck and Kasmut isn't someone you want to cross. Look, you can't keep chasing bandits your whole life. It's time to move on. Trust me."

The guard-leader looked into Yalu's eyes. Yalu thought of the duty to avenge his family. Had he done enough? Was it really time to move on?

"The wages are better." The guard-leader offered.

Yalu glanced over at Kasmut, eyeing him curiously. Then he nodded in acceptance and she led him away.

As they walked, Kasmut explained: "My husband, Rashidi, was recently appointed to oversee brick-making. The slaves are refusing to work, and some have rioted. I need soldiers to keep them in their place."

They arrived at a large estate in a part of the city in clear proximity and favor of the temple of Ptah. A limestone wall surrounded it, and guards stood watch at the large gateway. Yalu thought the house must have more than twenty rooms inside. The intricate paintings on the white-washed wall showed scenes of ancient heroes and numerous gods. On the South side of the house, a grove of palms cast shade. Yalu imagined the pool beneath the trees, and guessed that the house would have water inside as well.

"Return tomorrow at dawn. Rashidi will give you your assignment early in the morning." Then she gestured him away and walked through the gate.

Yalu took a few steps and then looked back. She entered the manor while shouting something at nearby slaves. The sun set in reds and purples behind wisps of clouds above Rashidi's manor. The darkening sky matched the darkness invading his heart.

Did I really make the right choice? He thought to himself. He felt angry at himself for abandoning his purpose so easily and wanted to kick something.

The feeling of something brushing against his leg startled him. When he looked down he saw a small cat. He stared at it as the anger burned in his eyes. Then he sighed and released a heavy breath. He crouched down and pet its back for a time. Then something caught the cat's attention, and it ran off into the darkness.

Chapter 2

Nebit crouched on the roof of a mud-brick building and surveyed the manor courtyard before her. Two guards stood at the gate with other guards casually patrolling around the walls twice her height. She saw only a few servants up and about this late inside the large two story manor house in the middle. The half-moon cast long shadows from nearby the horizon.

Her lips curled in a smile at the expectation of an easy assignment. Then she jumped down to the ground and landed silently. As she carefully approached the wall surrounding the courtyard she thought about the face of her target. She was hidden behind a drab tapestry so he couldn't see her, and could see him perfectly in the afternoon sunlight talking with her master.

But she always felt more comfortable in the dark. She followed the shadow of the building to the courtyard wall. She glanced to both sides before she leapt up and scaled the wall. Peeking over the edge she scanned the courtyard to make sure nobody was looking in her direction and then pulled herself over, hiding in the shadow of a small mud-brick storage building.

With her back to the wall, she waited for a couple of chattering guards to pass by. Her dark complexion helped her blend into the shadows. After peeking around the corner to make sure nobody was watching she darted to the shadow of the manor house itself. Then she jumped up to the window above her and climbed up.

The unlit room had a number of rugs laid out with most taken by sleeping servants. Moving her shoulder-length thin black braids out of her face, she looked at each person to make sure they were asleep before she silently slipped inside. She crept through the room out of it into the hallway.

Without difficulty, she found the stairs to the second floor where the room of her target would be. As part of her preparation, her master shared with her the floorplan of the manor. After ascending the stairs she found herself in a dark hallway with several unlit rooms on either side. But at the end of the hallway was a doorway aglow with lamp-light.

As she advanced through the hallway she heard the sound of footsteps on the stairs behind her. When she turned back and saw approaching light, she ducked into one of the dark rooms to the right.

"Well of course they wanted to see him, he has his father's cute cheeks," said a woman cheerfully.

"He may look cute but he sure has been a handful. Just like his father!" laughed another woman. "But he has your face."

"Do you think so?"

They continued to talk and, to Nebit's dismay, stopped nearby the doorway of the room she hid inside. Then she heard the sound of intelligible baby talk and of the women's soothing voices. She felt something stir within her and was compelled to risk peeking around the corner at the pair.

One of the women held a baby wrapped in fine linen and cuddled him to her face. The other stood close with an outstretched finger trying to play with him. His arms and legs moved helplessly while the sounds came from his lips. Nebit gaped with wide eyes fixed on the tiny little person.

A feeling came rushing up from inside her that she'd never felt before. Suddenly, memories of other women she saw at the temple of Ptah holding babies or being pregnant flooded her mind.

What would it be like to have one? Nebit thought to herself. *No! I can't do that. And why am I even thinking about it? I've seen them before so why am I having these feelings now?*

Then she gasped and put her hand to her mouth in horror. *Could this baby be HIS son? Do I really have to do this? I could tell my master I had to flee or be caught.*

Then she shook herself out of these thoughts and forced herself back to where she was. She slowly retracted the side of her face into her hiding place. The idea that just an innocent-looking baby could cause that effect disturbed her and wondered why this had not happened before. She took a few quiet breaths to regain her composure. After a few more moments, she heard the women continue down the hallway.

The women kept talking but this time a male voice joined them. Nebit waited. After a few minutes the women left the room and went down the stairs.

Nebit poked her head out. The hallway was empty. She crept toward the doorway with the lamplight, the predator stalking her prey.

As she approached the threshold of the doorway she heard a heavy sigh coming from inside which made her pause. She leaned her shoulder against the doorframe and leaned against it with her shoulder. She took a breath and then looked inside the room.

A large wooden bed sat in the corner on her left adorned with fine linen sheets. Across from it a window let cool air in. A man sat at a desk with a lamp on the far wall to the bed facing the wall. On his right was a reed basket with more linen. Laying inside was the baby and Nebit could see his sleeping face. She stared at the baby while the man busied poured over scraps of papyrus strewn across his desk.

It's not too late. I could turn back. Nebit thought, glancing back though the hallway, then her gaze returning to the sleeping babe.

No! This is who I am. There is no other way but forward. I must not let these feelings turn me from my path.

Nebit stepped inside the room. She slipped out one of her bronze daggers and held it in her hand as walked closer. Like so many times before, she stood behind her unaware target. She moved her dagger near his throat but outside his view as she readied herself.

Then she struck swiftly and silently. After a short struggle he lay helpless on the desk.

As she began to withdraw she heard a cry. In fact, a series of cries. She looked and saw the baby had awakened. Some blood splashed on the baby's face that likely woke him up from his peaceful slumber. Feelings of sympathy took her off guard and she instinctively took a step toward the baby intending to cradle him in her arms.

Just as suddenly, she heard footsteps approaching. Looking around, she decided her best way of escape was out the window. Her long thin legs took her there in two strides. Seeing shrubs on the ground below, she dropped down among them.

The very next moment a woman shrieked from the room she just left. From her hiding place, she saw guards in the courtyard turn and look up where she was and felt lucky that nobody saw her jump out the window. Her heart raced, hoping they wouldn't discover her. When the guards went running into the house to investigate, she dashed unseen to the wall, scaled it, and hid in the shadow of a nearby building.

She took a couple deep breaths, an attempt to calm herself down. But she could still hear the baby's cries and could not shake the intense desire awoken within her. The shouts and loud wailing would soon wake up the neighbors who would likely go to see what the matter was. But instead of completing her escape, she took a small risk. She climbed up the wall and pulled herself onto the roof so she could see what was going on.

Guards were running around searching the premises, including the shrubs she hid in before. She could also see the woman from the hallway cradling the baby in her arms as she wailed.

Why is the baby still crying? Nebit thought. *He doesn't know what happened... what I did... does he?*

She continued to watch people rush about frantically, trying to look for the assassin. She saw more women come into the room. Some were consoling the woman and others the baby.

What have I done? What's going to happen to the baby now? Would he grow up never knowing his parents like... like me? She took an uneasy breath, feeling hopelessly trapped in her own life.

Nebit sat on the rooftop and wrapped her arms around her legs. Her thoughts drifted back through her memories like the Nile in flood season as she rocked back and forth. The only mother she knew was her master at the temple who raised her and helped train her. Then she lifted her eyes to the moon above.

Maybe she can help? Nebit glanced one more time at the courtyard and left.

"Please come in, and welcome back," Her master, Halima sat at table, writing. Nebit entered the room and sat down on a wooden chair nearby. Papyrus was neatly arranged in piles on her desk as she wrote on a single piece with her reed pen.

Nebit waited quietly.

"Was your task a success?" Halima asked, moving the papyrus to one of the piles and looking at Nebit.

Nebit nodded.

"Then what is troubling you?"

Still under the affect of the events that night, Nebit told her everything that happened. She told her about these new feelings she never felt before. Halima sat in silence and listened.

"What am I fighting for? I'm just killing people they tell me to." Nebit took a deep breath and shook her head. "I can't keep doing this. I want.. I want a…"

"You want…" Halima began, "what every woman wants. You want the same thing I wanted when I took you in after your parents left you with the temple priest. Did I ever tell you why I came to the temple?"

Nebit shook her head.

"It wasn't out of piety or a devout service to the gods. I couldn't have a child. My husband tried to comfort me, but the constant teasing and insults from the other women were too much. Many nights I went to a solitary place to weep. I didn't want him to know. There was nothing he could do. The problem wasn't with him. It was with me-"

"But why is having a child so important?" Nebit spat.

"Hush and let me finish! On one such night I decided I couldn't take it anymore. And I left. I didn't say anything or leave any token behind. If there was one thing in my life I regret, it was that. But I didn't know what else to do. I went to the temple thinking one of the gods might have mercy on me. They didn't. But then you fell into my lap and I thought of you as the daughter I could never have."

At this a solitary tear escaped her eye and she quickly wiped it away with a finger.

"You would train your daughter as an assassin?"

"You'd best be careful not to cut yourself on your sharp wit. I may not be around to bandage you up." She scolded with an outstretched finger. "But now, to address one of your many problems, perhaps it's time for you to have one."

"Have one?" Nebit asked, "One of what?"

"What we've been talking about all this time!" Halima laughed. "Find yourself a husband and have a baby."

"A baby!" Nebit shouted. "It's too soon. I'm not ready."

"Nonsense." Halima dismissed with a gesture. "But you will need to be discharged from service to the temple so you can focus on your duties as a mother."

"My duties as a... what?"

"I'll talk to the priests about it. I'm sure with the exemplary service you've given them so far they'll agree to this basic need of yours."

"Are you sure?"

"Of course! Just leave it to your dear old mother." She smiled at Nebit and Nebit returned it nervously. Then she went back to her writing and Nebit left.

Nebit gripped the handles of her bronze daggers tightly in each hand. She bounced up and down to loosen her legs. Staring at her target she drew a slow breath and released it. Then she struck as a whirlwind. Her dark braids whipped around her face as she decimated the reed dummy in an instant.

Hearing the sound of clapping she was surprised to see a young woman in the doorway behind her. She recognized her as one of the cooks. Nebit smiled and bowed her head in acknowledgement. Her eyes rested on the large bulge in the woman's belly.

"I'm sorry, I hope you don't mind my watching." She said holding her hands behind her back, making her belly look even larger. "I've heard of the warrior woman and when I passed by I couldn't help myself."

"That's fine," Nebit said putting away her daggers and approaching her. "How long till it comes?"

"They say another three or four weeks." She said smiling, rubbing her hands lightly on her belly. "But my first baby came two weeks earlier than what they said. She couldn't wait to get out into the sun."

"Do you know if this one is a boy or girl?"

"From the test they say it's another girl. But the last time they said she was a boy. So I don't really know what to believe."

Suddenly they heard hurried footsteps from down the hall. Around the corner Halima appeared. She was breathing hard and her face looked frantic, almost scared.

"Nebit, come with me." She said before anyone else could utter a word. Then she grabbed Nebit by the hand and led her down the hall.

"What is this? Where are we going?" Nebit protested.

"Not now child," Halima said as she quickly turned and twisted through the stone hallways. Although Nebit could keep up just fine, her master moved with such speed that surprised her.

A few more turns and they got to a closed door. Halima opened it and led them inside. Nebit looked around at the room of stone slabs. With a number of crates piled on top of each other it looked like a plain storage room. A couple tables held lit oil lamps.

Then Nebit saw her take out a wooden key and placed it into a hole in the door. With a bit of a turn she heard metal scraping against wood.

"What are you doing? Locking us inside?"

"Listen to me," Halima grabbed her upper arm tightly. Her face was fearful and her voice was deadly serious. "You need to go... now."

"Go? Where? You locked us in an empty room."

Halima walked over to one side of the room, taking one of the lit lamps on the table. She grabbed one of the stone slabs on the wall near the ground and pulled it off as easily as pulling a lid off a jar revealing a dark passage behind it.

Nebit approached with her mouth gaping open. She saw that what Halima held was just a frame with cloth made to look like the other stone slabs of the wall.

"When I requested the priests let you go, all seemed favorable except one. Sakakwi, a very influential priest was against it and became angry as I continued. He burst out and said that it would disrupt his plans to let one of his best assets go."

"Then why are you doing this?"

Halima folded her arms and sighed. "You know I've always thought of you as my own daughter. I'm your master and yet... your mother at the same time. I raised you, cared for you, and brought the great warriors to train you. I love you, my child, and I want what's best for you. And right now, what's best for you is to leave."

"But what about Sakakwi? If he was so angry when you talked about letting me go then what's he going to do if I leave?"

"Not *if* you leave, *when* you leave. And don't you worry about Sakakwi, I'll deal with him. You have enough to do. There is an influential woman whose husband is in Pharaoh's court. She is looking for the best warriors and was intrigued when I told her about you. Seek her out. Her name is Kasmut."

"But you've done so much for me. How can I leave you?" Nebit could feel her eyes dampen and vision blur as a tear escaped.

Then they heard shuffling of feet outside the door. A voice called out, "The cook said they went this way. They must be around here somewhere."

Halima embraced Nebit tightly. Nebit put her arms around her and shed more tears. They could hear more voices outside and then someone banging on the door. Then she grasped Nebit's head in her hands and looked at her eyes. Nebit could see she was crying too. Halima handed her the lamp and whispered, "It's time to go now."

Nebit nodded and crawled into the tunnel. She looked at her mother's face one last time who quickly affixed the fake stone panel back on the wall. As Nebit started to crawl through the tunnel she heard wood cracking and then a loud crashing sound. She turned and was a little surprised that she could see through to the other side.

Halima faced three priests. The one in the middle stepped forward with a face distorted in anger.

"Where is she?" He growled.

"I told you I intended to let her go, Sakakwi. She's gone."

Sakakwi shouted in rage with clenched fists. He directed the other two to search the room. The opened the crates and searched them, throwing the vegetables and fruit stored in them all around the room. They toppled the top crates to the floor which broke apart. Some of the debris reached the fake wall hiding Nebit. Luckily, it wasn't exposed.

Then he accused her with a pointed finger, "Are you trying to undermine my plans? Do you know what you've done? There are men in Pharaoh's court sympathetic to those slaves and they need to be rooted out."

"Do not say such things to me. I've always supported you, and you know it." She replied confidently. "Nebit is a woman and needs to learn what that means. You have many such servants who can do your bidding."

"But yours has been one of my best and I won't lose her." Sakakwi came close to her. "Tell me where she is."

"I will not." Halima replied.

"Tell me where she is, or else," he growled, drawing even closer. Nebit could feel his anger repressed like too much water behind a dam that would break at any second.

"I will not." She repeated.

At this he released the fury building up within him and he raged at her. He took the khopesh at his waist and slashed her deeply across the chest. She shrieked in pain and dropped to the ground. Then hacked at her again and again, until he looked satisfied. The other two froze in shock.

He growled at her one more time as she bled onto the floor. "It's your own fault!" He yelled. "Had you done what I asked things would be different. I asked but you refused."

Then he turned around to the other priests with him. "She couldn't have gone far. You know what she looks like. See that she's found. Go!" The priests snapped out of it, looked at each other for a moment and ran out of the room. Sakakwi gave the room one last searching gaze before he left.

When Nebit could no longer hear footsteps, she opened the door of the secret passage and crawled over to Halima with tears streaming down her face. But she was too afraid to cry, someone might hear her.

She pulled on the shoulder of Halima who turned her head and their eyes met. Nebit cradled her head in her lap. With her final breath she whispered, "Go."

Then the life left her eyes.

"There you are!" boomed a voice. Nebit looked up with horror and gasped to see Sakakwi standing in the doorway. A painful lump lodged itself deep in her chest and she broke out in cold sweats. "I thought you might not have gone far. It was good I trusted my instincts. You will keep killing people I want until my aims are achieved. Fear not, I am a good and gentle master, as long as you do as I say."

He took some slow steps toward her as one would a scared animal. But when she gathered her wits she dashed toward the safety of the dark tunnel and he lunged after her. Just when she thought she made it, she felt a hand grasp at her ankle.

"Got you!" Sakakwi's shouted. "Now come like a good servant. I'm giving you the opportunity to participate in my plans. You should be thrilled at the chance!"

She kicked and kicked with her feet but his hands were too strong and he slowly pulled her out. Then she threw the oil lamp at him and he cried in pain, releasing her. Once freed, Nebit crawled as fast as she could. Sakakwi's voice echoed in the tunnel like a nightmare she couldn't awaken from while she kept going and going.

A T-intersection in the tunnels lay before her, but she didn't try to think about which way she should take. She just chose the way that seemed to take her farther away from him. She felt her way through the darkness as she came upon more twists and turns.

Ahead of her she felt a cold stone wall. A dead end. She was trapped. Whirling around she took her daggers in hand, expecting to see Sakakwi's face any moment coming around the last turn despite the total darkness. Nebit's mind raced to think of what she could do. Her heart pounded in her chest.

Moments went by and nothing happened. The moments stretched into minutes. The minutes stretched into what felt like eternity and nothing happened. The painful lump only seemed to grow. But nothing happened.

He's gone. I got away. I'm going to be ok. Nebit said to herself as she dropped her hands and breathed out in complete exhaustion. She leaned back against wall and panted to catch her breath. Nervously, she kept glancing down where she came even though it was pitch black. Then it dawned on her that she was lost and alone in the dark.

Once again, panic seized her and she cursed herself for throwing away her only light. She gasped and dropped her daggers on the cold hard stone. Flailing her arms around, she touched the walls, floor and ceiling around her. But she the ceiling felt a little different and something in her head told her to calm down.

Curious, she touched the ceiling above her head with both hands. She felt the grain of wood. *A trap door!* Nebit thought and felt relieved.

She took a deep breath and thought about her. The pain in her chest began to recede as the image of Sakakwi dissipated from her mind. She focused on Halima and her heart broke. She cried.

Wiping away the tears she whispered a vow, "I'll remember you and what you taught me. By my actions I will honor your memory. I will find husband and become someone who protects other people. You will live on in my heart... mother."

She looked up toward the wooden panel she couldn't see and giggled, "A trap door saved me from the trap."

Then she reach down to pick up her dropped daggers and felt a sharp stab of pain in a finger. She lifted it to her mouth then her eyes widened in realization. "Ok, I'll remember that too!" She smiled and shook her head.

After putting her daggers away, Nebit carefully pushed up against the wood. She felt a pang of fear as it didn't budge at first. But then she braced it with her shoulder and it slowly lifted.

Light flooded into the tunnel that blinded Nebit, but she welcomed it with elation. As her eyes adjusted she saw this was a storage room for scribes. Piles of empty papyrus lay on shelves lining the walls as well as tapestries going all the way to the floor showing the god Ptah. Best of all, nobody else was in the room. There were, however, a number of tables with lit lamps.

I better leave before whoever lit those lamps returns. Nebit thought as she pulled herself up.

Just then she heard footsteps. She quickly hid behind one of the tapestries as a couple men entered the room. Peeking around she saw a man lift up the wood trapdoor while the other looked down with one of the lamps. She slipped out the door when both their backs were turned.

"Do you see her?" One of the men asked.

"No, not here either." The other responded.

The first man groaned in frustration, "This was the last one! We have the other exits guarded. She must still be wandering around down there."

"Do you think she left before we got here?"

"If so then Sakakwi's going to kill us."

Seems all that man does. Nebit thought, shaking her head. *Then again, it's all I do too. Can I really change my ways? Or is it too late?*

As she continued down the hall she recognized the area and knew just where to go. She made a few more turns, carefully looking to make sure there were no surprises around the corner.

Peeking around one more corner she saw the side exit of the building that she was looking for. However, standing guard at the threshold was one of the men she recognized who was with Sakakwi. She quickly moved her head out of sight.

Images of them standing over her master's bloody body filled her mind. She could see Sakakwi's maniacal face again as he attacked her repeatedly. She felt the pain in her chest at the thought of killing another person for him.

A couple deep breaths calmed her so she could think clearly again. She looked around the corner once more. The man leaned against the doorway with arms crossed. Something outside the buildng held his attention. A khopesh leaned against the wall next to him. Two stone fire-bowls on either side of him lit the hallway.

After considering her options she drew a dagger, the same one she's used successfully countless times. Peeking one more time, she saw his attention was still elsewhere. Slipping around the corner she pushed herself against the wall toward his back.

Then she readied her dagger near his throat. Then anger swelled up suddenly and she sliced deeply. While still in shock, she was able to yank him back inside the doorway without too much trouble. But as she sliced the dagger deeper and deeper she felt greater and greater pangs of guilt. The pain in her chest returned with double the intensity.

She let him go and ran out of the door as fast as she could. As she did, and glanced back, the pain in her chest lessened. A glimmer of hope that she could escape her life shone as beams of the moon which rained down on her.

Nebit looked up at the large manor house before her with curiosity. She'd infiltrated larger, but not much larger. From her perch on a nearby building she could see the outdoor pool, large front yard, and numerous granaries.

Could this be the right one? She thought to herself as she dropped to the ground. The previous leads she had were dead ends. As with most of the manors she visited, she found no trouble bypassing the guards and entering the premises by scaling the wall.

She could hear voices coming from the balcony on the second floor. Climbing up from a wall, she hid next to the open doorway to hear.

"You had better!" hissed a harsh voice of a woman. "With more and more reports from my husband of these slaves refusing to work we need more help!"

"I'll keep trying, mistress." Said a male voice. "But with Pharaoh recruiting for his war in the South good ones are hard to come by."

"Find them wherever you can," replied the woman. "I'll be doing the same. You may go."

Then Nebit heard footsteps. She saw the figure of a woman come striding out. She put her hands on the railing and sighed deeply.

"Kasmut?" Nebit asked, stepping out of the shadows.

"Who's there?" Startled, the woman turned and stared Nebit in the face.

"Is your name Kasmut? Your husband is an official for Pharaoh?"

The woman regained her composure. She lifted up her nose and examined Nebit for a moment. "It is. And he does. What do you want?"

"My name is Nebit, I'm a… soldier. I heard you have work."

Kasmut turned to face Nebit. Her lips curled in a smile. "Ah, yes. I've heard of you. I suppose it wouldn't do for someone with your talents to call at the front gate. Tell me, how fares Halima these days? I haven't seen her in months."

"I'm afraid to say you won't see her anymore," Nebit said.

Attempting to restrain her emotions, but failing, Nebit told Kasmut about how Sakakwi killed Halima and how she escaped. Kasmut frowned and shook her head through most of it.

"That murderous boil on the flesh of the priesthood." Kasmut said once Nebit finished.

Nebit took a step toward her, "Is there anything we can do to right this injustice?"

Kasmut folded her arms and rested her chin in a hand in thought. "At the moment, no. However, should we bring this deed to light at the right time and you come forward as a witness it could severely damage him politically.'

She walked over and put a sympathetic hand on Nebit's face. "But think not of Sakakwi right now. He is very powerful and influential. We can confront him when the time is right. For now, I shall take you into my service as there is much that needs to be done. First, you must be hungry and tired. Come with me."

They walked back into the manor house and Kasmut took Nebit. She led her to a room with shelves and crates filled with salted meat, bread, fruit, and vegetables. In the middle were a number of low tables with reed mats to sit on.

"Take whatever food you want tonight," Kasmut began. Nebit did so immediately, starting with some of the meat. "You can sleep with the other female servants in the room down the hall from here. Just find an empty mat. Is there anything else you need?"

"You're offering so much already. But do you have a place to practice fighting?"

"The yard in front of the manor is where the soldiers and guards usually spar and train."

Nebit thanked her and Kasmut left to go back to her business. After eating for a little while, Nebit stopped and thought about all that happened to her tonight. Then she grabbed a piece of bread and a fig and headed to the front yard of the manor.

Numerous torches lit the gate and walls around the manor. But Nebit only needed the light of the moon. She finished the last bite of bread and unsheathed her daggers. Assuming a low stance with a dagger in each hand, she began to train.

An image of Sakakwi's face as he stood over Halima intruded in her mind and she felt the pain in her chest flare up again. It broke up the flow of her practice and she stumbled. The cold sweats came again.

She replaced that image with that of Halima as she knew her, as Halima would want her to remember her and she took a few deep breaths. She felt the pain lessen a bit. With one more determined breath she continued her training, but slowly at first and remembered her vow.

Chapter 3

Standing at the front door of his father's house, Tau breathed a sigh. He looked back the way he came. Rather than looking toward his meager house, his eyes were drawn to the temple of Apis some distance away. As he gazed toward the stone monuments and buildings glistening in the morning sunlight reaching up toward the heavens, he spotted an eagle soaring high above in the cloudless sky.

"If only I could join you up there," Tau said to himself.

Suddenly a voice boomed, "There you are my lad!"

Turning, Tau saw the bald head and gray beard of his father. He forced a smile.

"I was hoping you'd show up a little earlier. You probably got distracted on the way, didn't you?"

Before Tau couldn't answer his father said, "Look, I've got big news for you. I'll tell you when you're done training."

Tau trudged behind his father, looking down at the ground. They went around to the back of the house where a number of bundled reed practice dummies stood. To one side lay a pile of unbound reeds with another pile of cloth next to it.

"Here we are," his father said.

"So what are we doing?"

"Training!" His father put his hands on his hips. "I want you to use that technique I showed you yesterday."

"And you'll tell me the big news once I demolish those ten dummies?"

His father laughed, "That would be too easy for you. You're a head taller and stronger than most men. Today you practice endurance. Once you're done with these, bind another ten."

"And after those?"

"Keep binding them until, oh… the sun is half-way across the sky."

"Half-way?" Tau asked with disbelief. He looked over at the sun, shading his eyes with a hand. It was just a sliver above the horizon. When he looked back his father was already walking toward the house, probably to continue forging weapons. A highly skilled blacksmith such as him was never want for work. Tau shook his head and groaned.

He unstrapped the khopesh at his waist which was made larger than normal to fit his hand by his father. Then he walked up to the closest reed bundle. He settled into the stance his father showed him with the blade in both hands. He took a breath and then unleashed the four-fold strike. Cleanly cut sections of reeds landed on the ground.

Tau looked down at the reed fragments and grunted. Turning toward the next one, he focused his mind on the technique and unleashed it again. Again, and again he executed it. But each time he felt something like a wall in his mind grow making it harder and harder to focus.

When all ten lay in heaps on the ground he turned and looked back at the temple of Apis. Then he looked up and found the soaring eagle he saw before. He gazed at it again with longing in his eyes.

He walked over to the next bundle of reeds and stared at it for a moment. The sound of two rocks hitting each other startled him. When he looked up, he saw a grinning face peeping over the wall.

Grimacing, Tau looked back toward his father's house, who was nowhere in sight. He jogged over to find his three friends waiting for him.

"What are you three doing here? Didn't you take my father's warning seriously?"

Abayomi laughed, "He's so focused on his work! Do you really think he'd notice?"

"C'mon," said Sekani, "You should know today's our day out in the city. You started this tradition." He pointed to the small burlap sack hung over his shoulder.

"I don't know. I have duties to family now."

"You shouldn't have to change just because your father chained you to a woman," Nizm reached up to put a hand on Tau's shoulder. "Just one more go of it, for old times' sake?"

"Just one more?" Tau glanced again at his father's house.

"That's right!" Sekani nudged him with an elbow. "And besides, we need your help to get into the temple."

Tau grunted again. He crept back in the yard and looked around. Satisfied that his father was thoroughly occupied he started to walk away.

Passing by the reed bundle nearby him, Tau looked at them and said, "You get mercy today." He put away his khopesh and left with his friends.

They started toward the temple through the busy market street. The dirt under Tau's sandals was already packed down hard from all the people bartering and trading. Most of the goods on this market were fruit and vegetables. Tau stopped at one stall and traded for a handful of figs, she told him they were her favorite fruit. His friends waited for him impatiently.

Up ahead they saw the sprawling and bustling complex of the temple of Apis. Huge stone blocks stood upon each other as people stand on the traditions of the previous generations to complete an awe-inspiring structure.

As they walked up to the temple, huge stone pillars with ornate carvings greeted them. Numerous gold bands wrapped around each pillar. Tau looked upon the images of the bulls, a symbol of strength, and remembered the feeling of wonder the first time his father took him here for a festival. There were so many people. The bulls they kept were so large with long pointy horns. He sighed as he looked down upon them now.

Continuing through the main courtyard, they passed by a large number of people laying prostrate in front of the large stone bull statues. Nizm leaned to Tau and said, "I wonder why they don't bring real bulls to pray to."

"You see those small stone piles under that bull statue?" Tau pointed and Nizm nodded. "Real bulls don't drop stones."

Nizm muffled a laugh while the other two gave them looks saying to hush. This was the critical part. They turned left before the main temple entrance and found an unguarded doorway. Looking to make sure nobody saw them, they entered.

Taking a quick turn, they ascended a flight of stairs. As they walked along a hall Tau took a moment to gaze at all the people praying below from a window. Another couple flights of stairs and they were on the top floor. The wind tugged at the white shenti around Tau's waist as he breathed out in delight.

The whole of the city stretched out before him in every direction. The mud-brick buildings and trees filled the whole city, all the way to the white walls which stretched up high. Beyond them he saw the vast Nile River slowly flowing in its course. The greens of the shrubbery, trees, and grass on the banks looked so alive next to that big blue line in the sand.

Sekani already took the clay cups and poured the beer into them. He handed Tau one of them rather sloppily. Tau took it eagerly and finished his portion in one gulp.

"Ah! This is what life was meant for," Tau gazed at the beautiful landscape and took another breath as well as all of the worries and cares that burden. The other three gathered around him and they admired the view together.

Suddenly Tau saw movement from the corner of his eye. A temple priest was walking toward him.

"What's your business here? This place is off-limits."

Tau's mind raced for an excuse. "Sorry, we were looking for a place to pray and got lost. Can you tell us where to go?"

The man responded with a look of disbelief. Then his mouth open in shocked realization. "Wait, I remember you four from about seven days ago! I especially remember telling you to never show your crooked nose here ever again! Guards!"

Before the priest could react, Tau and the other three ran back the way they came. A guard came running and Tau thought quickly, "The priest calling for you is up those stairs. Run quick!"

The guard nodded his head thankfully and continued passed them. As soon as the guard's foot touched the first stair the priest appeared at the top yelling, "You idiot! After them!"

The guard looked confused for a moment, then turned toward the four running down the hall and gave chase with a rather annoyed expression.

They continued their escape down the flights of stairs and through the corridors of the temple. By this time the guards had mobilized. One guard attempted to block their exit at a four-way intersection. Nizm and Abayomi ran down one way while Tau and Sekani went the other way.

"Do you think they'll be able to get out?" Tau called while turning another corner.

"Don't worry about them!" Sekani said between heavy breaths. "Just run!"

Tau turned and saw they garnered quite a following of guards waving a wide assortment of weapons. Sekani moaned in disappointment and Tau looked up ahead to see two guards blocking their path from the exit. The guards behind them cheered in premature triumph in anticipation of catching their quarry.

Tau grinned and felt a rush of excitement come over him. He gave a magnificent roar and sped passed Sekani toward the two guards. Their expressions changed from confidence to panic as the charging lion came straight for them. He hit them fast and hard and they were knocked over like young saplings.

They continued out into the temple courtyard and passed the array of bull statues. Worshippers looked at them curiously. Tau turned and saw the other two running on the other side of the courtyard. Another, smaller group of guards were chasing them. He gave a call and a hand gesture so they started converging toward the middle where the exit lay.

Two more temple guards stood waiting for them. All the commotion inside alerted them. This time he brandished his khopesh and gave his warcry. The guards had spears at the ready but Tau was unphased. He focused his mind and transitioned the new stance his father taught him. To the astonishment of the guards, the heads and tails of their spears fell, cut cleanly, to the ground.

His friends ran by, each turning to give a nod of respect and thanks before scattering to the four winds. Tau gave another roar and grabbed the wooden shaft of one guard, while swinging his khopesh at the other to keep him at bay.

As the merging group of guards behind him came up to him, Tau pulled the guard off balance. Tau moved his grip to the guard's wrist and swung him around. His feet hit the other guard in the head, knocking him out, and then Tau flung him toward the large group behind him.

The ones in front, shocked, quickly dropped their weapons and caught the man. The others behind tried to get around, but it was too late. Tau ran off into the mazes of the market and they lost him.

Strutting toward his new home down the road, the burlap door came into view. It was a nice heavy fabric with reds and yellows, chosen by his wife. With a rough hand he tossed it aside, stooped down, and stepped in.

"What are you doing here?" Kesi asked with a start. Then she realized her loud words might've awakened the baby cradled in her arms and she began gently rocking it in her arms.

Without saying a word, he emptied the small sack into his hands. The figs easily fit into his hands. Instantly, her shock melted to delight, and her eyes brightened in anticipation. She gave him a warm smile. Tau beamed and casually sat down next to them.

"Little Ebo seems to be getting stronger than when I first saw him," Tau observed.

"Yes, I almost wonder if he knew what happened that night." Kesi closed her eyes and shuddered. Tau guessed she recalled the memory of her murdered husband. She opened here eyes looking sadly

at Tau's now step-son. She stroked Ebo's cheek
tenderly.

"You still haven't told me how it felt," Tau put
a hand on her knee.

She looked at him again and forced a smile. Tau
gazed deeply into her brown eyes. The black hair
surrounding her face hadn't been brushed yet this
morning. The colors put on her face were put on from
the day before.

"Let the past stay in the past," She said as she
looked down toward Ebo in her arms.

"How about I stay here with the little lion while
you go out for a bit? Didn't you say that you hadn't
seen your old maidservant in a week?" Tau offered.

She looked at him slyly, "Aren't you supposed
to be training with your father today?"

Tau turned his face to hide his guilty look.
From the lamp-light he saw the silhouette of his face
and his crooked nose. "I finished training."

"You've been with those men again, haven't
you?"

"What men? There are lots of people with
whom I associate."

"I warn you," She wagged a finger at him.
"Those men are a bad influence on you."

"I'm a worse influence on them!" He shot back
with a grin.

For a moment they stared at each other. Then
Kesi laughed and shook her head. "Don't forget you
have a duty to your family. Your father decided to
marry you proper and I intend to see it through."

Tau rolled his eyes. He replied, "Alright. I'll
go."

Before Tau could stand up he felt Kesi's hand
on his shoulder. She leaned over and kissed him on the

cheek. "Thank you for the figs." He smiled at her while running a hand through her hair. Then he left.

"I tell you the truth, my friend," Badru began. He put his arms behind his head while reclining in his wooden chair. "You need to stand up for yourself. A father needs to know his son will make his way own in the world."

"I try to do that. Only it never works out that way." Tau laid down on the cushions. He always liked this couch best. He rested on it a lot lately while talking with Badru. He breathed out heavily as he poured his troubles onto Badru. "I don't know what to do anymore. I hate this insistence on training. I don't want to be a soldier, doing the same thing every day. I want excitement and adventure!"

"Yes, all excuses I've heard before. I wonder though, are you trying to tell them to me or to yourself?"

As Tau groaned, they heard a squeal like that of a little pig. Then a little girl wearing a brilliant green dress with black puffy hair ran into the room and jumped on Tau. Tau groaned again.

"Unky Tau!" she exclaimed as she positioned herself on his lap. "I didn't know you were coming. Daddy taught me the word for reed this morning. Look here, I drew it. Do you have a piece of papyrus? I'll teach you to draw it."

Caught off-guard, Tau looked around. He replied, "Sorry Amahl, I have no papyrus with me. Nor do I have anything to draw with."

She furrowed here dark black eyebrows in displeasure as Behati entered carrying her other daughter Omphil in her arms. She sighed and shook her head at Tau. When Omphil saw her sister playing with Tau, she managed to wriggle out of her mother's arms and climb up onto him too.

Behati gave a sideways glance to Badru who looked at her with an unreadable expression. Then she quietly sat in a cushioned chair opposite him. While the girls talked to him unendingly, Tau could feel the tension between Badru and his wife.

Between Omphil trying to hang from his arm and Amahl asking about his latest exploits he caught the conversation between Badru and Behati.

Behati accused, "That is beside the point, you bartered for too many!"

"Beside the point?" Shouted Badru, "It is the point! Those silver items were a very good deal. We'd be able to trade for twice the value in a year."

"And what are we supposed to use for to feed the servants if our fields on the Nile don't produce? They don't eat silver."

"That should not happen. You know very well we had good flows last year. And if something does happen, we can barter."

"At half the value you got it for!"

They argued before when Tau was there. He always wanted to say something to help, but could never think of anything. He got up to leave and Tau managed to convince the girls to stay with their mother so he could follow.

When they entered the room, they saw his father sitting down next to another man. Badru gave an elaborate bow and Tau tried his best to copy it.

"Ah good, Tau is with you." His father said. "Our friend here will need likely need men of both your talents."

"Indeed?" Badru asked. "And what can we do to help you, Sakakwi?"

Sakakwi stood up. He was taller than Badru, but not Tau. It was then that Tau noticed burn marks on the corner of his eye. He forced a smile for them, but all they could see was a dark gleam of malice from his eyes. He got bad feeling from the man, but Badru seemed to trust him.

"I require records," Sakakwi said bluntly. "These are very old records. It was unfortunate they were moved from the library to the ancient archives long ago."

"I haven't been there before," Badru rubbed his chin with his index finger. "The Medjey should honor my seal of authority and allow us passage into the tunnels underneath Pharaoh's palace. Tau, are you ready for a little adventure?"

Tau glanced quickly at Sakakwi with a look of concern. But then he looked at Badru and the thought of braving the unknown depths excited him. He grinned and folded his arms, "Dark is the day when I'm not ready for an adventure."

Holding the torch in front of him in one hand and his large khopesh in the other, Tau confidently walked ahead of the others. Badru and Sakakwi chatted idly as they walked. And a guard with a blade took up the rear.

Tau led them down the dark and musty passageways while Badru or Sakakwi would shout which way to turn. Then Tau spotted a pair of twinkling eyes up ahead.

"One of those wolves that Medjey guard warned us about decided to show up." Tau said as he raised his blade to strike. But then as the light showed the wolf, another five pairs of twinkling eyes appeared. Tau cleared his throat. "And he decided to bring his pack with him."

Badru drew his mace and explained, "When fighting wolves it is best to attack as a group since they-"

"For glory!" Tau roared charging forward. Not wanting to be left alone, the others followed behind.

The first strike from Tau landed on the side of one wolf's head sending it sprawling against the wall of the tunnel. The wolves snapped back at the other men. Badru's mace and Sakakwi's khopesh dispatched two more.

Seeing that the other four wolves were grouped together, Tau saw the right opportunity for his new technique. He settled into the stance with both hands holding his khopesh. With battlecry, he leapt forward and unleashed his fourfold strike. The wolves melted before him.

"Four more over here!" Shouted the guard from the behind them.

"Not a moment's peace? Just the way I like it." Tau shouted with a laugh.

"The loud noises must have roused them," Badru said.

As Tau, Badru, and Sakakwi came back, the wolves had already encircled the guard. One wolf bit onto the guard's leg but as the other wolves came in for the kill they were easily killed. The guard rammed his spear into the chest of the wolf that bit him and now all of the wolves lay dead.

"A well-earned victory," Tau said. Sakakwi nodded to him approvingly.

The guard leaned against the cold hard stone of the passage wall as he held his leg in pain. The others came around him. Badru crouched down at the guard's leg. "I'm fine," The guard dismissed him with a gesture.

"Let him take a look," Sakakwi put a hand on the soldier's shoulder. "He wouldn't boast about it, but he's one of the most skilled physicians in Egypt."

Badru carefully prodded and poked his leg. Then he took out a leather pouch with medicinal supplies. He applied some ointment to the bite wounds and bound it with some straps of cloth. Then gestured they were ready to go.

Tau took the lead and they went onward. Soon they entered a large room with stone statues arranged in two rows stretching almost as high as the ceiling which was about twice Tau's height.

"I think we're almost there," said Sakakwi, looking around for more signs of animals.

They walked in the middle of the rows. Tau moved his torch closer to the statues so he could see who they were. He saw all of the strong gods represented.

"Badru," Tau said. "Remember when we were young and I convinced you to paint horns and red eyes on the statue of Ptah in the temple?"

"No," Badru replied.

"How could you forget?" Tau smiled. "I couldn't stop laughing."

"I did not forget, but choose not to remember." Badru corrected him.

Continuing on, they came up to an intersection where the row of statues met columns of statues arrayed horizontally in front of them. In the center were large slabs of stone on the floor that looked different than the other floor tiles.

"Wait a moment," Badru rushed forward and grabbed Tau's arm. "There is a trap here."

"A trap? Are you sure?" asked Sakakwi.

"Deadly sure," he replied. "Some of these tiles are fake. Stepping on them will send you into a pit of spikes. Let's walk around the side."

As they passed around the side and crossed through the column of statues Tau asked, "How did you know there are spikes underneath the tiles?"

"I remember that on this formation the text says there are deadly traps which usually mean spikes."

Badru explained. "Would it make you feel better if they were filled with poisonous snakes?"

"Maybe it would," Tau laughed. "But why have traps just for some old papyrus scrolls?"

"The archives are not the only place here." Badru explained. "There are secret burial chambers of the Pharaohs of old. They must be protected."

"Some knowledge must to be made secret," Sakakwi added in a deadly serious tone.

They continued onward passed the statues and through more dark passageways. Cobwebs and a dank musty smell greeted them as they came to a fork ahead. From the torchlight they could see both tunnels led to rooms with empty coffins. Badru looked around with a confused expression.

"Did we make a wrong turn?" Badru asked himself.

"Something feels odd," said Tau. "Could there be a secret passage here?"

"Ah, yes." Badru lifted a finger in epiphany. "Those are fake tombs. A hidden trapdoor should be located in this area. We just need to find it."

Badru started touching the ground near him and soon all of them were touching the floor and walls to help look.

"I think I found it!" Tau laughed as he searched a wall. The others crowded around him. There was a small square stone twice the size of his thumb. He looked back at Badru who nodded his head. Tau pushed it and it went in.

Suddenly the floor underneath them dropped and they found themselves sliding down a steep slope. Luckily the ground wasn't far. They all landed in a heap. As they stood up and dusted themselves off they found themselves in a small room with a passage leading forward.

They took stock of themselves and then looked around the room. It had four large pillars with elaborate paintings on them.

As they walked down the passage they entered a large room. Ornate statues and pillars with more paintings populated the middle of the room. Shelves of scrolls lined the outside of the room. Two ornately carved doorways were on either side of the room, with more little passages like the one they entered through.

"Yes! You've brought us to the right place. Now I need to find the right records." Sakakwi said as he and Badru started looking through the scrolls.

The guard leaned up against one of the pillars, as though afraid to touch anything. Tau, however, began an investigation of his own to see every painting and ornament that can be found in the room. And there were many. He found images of nearly every god in their popular stories.

One such painting brought up memories of when his father took him and his older brother to the temple and told him about how Ptah created the world. Tau smiled as he remembered looking on the statues and shining gold overlaid upon stone and wood.

A cry for help interrupted his reverie. He turned and saw an enormous lion approaching the others from the other side of the room. It started growling at the armed men. Tau readied his khopesh while running to them.

"The lions down here must have slipped the Medjey's minds." Tau said as he brushed his shoulder against Badru's.

"Indeed," Badru responded. "We ought to refresh their memory when we get back."

"Shouldn't be too hard for the four of us to cull a lion," remarked the guard. Just then two lionesses appeared behind the giant cat, and the guard's confidence dropped like a stone in the Nile.

"Do you have the scrolls we came for?" Tau asked.

"They're here," Sakakwi tapped the rolled papyrus tucked underneath his arms.

"Everyone keep calm. If you run, the lions will chase. And they will run faster." Badru explained.

The four retreated slowly through the room as they faced the advancing predators with weapons in front. The lionesses spread out to try to encircled the group, but they retreated back all the faster. The lion tried snapping bites here and there but the blades dissuaded it.

Once the group got to the other end of the room and slipped into the corridor, all three of the large cats walked abreast. Suddenly, the lion let out a paralyzing roar that echoed through the hall.

The other three felt as though they might die, but Tau never felt more alive. He whispered into Badru's ear, "I think now's the time for some of your magic."

Badru shook himself from his daze. He reached inside his black robes and produced a small bag. Then he hurled it and create an explosion of dust when it hit the lion square in the face. The lionesses were caught up in it as well. All three gave painful groans and roars.

"Withdraw!" Badru shouted and the four of them turned and ran down the passage with Tau in front with his torch.

After a few moments, however, they could hear the claws and growls of the cats in pursuit. Badru ran right behind Tau, giving him directions. Sakakwi ran behind him, trying not to drop or damage the scrolls. And the guard in the rear ran while frequently looking behind him, expecting to see a lion ready to pounce on him at any moment.

Eventually his fears were realized as he saw the lions were keeping pace with them. Up ahead, Badru directed Tau to turn right and into a room. They all stopped dead in their tracks when they saw the pit up ahead with a bridge made of two ropes strung across. The other side was about two lengths of a man. The light from the torches showed a large number of snakes on the floor beneath it.

"It would seem fortune brought you your pit of snakes," Badru said to Tau.

"How very kind," Tau frowned. "But I don't remember asking for the lions."

An intense and fierce growl from behind them caused them to turn their heads. The lion and one of the lionesses crept up on them.

"Let the guard go across first," said Sakakwi. "We need to make sure that bridge will hold us."

The guard looked at him with horror. Then he looked forward trying to figure out if he feared Sakakwi more than the snakes. With a shove, Sakakwi made his decision for him and the guard grappled onto the ropes.

He took a step. The ropes held. He took another step. And another. They still held. Then he kept walking and crossed to the other side. Then Sakakwi crossed over. All the while, the Tau was contending with the lions, using his large khopesh to keep them at bay.

After Badru crossed, Tau slowly made his way onto the rope. He held the rope to balance himself with the hand that also grasped the torch. Just as he made it a few steps across, the lion swiped at him, missed, but cut one of the ropes with a claw. It dangled loosely in Tau's hand. Gambling on his balance, he turned and tried to run to the other side on the rope beneath his sandals.

On his second step he felt his feet drop as the rope snapped from the pressure. Desperately, he grabbed onto the rope ahead of him with all his might. On it, he swung down and smashed into the side of the pit. His khopesh clanged loudly on the floor, disturbing the snakes. His torch also hit the ground and the serpents nearby slithered away from it.

Looking down, Tau picked up his legs so any opportunistic snakes wouldn't have a target. Tau looked back and saw both of the lions on the other side staring back at him. He looked back at his khopesh and sighed as he realized he would have to leave it. Then he climbed up.

Badru gave him a hand to help him up, "Thank goodness you're alright. When I saw the ropes break I feared the worst."

"Those lions were nothing. I guess you can thank whatever gods gave me my tremendous muscles." Tau flexed with pride.

"They're gone!" The guard shouted.

Tau looked at the guard and sternly said, "I assure you my muscles are not-"

"No, the lions," he said pointing behind them, "Where did they go?"

Everyone looked back to the side they came from. Ropes dangled from their places. The snakes still slithered around the torch in the pit. But the lions were gone.

"They probably just went back to wherever they came from," Sakakwi suggested. "Come, let's leave this place."

They continued on with Badru guiding their path. They made a few more twists and turns in the cold stone passages. Without Tau's torch it was darker. And without his khopesh it felt darker.

Finally they came to an intersection they recognized. They all breathed a sigh of relief.

"You've all done well for me this day," Sakakwi said to them. "You'll all be rewarded well. Tau, I shall make sure to replace your lost khopesh with the best one I can buy."

"You see, my father is a blacksmith." Tau explained. "If you just get me the best quality bronze he can make me another one."

"Very well, I shall do-" Sakakwi was interrupted by a fierce roar.

Just as they turned to look, a lioness came out from the dark with claws outstretched. She pounced on the guard before he had a chance lift his shield up. The three backed away with horror as the man was mauled.

Tau stepped forward but Sakakwi grabbed his arm and said, "What are you going to do? The gods have sealed his fate. We run." And Sakakwi ran with Badru behind him.

Turning back, Tau looked as the three lions started to eat the guard alive and listened to his screams. He stared at his empty hands and considered Sakakwi's words. Then he cursed himself and ran to follow Badru and Sakakwi.

Standing at the front door of his father's house, Tau breathed a sigh. He looked back the way he came. This time he looked passed the market, passed the temple of Apis, and even passed Pharaoh's palace. His thoughts went back to that ancient archive with all the paintings and stories. He wondered how many other places like that are out there for him to explore.

Then he shook the sack slung over his bag and smiled at the clinking bronze nuggets inside; the only proof he had of his little adventure today. He hoped these prizes were enough to satiate his father.

"Where have you been?" Boomed a voice.

Tau turned and saw the angry look on his
father's face. Tau responded with a smile, but this time
a sincere smile.

"And where's that khopesh I made for you?"
His father asked.

Tau took the bag and dropped it at his father's
feet. Hearing the sound of metal, his father opened the
bag and inspected it.

"This is some of the finest bronze I've seen!
Where'd you get it?" His father looked up at him
amazed.

"It's a long story," Tau said. "But I've been
wanting to hear your big news all day. Will this take the
place of my training?"

His father picked up the bag and examined it as
though calculating its value. Then he looked at Tau
sternly, "Nothing can take the place of discipline
learned from training hard. I found a job for you. It
may not be the job you like but I think it's the job you
need. You won't be winning glorious battles, but favor
in the eyes of Pharaoh's court. The official's name is
Rashidi and you'll be helping keep slaves in line."

Tau agreed, "Decidedly not glorious."

"Glorious or not, you must learn to do your
duty." His father put his arm around Tau's shoulder
and walked him inside. "Now come inside because I
have a lot to tell you about duty." Tau sighed dejectedly
as he walked inside with his father.

Chapter 4

Rashidi stood with arms crossed in front of Yalu and two other soldiers. The black hair of his wig jostled as he moved his head to examine each of them in turn. His gold earrings sparkled in the morning light, as well as the necklace and bracelets awarded him for his royal service. His expensive cinnamon fragrance drifted out with the gentle breeze the tugged at his white fine-linen shenti. Along with the fragrance came the dull roar as foremen behind him quarreled among themselves.

He sighed in front of them and asked the Kasumut who stood next to him, "Are you sure these are the best?"

"The best available," She clarified. "You know with war brewing in Kush to the South that Pharaoh is drafting all the best warriors. Lucky for you, your wife knows where to look."

He turned back to three standing before him and looked them over again. Yalu glanced at the tall man to his left who stood more than two heads taller than him. The khopesh at Yalu's side looked almost like a toy in comparison to his own.

Glancing to his right stood a woman. She stood confidently with her dark complexion and thinly braided hair. He was interested to note the absence of any jewelry on her. He wondered if the two daggers at her waist were for show, or if she really knew how to use them.

"Very well, you are now in my service." Rashidi quickly. "As you know, numerous groups of the Hebrew slaves are rioting. Kasmut has assigned you a location and will take you there. Do whatever is necessary to get them back to work. If you need to make a few examples then I'll understand. Am I clear?"

"Yes, Master Rashidi," The three replied.

"Good. Report back when your task is completed," Rashidi instructed before turning to yell at the group of foremen behind him as Kasmut led them away.

"Our first assignment." Yalu spoke softly as though Rashidi might overhear, "This will set the tone for the rest of the job."

Tau grunted dismissively and shook his head. Nebit said nothing but followed in line behind Kasmut.

She took them out the North gate of the city. Slaves here on either side of the main road were in different stages of making the mud-bricks. The Nile sparkled in the sunlight to their right. Up ahead they saw a dozen men shouting at one of the foremen in a language they couldn't understand. About twice as many more loitered in the area.

Recognizing Kasmut, the foreman, wearing a white tunic and girdle browned by all the dust, ran to her.

"Finally! Do something! I cannot get them back to work," he pleaded through his dark and bushy beard.

Kasmut turned and looked at Yalu. Then she gestured with her head that he should take charge. Just as quietly, she turned and left.

Yalu stepped forward and gripped his weapon. Behind him, Nebit and Tau did the same. The sight silenced the angry slaves. Their eyes showed fear and desperation explained by recently inflicted bruises and scars.

"I was told by your overseer that I could make an example out of you if you refused to get back to work," Yalu told them brandishing his khopesh.

None of the slaves broke the silence.

"Volunteers?" He pointed at them with his khopesh and the hint of a roguish grin on his face.

Finally one of the slaves spoke up, "He stopped sending us straw and told us that we have to find our own. And yet he still expects the same number of bricks!"

Nebit replied, "Perhaps the straw was delayed, or stolen. A lot of things can happen. He didn't necessarily stop the straw on purpose."

The slave dismissed her words with an annoyed gesture, "Ask the overseer. He gave the orders." The rest scoffed in agreement.

"I will talk with him and find out what happened to the straw. Until then, get back to work."

"Look," one of the slaves stepped forward and showed them the whip lashes on his back and the bruises on his arms. "These are what we received in place of the straw. They will work us until we die!"

"You can trust my word, we will investigate this matter. But for now get back to work. If you don't, you can trust my word about making some examples."

The crowd wouldn't budge. Despite Yalu's most intimidating expression and threatening weapon, they wouldn't get back to work. He started thinking about Rashidi's words of making an example.

Shall my blade continue to bath in the blood of the undeserving? Yalu thought.

Just then he heard a loud irritated grunt from Tau at his side. Tau leaped forward and roared, his face plastered with reckless abandon. The crowd startled in unison. Tau swiped the air with his khopesh a few times.

"You!" Tau pointed at a man in front with his weapon. "Step forward."

The man trembled and stood still as though paralyzed. His eyes wide and mouth gaping open.

"Now." Tau growled.

This prompted the man to obey. The crowd looked on with fear in their eyes.

Bringing him close to his face, Tau asked him quietly but sternly, "You don't really want to be an example, do you?"

Trembling with fear, the man shook his head.

"Good, I don't want you to be either. I'm sure duty is important to you." Tau turned the man around to face the others. "Now, can you tell your friends over there to do their duty?"

The man nodded and Tau nudged him forward. The man walked slowly, still trembling. When he rejoined the others he looked back at Tau who didn't budge. The man gestured to the others went to his work area. The crowd seemed finally resigned, and begrudgingly went back to making bricks.

As the last slave was leaving, he looked at them sternly and warned, "I believe that my god, the god of my ancestors and of me, made oaths to my forefathers. I also believe that he keeps his oaths. And I will pray that He keeps you to yours."

The three of them went to each group of slaves as well as individuals until the all of them were busy doing their work.

The foreman approached the three and said, "I am in your debt. You have succeeded where I have failed. When you said you'd make some examples I feared the worse. But things didn't turn out as I expected."

"Things rarely turn out as you expect." Nebit said. Yalu felt painful memories resurface. When he looked at her it seemed she felt the same way.

"What do you know about the missing straw?" Tau asked the foreman with arms folded.

"Rashidi told us that the slaves were to gather straw in addition to molding and baking the bricks," he answered.

"Why?" asked Yalu.

"He didn't say," the foreman replied with a sigh.

"You didn't ask?" Nebit stepped closer to him.

"I don't think he would have told us. And I'm sure certain punishment awaited anyone who asked."

"I'll ask in your place. I gave them my word and intend to keep it." Yalu said.

"If you say so, but I need to tend to the slaves. I pray you fare well!" He waved goodbye to them and said, "May our god go with you."

"Which god?" Yalu responded blithely, "Ammon-Ra?"

"No. The god of my ancestors, of the Hebrews."

"What do you think happened?" Tau asked after he had left them, and as the three huddled to speak privately.

"I don't know," Yalu brushed the contour of his jaw with his fingers. "Rashidi knows more than he's telling. We need to ask him."

"You don't think he really did deliberately stop the straw, do you?" Nebit wondered aloud.

"Something isn't right here," Yalu released a deep breath, "We were hired to protect Rashidi's quota of bricks from the slave riots, but I feel it's the slaves who need protection."

"Protection? From whom?" Tau asked. "What about our duty to Rashidi?"

"And what about our duty to conscience?"
Yalu shot back. "Perhaps its just my nature now, but
after years of protecting others I've acquired an eye to
see banditry."

"Are you suggesting Rashidi's robbing these
slaves like bandits?" Nebit asked with a curious eye.

Yalu shrugged, "Perhaps not, but I think it
deserves asking the question."

Nebit regarded Yalu and a smile appeared on
her lips.

"One thing is for certain," Yalu began. "This is
bigger than some missing or stolen straw. For now, all
we can do is return to Rashidi and ask if he will tell us
anything. We are returning with good news, so he may
feel inclined to tell us."

They agreed and returned to Rashidi's manor.

They found him busier than ever arguing with
other foremen about more rebellious Hebrew slaves,
trying to complete their business before evening. When
he saw the three he excused himself and motioned for
them to come. "Well…?"

"Master Rashidi, all the slaves are back to work
and following the foreman's instructions." Yalu
reported as a smile grew on Rashidi's face.

"Well done!" Rashidi exclaimed. He addressed
everyone present, most especially the foremen. "I
finally have some good news! These servants of mine
have actually done the job assigned them. You should
learn from their success." The foremen all scowled, but
kept their murmurings quiet.

"Master Rashidi," Yalu said, "the slaves will be
ready to work at full capacity once they receive the
straw they need to make the bricks."

"The straw..." Rashidi trailed off. His demeanor changed from jubilant and proud, to serious, "they won't be getting any more straw."

"No more straw?!" Nebit asked with surprise.

"That's what Pharaoh ordered," Rashidi replied honestly, "He's redirected the straw for the Hebrews to other slaves."

"Why did Pharaoh do that?" Yalu pressed.

"Pharaoh has his reasons. Go collect your wage and celebrate your success! If I see you three too early tomorrow then I'll know you disobeyed my command." He finished with an unreadable smile. Then, just as quickly, he turned and continued arguing with the foremen.

As they walked to the clerk, Nebit contentedly concluded, "I guess Pharaoh needs to show those Hebrew slaves that he rules in Egypt. Our little mystery's solved."

"But," Yalu said and they both turned to him. "If Pharaoh's reason is to make the Hebrews worship him as they ought to... Why now? Why not a long time ago? Why the sudden change?" The other two silently walked with him.

Their minds raced to think of possible answers. Tau offered, "Maybe they provoked his wrath somehow."

Yalu pursed his lips and scrunched his eyebrows, "If they did, then I would like to know about it. Rashidi hired us to keep them in line and I don't like that they're keeping information from us."

They found the clerk at a storehouse. He searched through his papyrus scrolls, measured some vegetables, drink, and payment in barley, and sent them on their way.

Tau looked at his wage with some displeasure. "I think I can barter in the market for food more to my liking. Do you two want to come with me?"

"I could use another sword," Yalu confessed. He took it out and showed them. It was bent in some places and chipped in others. "Perhaps Rashidi will fit us with new gear."

"Perfect! My father is a master blacksmith. If you find one you like then maybe you can ask Rashidi about it tomorrow."

"I also need a good armorer," Nebit grinned. "Let's go."

As they walked on they passed the massive temple to Ptah the Creator, marked by tall pillars in front of the doorway. Rings of gold overlaid on them spanned about a fist in height and about half a man's length apart. Images of the great god creating the world adorned them.

Arriving at the market, Tau led them to his father's house. Four tables carrying carefully placed khopeshes, swords, daggers, and shields as well as the counter in the middle with various weapon-crafting tools easily fit into the large room. Three standing racks along one wall held spears.

"My son returns!" Tau's father greeted them smiling. He wore polished scale armor, and a small silver lion dangled from his ear. "Welcome to my shop. You know these are the best quality, forged by a lion!"

As Yalu and Nebit browsed the weapons and armor out on display, Tau stood nearby his father who went back to sharpening a blade.

"How is that new weapon coming along?" Tau asked.

"Slow going. That bronze you gave me is very stubborn. Yet I feel it will yield some of my best work That piece of trash will have to do for now. If I've told you once I've told you a thousand times, treat your weapon as yourself. Never lose it!" His father responded without looking up. He motioned with his head toward Yalu and Nebit with a small amount of displeasure, "More friends of yours?"

"We work together for Rashidi," Tau explained. "We just finished our day's work and decided to go to the market."

His father smiled and nodded approvingly, "Good. I'm glad you're taking your duty seriously. That reminds me, your friend Badru came by asking for you. He mentioned a great opportunity."

"Did he?" Tau asked with surprise. "Where did he go?"

"Around the market somewhere," His father replied.

"Let's go!" Tau shouted to Yalu and Nebit who dashed off with him.

As they approached the market, they noticed more and more people on the streets and the sound of bartering filled the air. "Give me a few minutes to find Badru. It shouldn't take me long. Wait here." Tau said as he ran off.

As they stood waiting, a man carrying a sack full of figs ran into them from behind and knocked both of them down.

Yalu lifted his head after regaining his balance to see the ground littered with figs. He cursed, then rolled off of his flattened companion. He stared into her startled brown eyes. For a moment, his face flushed in embarrassment.

"Are you injured?" He finally asked, but she didn't reply. So he pulled himself to his feet. He offered a hand to help her up.

"Aaaaiiiii! My master's figs!" screamed the man carrying the figs. Yalu turned to look at him.

When he looked back he saw his wife, beaten and bloody, reaching her hand up at him. He felt the anger in her eyes and he jerked his hand back.

Nebit looked up at him with surprise, wondering if she did something wrong. Then she saw Yalu's grow pale, almost as though dead. He panted like he was running from a crocodile from the Nile. Then he shook himself awake and gave her his hand to help her up.

The man carrying the figs crouched on the ground, gathering them up. He wore a brown turban with darker brown robes. A piece of cloth around his waist fastened his robe together.

Nebit stood over him, "Have you any eyes at all?"

He didn't even look up; he just kept gathering his scattered figs.

Tau spotted Badru directing slaves on the other side of the market. Badru looked nothing like his friend. His body was slim with ebony skin, darker than Nebit's. He wore a brown kalasiris robe and a like-colored hat. They greeted each other with a hug.

"How does your home fare today?" Badru asked.

"My wife is happy. Little Ebo seems to be recovering from his ordeal. And seems my father is satisfied so long as I keep away from anything I like to do." Tau said with irritation. Then he winced and asked, "How about yours?"

Badru moaned and shook his head. "Not well, as I am sure you have guessed. Last night the arguments seemed to come as soon as our daughters were in bed. And the worst part is that we seem to argue about small things."

"Sometimes the small things are the ones that matter most," Tau grunted. Then he motioned toward the market unfolding in front of them. "And what are you doing here?"

"My father sent me to purchase some food and supplies with some slaves to carry them," Badru glanced behind him to the three men following a few paces behind.

"Isn't that steward's work?"

Badru sighed, "My father's talking about death again. He thinks I need more experience running the household. So he recommended I handle this personally. I'm not sure I really need it, but it sets his mind at ease."

"If you want more experience you should spend more time with me!"

"Time spent with you is certainly an experience," Badru put his palm to his forehead. "In all the times I walked the cold stone passages not once was I attacked by lions. Tell me, does trouble follow you around or do you actively look for it?"

"Bah! It's not so hard to find when you spend so much time with it. Now what's this great opportunity?"

"Pharaoh's magician, Haji, is to give a demonstration."

"A demonstration!" Tau exclaimed. "I'd love to see that."

"Yes, I know. In the courtyard of Pharaoh's palace. Pharaoh himself will preside over it," Badru's brown eyes beamed, "tomorrow, at mid-day."

"May I bring friends from my new job?" Tau asked.

"If they behave like your last group of friends it would be my head!"

"No Badru! Sekani and them are good to drink a beer with. These two seem like serious soldiers to me, very cool and collected. A man and a woman."

Badru blinked, "Does the man have an old beat-up khopesh and a small dented shield slung on his back?"

"Yes, he does!"

"And does the woman have shoulder-length braids with daggers strapped to her back?"

"Is this magic?" Tau asked with astonishment.

Badru pointed straight ahead. He looked up and saw Yalu and Nebit arguing with a third man.

"Oh! So am I foolish because I'm a slave or because I'm a Hebrew?" the man shouted angrily.

"Both! Anyone can see how foolish you are," Nebit shouted back.

As the man finished picking up the last fig he said, "Well I heard from someone that our god will bring us out of Egypt and into a much better land." He stood up and stormed off with his figs.

Just as Nebit was about to shout something back to him, Tau interrupted by introducing Badru: "He is apprenticed to Pharaoh's magician Haji."

"Greetings, friends of Tau are friends of mine," Badru performed an elegant bow. Yalu and Nebit, noticing his fine robes, bowed lower to show respect.

"My name is Yalu and she is Nebit." Yalu noticed several royal symbols embroidered on his cloak. He wasn't sure how Tau knew such a man, but thought he better be as respectful as he could.

"Badru invited me to a demonstration by his master Haji. Would you like to come as guests?"

"I could not help overhearing your," Badru paused to choose the right word, "disagreement."

"That was just a thoughtless slave not paying attention to where he was going," Nebit dismissed with a gesture.

Badru gave Tau a skeptical eye who replied with an innocent smile. He turned and told them, "Be sure there are no disagreements when you come to the palace."

"Yes sir Badru," Yalu said. "It would be an honor to be in your escort."

Tau slapped his hands and rubbed them together, "Then it's settled. We'll meet at the gate of the palace tomorrow."

Badru bowed again, "Then I shall return to my task. I look forward to see you all tomorrow." They said also bowed, their goodbyes to him, and he left.

As they left the market Yalu said, "I wonder if we keep our ears open that we might be able to learn more about Pharaoh's order to redirect the straw from the Hebrew slaves."

"Clever," Nebit complimented. Yalu glanced at her and their eyes met for a moment.

"Friends!" Tau asserted, "We're ignoring Rashidi's command. Must I remind you what we've been ordered to do? I'll wager I can put down more beer than both of you put together!"

Yalu and Nebit looked at him surprised. Then looked at each other, wondering what the other would say. Finally, Yalu said, "I accept your challenge."

Yalu and Tau turned to Nebit but she raised her hands in surrender. "I cannot. I need to train."

"Train?" Tau asked. "We look after slaves. What do you need to train for?"

Nebit raised her lip in a scowl. Turning to walk away she answered coldly, "Looking after slaves. Yalu, take care not to drink too much."

Yalu grunted in acknowledgement and he watched her leave. Her dark thin braids swayed with each step. He thought the way she carried herself, she must know how to use those daggers.

"Sure, go wear yourself out training!" Tau called out to her. She didn't respond. Then he turned to Yalu and grinned, "Let's go have a good time."

Chapter 5

From nearby the gate to the palace, Yalu waited, rubbing his head with his hands, hoping the ache would leave soon. As he touched the roof of his dry mouth with his tongue he shook himself to try rid himself of the sleepiness.

He tried to take his mind off himself by admiring the palace structure. Many of the stones on the wall depicted Pharaoh or one of the other gods. The palace of smaller stones stood about as high as six or seven men. The early morning light shone on the gold overlaying the intricate patterns of the massive main entrance. Four guards in heavy white shenti, sandals, and carrying large spears eyed Yalu suspiciously. It made him uneasy.

He saw the guards at the gate talking amongst themselves. Then one of them began walking in Yalu's direction. At first, Yalu pretended not to notice, but turned to face him when the guard approached. He towered over Yalu. He was almost as tall as Tau.

"What are you doing here, soldier?" He asked cautiously.

"Personal invitation," Yalu replied. "I'm Badru's guest for his master Haji's demonstration today."

The guard thought for a moment. "What you say is true." Then the guard cocked his head and said, "The others seem to think you were somebody. Are you known as Yalu?"

Yalu nodded.

The guard harrumphed and looked down at him haughtily, "If I beat you in a fight then I might get the recognition I deserve."

"Good thing we've no reason to fight."

"Yeah, good thing." The guard responded. "Unless you make a mistake. If that happens, you can wager your best beer I'll be right there." The guard chuckled as he walked back to his post.

"You can have it," Yalu muttered as he remembered his condition. Then he spotted Nebit appear from around a corner.

She walked to him and stated the obvious, "You look awful."

Rubbing his face with his hands, he admitted, "That's because I feel awful. I guess I drank too much beer last night. I forgot what it felt like. Every time! It's like I need to keep doing that to remind myself how bad it is."

She asked. "Where's Tau?"

At that moment he saw Tau appear from around a corner and he pointed toward him. He was in a similar state as himself. Yalu was impressed how much beer the man was able to hold.

After waiting a short while, they saw Badru exit the palace doorway. He descended the steps and approached them through the gate. "Good morning. I see all of you wanted the…" he stopped after looking twice at Tau and Yalu and then continued, "beer-drinking contest. Tau suckered you into it, yes Yalu?"

"It's my own fault for accepting," he threw up his hands.

Badru smirked, "I made that mistake once… once." He motioned for them to follow him. "We have some time before the demonstration. I can show you the arboretum, the indoor pool, and oh! The hall of Pharaohs is particularly interesting."

As they followed him, Yalu glanced at the guard and strolled past with a bravado he did not entirely feel.

As he turned a corner, he heard the dreaded, "Stop there!" Yalu glanced back.

But the guard had stopped two old men with long white curly beards as they approached the palace. One of them looked short compared to the guard but the other was about as tall, and the wrinkled faces of both showed determination and courage. The brown robes and white linen turbans reminded Yalu of the Hebrew slaves. One leaned on a staff as they stopped in front of the palace entrance.

"We are here to speak with Pharaoh," the taller man said in a familiar accent. Badru and the others stopped to listen.

"State your name and your business," One of the guards demanded.

"My name is Aaron, this is Moses, and we have a message for Pharaoh from our god. Let us pass." The guards looked at each other a little fearfully for a moment.

Badru whirled around to look at them. Yalu and the other three did the same. As the guards talked amongst themselves, Yalu could see Badru was studying the old men carefully.

Nebit leaned toward Yalu and said, "I think these men are Hebrews."

Suddenly a light of realization shone on Yalu and he whispered to her, "Perhaps we can find out what happened to the straw from these men."

Her face lit up and she smiled.

Then one of the guards directed the other two to stay while he and another accompanied these elder Hebrews. As the guards escorted them, Yalu and the others quickly climbed the steps into the palace and escaped into a room on the right.

"Friends," Badru whispered, "Follow me." He led them through the massive entryway into the palace. The cool of the stone felt even more so as they came from the hot sand outside.

"Sir Badru," Yalu began, "Would it be possible for us to listen to what those men have to say to Pharaoh?"

"You mean spy on them?" Badru turned while walking but showed a knowing expression, "I know of a secret room where we can watch what happens inside Pharaoh's audience chamber. It is a secret for the magicians and priests; be sure you tell nobody of this place." They nodded in agreement and he took them down a hallway.

An old man with priestly robes walking the opposite direction gave them a curious eye.

"You there!" He stopped them, "What are you doing in this part of the palace?"

"I am the apprentice to master magician Haji," Badru took out a gold token from a pocket in his robe and showed it to him.

After examining it carefully, the man nodded to affirm its authenticity. Then he looked around at the other three and warned Badru, "Just remember that you're responsible for these soldiers. If they do anything then you will be held accountable." Badru smiled and bowed to him as he continued on his way.

They made a few turns in the hallway and arrived at an empty banquet hall. A large bare table with chairs sat at the center of the room. Badru stood next to one of the walls and Tau asked, "So how do we get there?" But Badru simply smiled and moved his hand behind one of the tapestries. The tapestry was draped from the ceiling to the floor and was as wide as four persons. It was bordered with purple and gold, depicting the god Ptah creating the world. They heard a click and then the sound of stone rubbing against stone. Then Badru slipped behind it and vanished.

"Flesh and fire, a secret passage?" Yalu whispered.

Tau followed behind him with Nebit after him. Yalu looked over the banquet hall one last time before he entered. He continued, "I suppose I shouldn't be surprised by-"

Badru hushed him. "We are almost there and do not want to be heard." They walked along the dark passage, feeling the wall as they went. The ceiling was barely tall enough for Badru, Yalu, and Nebit, but Tau needed to hunch over. After a quick turn of a corner, they saw light coming from their left. When their eyes finally adjusted, they saw Badru pointing toward the holes on the wall from where the light came. They all looked through.

From behind the wall they had a perfect view of Pharaoh's audience chamber. Eight golden lampstands encircled Pharaoh's throne of wood overlaid with gold. Numerous stone pillars also overlaid with gold in parts held the ceiling about three lengths of a man high. Sunlight entered the chamber through holes in the ceiling.

Pharaoh's heavy purple skirt with gold trimming spilled over from the throne. The gold jewelry, amulets, and belt looked impressive enough, but weren't the most impressive. The centerpiece of Pharaoh's regal attire was the red and white double-crown symbolizing a united Upper and Lower Egypt resting on his head. A particularly menacing cobra protruded from its front, rearing to strike and take the life of any who trod carelessly before Pharaoh.

Haughty men on either side of him looked smug in their white linen skirts and gold jewelry. Each had a headdress with black locks of hair flowing down from it. The two men they saw earlier stood solemnly and silently in front of Pharaoh. A handful of the palace guard stood in-between them and Pharaoh with his entourage.

Sitting tall on his throne, Pharaoh's comical expression showed his amusement at the two Hebrew men standing before him. "He told you to say that, did he? Hmm…" Pharaoh looked at them blankly. Then a devious smile grew on his lips. Leaning forward he said playfully, "I have news for you. Some of your fellow Hebrews came and appealed to me concerning my edict about the straw. They thought to trick me by blaming my own people. But they did not know I saw through their simple trick to stop working. What a lazy people you Hebrews are. They just needed more work to keep themselves busy." Pharaoh chuckled as the two men kept silent.

Pharaoh's smile vanished when the silence extended awkwardly. "Your purpose with this request is foolishness. You people have no right to worship another god when you should be worshipping me like the rest of Egypt. Moses, I recognize that you are a man of great influence and I understand your concern for the Hebrews. I will make you this bargain: give up your request and then I will give you a position in my palace. I may even reconsider my edict about the straw. What do you say?" The men continued their silence.

Allowing his agitation to show, Pharaoh declared, "I… am the most powerful god in Egypt. Where is this other god you keep telling me about? Can you even tell me his name? Why should I believe you?" Anger filled his face as they maintained their silence. Just as quickly a smile replaced the anger as an idea came to him.

After a deep breath Pharaoh said, "If your god truly has power here then let him perform a miracle.

Perform a miracle!" Pharaoh laughed and soon all his entourage laughed with him.

Then the two men turned their heads and nodded at each other. The tall Hebrew man raised his staff into the air. Guards readied their weapons to defend Pharaoh from this blatant threat. Pharaoh himself leaned forward, intrigued by this unexpected action. But instead, the man threw the staff on the ground. The sound echoed off the stone chamber until it was replaced with silence again.

"Is that your surrender?" Pharaoh asked. But as everyone looked back a second time they started to panic and flee as they realized the staff before their eyes had transformed to a giant snake. Dark brown speckles covered its light brown hide. "What... What sorcery is this? Su. . . Summon my magicians! Summon Haji!" Within seconds a man appeared from the other side of the room. As soon as Pharaoh saw him he motioned toward the giant snake in front of him, "Haji! Do something!"

The flaps of his black kalasiris robe brushed the floor like a shadow as he calmly walked to Pharaoh and bowed courteously.

"As you command, my Pharaoh."

He turned and looked defiantly at the snake. By then, it had reared up and was standing as tall as him. He held himself confidently and gazed at the snake, attempting to size it up. Then he focused on the men behind the snake.

Haji held up his staff, "Oh great Wadjet, protector of Lower Egypt! We call upon your power here in our time of need. We call upon you in the name of Pharaoh. Give us the power we need to defeat your enemies. Come now and take possession of my staff!" Throwing down his staff, he produced a flash of light, and smoke. As the smoke cleared, everyone could see that Haji's staff had transformed into a snake. The other magicians cheered and praised Wadjet.

Yalu gaped in wonder of this magic. He'd heard the magicians of Pharaoh's court could perform great deeds but he was awestruck to witness it in this way.

One after another, each one of them threw down his staff, and in a flash of light and smoke, everyone saw that Wadjet transformed their staves into snakes. Each time, they cheered and praised Wadjet, the protector. Pharaoh reclined on his throne, pleased with his servants. The smile returned to his face as he pointed out to them in a tone hinting of boredom, "As you can see, Moses, you're not the only magician in Egypt."

Haji inserted, "You are now face-to-face with Wadjet, the goddess of snakes." The guards and other magicians laughed and started scoffing. One man shouted, "Your tricks are nothing before Pharaoh." And yet another, "Your god must now submit before Pharaoh."

The snake from the Hebrews spanned almost four lengths of a man while the snakes from the Egyptian magicians barely spanned one. Once the large snake saw the others, it slithered over to them. As it did this, the magicians jumped backward in fear. They watched in horror as it opened its mouth and swallowed the first snake, head first, that it came upon. The snake flailed its tail in desperation, but to no avail. Soon the entire snake was consumed.

"Nooo!!!" Badru screamed. The other three stared at Badru, shocked at his outburst. His mouth and his eyes gaped wide.

Realizing that trouble had already begun, Yalu took a breath and calmed himself. He glanced at Nebit and Tau and said, "We have to get out of here… Now!"

Tau grabbed Badru by the hand and yanked, but he resisted and wriggled his hand free. After Yalu encouraged Tau with hand gestures, Tau wrapped his arms around Badru's waist, lifted him up like a wooden statue, and ran after the other two. Badru struggled in futilely in Tau's grip. Tau ran around the corner and through the passage, still awkwardly stooped because of the low ceiling.

Luckily, nobody was present in the banquet hall when they exited the secret passage, but they heard shouts from people coming from all directions. As they started back down the hallway, they saw the entire palace in an upheaval. As they ran through the winding maze of halls, the images of gods and goddesses on the walls seemed to reach out to them, as though to stop them. Suddenly, a turn of a corner left Yalu startled to see a man with arms stretched out to grab him.

"What you scared of?" Tau asked as he tried to get a better grip on Badru. "It's just a statue."

Yalu released a tense breath and led them on. Another couple twists of the hallway took them to the main hallway leading out. But before they exited the great golden doorway, Yalu saw the guard who had harassed him earlier barring their way. As the guard recognized him, his face scrunched with anger. Charging he shouted, "You! You must have led Moses here. All this trouble is on your head!" Yalu drew his sword and shield just in time to deflect the huge spear. Slinking to the side, Nebit drew her daggers as Tau put Badru down so he could engage in combat.

Yalu shouted and feigned an attack with his shield to get the guard's attention. His attempt succeeded as Tau and Nebit flanked the guard. But the guard saw Tau coming and used the blunt end of the spear to keep him at bay. Nebit, however, slipped in close and drew blood with a couple pierces from her daggers. The guard yelped in pain and turned to face her. At this moment Yalu saw his opening and bashed the guard across the backside of the head with his shield, knocking him to the floor. With their final obstacle cleared, they ran through the doorway, down the stairs, and made their escape.

For a while, they just ran away without care for where they went as long as it led away. When they got some distance from the palace, they slowed to a walk. Nebit asked through panting breaths, "What do we do now?" By this time Badru had given in to complete panic, shouting only nonsense. "I say we just leave him here and find a place to hide."

"We can't leave my friend here like this!" Tau objected. "We must take him with us. Something bad might happen to him if we don't."

"As long as you carry him, I care not if we bring him," Yalu replied. "Follow me. We can go to the house of my mother. Once there we'll decide what to do." Nebit and Tau nodded in agreement and continued following him.

All throughout the market and the streets the people gave them curious stares because of Badru's bizarre behavior. Nobody here yet knew of the things going on at the palace. Making their way through one of the common districts, Yalu finally stopped at one of the mud brick houses.

Tau put Badru down and asked, "Are you going to be good now?"

"Yes. I have control over myself now." Badru sighed and shook his head, "It... It is just... I cannot believe what has just happened."

Yalu lifted up the heavy brown cloth door and entered the house followed by everyone else. They heard a surprised gasp from a woman inside. Her light brown dress flew as she turned around. But after seeing her son she gave a sigh of relief. "Boy, you scared me half to death! I thought you were a thief. Who are they?"

"These are. . . my new friends," Yalu said and introduced them.

Nebit, Tau, and Badru went over to the right side of the house to sit down. His mother went over to the cooking fire on the left side of the house and before Yalu knew what happened she tugged his arm, pulled him along and whispered to him, "She's cute! Have you finally decided to build a new family?"

"She works with me," Yalu explained quietly, looking back to see if the others heard.

"I would like to see grandchildren this side of the Reeds of Paradise."

"Please mother," Yalu firmly squeezed her arm as his face reddened. "A lot has happened today. Can this wait?" Sighing and rolling her eyes, she continued preparing the food. Then he walked back into the common room and made himself comfortable on one of the reed mats. Badru paced restlessly from wall to wall.

"It's over, Badru!" Tau put his hands behind his head and leaned against the wall, "Sit down and take a rest."

Badru glared at Tau and took a deep breath before asking, "Do you know what happened back there?!"

"A competition of magic, yes?" Yalu leaned forward, "Seemed to me the Hebrew magicians won."

"Pharaoh's magicians looked like fools," Nebit looked at the ground and frowned.

Badru lowered his gaze and shook his head.

"Yes, they did. But what power do they have to best the greatest magicians in all of Egypt? Where could they get such power?" Badru finally sat down as he started thinking, and rubbed his temple with two fingers.

"And the snakes! They defeated them too."

Tau stood and put a large hand over Badru's shoulder consolingly. "It's just a few snakes. What does it matter?"

Badru removed Tau's hand dismissively and turned. "Do you remember what Haji said? 'You are now face-to-face with Wadjet.' As an avatar of the goddess herself, that snake not only represented Wadjet, but was possessed by her."

"So not only was it a defeat for Haji, but also a defeat for our goddess?" Nebit looked up curiously.

"Precisely," Badru turned and pointed at her, "But where is this going? What is the purpose of this attack?"

"It's not all that important," Tau gestured with a hand. "So this Hebrew god defeated one of ours. We're not in the desert without any water. We have plenty more gods!"

"But Wadjet is the... or was the protector of Lower Egypt." Badru stated solemnly, "Her defeat leaves Egypt vulnerable." Then his face lit up. "Of course their god changed to a snake! His aim was to lure Wadjet out of her nest and swallow her whole! Not important, you say? I say this should matter to all of us who bow to our gods."

Yalu's mother entered the room with a plate made of straw and handed everyone a piece of bread. Keeping a little for herself, she found an empty reed mat and knelt on it. The two small silver earrings that dangled from her ears caught the light as she shifted. She moved her hair out of her face and nibbled on her portion of bread.

"Didn't Rashidi say," Yalu looked at Nebit. "That the Hebrews worship another god instead of Pharaoh."

"That's right," Nebit affirmed. "They don't even regard Pharaoh as a god."

"Another god…" Badru repeated, "The Hebrew god…"

Nebit grabbed Yalu's arm, "Do you remember that Hebrew slave who bumped into us in the market yesterday? He said that his god was going to take him out of Egypt."

Yalu replied, "Yes, I remember. And then one of the rioting slaves said their god made oaths to them."

"Oaths, you say?" Badru looked at them quizzically. Then he theorized, "What if this god of the Hebrews made an oath to take them out of Egypt? And what if that same god is making good on it, right now?"

"Take them out of Egypt?" Tau asked disbelievingly, "If the Hebrew slaves leave Egypt, who will make bricks?"

"More importantly, how was the Hebrew god able to defeat Wadjet? Is this only the beginning of… something?"

Nebit shook her head and sighed, "Can't the Hebrew slaves just accept their place and worship our gods? Defying the gods was something heroes did in stories of legend. Why does it have to happen now?"

"Why not now? Didn't the stories of legend have to happen at some time?" A small smile adorned Tau's face. "I never imagined I would live through a battle between the gods themselves, like when Horus took revenge on Seth for the murder of Osiris."

"Flesh and fire! Battles between the gods? It makes me feel so small." Then Yalu looked up as though startled. "It's almost mid-day! Rashidi is sure to have work for us."

"Right, we should go. But what about you, Badru?" Tau asked. "What are you going to do? Are you alright by yourself?"

"I will go back to my home. My father is probably worried about me. I feel like the earth quaked." Badru heaved a sigh, then stood up and left.

"Who is this Hebrew god?" Yalu's mother asked. "I know some of the slaves who came back from the last war brought gods with them. But nothing like this has ever happened before. What's different this time?"

Yalu got up to leave, prompting Nebit and Tau to do the same. Then he turned back to her and shook his head, "If what Badru said is true, then I feel that we'll know soon enough."

They left Yalu's mother solemnly and exited the house. Inscribed above the door they passed through were the words "Geb bless this house". It had been there as long as Yalu remembered. He wondered if other gods like Geb would be able to stand against this new god? Or will they meet the same fate as Wadjet?

Chapter 6

Nebit stopped in front of Rashidi's manor behind the other two. It looked like a hive of bees that had just been disturbed. Servants and slaves ran this way and that. As the group approached they saw the man in charge.

Yalu leaned over to her and said, "He shouts and they run off as if Anubis himself were at their heels."

"Anubis may be chasing us next." she warned.

As soon as Rashidi saw the three soldiers, he gestured violently for them to approach. They broke into a run towards him and when they were within earshot, he shouted to them, "Follow me, I have another task for you." He led them inside his great house. They heard more shouting up ahead: people arguing about something in heavy Hebrew accents.

Before they got there, Rashidi pulled them aside into a small storage room. "The normal flow of operations is interrupted," he began, "Pharaoh told me that a man named Moses came to his palace and caused trouble. Since the man is a Hebrew he ordered me to find out more about him. I want you to find this 'Moses' and observe him. In my audience room I have gathered my Hebrew foremen. Try to get information from them. This is Pharaoh's request, so I need not remind you of the consequences for failure."

When Rashidi entered his audience room one of the foremen banged his fist against the wooden table featured in the center of the room, "We already told you everything we know about Moses. Why do you insist on keeping us here?"

"Do not question my wisdom," Rashidi snarled as he approached deliberately. The three soldiers fanned out behind him. "Defy me and I will have you thrown into the prison pit!" At this threat, the man's face lost its anger and he backed away. Having sufficiently silenced the foremen, Rashidi nudged Yalu.

He stepped up to the table and asked, "Where can we find this man, Moses?"

The same foreman heaved a sigh. "I don't know."

"Have you ever seen him?"

"Yes, at one of our meetings."

"Where and when is the next meeting?"

"I don't know."

"You better not be lying to me! I will personally throw you in the prison pit if I find out otherwise."

The foremen glanced at Rashidi and cringed. The only response given was a cold glare.

Yalu paused to think of more questions. Nebit could see sweat beads appear on the side of his face. An idea came to her and she raised her voice, "Who can we ask to find out?"

There was silence as they considered her question. Then one of the foremen in the back spoke up, "I may know somebody."

Rashidi brightened up, "Come forward."

He cautiously approached Rashidi and the three soldiers.

"Who do you know?" Rashidi asked.

He answered, looking uneasy and shifting his weight from side to side, "Well, a friend of mine is a servant to one of the elders. The elders go to all of the meetings with Moses. He might be able to tell you where you can find him."

"Well, be off then!" Rashidi commanded as he wiped some sweat from his brow with a white cloth.

The other foremen hastily exited the room. Then Rashidi tossed Yalu a leather pouch, "If the man won't give the information freely, then use this."

"Yes, master Rashidi." Yalu took the pouch and opened it. It was full of small pieces of metal jewelry: copper rings, a few silver pieces, and even one or two flashes of gold.

Rashidi fanned himself with his hands and breathed heavily. Tau came up alongside of him and asked, "Master Rashidi, are you well?"

"I'm fine." Rashidi blurted out. Then he sat down and put a hand to his face, "Just fatigued. Fetch me water!" He shouted toward the kitchen.

"Yes master." A woman's voice responded. A few seconds later they heard a scream and a crash. Nebit rushed into the kitchen to see her gazing at the floor with her mouth gaping open. Then she saw the pitcher that she had dropped. Blood drenched the ground next to it.

"What happened? Where did all this blood come from?" Nebit asked as he looked for signs of a wound. The others entered the kitchen now as well.

"No, I'm fine." She regained her composure, "I dipped the pitcher into the basin of water, but when I looked in the pitcher, it wasn't water, it was blood!"

Nebit and the others stood speechless as she explained, staring at the blood spilled on the floor. Nebit went to examine the water basin. Her eyes widened and she gasped.

Everyone rushed over to see. And to their surprise, it was indeed filled with blood. Soon, the entire kitchen reeked of it and everyone covered their noses. Rashidi grabbed the servant's shoulder.

He demanded, "Where was this basin filled from?"

"The Nile! We always carry our water from the Nile."

Rashidi loosened his grip, pondering her answer. She wriggled herself free of his grip, and backed away from him.

"The Nile. . ." Rashidi repeated to himself.

Another servant rushed in and shouted, "Master Rashidi! The water in the pool outside… It changed to blood! And others in the neighborhood are shouting about the same thing. What do we do?" Everyone remained silent for a moment.

Once again, everyone rushed away, this time outside to the pool. A large crowd gathered around it but parted to let Rashidi through. It glistened a deep and dark red in the morning sunlight. Onlookers remained silent with mouths gaping.

"What happened?" Rashidi looked around for someone to answer. Yet nobody did.

"Did not Moses perform magic today at Pharaoh's palace?" Nebit asked. Her face felt hot when everyone looked at her. Then she realized others didn't know she, Yalu, and Tau were at the palace. She added, "Or so I heard."

"Moses! Yes, it all makes sense." Rashidi growled. He took Nebit, Yalu, and Tau aside and said, "Can you see it? Can you smell it? This is what that man is doing to Egypt. This is why he must be stopped. This is why you need to find him and figure out what he is up to." He turned to his servants and ordered, "Find some water somewhere."

The servants acknowledged him and left.

He continued: "Do not trust the Hebrews. I will pray to Anuket to reverse this plague. I don't understand how the goddess of the Nile could let this happen."

They left Rashidi's manor and found the Hebrew foreman waiting. He wore a sack on his back, a wooden mace with metal studs on one side of his waist, and a sling on the other. "Have you asked Rashidi about the straw yet?" he asked, shielding his eyes from the sun.

Nebit, Yalu, and Tau exchanged guilty glances. Then Yalu just silently shook his head.

He nodded, but changed the subject: "My friend, Yadid, is the head servant of a man named Nun," he explained.

"Who is Nun?" Tau asked, stepping up to walk alongside the foreman. Nebit and Yalu closed the distance to listen.

"One of the elders in the Hebrew community. His household is very prosperous and respected. He is sure to be a part of any meetings with Moses."

As Tau and the man talked, Nebit couldn't help but notice all people running about them. Some people were wailing. Others shouted that they were thirsty and needed something to drink. More than one person lying prostrate on the ground, crying out to Anuket for water. Then, the reek of blood overwhelmed them.

"This is horrible!" Nebit cringed while covering her nose, "If all the water in the city changed to blood then how do we satisfy our thirst?"

"Look ahead!" Yalu pointed. Tau and the foreman stopped to look as well. A large crowd gathered around several traders, shouting at them. They ran up to see what was going on.

"Trade us for your beer; you have plenty left," One man in the crowd yelled.

The trader shouted back, "This belongs to Pharaoh, for his overseers!" Bodyguards and soldiers for the tradesmen kept the crowd at bay as they packed up their barrels.

They moved on and eventually found themselves among the brick-makers again, and approaching an estate similar to Rashidi's: perhaps a little smaller. A man standing watch and armed with sword and sling came to greet them. The two Hebrews spoke anxiously in a language the other three didn't understand, then the guard opened the gate, which was closed again behind them after they entered.

The foremen told them, "He said some misfortune befell Yadid, but he doesn't know what it is. He told us to wait here. I trust it's not serious."

Nebit felt the conversation held more than the Hebrew foreman would admit and eyed him suspiciously.

They entered the manor house and were escorted to a room with a low stone table sat in the middle. While they waited, they examined various murals that adorned the walls. Nebit was intrigued by the scenes depicted. In the prison pit, one of the prisoners dreamed about squeezing grapes into a cup. Another prisoner dreamed about birds eating bread. A third prisoner was shown between them and talking with them. Another painting showed a man wielding a rod as emblem of his power. He pointed at a storehouse, and people carrying sacks on their backs walked toward it. Still another painting had the same man standing between a storehouse and another eleven men.

Nebit opened her mouth to ask what the paintings meant when a man entered the room. He tugged his long gray beard, and the wrinkles on his face showed his weariness.

"I am Nun, of the household of Ephraim. I understand you came to see my servant Yadid. Regretfully, I must tell you he was kidnapped. With all the trouble Moses is causing it, I fear it only adds to our sufferings."

"Not so!" came a shout from inside. A young man with dark curly hair and piercing blue eyes entered.

Nun sighed.

"Our god sent him to free us from this suffering."

"If he indeed was sent by our god to free us from suffering, then why do we still suffer? Sit down, my son." Nun dismissed him and the younger man reluctantly obeyed. Then Nun turned to his four guests. "Please pardon Hoshea. But as you can imagine, we're frustrated by these recent events. We tried to hire some soldiers to rescue Yadid, and we could only find one ready and willing. My son offered to go himself, but it is much too dangerous. Then I heard that you had arrived right at my front door to help us and I believe it is a sign from our god."

Nebit interjected. "We're here on other business."

"Oh?" Nun's eyes showed disappointment.

"We're Egyptians," Tau tried reasoning. "I don't think a Hebrew god would send Egyptians to help."

"Actually, he did send us," Yalu said suddenly.

Nebit turned and looked at him in shock with her mouth gaping open. Glancing at Tau she saw he was doing the same thing as her. She hoped he a good reason to assume the intention of a god.

"We'll rescue Yadid," he insisted.

"Praise the god of my ancestors! I knew it," Nun exclaimed, raising his hands into the air. Then he calmed, "Yadid was at the market square just down the street. Perhaps you can start there."

"I am Yalu. My companions are Nebit and Tau. We will see what can be done."

Nun repeated their names, bowing to each one. "I know that my god will see you through to the end." The wrinkles on his face rearranged as Nun attempted a small smile, "Wait at the gate while one of my servants fetches the soldier. Farewell."

They left the house with Tau and Nebit giving sideways glances at Yalu. But he just smiled at them contentedly. The foremen left to tend to his slaves. Nebit put a hand on Yalu's shoulder and asked quietly, "What was that about with their god?"

"We came to get information from Yadid, and we can't very well do that if he's captured." Yalu told her.

"Information about Moses," Nebit clarified. "We could've saved the trouble by asking Nun."

"Some Egyptians asking about their god's emissary would've made him suspicious," Tau said. "He might have ended up turning us away."

Yalu sighed, "I don't know, maybe it was a bad decision. I've made our bed of straw and now we need to lie in it. What was I thinking? The chances we're going to find that Hebrew are next to nothing!"

Nebit put a hand on Yalu's shoulder to try and comfort him. But he just frowned, gazing toward the ground.

Then Yalu looked up. A man with a ragged brown cloak, a pack on his back and curly gray hair exited the house. A sword hung from his belt on one side and a sling on the other. Yalu grinned, "Then again, maybe not."

Nebit looked at Yalu confused, as did Tau. The man walked up to Yalu with a smile of his own and they embraced each other. "I didn't think I'd see you so soon. How did you get mixed up with this rescue?"

"Another job fell to me." Then he turned to the other two and said, "Lior and I fought together before. We can count on him. Let's go."

Arriving in the bustling market, they found tightly-packed mud houses: most residences were inhabited by families. They displayed their wares and crafts on tables or in baskets, or strolled with baskets or sacks in search of something they needed.

Tau looked up and down the market street, "With so many traders here, it will take hours to talk to them all."

"You're right. Let's split up." Yalu said. Then he pointed to a statue of Pharaoh, "Let's meet there in two hours."

Nebit nodded in agreement. They divided the market into sections and they each took one.

Yalu studied his section of the market. At first glance, it looked like everyone was busy. But after watching, Yalu could see that some traders were more passed by than others. After a few minutes, he spotted just the one he was looking for. The plump man had been sitting on his stool without a single customer. A brown turban rested on his head and a like-colored robe covered his body. Various bottles and boxes decorated the table he kept close watch over.

Yalu approached him, "I have some questions for you."

The trader looked at him with disgust and replied, "I don't have time to waste on your questions."

"Yes, I can see that your bottles are in high demand today." Yalu smirked, but the trader just frowned at him. Then he picked up a bottle and asked, "What is this?"

The trader snatched it out of his hands, "This perfume is worth ten deben of wheat."

Yalu did not have so much grain. He turned away.

"Wait," the trader said, "I will answer your question."

"A Hebrew man named Yadid, the servant of Nun, was kidnapped somewhere near here. I'm trying to find him. Have you seen anything?"

"Yadid?" The trader perked up in recognition of the name. "I know him. He stops by every couple weeks to buy something for his master or mistress. In fact, he came today."

"Did he buy?" Yalu asked.

The trader nodded.

"Which perfume?" Yalu asked, "Do you have any more?"

The trader gestured to a small clay bottle. Yalu opened it for a moment and smelled sweet herbs in oil.

Then he remembered the pouch of jewelry from Rashidi. The perfume could help him find Yadid, and Yadid could lead him to Moses. It wasn't exactly what Rashidi had intended the gold for, but it would get them closer to it. "Would you trade it for a silver bracelet?"

The trader's eyes narrowed. "Only gold or grain. I must feed my family."

Yalu took out a small gold ring so the trader could examine it.

The trader nodded reluctantly, and accepted the payment. Yalu took the perfume bottle and turned away. The spices were not rare, but they were in a pleasing proportion, and Yalu opened the bottle again, to remember it.

Lior walked inside a tent full of figs, dates, and other dried fruit. He recognized the trader from the other market, and waved. The man waved back with a forced smile.

"Greetings, did you hear about Yadid?" Lior asked as he walked toward the counter of woven reeds in the back.

"Hear?!" He leaned forward and lowered his voice. "Why, I practically saw it with my own two eyes. Ruffians made a scene not fifteen paces from my tent and then grabbed him. It's a tragedy! I tried to stay hidden. Wish you had been there! But I did get a few peeks, and I heard everything. There must have been eight or ten of them."

"Did you see where they went?"

"They took him up that way," he pointed westward, "and said something about the temple of Ptah? Unfortunately I don't know more than that. The Lord go with you."

"I will," Lior affirmed with a pat on the trader's shoulder. "Forgive my haste, but I must go. The Lord protect you and your family."

Tau grunted with irritation. He looked behind him at the traders who gave him no information and frowned. As he was about to give up and go to the statue, he saw his friend Nizm standing nearby the entrance to a tent. He walked over with a big smile.

"Tau," Nizm greeted him shyly. "What are you doing here?"

"Looking for somebody," Tau answered, "How about you?"

Before Nizm could reply, Sekani and Abayomi both exited, each carrying large burlap bags. Tau couldn't tell what was inside. They looked pleasantly surprised to see him.

"I thought our prior outing would be our last. Did you come to help us?" Sekani asked.

Tau tilted his head curiously, "What did you need help with?"

Confused Sekani turned to Nizm, "You didn't tell him?"

"I didn't know he was going to be here!"

"You didn't invite him?"

"No!"

"If you didn't come to help, then what are you doing here?" Sekani asked and the three looked at Tau expectantly.

Tau put his hands on his hips and replied irritably, "I'm working! Now tell me, what are you doing here?"

The three gave him a guilty look. Then Abayomi put a hand up around Tau's shoulder and they walked together. They gave Tau and Nizm each a bag to carry. They all swung them over their shoulders. Tau looked down at him, preparing for the worst.

"You see, we ran into a little bit of a problem." Abayomi began. Tau could hear the tension in his voice. "We wanted to keep our little tradition going, but since they'd recognize us at the Apis temple we thought we try the temple of Ptah."

"That was your idea." Sekani blamed with a pointed finger.

"We all agreed to it!" Abayomi defended himself. "I thought you said it was brilliant."

"I did not!"

Nizm jumped in, "You said it. I heard you."

Sekani grimaced, "Then I must've drunk too much beer and wasn't thinking clearly."

"Anyway," Abayomi continued, "We made our preparations and broke into the temple courtyard. We got all the way to the main building and thought we weren't seen."

"They spotted Nizm and started shooting arrows at him," Sekani interrupted.

"It wasn't my fault!" Nizm said. "The clay statue never would've fallen over if you hadn't made me carry that huge sack."

"Let me finish the story!" Abayomi shouted at them. "So, they started chasing us and lobbing arrows at us."

"You don't lob an arrow, you shoot it." Nizm posed as an archer. "I think these guards must have had recurve bows because those arrows went by really fast."

"Fine, shooting arrows at us and chased us up some stairs. But before we knew it, we were trapped. There were guards on one side and the edge on the other. An arrow flew and Sekani fell off the edge. We thought he died."

"I didn't."

"Yeah, we can see that." Tau laughed.

Sekani explained, "There was a ledge underneath and I fell on that."

"After that they caught us and took us for questioning," Abayomi shook his head. "I prefer not to talk about that. But to do right by them we needed to help them out. So here we are."

"I see," Tau said in a concerned tone. "And how are you helping them."

"That's the easy part of the whole thing," Abayomi smiled. "All they said we had to do was pick up these sacks and deliver them and we're free to go."

"Does sound easy," Tau agreed. "What's in the sacks?"

"That's not for the uninitiated to find out." A voice called to them. They whirled to see a man with a cloth around his nose and mouth.

Sekani stepped forward and dropped the bag in front of him. He said, "We did what you asked. Here are the bags."

Tau and the others dropped their bags and stepped back. From the shadows, about five others came and inspected the contents. When they each nodded toward the man he said, "Your debt has been paid. You're free to go now."

With sighs of relief Sekani led the three away. However, Tau glanced among the men with the bags curiously. He wondered if they had something to do with Yadid's disappearance.

After they got out of earshot of the other group, Tau whispered to his friends, "Don't wait up for me. There's something I need to do."

Toward the outskirts of the Hebrew neighborhood, Nebit decided to change her approach. Traders were suspicious of a warrior woman, but might be more helpful if she had wares, or a more familiar role. Her best seductress routine had achieved nothing. She thought: "Perhaps if I act like a Hebrew I might have better luck."

She found a weaver selling the robes she had seen Hebrew women wear. She approached and browsed among the wares and casually asked: "Would you take two weight of rye for this robe?"

He turned and tried replying in Egyptian. After a few failed attempts, he managed, "Five, or I could use three cruze of wine."

She did not have enough. Frowning and disappointed, she left the weaver. But twenty paces away she raised her eyebrows and turned her head to glance at him with a sly look. He was distracted by other interested traders, so she slipped back unnoticed and hid behind the pile on top of which lay her chosen clothing. When she was sure nobody watched, she quickly grabbed it and stuffed it into her sack. Then she followed the shadows of people passing and left the weaver none the wiser. Then, feeling a twinge of remorse, wished she had had the forethought to ask Yalu for some of the jewelry in Rashidi's pouch.

Donning the brown robe in one of the alleyways between mud brick buildings and an adjacent tent, she tried walking. It jutted and bulged oddly over her weapons, but that could not be helped. Once she felt ready, she left the comfort of the shadows to find her mark. She looked to one side of the street, and one tradesman who wasn't busy looked promising, but she changed her mind as a woman approached him. Scanning the other side, she saw only traders busy selling their goods. She walked on a little way and then spotted the trader she was looking for.

He watched people pass by, unable to catch their attention with his baskets and woven figures inscribed with prayers.

She chose a role carefully as she approached him, acting a girl in need of something. He noticed her immediately and started speaking to her rapidly in the Hebrew language. She could only shake her head.

"Yadid?" She said attempting a Hebrew tongue.

The man continued to address her in Hebrew.

She kept the question on her face, repeated the name, and pointed to the four directions, hoping that the man would tell her which one was correct.

Instead, the man, still speaking, put his hand on her shoulder and his tone implied that he was trying to talk about her something else. She thought quickly, looked down the street, and yelled, "Yadid!" pretending she had seen him, and left him to his disappointment.

Ducking into another alleyway, she leaned on a mud brick building and sighed. The two hours were almost up, and she had no clues at all. Her mind raced for some other way she could get information, determined not to return empty-handed.

Suddenly, a voice called to her from further down the alley.

She glanced toward it and saw two armed Egyptian men walking toward her, leering expressively.

"I think we have found a playmate," the one with the khopesh at his side said to the man with the spear on his back. "Shall we take her back and play some games with her?"

A flash of panic instinctively erupted from her middle. But then she curled her lips back as she regained her courage. Uncovering her head, she smiled at them toothily, "Games are for children. I like something a little more ill-behaved."

At first they were startled by her attitude, but it didn't deter them.

"Ill-behaved?" saids the other, taking a step forward, "We can be very ill-behaved."

She tilted her head, "But you two seem so . . . upright," she opened her eyes wide in false innocence, aware of the innuendo's effect on her aggressors, but keeping her eyes on their faces.

The slower of the two objected, "We have an eyewitness to the contrary. Would you like to join him?"

The quicker-witted Egyptian shot an elbow into his ribs, and corrected the error, "You should see for yourself, either way." He played with the hem of his tunic.

"No, no. Where is this . . . eyewitness? I should be asking him first, to be sure." Nebit could not believe her luck. Could they really be talking about the kidnapped Yadid? It was too absurd to be true.

The slower man said eagerly, "You want to meet him?"

"He would tell me how ill-behaved you are? Where is he?" She glanced behind herself, making sure she had a clear escape route.

"If he could speak through his gag," the slower one murmured gloatingly to his friend. "Just south of the temple of…"

The cleverer of the two punched his stupider companion's arm.

"Quiet!" he growled. "We can't just blurt secrets to every pretty face."

But the man dismissed him with a hand gesture.

"Come with us and we'll show you how bad we really are."

As he put his arm around her shoulder he felt a sharp pain at his side. By reflex, his hand grasped the rib and when he looked down he saw blood: his blood. He looked up at Nebit, whose robe swirled through the air before it fell to the ground. He drew his Khopesh just in time to defend against the woman's attacks.

As the two swung their blades at each other, the other man watched and waited with his spear at the ready, waiting for an opportunity to strike. Nebit struck furiously with her daggers, and the man retreated with his back to the building. Her blades tore into his cheek, forearm, and leg. Then one of them found itself in the man's chest and he fell.

Nebit pointed her daggers at the other man and readied herself to pounce on him. Just then, nine more brutes appeared behind him. Nebit saw some of them wielding khopeshes and the other bows. She stared at them for a moment with wide eyes, then turned and ran away as an arrow sliced through the air where she had been.

Yalu stood at the statue of Pharaoh chatting with Lior while they waited. Suddenly, a fleeing Nebit ran past them.

"Look out! They're after me!" She yelled as she hid behind Yalu.

Yalu looked behind her and saw five armed Egyptians chasing. He turned around and glared at her. "What did you do?!"

"Nothing!" She tried to show open palms to indicate her innocence, but each hand held a dagger, and both were dripping blood. "I was just gathering information. Now isn't the time to talk about it."

Yalu grumbled as he begrudgingly drew his sword and shield just in time to deflect an arrow. The traders and passersby in the area heard the clang and fled in a panic when they saw the fight break out.

Taking a couple steps back, Lior readied his sling with his right hand and took a few rocks from a pouch at his waist with the other. He slipped one of them in the sling's cradle and after a couple swings he launched it and hit one of the thugs carrying a bow, knocking him down.

Yalu charged forward with his shield at the ready to meet assailants in combat. But one aggressor ran past and headed straight for Nebit. She recognized the clever man from the alley. He engaged her with his spear and a cry for vengeance.

While Lior brought down the second bowman with his sling, Nebit danced around the Egyptian's spear. He thrusted towards her abdomen and she contorted to dodge. He thrust toward her head, a blow she deflected with her dagger. Then she leapt toward him and sliced up into his jaw and then back into his throat. He fell with a nauseating gurgling sound. Yalu and Lior quickly defeated the others.

As Nebit walked up to them, Yalu asked her, "Vengeance?"

She shook her head and smiled innocently.

Just then they saw Tau emerge from the alley and strut toward them. He carried the oversized khopesh over a shoulder and a grin on his face.

"There were more of those brutes there. What happened?" Nebit asked.

"You don't have to worry about them anymore." Tau gestured dismissively. Then he handed her a brown robe. "I think you dropped this."

Nebit's face flushed red. She swatted it from his hand and warned him, "You better not tell anyone."

"So, there is more!" Yalu accused, pointing his finger at her.

Lior put a calming hand on Yalu's shoulder. "A trader friend of mine said that he heard the thugs who took Yadid talk about the temple of Ptah. So that narrows it down somewhat. But it will still be hard to find out which house they're keeping him in."

Yalu pulled out his bottle of scent from a pouch on his belt, "Let's hope this will narrow down the search even more. Let's get going."

Yalu led everyone out of the market and to the grounds of the temple. The sun cast its last ray of light over city walls and twilight loomed in the air. They gazed southward at the neighborhood of dense houses spanning before them.

"Hmm..." Yalu rubbed his chin as he considered the paths. Then he concluded, "We need to explore and then we can choose what to do."

"Yalu, can we smell that perfume?" Nebit rubbed her hands together in excitement as Yalu took the bottle out and opened it. The sweet-smelling fragrance almost overwhelmed them. "I have never smelled perfume like this before. Close it now. We don't want to smell of it ourselves," she suggested.

Yalu closed the bottle and stashed it away. "I have a good nose, so with any luck I'll be able to sniff out the right house."

As they crossed back and forth through the area, the half-moon appeared over the horizon and cast menacing shadows into the dark city neighborhoods. Windows glowed as people lit lamps to see. Some passersby wielded torches to fend off the encroaching darkness.

After climbing through alleys for miles, Tau ran into Yalu.

He walked over to Yalu and asked in a whisper, "Do you smell it yet?"

Yalu matched his whisper, "Not yet. Do you?"
Tau shook his head. "This might be a long shot. But
let's keep searching."

They continued.

When Tau and Nebit met in a dark alley, more
than an hour later, at first they startled each other, but
soon each recognized the other. Nebit said quietly, "I
haven't smelled it yet. Have you?"

"No, I haven't." Tau replied, "Do you think we
will be able to?"

She shrugged and they both went back to
sniffing houses.

Deep into the evening hours, Yalu and Nebit
met.

"I doubt we're going to find him. Sniffing for
houses for perfume that we'd find the right one by
chance is a fool's errand. I can't believe we're doing
this," Yalu admitted, and Nebit laughed to herself, not
wanting to gloat that she had thought so all along.

"Well, we could go back to Rashidi and tell him
we can't find Moses." She leaned casually against a mud
wall.

"Let's keep searching for a little longer and
then come up with a new plan."

Nebit nodded and started sniffing around the
next house.

Yalu turned to check around another house.
Suddenly, he heard Nebit's gasp from a few yards
behind him. He whirled around to see amusement on
her face as she pointed enthusiastically at the house's
window. Yalu crept over, and from the window he
could smell a faint fragrance that matched the one from
the bottle he bought. The unfortunate servant must
have dropped the bottle for the aroma to linger for so
long. Glancing inside, they saw a Hebrew man
crouching in a corner. Egyptians lounged around,

casting him the odd glance to make sure he hadn't moved. They held spears, bows, khopeshes, etc., and more weapons lay in a pile near the door.

Yalu motioned for Nebit to follow, and they went in search of Tau and Lior. Yalu then explained to them what he saw in the house.

Tau crossed his arms, "If we break open the front door they're liable to kill the poor man."

"I've been thinking of a plan. Tell me your thoughts." Yalu crouched on the ground and drew in the sand. After his explanation, they squinted at the barely visible diagram for a few more moments.

"I like it," Nebit finally replied. She smiled as she said, "Letting Tau be the main target will allow me the freedom to sneak around."

"Reminds me when we joined those bandits only to flee with the loot they stole." Lior chuckled.

"I suppose these are merely a different kind of bandit. Let's do it," Yalu stood up and the others followed.

As they walked back to the house Yalu relieved Lior of his weapons. "You won't need those."

"Oh yes I will. And I'll thank you to return them when the time is right."

Yalu finished the preparations by binding Lior's hands together with a piece of rope Lior kept in his pack. Then Yalu took the pack from him as well.

Reaching the house again, they found their arranged positions. Nebit set herself up by the window. Tau crept near the door, but within line-of-sight to Nebit. Yalu approached the front entrance with Lior beside him. The door of tightly bound reeds showed their desire for privacy. Lior took a deep breath, turned to Yalu, and nodded. Then Yalu knocked on the mud-brick building.

Voices murmur behind the door. A few metal and wood clanks interrupted the evening silence. After a few moments, a man asked, "What do you want?"

"I want to join you." Yalu replied in a tone of mock-conspiracy.

The man looked Yalu over, then turned his head to Lior, who showed his face downcast, and asked, "Who is he?"

"My prisoner." Yalu yanked the rope prompting Lior to yelp.

The man looked at the two one more time and closed the door. Muffled discussion took place. Suddenly the door swung open and two men greeted them. One had a big smile on his face, and the other held a khopesh, trying to look intimidating. "Come in, friend. And tell me about your prisoner." the happy one invited.

"Gladly," Yalu stepped in and jerked the rope hard enough to make Lior stumble through the doorway. "This man's a trader with connections to a wealthy Hebrew family. I'll wager we can get a lot for his ransom."

"Our master decides the ransom. Lucky for you he should come tonight. He'll get you recruited properly." The same man sat and started talking with Yalu.

The intimidating man took Lior and sat him down next to Yadid. Lior leaned over and muttered into Yadid's ear, "Stay safe when the fighting starts."

Yadid's face turns to shock. "Who are you?"

"No talking!" One of the guards shouted and jabbed Yadid in the side with the blunt end of his spear. Yadid yelped to their amusement.

Outside, Tau motioned with his hands as he mouthed, "Ready yet?" Nebit shook her head. Then she turned her head to watch the room through the window again.

Tau sighed as silently as he could, and Nebit kept a close eye on him as well as inside the house. The impatient soldier paced in a circle. Then he grabbed his khopesh and pointed inside the room. He swung his blade, grinning fiercely, careful not to hit anything or make noise. After a few fierce blows on the air, he raised his arms above his head in triumph. Nebit could almost hear his silent roar, but she definitely heard his exerted breathing. She stifled a laugh.

Suddenly she raised her hand with her palm toward Tau. He paused. Both hands gripped his khopesh tightly as he focused on Nebit's hand. Once the majority of the men on the inside went to sleep, she gave Tau the signal. His grin widened from ear to ear as he carefully raised his khopesh over his head and to the left. Then, with all of his might, he roared wildly and swung it downward.

The attack ripped the door into pieces and flung them into the room onto the few occupants. Some of the men close to the door scrambled backward. "I am Tau!" He declared as he stepped into the room.

In his battle rage, Tau didn't hear the shouts. Finally, the men shook themselves from their stupor and grabbed their weapons and rallied. He grinned as he provoked them, "Come here. I can take you all at once." He lowered his stance and set his khopesh parallel to the ground ready to charge forward.

Then Yalu stepped forward, turned his head towards the men cowering behind him and said, "I'll show you how to handle a big brute like this."

They cheered him on in great relief as he assumed a defensive stance with his shield held out and his sword behind it. He nodded, and Tau took a deep breath and roared as he charged. Just before Tau trampled him, Yalu tucked and rolled out of the way. The soldiers behind him gasped in terror as Tau continued toward them and slashed one of them before they had time to react. Then, after Yalu had risen from his roll, he joined Tau in the attack.

At this point, chaos broke out, just in time for Nebit to jump in through the window. She bolted over to the thugs guarding Yadid who were too focused on the battle to notice her. A little work with her daggers rendered them no longer a threat.

"I'm very glad to see you," Lior confessed as Nebit cut his bonds.

When Nebit cut Yadid's bonds he started talking, "Thank you, thank you, thank you, thank you so much! They've done so many things to me I was afraid they were going to kill me. I never thought I'd be rescued, especially by Egyptians."

Nebit finished her work quietly, but when done, she pointed one of her daggers at him which shut him up, "Stay out of the way and keep silent. Try not to get yourself hurt." He nodded emphatically and stood with his back to the corner as she turned and joined the fray.

Yalu raised his shield and took a step in retreat as he saw Nebit and Lior. Tau followed his lead and the few remaining enemy filled the gap and completed the trap. The two in the back fell to Nebit's subtle slashes and Lior's sword. Their screams caused two of the men fighting Yalu and Tau to turn and face them.

At this point, Yalu banged the side of his sword with his shield and shouted to them, "Drop your weapons and we'll just leave with Yadid."

A small silence preluded the first thug to drop his spear. The others reluctantly followed.

"A well-earned victory," Tau hooked his khopesh back to his belt.

Yalu glanced among them and saw only minor cuts and bruises on all except for a deeper cut into Lior. Yalu asked, "Are you alright?"

Lior leaned against the wall and breathed a heavy sigh. With the back of his hand pressed against his forehead he said, "It burns and makes me feel faint. I need you to carry me back on your shoulders."

"Flesh and Fire!" Yalu cursed and Lior burst into laughter.

The others looked on bewildered. Tau offered, "If you need help then I can carry you."

"Let the crows have him!" Yalu dismissed Lior with a gesture. He walked over to Yadid, "What about you? Are you well?"

Yadid nodded and then approached Lior with gratitude and spoke to him in Hebrew.

Lior put his arm around Yadid's shoulder and motioned toward the others. "It was Yalu's plan that saved you. He, Nebit, and Tau deserve the lion's share of your thanks."

"Save the thanks for later. We need to head back to Nun's manor, first." Nebit pointed out.

Lior and Tau took his elbows and led him out the door.

As they headed back Yalu told him, "We're going to call in that favor pretty quickly. We need some information from you."

"I will help you any way that I can," Yadid agreed.

"We need to know about Moses."

Yadid stumbled but Lior and Tau helped keep him from falling. Then he stopped walking and asked cautiously, "Why do you want to know about him?"

"We saw his miracle with the snakes."

He searched Yalu's face, but it couldn't find the reassurance he was looking for. So he turned to Lior

and they talked briefly in Hebrew. Then he turned back
to Yalu and asked, "Why do you really want to know?"

Nebit moved forward, "We have been tasked
with finding out. We rescued you for this information
because a powerful Egyptian is afraid of him."

Yadid looked into her eyes as well, and decided
she was telling the truth. It weighed heavily on him.
"Do you realize this would betray my own kin?"

"Trust me," Lior said reassuringly. "They
rescued you. This is a good lot. It's for the best."

Yadid glanced back at Lior and they smiled at
each other. Then he stared into Yalu's eyes for a few
moments. Finally he nodded.

"We heard Moses holds meetings. Where do
they take place? And when is the next one?"

"My master Nun attends them," Yadid folded
his arms and rested his chin on his fist. "See me
tomorrow."

Yalu expressed exasperation: "Our master
expects a report tonight."

"You need to be patient," Yadid assured him.
"I cannot gather this kind of information so quickly."

Tau shook his head, "I hate waiting."

"I'd think a soldier should be used to it." Nebit
said with a smirk and Tau scowled at her.

"Enough," Yalu turned around and put a hand
on each of their shoulders. "Let's get him home. I think
what's happened may be explanation enough for our
master."

Chapter 7

Upon hearing the good news of Yadid's rescue, people in the manor came flocking over to see. Soon the soldiers found themselves enveloped in a crowd of Hebrews greeting and thanking them. They made way for Nun, his son following close behind him. When he saw them he clapped his hands and smiled widely. With each step Tau felt the crowd growing. He breathed the air and really felt alive. Finally, they enter the gate and Nun embraced Yadid, who shed tears of joy to be reunited with his master and safely back home one again.

Hoshea embraced Yadid as well with many pats on the back. Then Nun faced the soldiers, "I praise the Lord our god that we can see Yadid alive again. Let me offer you my warmest thanks. Yadid has been a friend and servant for many years. Come! I will host a banquet for you and everyone in my house! I can see that your weary bodies are in need of refreshment," he called for his physician.

Yalu cradled some bruises on his shield arm making Tau think of a cut he'd received on his arm. They gratefully followed Nun and Hoshea into his residence. As they passed by, the crowd continued their appreciative cheers.

Tau couldn't wait as Nun led them to his pool. This cool bath was square, about two lengths of a man, and the foundation of the pool was laid in stone. It was about waist deep with smooth sitting stones around the edge. He motioned toward the pool, "Please use this to refresh your spirits. My physician will be here shortly to tend to your wounds. Excuse me." He left.

"Don't be shy," Hoshea said as he took off his robe to enter the pool. Then he gestured, "Come on in."

Yalu found a place in the refreshing water and Nebit sat next to him. Tau stepped in next to Hoshea. The water felt cool, soothing his wounds and relaxing his muscles.

"Ah." Tau put his hands behind his head and leaned back against the edge of the pool. He couldn't remember a time he felt more at ease, even at Badru's estate. "This is just what I need."

"Please," Hoshea motioned with his hand, "Tell me about your heroic adventure."

"It all started in the Hebrew market," Tau began. "Through fate or chance, I don't know which, I was able to find the men responsible. There were about fifteen of them in all, so I waited for my chance. But as luck would have it they were…" He trailed off to look around at the others. As his eyes scanned over Nebit he saw her shaking her head slightly.

Smiling, and with a bit of a chuckle, Tau finished, "busy." He then recounted finding the house, tricking the kidnappers, and the fight in vivid detail.

"But Yalu is the mastermind," Lior pointed to him, "He came up with the whole plan."

Yalu commented, "It was a team effort. We all had our job and executed it well."

Tau bowed his head with a smile and gave Yalu a few claps from his hands. Though he knew his job was critical, he couldn't help feeling that Yalu helped give him this opportunity.

The physician entered the room and Yalu volunteered Lior as first to undergo treatment. He grunted and groaned as the physician applied ointment.

He called Yalu next and tended to the cuts on his upper arm. He used a different kind of ointment on the bruises, and Yalu winced with his own grunts and moans.

Tau's turn was next. He made it a point to recount his prior adventure with his friends breaking into the temple of Apis and their escape. From Badru's treatments, he learned that if his mind was occupied then the stinging and soreness would feel less.

The physician approached Nebit last. After examining her, he declared, "You have only bruises. Are you protected by a god?"

She looked around at the others and gloated, "Some people know how to avoid getting hurt."

Hoshea turned to Nebit, "How did you learn to fight? That isn't taught to Hebrew women."

"Yes," Yalu turned to her. "I've been meaning to ask that too. You took care of yourself very well back there."

Nebit opened her mouth to answer but looked away and sighed. "I'd rather not talk about it."

There was a pained look in her eyes. Yalu walked over to her and put a hand on her shoulder. She looked up into his eyes and a single lonely tear escaped. She quickly wiped it away.

"Before I forget," Hoshea changed the subject and leaned forward. Ripples broke the surface of the water. Light from the torches refracted through it, and cast moving shadows on the floor of the pool. The others leaned forward too. He continued in a slightly quieter voice, "I don't think any Egyptian has helped us the way you have. But many more great things will come to pass in the days ahead. You might. . . well. . . " He trailed off.

"Might what?" Tau asked.

They heard footsteps approaching, and Hoshea turned his head for a moment, then looked back at them.

"If you need anything, ask my family."

Nun entered and announced, "The feast is
ready. Come, let's eat and drink!" Everyone stood, their
legs shaking as they quickly dried in the warm air, and
put on their outer clothes. They followed Nun into a
much larger room with a stone slab on which were laid
cups of wine, roast bird, grilled lamb, with fresh garlic,
onions, figs, and dates.

"What a feast!" Tau proclaimed, staring at it all
and licking his lips.

Others in the room sat near the food but
waited for the mercenaries to commence. Nun gestured
welcomingly, "Sit!"

Each found a seat in a place of honor. Tau
immediately got to work on a large juicy chunk of
lamb. He turned to tell Yalu how good it was, but Yalu
seemed transfixed by Nebit tearing into a good-sized
bird's leg with her teeth. When she noticed them
looking at her, she shrugged with a smile and
continued.

Nun stood up and pulled Yadid up with him, "I
want to extend my thanks once again to Lior, Yalu,
Nebit, and Tau for rescuing my servant and friend,
Yadid. Let's give them a good cheer!" Everyone thrust
closed fists into the air shouted cheers. After a few
seconds, Nun gestured with his hands for quiet, and
began telling stories about Yadid.

Tau continued guzzling wine and was surprised
to find it empty after only a few bites of lamb. As he
stared into his empty wine skin he heard a woman clear
her throat above him. He looked up and his eyes met
the biggest brown eyes he had ever seen. They were
accompanied by long, curling lashes, and curly black
hair that draped down over her shoulders.

"More wine?" she asked.

Tau emphatically nodded his head.

She leaned over to pour wine from her clay jug.

After it was filled, he took another drink, then looked up to thank her, but she had gone.

Tau stood and announced, "I'll wager I can drink more than you! Any challengers?"

Yalu replied with a laugh, "The beer last night taught me my lesson. You didn't learn yours?"

"Lesson? What lesson?!" Tau shouted, "I can drink more than any two people here!"

Hoshea stood and started to say, "I'll take you…"

"No you won't," Nun replied, grabbing his son's robe and pulling him back to his seat. Everyone laughed and Tau laughed the loudest. Hoshea made a helpless gesture toward him.

When the food and wine were gone, Yalu stood up and said, "Thank you Nun, for your hospitality. It is good that your servant was found whole and well. The sun shine its favor on you tomorrow."

Nun nodded and stood, "Yes, it has been a long night I thank you all again for your efforts. I pray that the Lord our god blesses you abundantly."

Tau was reclining comfortably against the table in the middle of the room. He could feel his senses slowed as an effect of the wine and took his time getting up. He stretched his arms up in the air and staggered out with everyone else. He noticed Yalu give Yadid a look and, in turn, replied with a nod.

After all the trouble we took rescuing him, helping us is the least he can do to repay his debt, Tau thought.

Lior walked with them up to the gate and told them, "This is where we part ways for tonight. A good deed done and we live to fight another day!" He gestured with his hand, staggered, and almost fell to the ground.

Yalu caught him and helped him regain his balance. "Perhaps you should think about walking to your bed first."

They all laughed together. Tau added, "It was a good fight tonight, the feast was excellent, and the stories were captivating."

"Captivating indeed! You're quite the storyteller yourself. I'm almost convinced you've had more adventures than Yalu and me." Lior said. "But yes, I must rest for tonight."

"Good night, Lior," Yalu said.

"Very well." Lior embraced Yalu. "Good night, bandit-hunter Yalu."

Then Lior embraced Tau and Nebit before he left them. As the three walked out of the Hebrew district the moon above accompanied them.

"Bandit-hunter?" Nebit asked.

Yalu groaned. "The man's nickname for me. I'm not really a bandit hunter. For the last few years I've guarded caravans crossing the desert."

"Then how did you get it?" asked Tau.

"Well, I suppose I did get a reputation for some risky rescues." Yalu told them about rescuing the maidens from the bandits at the ruins.

"You are a protector then?" She stood in front of him with hands clasped behind her back. "Can you show me how to protect people? I've spent all my life taking the lives of whoever my master wished. And I hate it!"

"It's not that hard," Yalu looked awkward as he replied. "Maybe it comes naturally to me."

"Then can I fight alongside you?" She asked, leaning forward, close to him. "Maybe I can learn from you."

Yalu paused. Tau thought he looked like a startled gazelle whose eyes are searching for a predator. The eyes revealed a pain hidden until now. But then Yalu shook it off and he nodded.

She smiled broadly and grabbed Yalu's hand with excitement. "I shall hold you to it." Then she ran off in the night. As he watched her go she turned and waved at him. He waved back at her, with a smile on his face.

Tau stood watching with interest. Suddenly, Yalu turned to him and his face flushed red. Tau laughed, "Did you forget I was here?"

"No, I... Well, maybe." Yalu admitted. They laughed together and walked down the shadowy road.

"I was thinking on our way back," Tau started. "You were lying to Nun before about their god sending us. But now I'm not sure. Was it really mere coincidence?"

Yalu looked ahead but didn't answer. His face was contorted as though in thought. Then he said, "No. I think its more likely that one of our gods is helping us so we can spy on Moses."

Tau grunted and they continued. Yalu turned down the road to the house of his mother. Tau waved goodnight to him. Then he walked the road back to his own house. Kesi and little Ebo were already asleep. He smiled at them and then settled down to sleep himself.

The next day, Tau met the others at Rashidi's home, and they headed to the outer parts of the city again. As they approached the edge of the city they saw a familiar dark-skinned face wearing a black kalisiris robe, a sack on his back, and a bronze mace on his belt.

"What are you doing here, Badru?" Tau asked and walked up to him. The other two followed behind.

"Are you going to look for Moses?" he asked in return. Dark rings around his eyes betrayed his lack of sleep.

"That's our task from Rashidi," Yalu answered from behind. "Why do you ask?"

Badru took a deep breath and released it. "You can see the results of the latest battle between the Hebrew god and the Egyptian gods."

"Battle!" Tau said with surprise. Then he asked with confusion, "What battle?"

"Surely…" Badru looked at Nebit, "You saw the blood of Anuket. It is there, spilled for all of Egypt to see!"

"Anuket, the goddess of the Nile," Yalu elaborated, "Rashidi went to pray to her for the blood to go away."

"His prayers are in vain," Badru said grimly.

Feeling more confused than ever, Tau asked, "Why?"

Badru explained, "Anuket, who embraced the fields along the Nile to the blessings of a bountiful harvest, now embraces her own death. Anuket is the next god to fall before this Hebrew god."

"But at the festival of Anuket. . .," Tau recalled, "Does that mean the bronze shards we sacrificed to her were wasted?"

Badru nodded and asked "Can I come with you? I want to speak with Moses, to learn more about their god. How can he have the power to defeat Wadjet and Anuket? I must understand."

"Of course you can join us!" Tau flung an arm around Badru. "We'll get you your chance to talk with him even if we have to…" Tau gripped the collar of Badru's robe and tugged it upwards, growling.

Badru protested, "Put me down you overgrown water cow!" A smile cracked his expression as his feet met the ground again.

"I don't know about this," Nebit shook her head. "Rashidi might object. And how did you know we were going to Moses?"

Badru gave a sideways glance at Tau, who innocently scratched the back of his neck. Then he turned to her, "I give you my word that I shall not interfere with your task. But I must have my questions answered."

"I understand," Yalu said. He exchanged glances with Nebit who hesitantly nodded in agreement.

When they arrived at Nun's residence, Lior waved at them from the gate. Yalu asked dryly, "Did they promote you from hero to gate guard?"

"No kidnappings today, sir. We'll see about tomorrow." He cracked a smile. Yalu returned it.

"We're here for Yadid."

Lior turned around and whistled to a nearby servant. "Sarah, fetch Yadid. The Egyptians are here." She ran inside, and her long curly black hair jumped with every step. Tau remembered her who filled his cup the during the feast last night.

After a short time, Yadid emerged. He approached them and his eyes looked over the group. When they got to Badru, Yadid asked, "Who is he?"

He stepped forward and answered before Yalu had a chance, "My name is Badru. I have seen the wonders that your god has performed and want to talk with Moses."

Yadid nodded and led them away from the estate.

They walked for a while without saying anything. Yadid glanced around, keeping stock of their position. Then, when he was satisfied, he walked into an alley and turned around.

"There isn't another meeting, but I know where Moses is staying. His brother's family has a home here."

Yadid gestured them to follow. He walked out of the alley but then stopped and turned around. Tau could see his anxiety. The man had clearly not slept well after the feast.

"What are you really planning?" Yadid's eyes searched theirs.

Yalu held up his open palms as though they showed he had no hidden intentions. "We really just want to learn more about Moses and his god. And Badru wants to speak with him."

Yadid searched Yalu's face for a moment and then turned to Badru. He sighed and then nodded toward the ground. He looked up and into the eyes of each person before he turned and continued. It made Tau feel guilty, though he didn't know why. He wondered if he should be doing this. Then his father's voice boomed in his head, "Do your duty!" He quickly dismissed the feeling.

Their Hebrew escort stopped next to a mud-brick house and pointed to a larger house a little way down across the street. The four looked at the tall, two-story house surrounded by a stone wall. While the others struggled to see over the walls, Tau could easily see a second structure inside. He also saw a few servants go about their business.

Yadid took a step back, "I've shown you what you wanted."

"Yes Yadid," Yalu answered, still examining the area, "This is all we need."

Before he turned to go, Yadid put a hand on Yalu's shoulder, "I met you last night, but you were a ray of light in that dark place. I pray the Lord our god blesses you."

"Your god bless you as well," he replied as Yadid left. Staring at the estate Yalu asked, "So what now?"

"We approach the gate and ask to speak with Moses," Tau suggested.

Nebit opened her mouth to criticize him then shut it just as quickly. Then she commented, "I guess it could work."

"We're heroes! We rescued their kin," Tau reasoned. "They've got to recognize us since we've proven ourselves."

"That was only last night," Nebit reminded him, "Do you really think word spread that fast?"

"Moses isn't hiding." Tau reasoned. "Why shouldn't he see guests who call upon his door?"

Nebit looked at Tau skeptically. Then she finally shrugged, "Ok, let's call on his door. Let's see what happens."

As they walked up to the gate, the two guards eyed them. They wore bronze helmets, straps of leather for armor, and straight swords attached at the waist.

With his sword before him a guard asked, "What's your business here?"

Yalu smiled shallowly and folded his hands across his waist nonthreateningly. He answered, "May we speak with Moses?"

"No. Go away Egyptian," he motioned with his hand. Nebit gave Tau a quick smile of victory.

"Were you the last to hear?" Tau raised his voice. "We rescued Yadid!"

"Yadid?" the man turned to Tau, "Who is Yadid?"

Yalu answered quickly, "A servant of Nun, kidnapped not long ago."

"Oh yes! I heard the story of his rescue this morning. That was you? Of course! I'll go get Moses right away." He went inside the large house. Tau flashed a grin at Nebit, who folded her arms with annoyance trying to ignore it. They waited for a few minutes before he returned.

"Sorry, no."

"Why not?"

"That's all I know."

"Is there anything you can do? This is urgent," Badru interjected.

"I wish there were," he said, "I do thank you for your service to Yadid. You are rare Egyptians, indeed."

They left the gate. Nebit shot another grin towards Tau, who grunted irritably. His mind raced to think of something. Badru sighed dejectedly.

Yalu whispered to the group, "What do we do now?"

Nebit perked up, "We know where he lives, so we stay and wait until we see him and then follow where he goes."

"Stay where?" Yalu looked around.

Tau pointed up at the two-story house behind him without looking. "What about this place? If we can get a room in there, we can see over the wall and find out what they're doing."

His companions saw that the home across the narrow path had a window which overlooked the wall on the second story. They all smiled at him, except for Nebit. He felt good.

Approaching the door, Tau saw the dirt ground inside covered with reed mats. Next to them rested two clay basins full of water. Two men in the right-hand corner wearing robes and turbans sat down on the mats, one older and another much younger looked the group over. Their expression turned fearful once they saw Tau.

"We want to stay in a room here. The one on the second story right above us." Yalu broke the awkward silence. Then he took out a jewel from his pouch. "We can barter. How about this for a week's stay there?"

The younger man continued to sit and looked to the older man who seemed to be his father. The older man stood up, walked over, and examined the jewel. When the man looked up at Tau again, Tau tried to smile as warmly as he could.

"Very well. My son will show you the room." He pocketed it with a smile. "Be sure to wash up before you enter your room. But you'll be on your own for meals."

After they washed their feet, the man's son motioned for them to follow. He led them through a door in the back and through the kitchen to the outside. Then he took them up a flight of stairs to the second floor. A small hallway with heavy burlap for doors opened ahead of them.

Leading them all the way to the end, he held up the burlap for them. He stood by the door and continued to hold it open as they enter. Tau almost had to crouch to get inside.

Scanning the room, he saw a few reed mats on the ground. A low mud brick table occupied the center of the room, and a single window let the light shine in from the opposite side.

Yalu walked over to the window and looked out at the streets and the house opposite them.

"This is perfect," Yalu looked over at the young man and nodded. With that, he quickly bowed to them and left.

Everyone's attention immediately focused on the window and they gathered around Yalu to see. Tau could see the goings-on over his head. Scanning the manor, he saw various Hebrew servants fetching water and moving heavy sacks of grain, among other things. The main building was a little smaller than the one in Nun's residence. A second building appeared to be a home for the servants. Numerous smaller granaries dotted the inside as well.

"What are they doing now?" Badru put his hand on Yalu's shoulder and peered over it.

"It looks like they're filling their granaries. They're stocking the entire place with food, water, and other supplies," Yalu replied, "But I don't see the men we saw talking to Pharaoh at the palace."

"Do you think that Hebrew showed us the wrong building?" Badru asked. "He seemed rather hesitant."

Yalu shook his head, "I trust him."

"Tell me about this man, this Yadid." Badru said as he walked over to the table and sat down cross-legged.

Tau sat down at the wall on the other side of the table of Badru and leaned against it to get comfortable. He told Badru that Yadid is the chief servant at Nun's household and recounted the rescue.

Badru looked inquisitively at Tau, "Tell me about your rescue of Yadid. Did you notice if the abductors had a brand of an eye on their skin?"

Tau shook his head. Badru looked at Nebit, and she repeated the gesture.

Then Yalu spoke up while keeping his gaze on the manor, "An eye? You don't mean the eye of Ptah, do you?"

"I do," Badru started, "Before I left my home today I overheard a conversation between my father and one of the leaders at the temple. They talked about plans concerning the Hebrew slaves. Then I heard something about frustration over three Egyptians and a Hebrew who slew some of its new members during the night. You seem to fit the description," he leaned back against the wall and gravely made his accusation.

Nebit shook her head furiously, "There's no reason to suspect those men were from the priesthood."

"Actually, there is," Tau recounted his little adventure with his friends who ran afoul of the priesthood. He told them how, after his friends gave the sacks to the men working for the priests that he got suspicious and followed the men.

"So that's why the whole lot of them didn't continue after me from the alley," Nebit concluded.

When Badru looked curiously at her, she filled him in on the fight in the Hebrew market. Then he asked, "So what do we do now? Shall we wait until Yalu spots Moses leave the manor house?"

Yalu shook his head and sighed, "We've no idea when he's going to come; it may be too much for one person. Let's watch the manor in shifts. If it gets too hot, we can watch from the roof or the road. It's already noon, so I'll watch for a few hours. Then Nebit can watch until twilight. After that, Tau and Badru take turns during the night. Agreed?"

"What about tomorrow morning?" Badru inquired.

"Two shorter shifts per person," Yalu answered.

"That sounds fair to me." Nebit said. "The watcher must be alert so as not to miss any opportunity."

After a short silence Tau felt his empty belly and said, "If we're going to be here for a while, we'll have to go buy food. I saw some of the merchants in the streets selling bread and figs. They looked good."

All of them, even Nebit, agreed. Yalu settled into a more comfortable position at the Window and Nebit kept him company. Tau went down to the market with Badru in anticipation of the aroma of fresh baked bread and the taste of sweet figs on his tongue.

Disappointed to find a ripe-looking fruit smell rotten, Tau thought of Badru and his wife. He leaned over to Badru browsing next to him and asked, "How are things going with Behati?"

"Still not well," he answered. "She seems intent on questioning my every decision on our wealth. I do not understand it. We have enough for what I want to do with it and what she wants. I feel like she has no trust in me."

Tau listened, trying to think of something to say that might help. An idea came to him and he said, "Have you tried explaining why what you want to do is a good decision?"

Badru nodded his head with annoyance, "Yes, of course. I told her about trading much of our fine linen for some cattle, but she would have none of it. I told her about growing a herd and all of the benefits, but it was for naught. She seems set against me."

Tau frowned having realized it was the wrong thing to say. Then he thought of something else, "Maybe she isn't like that, but thinks something else is better."

"That is for certain," Badru huffed. "She always thinks that my decisions and ideas are bad, no matter what I suggest, she has something to say."

Tau started feeling he was doing more harm that good, so he left that topic alone. "What about little Amahl and Omphil?"

Badru laughed, "They keep asking when 'Unky Tau' is coming to visit, much to Behati's chagrin."

Tau laughed with him and they continued bartering for the supplies they needed and returned to the room.

Chapter 8

Yalu awakened with a gasp. As he caught his breath, he found himself in a dark, strange, mud-brick room. Looking around he saw Nebit sleeping on a reed mat nearby and Tau sleeping next to an empty mat in the opposite corner. Badru sat by the window, looking out. A small beam of moonlight slipped through it and cast his shadow on the floor.

"Are you alright?" Badru turned his head for a moment at Yalu's sudden outburst.

"Just a dream," Yalu stood up. Then he rubbed his eyes as he walked over to Badru. "Still nothing?"

"Still nothing," he confirmed. "Everyone is still sleeping. Tonight is no different from any other thus far. They continue to bring grain and build more granaries. They are preparing for something, but I know not what."

"Five days we've been watching the house and neither Moses nor Aaron have come out," Yalu shook his head.

"Yes, my patience is wearing thin as well. But after the stir he caused at Pharaoh's palace, hiding may be his aim. I must know more about this god of his. During my training I have studied many gods and learned their ways. But… this one is different." Badru's frustration showed in his tone.

Yalu's mind went back to what he said to Nun about being sent by the Hebrew god. He asked, "Do you think it's possible this new god could make people do things without them knowing?"

"Hmm…" Badru rubbed a finger to his temple in thought. "I suppose that is possible, though usually the gods do not take such care for subtly with us lower beings. If a god wants to turn a commoner into a queen, then they'll send an eagle to snatch up her sandal and drop it in Pharaoh's lap."

"I see," Yalu nodded. He felt more at ease and started to admire Badru. "Thank you for your wisdom."

Badru grunted and nodded his head in response. Then Yalu patted his back to encourage him to be vigilant as he turned to go back to his bed.

"How long until its Tau's turn to watch?" Yalu asked as he lay down.

"I shall awaken him in about an hour," Badru chuckled, "Last time I woke him he almost got me again with that right fist of his. Unfortunately, the first couple of nights I wasn't expecting it," He rubbed a dark bruise on his left cheek carefully.

"I wish you luck this time," Yalu smiled as he rested his head on the clump of reeds at one end of the matting. Closing his eyes, he took a deep breath and released it. The firm reed mats felt good to his shoulders and back. As he established a slow and steady breathing rhythm, everything around him faded away.

The next thing he knew was a sudden jolt on his chest, which awakened him violently. He opened his eyes to discover the daylight. Through squinting eyes, and after a little time for adjustment, he saw Tau standing above him.

"You're awake? Good," Tau yawned as he stretched his arms. "I need to sleep. No movement from Moses last night. What a bore, doesn't he ever go out anywhere?"

Yalu yawned right after Tau. Then after mumbling some incomprehensible words, he crawled out from underneath his blankets and stood up.

"Have a good rest," He patted Tau on the back and walked over to the window. His eyes glanced over the wall.

Through the window he could see the Egyptian dawn painted with orange and gold intermingling with a dark sky becoming deep blue. As Yalu scanned from right to left through the southward facing window, he saw the sun creep over the sand dunes at the horizon. Shadows of buildings, palm trees, and the great, white wall of the city stood out in contrast to the growing light of day. Every once in a while, somebody walked by on the street, even at this early hour. Soon, dawn gave way to morning and the streets bustled with people. In the distance he could see the sunlight reflecting off the Nile. It sparkled. His mother had told him that was Anuket's way of showing favor to the people of Egypt.

"Is nobody showing us favor now?" Yalu muttered.

"There may still be." He heard Nebit's voice from behind him.

Startled, Yalu turned to see her stretching over her bed. She smiled at him and he felt reassured. Conscious of his task, he turned back to the window.

"Who?" Yalu asked.

Nebit didn't reply. He glanced again at her to her stretching each of her legs and arms individually. She reminded him of a leopard. He heard her footsteps walk near to him. She bent over with her face next to his, looking toward the manor.

"Any sign of them yet?"

"None at all," Yalu replied with a sigh.

A moment of silence passed.

"I've been meaning to tell you," Yalu began. "I've not seen anyone as adept as you with those daggers in all my travels back and forth along the sands. Most just use them as a backup weapon, or when preparing food, even me. But you use them expertly as you weapon of choice."

He glanced over to see her smiling, but her expression seemed bittersweet. She replied, "I've had good teachers and a good master."

Then she leaned her back against the wall next to him and stared blankly against the wall in front of her. After a moment she slid down along the wall and sat on the ground with her knees folded against her chest. From the corner of his eye, Yalu noticed her dark braids sway with her movement.

"Most people seem either put off or amazed to learn of a fighting woman like the son of Nun," Nebit said. "But you seem to be different. Why is that?"

"I suppose it's comforting to meet a woman who how to fight," Yalu said. Just then, images of his dead wife and family flooded his mind. He put a hand to his forehead as guilt overwhelmed him. Not wanting to betray his feelings he tried to quickly think of an excuse. As he turned to tell her he saw from her face that she already saw.

Her deep brown eyes made him feel more at ease. She cocked her as she looked at him. Her lips seemed full and her nose wrinkled in curiosity.

"I told you that I wanted to be someone who protects people," She changed the subject. "You said you would teach me. When is that going to happen?"

"Hush." Yalu's head turned quickly back to the manor.

Nebit instinctively drew a breath and readied for action as she stared at the one green eye she saw in his profile.

"I saw them. And it looks like they're coming outside of the wall," He turned and shared a smile of excitement with her and she returned it warmly.

"Wake up you two sleeping water cows I spotted them! We need to go now." Yalu bolted over to Tau and Badru, tapping their shoulders with his hands. Then he remembered what Badru had said and readied.

"What…" Tau yawned and instinctively tossed his fist at Yalu, but hit only air. He commented, scratching his chest, "Feels like I just got to sleep."

"Huh? You spotted Moses and Aaron?!" Badru jumped up from his mat, "Finally!"

"Let's go," Yalu dashed out the door, closely followed by Nebit. Badru grabbed Tau's hand and attempted to pull him up from his bed. Tau resisted, but eventually gave in, getting up and following Badru out the door.

They joined Yalu and Nebit in a small alley between the buildings. As they looked, they saw Moses and Aaron walking down the South side of the street. Both wore earthen cloaks, and Yalu recognized Aaron holding the same staff that transformed to a snake in front of Pharaoh.

Yalu turned to the others and instructed, "Don't do anything to get their attention." Then he left the shelter of the alley and followed them at a distance. The other three fell into line behind him.

They continued their pursuit through the city to the gate of Pharaoh's palace. They saw Aaron and Moses talk with a guard at the wall for a few moments, but instead of going inside to the palace, they headed east.

Moses and Aaron led their entourage, and the quartet of investigators, to the Nile. No trace of the blood remained. Even the stink of dead fish had gone. Pharaoh, his guards, and a few nobles loitered at the shore underneath the royal pavilion as they watched laborers ready his barge. Moses and Aaron approached Pharaoh. The guards blocked them briefly, but soon they pushed through and began conversing with Pharaoh.

Yalu took the others behind some large shrubs underneath a palm tree.

Tau blurted out, "Why are we stopping here?" The others hushed him. He whispered, "Why don't we get closer?"

Yalu peered through the shrubbery and replied, "If we get closer, we may lose the advantage of stealth."

"I see Master Haji with Pharaoh," Badru exclaimed in muffled excitement. "I wish I could hear what they say."

Tau and Nebit peeked at the scene as well. They saw Pharaoh dressed in a loose purple garment with golden trim. He reclined in a well-cushioned chair with his magicians and nobles standing to either side. Haji stood at Pharaoh's left hand with his black kalasiris robe waving in the cool morning breeze. In front of them, the Nile contained the myriad of boats that common people use to fish, gather reeds, and transport themselves from one side to the other.

Men carefully carried supplies onto the wooden barge and into the small house at one end. Other men carefully inspected the boat for cracks and holes, or made ready the canopy to shade Pharaoh as he sat underneath. Ten men stood at the ready with long punting poles.

Near the royal pavilion, Moses and Aaron turned from Pharaoh and walked away toward the shore. As they stood on the shore, Aaron raised his staff over the water. Pharaoh and his officials looked toward them, waiting for something to happen. Slowly, waves appeared at the shore: not normal-sized waves, but larger. At first, it looked like the water advanced further and further onto the shore. As it advanced, it looked to the onlookers less like water: it didn't move like water. The undulations advanced to Pharaoh's encampment. One jumped onto Pharaoh's lap, causing the man to thrust it away from him with an energy born of anger or fear. Pharaoh turned and shouted to Haji, who started his incantations.

"I think... If my memory serves me correctly, those gestures are intended to call upon Heget," Badru explained.

"Patron goddess of frogs, and the womb," Nebit recited. She thought of the advice her master gave her.

"I thought you weren't talking to Badru," Yalu smiled at her.

She turned quickly to give him a squelching look.

Badru ignored the exchange; "Pharaoh has called upon Haji to match the miracle," Badru explained. "Haji is summoning Heget."

While Haji performed his incantation, they heard noises in a nearby mud brick house. They watched an army of frogs emerge from the building. The frogs of Heget hopped out to do battle with the frogs of the Hebrew god. Pharaoh appeared pleased with Haji, and gave a shout of praise to Heget. In response, Haji and the nobles gave praise to Heget and bowed to the ground towards Heget's frogs. Then Pharaoh, Haji, and their company returned to the palace.

Moses and Aaron remained in the midst of the frogs for a few moments longer. Aaron put his hand on Moses' shoulder; Moses shook his head.

The four watched as the frogs brought by the Hebrew god engulfed Heget's frogs by sheer volume.

Then Moses and Aaron left back the way they came, toward them.

Yalu turned back and looked at the others and motioned for them to follow. He left the cover of the bushes followed by the other three. When Moses and Aaron saw them they stopped abruptly and eyed the group cautiously.

"Who are you?" asked Aaron, "What do you want with us?"

Yalu introduced them. "We've seen what you're god has done and were hoping you could spare some time to talk with us."

They looked at each other and shrugged their shoulders. As Aaron turned back to Yalu he asked, "You look familiar. Have I seen you before?"

"We met in the caravan from Wadi Meghereh."

Aaron's face lit up, "Now I remember. You came to our aid. And my brother was in your caravan."

"I also heard from Nun's son that you're responsible for rescuing his family's chief servant." Moses added, "A very brave rescue I'm told."

"Then we've found favor in your eyes?" Yalu pressed.

Moses and Aaron nodded.

Badru stepped forward and asked. "First, who is your god? What is his name?"

"Hmmm." Moses looked toward the ground and smiled as he pondered his answer.

Yalu remembered how they remained silent when Pharaoh asked this exact question. He wondered how they would respond with Badru asking it.

"He… is."

Badru waited a moment and then motioned for Moses to continue, "He is what?"

"He simply is." He replied with a laugh, as if he had just told the universe's best joke.

Badru's expression showed only dissatisfaction. Yalu looked around at Nebit and Tau. They seemed to share his confusion.

Moses said in a compassionate tone, "When you pray to one of your gods at a statue at one of the temples. You bow down, recite a prayer, ask for whatever it is you need, and then you leave. When I speak to mine, He speaks back."

After a short pause, Badru said, "And what is your god's realm? He is a god of what?"

"Everything," Moses answered.

Badru lowered his eyebrows. Yalu thought he seemed like a young wildebeest being toyed with by a lioness. From his expression he didn't seem to like it at all. He asked, "What do you mean?"

Moses explained patiently, "He created the world and all people from every land; the animals, fish, birds, and frogs." They glanced involuntarily at the measureless amount of frogs pouring forth from the river. Nebit looked concerned.

"The Priests tell us that Ptah created the world," Badru countered. "It was like a mother giving birth. He grew the world inside of himself and at the proper time spewed out light and water."

"That's not what I heard," Nebit shook her head with a dissatisfied look on her face. "Ptah created the world from a big block of stone. He carved it using his fingernails. The deep places filled with water and became rivers and oceans."

"But I was told that Ptah simply willed the world into existence. He used his powerful mind to shape the mountains and valleys," Yalu told them honestly.

"My father told me that Ptah flexed, like this," Tau bent his knees and stretched his arms above his head in the shape of a circle. Then he flexed all his muscles and released a muffled roar. Everyone chuckled a little, "Then the world just appeared in between his arms."

"The details are unimportant," Badru dismissed the others with a wave of his hand, "The point is that everyone believes that Ptah created the world. And yet you tell me that your god did. They cannot both be creators."

"You are right," Moses nodded. "But it is my turn for a question now. How has Ptah demonstrated his power to you, personally?"

As Badru tried to think of something Moses leaned forward, "You've already seen the blood and the frogs. He won't stop until Pharaoh lets us go."

A moment of silence passed. His words weighed upon Yalu as a burden on his shoulders. He glanced to the others and it seemed they struggled with it the same as he.

After a few moments Moses asked, "Do you have another question?"

Yalu said with a little doubt in his mind. But he felt he simply must know. "Yes, could your god have people do his bidding without them knowing it?"

Moses nodded and answered thoughtfully, "I think so. If you're talking about Pharaoh, I feel our god hardened his heart and he won't let us go worship and sacrifice to our god. Pharaoh wants all people in Egypt to worship him as God. My people can't do that. We need to leave Egypt."

Yalu's thoughts went back to his words to Nun and he wondered about them.

"If he won't let you go then what will your god do next?" Badru asked.

Moses took a deep breath, "Only he himself knows and will tell me when he's ready."

"My apologies, but didn't we agree to meet with them after?" Aaron asked him aside.

Moses nodded. Then he looked up at the four and said, "I'm sorry, we must be going. Perhaps we can continue talking later." The four said goodbye to Moses and Aaron who walked away toward the Hebrew district.

Nebit cleared her throat and nudged Yalu, and the others turned to look at her. She pointed toward the frogs, "They're almost here!"

Indeed, the creeping frogs had advanced, and were nearly two paces away. On the Nile, the frogs overran the boats and the frustrated boaters attempted to toss the frogs back into the river. But as they did, more frogs jumped onto it. The frogs continued to advance on land.

"Let's go back to Rashidi. We finally have something to report to him," Yalu suggested. Then he turned to Nebit and said, "I don't think the frogs will bother you that far from the Nile."

The laugh she replied with seemed insincere and tense. They left the river and walked through the city to Rashidi's manor.

Badru stopped before the entrance.

"I shall stay here," Badru leaned against the wall. "I want more time to think on Moses' words."

They reluctantly left him, and continued to Rashidi's estate.

While walking the grounds looking for him, Yalu heard the sound of metal against metal. Then he heard footsteps. He turned and saw man holding a khopesh in each hand. The man rubbed them together with a maniacal gleam in his eye.

Yalu's gasped as he realized this man was the bandit he crossed khopeshes with before. Grabbing his own khopesh, Yalu swung it out to threaten him.

"Why raise your blade against me now? We're on the same side now, you and I. Surely I don't deserve it." The man smirked. On his left was a short fat man carrying a spear. To his right was another with a spear. Behind them was a tall thin man who carried a recurve bow.

"You!" Yalu spat out. "You deserve death."

"Oh?" The man chuckled. "And you think you're skilled enough to give it to me?"

Yalu scowled. The others started to ready their weapons too. The thought of seeing the man lying on the ground dying in a pool of his own blood as punishment for his wicked deeds filled him with satisfaction. But he also knew he was disadvantaged of having three against four.

"Stop!" Kasmut screamed and ran to them from the house. Everyone on the premises complied with the order and looked at her, but heaved a sigh of relief when she wasn't speaking to them. Yalu and the other man stepped away from each other. She stood between the two groups and said, "Do not dare fight in my household! You both are in the employ of Rashidi."

"Exactly," said the man with the khopeshes, "I was telling that to your hot-headed servant over there, but he only drew his khopesh."

"You drew yours first!" Yalu retorted.

"Gahiji, these mercenaries are on a special assignment from Rashidi." Kasmut explained with an angry look. "I know not what happened but I would have you keep your distance from them."

Nodding subserviently to her, Gahiji folded his arms, and tilted his head upward haughtily, saying, "Very well. I will honor you and your household."

As Gahiji turned to leave he shot Yalu a knowing glance as though to say Kasmut saved him. It infuriated Yalu, but he repressed it. Partly because he didn't want it to show in front of Kasmut, and partly because he suspected that it may be the truth.

When they had gone, Nebit leaned over to Kasmut and asked, "Who are those coiled vipers?"

"They were sent to us," Kasmut shook her head with a sigh. "The leader, Gahiji, is an unprincipled and uncouth man. Even with my numerous contacts, I don't know where he came from."

"He's a bandit." Yalu folded his arms, looking cross. "Not ridding the world of him is one of my regrets. I can only guess how many innocent travelers he's slain. Who sent him?"

"Sakakwi." Kasmut answered.

Yalu's eyes followed Gahiji to the other side of the manor courtyard where he and his group sat down under the shade of a palm tree. He growled underneath his breath as he committed both names to memory.

"We could have taken them," Tau huffed and patted Yalu on the back.

"Bandit or no, I'll have you both punished severely if I hear about any fighting," Kasmut warned. "Now why are you here? You have something to report to Rashidi?"

Yalu nodded.

"I'll take you to him."

Kasmut led them inside to a hall where Rashidi sat on one side of the table, and three of the Hebrew foremen sit at the other.

"Rashidi, your soldiers are here to see you."

As he was about to thank her when she said, "Those bandits you insisted to keep almost broke out fighting in my courtyard." Then she left the room briskly.

"They're not..." Rashidi started but then walked to the door to shout at her, "Rumors only!"

Rashidi heaved a heavy sigh full of frustration. He dismissed his foremen. After they had gone, Rashidi motioned for his three soldiers to sit at the table. He cued them with his hand, "Tell me what you learned about Moses."

Yalu began, "He finally came out of hiding this morning. We followed them to the Nile where they met Pharaoh. There was another confrontation with Pharaoh's magicians, except this time an army of frogs appeared from the Nile. We learned that he is a messenger from his god. They are trying to convince Pharaoh to allow the Hebrew slaves to worship his god."

As Yalu spoke, an anxious look grew on Rashidi's face. He sat listening with his mouth agape and his eyes wide. When Yalu finished, he sat lost in thought.

After a few moments he asked, "Surely, there must be some other motive that Moses has. Is it power that he wants? Does he want to be a head priest in one of the temples? Or perhaps he is displeased with the Egyptian gods and has decided that he wants to follow this other god."

Yalu shrugged, "It may be as you say. But we haven't been able to find any motives besides wanting to let the Hebrew slaves worship their god."

"Then you need to look harder!" Rashidi's held Yalu with his eyes.

Kasmut barged suddenly into the room breathing heavily, disrupting the tense moment. A shocked look painted her face.

She consciously regained her composure and stated, "Pharaoh sent a messenger for you."

With a look of concern he said, "Very well."

He left the room with Yalu and the others in his train. In front of the home, Yalu saw a man on a chariot with two horses, wearing a white skirt with gold trim and sandals. Badru watched, still leaning on the wall.

The sound of croaking surprised Yalu. He saw an armful of frogs sitting or hopping aimlessly. The servants hurriedly tried to get rid of them, or at least keep them outside. Coming from all around the neighborhood, he heard muffled cursing and cries to Heqet.

When Rashidi approached the messenger, he began, "Rashidi, his greatness has summoned Moses to the palace. I was told that you know where Moses and Aaron are. Go and tell them that they must come to see Pharaoh now." Then the messenger rode away as quickly as he had come.

Rashidi turned and looked surprised to see the three soldiers behind him. Yalu figured that all of this was a lot for him to take in. He quickly regained his composure.

"You heard him. Go to Moses and Aaron, and bring them to Pharaoh," he released a tense breath as he stormed back inside where Kasmut waited with reports.

Badru walked up to the three and chuckled as he said "Well, just when we thought we were done, here we are. It would seem that Pharaoh decided this humiliation of Heqet needs to stop. May I accompany you again?"

They agreed and hurried to the Hebrew district. Yalu walked alongside Badru and said, "A thought has been festering in my mind like an open wound since the Nile changed to blood. I saw many people praying to Anuket for help, but she provided none. It lasted for a week! I'm sure Pharaoh wants Moses to stop the frogs from his urgent summons. The stories tell about how powerful the gods are. Why aren't they showing their power now?"

"I do not know," Badru said with a sigh. "But I fear for Egypt if these things keep going on."

Yalu thought about it as he hopped over a rather large patch of frogs.

Tau ploughed through them as if they weren't there, scattering them with every kick, or squishing them under his sandals. Yalu and Badru made unpleasant faces at him, but Nebit shoved his shoulder.

"Watch where you step, you big elephant! Are you planning to have roast frog tonight?"

Tau flashed her a mischievous grin. Looking at the smile paired with his crooked nose, Yalu and the others couldn't help but laugh.

They continued their pace through the frog-infested city. Arriving at Aaron's manor they walked up to the gate.

Yalu stated to the guard, "Pharaoh has summoned Moses and Aaron to the palace."

He nodded and ran to the house. A few minutes later he returned, accompanied by Moses and Aaron.

Behind them, Nebit also caught a glimpse of a fair-skinned woman peeking out from the reed door.

Moses guessed, "He finally decided to let us go?"

Yalu, caught off guard by the question, stuttered, "I don't know. We're just running Pharaoh's errands."

"From one servant to another, let's go." Moses said.

As they walked, Badru slipped alongside Moses and asked, "I noticed that you knew the proper etiquette when in the presence of Pharaoh. Yet you are a foreigner."

"Hmmm..." Moses flashed a nostalgic smile, "I was part of the royal family of Pharaoh once. I had food and gold. I had power to tell people to do my every whim. My mother, or rather my Egyptian mother, would have seen to it that I became Pharaoh."

"What happened?" Tau interrupted.

"I gave it up," Moses stated frankly.

The four stopped dead in their tracks. Moses was pleased when he saw the astonishment on their faces and mouths gaping open. He quietly looked at them.

Badru broke the silence, "How could you give up that kind of power?"

Moses' smile faded and they could see his face distort as though he were in pain: "I saw the suffering of my people. I couldn't sit by and do nothing. I..." He trailed off, as though a painful memory resurfaced. He tried to speak a few words but his throat choked up. Attempting to hide his emotion, he pretended to cough.

Badru opened his mouth to follow up, but Tau put his forearm to Badru's chest. Badru looked up at him, but Tau just shook his head. They continued the rest of the way in silence.

When they arrived at the palace gate, the guards immediately recognized Moses and eagerly let them through. Frogs infested the area, and servants ran back and forth with bushels, trying to remove them. The four companions and Moses entered the palace, heading straight for Pharaoh's audience chamber. The frogs had invaded the inside the palace as well. The guards and most of the people who passed by stopped and looked at Moses with contempt. One man muttered something under his breath. Another one whispered something to the man next to him. This continued as they walked down a large hallway until they finally reached the chamber. A handful of armed men guarded the double doors. Closed and ornately decorated with gold plating, they depicted images of pharaohs of the past.

The guards, most of whom carried spears, stopped them as they approach. Aaron raised his hand, "Pharaoh summoned us. Let us in."

One of the guards opened the doors while another guard instructed, "Enter Pharaoh's Chamber."

They allowed Moses and Aaron to enter but barred the way for Yalu and the others. They shut the door behind them, and the four stood in the hallway in sudden darkness and silence.

In the silence, the croaking emerged. Now that they had a chance to really listen, the sound of croaking frogs echoed throughout the palace. It unsettled Yalu. He heard nothing like it before.

The audience was short, and finally, the doors opened, and Moses and Aaron walked out. A restrained grin could be seen through Moses' beard. The four followed them, walked back down the corridor, exited the palace, and out the gate.

As they walked down the road Tau asked Moses, "Well, what happened? What did Pharaoh want?"

"Pharaoh agreed to let us go and offer sacrifices to our god after I pray tomorrow so that Egypt may be rid of the frogs," Moses said, and some hope shone in his smile.

"That's too bad. I was getting used to not being able to hear myself think," Tau quipped.

"May I ask a question," Asked Badru politely. He continued when they nodded. "Would not a wave of your staff command your god to remove the frogs? That is how they were brought forth, after all."

"If I commanded my god things would've happened much differently," Moses confessed. "No, he is the one who commands me."

"Commands you? Like a slave?" Tau asked.

"Yes, like a slave."

"How is that better than being a slave for Pharaoh?" Badru pointed his finger at Moses. "A slave is still a slave no matter who the master is."

Moses stopped and leaned on his staff, thinking how to answer. Aaron answered for him, "Tell me Egyptian, is it better to be a slave to a man or a god? But Pharaoh says he is a god, and I'm sure that you, like any other good Egyptian, believe him. I will point out to you that Pharaoh will grow old, whither, and die like the grain in the fields. Or perhaps Pharaoh may be struck down by the sword or arrow on the battlefield. Then a new pharaoh will take his place. The old pharaoh is said to go into the afterlife as a god, then the new pharaoh becomes another god. The problem is if you do something that pleases the old pharaoh, it will be forgotten once the new pharaoh has come. The Lord my god does not grow old, and will not be struck down on the battlefield. I would rather please the Lord, because once I have his favor he will guard and protect me for the rest of my life. He will rescue me when I'm in trouble, and show me the way to be free from evil."

"Free from evil?" Badru wondered, "What evil do you mean?"

Nebit squeaked as she narrowly missed stepping on a frog, garnering everyone's attention for a moment.

Badru continued, "But the important thing is that the frogs will be gone tomorrow. I wonder why Pharaoh didn't want them gone today."

The others just shrugged and shook their heads.

"I think that we should go back and report to master Rashidi," Yalu changed the subject. "He will want to know what has happened at the palace."

"Yes, go back to your masters and I shall go back to mine," Moses grinned. "He should be pleased with servants such as you." Then he turned down a street and back toward his brother's home.

Yalu and the others stopped for a moment to watch as Moses walked down the street. The heat of the day had started to cool off, now that the sun faded into the horizon behind them. Their long shadows reached after Moses, as they themselves had done earlier this morning. Then Yalu turned and led them back to Rashidi's estate.

Chapter 9

Rashidi stepped inside Pharaoh's palace nervously. He had an idea why he had been summoned, but no details. The slaves he oversaw hadn't been meeting their quota of bricks. Rashidi rehearsed his list of excuses in his mind. *First, Moses is causing a stir among the Hebrews that disrupts their work. There is nothing I can do about this because of the high regard they hold him in. Second, the diverting of the straw caused the slaves to work slower. But that might suggest that I am putting blame on Pharaoh's decree. I should emphasize how the foremen aren't forcing the slaves to work harder.* The only thing that didn't make sense was why Pharaoh had summoned him after dusk: a time for political intrigue.

The frogs still seemed to be everywhere. No matter how much work the servants did to remove them from the palace more frogs kept comig. Finally he reached the doors to Pharaoh's inner chamber. The handful of guards present recognized him. Before one of them opened the ornate wooden door overlaid with golden patterns, Rashidi adjusted his wig and took a deep breath. Then he gestured with his hand for the guard to open the door.

Rashidi walked into the room and bowed low to the ground. Pharaoh stood behind a table filled with papyrus scraps and scrolls. Several servants stood fearfully behind Pharaoh holding more papyrus. As Rashidi rose to his feet he could see hints of anger and desperation on Pharaoh's face. The double-crown lay on the table. A moment of silence passed between them as he and Pharaoh stared at each other. The only sounds came from the frogs.

Deciding to seize the moment, Rashidi broke the silence, "Pharaoh, as I was walking here I wanted to tell you that Moses has been causing trouble among your slaves. You see, he…"

"Moses," Pharaoh growled and Rashidi stopped to listen. The tone instantly put fear into his heart. Pharaoh closed his eyes and took a deep breath. Then looking back at Rashidi, he said "I summoned you to tell me what you learned about Moses so far."

"Yes, Moses…" Rashidi gathered his thoughts, "On the surface, Moses appears to be doing the will of his god. The people seem to like the idea of a god who wants to take them out of Egypt and keep them from working for Pharaoh, so Moses is telling them what they want to hear. This is why they're not fulfilling their quota. The slaves look to…"

"Do you know why Moses is doing these things?" Pharaoh interrupted. Rashidi heard frustration in his voice.

Rashidi thought for a moment, "It is my suspicion that this man has ambitions. He wants to rule over those slaves as Pharaoh. Somehow, he must have made a pact with a foreign god to give him all of that power."

"He keeps telling me that the people need to leave to go worship the Lord, their god." Pharaoh said. Then he shook his head and sighed, "The Lord is a powerful god, perhaps more powerful than any other god in all of Egypt. But if allowing them to worship him will end this madness, then so be it. I don't want to be distracted with this while there are still preparations to make for the war in Kush."

"The war in Kush—That must be why he needs the slaves," A smile grew on Rashidi's face as he spoke. He watched as Pharaoh's brow rose in interest. He continued, "The Lord must be a Kushite god.

Moses and the Kushite god must have made an agreement that if Moses provides worshippers to the god; then that god would provide him power. The loss of such a large number of slaves would disrupt Pharaoh's war preparations. My lord Pharaoh, this is an attack on Egypt!"

Pharaoh's lip curled as he listened to Rashidi. Then he banged his fist on the table causing papyrus to fly about. The servants around him jumped back in fear. "Those Kushite vipers! Your wisdom comes through yet again, my good servant Rashidi. I will not allow Moses and his god to beat me. Tomorrow, after I see that the frogs are gone I will issue a decree forbidding the Hebrew slaves to leave Egypt. And then Moses must be dealt with."

"But since the Hebrew slaves hold him in such high regard, if we did something to him then they might rebel against us. That would hinder Pharaoh's war preparations as well." Rashidi pointed out.

"Yes," Pharaoh started to share Rashidi's smile, "We mustn't do anything rash because the Hebrew slaves are too many. We must be patient like the crocodile and just as vicious and cunning. If we deal with him in the shadows we can even blame Moses' death on Kushite assassins. Then their trap would be completely disarmed."

"Excellent plan Pharaoh. You are wiser than I or any," Rashidi affirmed with a bow. "Is there anything your humble servant can do to aid you?"

"Yes," Pharaoh looked Rashidi in the eyes, "I want you to continue to spy on Moses. Find out the best time when we could get the job done. Once the time is right, send your best servants to do it. I'll send you more help from the priests of Ptah."

"Very good, the other servants from them are working perfectly," Rashidi gave a good belly laugh. "Fear not Pharaoh, this problem will soon be resolved.

With your leave I will make the necessary
preparations." Rashidi bowed again.

"Yes, you may go now," Pharaoh read his
scrolls again as Rashidi got up and left the room.
Servants scrambled trying to pick up each scrap and
carefully place it on the table. Rashidi paced past the
guards and quickly exited the palace, his mind already
planning.

Rashidi saw Kasmut and a number of his
personal soldiers waiting for him outside the gate.
When she saw him approach, she picked up a lantern
and pressed the wrinkles out of her dress.

Rashidi said as they started the journey back,
"We have work to do."

The tip of Badru's robe glided across the carpet
of the stone floor as he followed closely behind. Stone
statues of the pharaohs from ages past lined the walls.
The echo of croaking filled the chamber. Suddenly the
footsteps in front of him stopped and the face of his
master startled him. Haji asked with slight annoyance,
"Were you paying attention?"

"Of course master," Badru bowed his head.
"The power over life and death is great, but is eclipsed
by acquiring knowledge of one's situation."

Haji stared into Badru's eyes with a searching
gaze that made him feel uncomfortable. After a few
moments Haji nodded and continued forward. Then he
asked, "Tell me what troubles you. I can see it in your
eyes."

"Recent events. The appearance of all these
frogs is an attack on Heget. Anuket's blood spilled in
the Nile. Wadjet swallowed whole! What does it all
mean?"

Haji nodded approvingly, "I see you have
already looked into this and applied my teachings. You

ask the right question." Then his voice grows stern, "However, your inability to answer proves you are not ready to take my place yet."

They continued on to the next chamber. "Those defeats were humiliating, this much is true. And there is no doubt that other gods will use this as an opportunity to improve their standing. Once this foreign god meets his match and is defeated then he will find his place among the other gods."

"What happens if he doesn't meet his match?"

"Come now Badru," Haji scoffed. "Have more faith in our gods. I have worked as chief magician to Pharaoh for many years and have seen many foreign gods come and go. These events will pass into your memory."

Badru followed behind him with a feeling of lingering doubt.

Up ahead, Sakakwi turned a corner into their view. He grinned when he spotted them and approached. The golden holy symbol he wore marking him as a priest of Ptah swayed with each step. He addressed Haji with a bowed head, "Greetings venerable Haji. It is good to see you again. I hope you are well. Today I come with a task for your apprentice here."

With raised eyebrows Haji turned toward Badru, "I have nothing for him at the moment. Badru, go and do as he asks."

They both bowed to Haji and left him. Walking through the chambers Sakakwi began, "It was decided to that you join a small group to assist in dealing with a... threat."

Badru shook his head, "What threat?"

"These frogs, for one," he motioned with his hand at the slimy amphibians they passed by on the floor, "The problem goes deeper than mere frogs, however. It is a religious problem and Pharaoh himself wants us to resolve it. The leadership decided the task falls to you."

"What task? Why me?"

"As chief magician, Haji knows about all the different gods and how to appease them. We need someone with those skills to investigate this Kushite god responsible for all this trouble and find out how to defeat him. There is already a scouting group watching the religious leader for this god. Haji's place is beside Pharaoh. But being his foremost apprentice you are best suited to discover anything."

"You flatter me. I'm not his foremost apprentice," Badru said, trying not to step on any frogs walking down the palace steps. "Who are these scouts? And who is this religious leader?"

Sakakwi flashed Badru a devious grin, obviously pleased with himself. "Do you want to know the secrets I learned from the records we obtained?"

Eyeing curiously as they walked, Badru nodded.

"The leader is a rebellious nobleman named Mutmose who now calls himself Moses. He is a murderer and a traitor. According to Ptah's elders, he was in line to become Pharaoh one day, but all that changed when he decided to betray our people by slaying an overseer in cold blood. Pharaoh ordered that he be executed for his crime, but somehow he fled. That was forty years ago. Now, he comes to our Hebrew slaves with the help of this Kushite god to take revenge on us by disrupting Pharaoh's war preparations. The spies… are inconsequential, just some rabble assembled by one of Pharaoh's overseers. You need to make sure that the interests of the priesthood are maintained, and use your talents to assist the spies in gathering the information."

"I see…" Badru continued, "You said that the god is from Kush? If that is so, then why does this god manifest frogs? The Kushites are herders, and all of their gods are cattle gods."

"So are the Hebrews," Sakakwi replied as they stopped at the gate to an estate. Badru recognized it as belonging to Tau's master. "The overseer here handles the scouts. His wife Kasmut handles much of his affairs. I also wish to give you a word of caution about her. I have reason to believe she may be a Hebrew sympathizer. Don't tell her any critical information, save that for me or someone else whom you trust."

Badru nodded. They arrived at Rashidi's estate and he quickly scanned it for Yalu, Tau, and Nebit but didn't see them. Kasmut, however, did see them and approached with a wry smile on her lips. She approached them and asked, "My good priest Sakakwi, I hope you are in good health. Do the band who slew your servants continue to elude you?"

An angry look flashed across Sakakwi's face. His lip twitched as she spoke. Then he said in an irritated tone, "Not for long. I have new men out searching for them. Justice will prevail."

"Of course it will," She smiled.

"And what about you?" Sakakwi pointed a finger at her. "I've heard the wife of Rashidi is plotting against me. How do you respond?"

"My husband and I have only ever supported your efforts," she crossed her arms and said indignantly. "Whoever claims otherwise is a liar and I'm insulted that you would believe them."

Sakakwi held her in his gaze as though he could look into her heart to determine the truth. After a moment he replied, "No insult intended. I never said I believed such claims, only that I've heard them. As you know, I reward loyalty but punish those who go against me."

She listened with an unreadable expression. She responded, "As do I. Now tell me, what is your business here?"

Sakakwi turned and put a hand on Badru's shoulder. "I've decided that the spies in your husband's employ need help to get more information. With the new plans we need as much as possible."

Kasmut sighed and shook her head, "They've been providing sufficient information so far. And the others you brought to 'help' have mostly caused trouble in my household."

"I shall be the judge of what is sufficient," Sakakwi snapped. "This man is most knowledgeable in the dealings between gods and men. He is the apprentice to chief magician Haji. And you will accept his help."

"Very well, if you judge this to be necessary then we will see it done." Kasmut gave a courteous bow.

"Good. I have other business to attend to now."

Sakakwi left and Kasmut led Badru inside the house. She took him to a room where Rashidi reclined behind a slab table. Yalu, Nebit, and Tau stood near the doorway, clearly surprised to see him.

"This is Badru, more help from Sakakwi," Kasmut introduced in an annoyed tone.

"It is my pleasure to help in any way I can," Badru steps forward. "The priesthood is very concerned about this new god. I look forward to working with your scouts." He looked over Tau and Yalu as though sizing them up, but let his eye pass over Nebit as if she were not there.

Then Badru cocked his head in realization, "Does everybody else hear that?"

The others in the room shook their heads and looked at each other puzzled.

"The frogs have stopped croaking."

"Finally!" Nebit shouted in joy, "Moses must have prayed to his god."

"But they're all still here," Tau observed." He stooped over to look at one of them. He poked it with his finger, then stood up and shouted with surprise, "They're dead. They're all dead!"

Rashidi at first looked shocked, but then he leaned back again. "It seems like whenever I have a meeting here with you people something bad happens. First it's the blood and now this," Rashidi shook his head.

Kasmut folded her arms and shook her head with disgust, "I will see these things removed. I don't want them reeking inside my house."

She left them in a hurry.

Rashidi continued, "Last night, I was summoned by Pharaoh. Moses is the foremost subject on Pharaoh's mind. Because of all these frogs, as well as the other trouble he has caused, we're going to confront this problem in the shadows. We are to use Badru wisely. Keep a watch on Moses. Learn his habits, where he goes to pray to his god, who is closest to him, and anything else you think is important."

Yalu nodded, "Understood. We can return to the room that overlooks Aaron's home. But I heard that Pharaoh was letting them leave to worship. Is that not the case?"

"No," Rashidi shook his head, "Pharaoh has forbidden it. He will not lose so many slaves."

"But didn't he say…" Tau started but a glare from Rashidi stopped him.

"Report to Kasmut each night. Leave nothing out." Rashidi pointed at them as he spoke. After he finished he flicked his wrist in a signal to leave.

On the way out, Badru noticed Rashidi's servants gathering the frogs into baskets, and bringing them outside. At the gate were large pile of dead frogs. Looking down the road, he was dismayed to see that this pile was one of many such piles.

Badru cringed as they rounded a particularly large pile, "There will not be a single bottle of perfume left in the city after this."

"I can already smell them." Nebit covered her nose with her arm, making a face behind her elbow. Then her face brightened suddenly. She turned to Yalu and asked, "Do you still have that bottle from when we rescued Yadid?"

Yalu tapped his chin in thought for a moment then raised his eyebrows. Looking through the pouch on his belt he fetched out the small bottle and tossed it to her. She caught it and cradled it like a baby in her arms for a moment before she opened it and sniffed deeply, then applied the oil to her temples, and along her collarbone. She gave Yalu a smile of gratitude and he returned it.

"Since Pharaoh decided to keep the Hebrews, I wonder what their god will do next." Tau said innocently, but the others stopped walking and turned to look at him. "What?"

They shared a moment of awkward silence and looked at each other uneasily.

"In my heart I am afraid of that," Badru said sincerely. "But there is no point dwelling on that now. We will just have to wait and see."

As they continued walking, Nebit asked, "Didn't Moses say that the frogs were going to go away? Why did they just die where they sat?"

"Maybe since Pharaoh forbade the Hebrew slaves from leaving, the Hebrew god forbade the frogs from leaing." Tau gave a laugh.

Just then Badru saw a couple arrows hit the ground amongst them and heard a loud clang as one ricocheted off the shield on Yalu's back. While the four looked around to find who shot them, four men drew khopeshes and charged. Everyone else in the vicinity fled.

As Nebit deflected an attack with her dagger, she called out, "Bowman, forty paces ahead!" An arrow narrowly missed Badru's chest and got lost in one of the piles of dead frogs.

"Another, thirty paces behind," Yalu blocked a slash with his shield and thrusted underneath with his own khopesh, drawing blood.

Knocking a blow away with his mace, Badru reached into his robe with his other hand to grab a handful of dust from one of the pockets. When the attacker started to swing again, Badru grinned and tossed the dust toward the man's eyes. The man cried out in pain and Badru knocked him over the head with his mace. He fell to the ground.

Badru looked over at Tau who roared at two men and swung his khopesh widely, forcing them to back off. One of them lunged at Tau after his swing, but was met with a powerful kick to his gut. He collapsed in pain. "I don't see the third bowman!" Tau shouted over his shoulder as he parried the other attacker.

"Keep looking," Yalu shouted back. After a failed attempt to counter his opponent he cursed, "Flesh and fire."

Badru circled around and flanked the other man engaged with Tau, narrowly escaping another arrow. He was too focused on the big brute in front of him to notice. As the man slashed at Tau, Badru brought him down with his mace.

Nebit pursed her lips as she danced the familiar steps of combat her partner was so faithfully repeating.

An arrow whistled through the space her head had
occupied all too recently. In a pause between sets, she
pounced on him suddenly, slashing at his chest and
throat. He fell, grasping his wounds.

The man fighting Yalu turned to run. As Yalu
took a deep breath to run in chase, a dagger flew past
his head and into the man's back and he hit the dirt
with a cry of pain. Turning around, Yalu flashed Nebit
a smile of gratitude. She returned it. Upon seeing the
swordsmen fall, the bowmen withdrew.

"Rashidi neglected to mention there would be
fighting," Badru muttered as he put his mace away.

"But you handled yourself well," Tau patted
him on the back.

"Tau, are you injured?" Yalu asked, and pointed
to some blood on the side of his waist.

"Huh?" Tau looked at it. "This is nothing."

Badru slipped under Tau's arm and examined
the wound. "I can easily treat such a small wound. Let
me get my ointment."

"Badru, you said that priests of Ptah have the
eye branded on them, right?" Yalu crouched down and
looked at one of the fallen attackers.

While looking around in his pack, Badru said
"Indeed they do. The eye of Ptah is usually branded
into their right palm." He found the ointment from his
pack and opened the jar.

"I really don't think that's necessary," Tau
waved his hands dismissively. "It will heal on its own.
You don't need to waste your ointment on it."

Yalu picked up the dead hand of one of the
attackers and pulled the khopesh from it. He stared at
the palm for a second in deep consternation. Nebit saw
his look, and glanced over his shoulder.

"Any friend of mine must get the best
treatment I can offer," Badru dipped two of his fingers

into the jar and pulled out a generous amount of the ointment. "Hold still."

"Badru, the right hand bears the eye of Ptah," Yalu stated and dropped the hand on the ground. Nebit walked away from them and leaned against the mud of a nearby building.

Tau muffled a gasp as Badru applied the ointment. When he was finished, he turned to Yalu and said seriously, "This is very bad."

"Ow! That's the truth! I've met scorpions whose sting hurts less than your 'healing'." Tau complained.

"What does this mean?" Yalu asked, "Is this because we rescued Yadid? And why is the mark on their hand?" Yalu asked. "Ptah is the creator and god of knowledge. Shouldn't it be over their heart?"

"Ah but he is also a god of craftsmen." Badru explained. "Craftsmen work with their hands to create."

"Aren't you a worshipper of Ptah? Do you have any influence?" Yalu asked hopefully.

"Not officially," Badru admitted. "However, I do have friends in high places. If we tell them of our mission from Pharaoh, then they should relent."

"Let's try next time." Yalu stood up.

They returned to the street of Aaron's house and found the home they had stayed at before and after washing their feet in the basin, they headed up the stairs to the room. The man's son didn't bother to show them the way this time. They sat together talking to each other in their own language.

Upon entering the room Yalu said, "I think it's your turn to watch, Badru."

Badru walked over to the window and settled in. He glanced behind him and saw Yalu and Nebit sitting on their reed beds sharpening their weapons. Tau got started on a well-deserved nap. Badru began his watch with a deep breath. He was looking forward to this time alone at the window so he could think of all that had happened.

That evening, Nebit left the others to report back to Kasmut. Remembering their earlier encounter, she kept a careful eye on her surroundings. Fortunately, she arrived at Rashidi's home without incident.

When she got there, Nebit approached Kasmut as she gave instructions to a handful of servants. When she looked up at her she said, "I'm ready to report."

She nodded to Nebit who told her the events of the evening. When she was done, Kasmut said to her, "Good. Now I want you to show me where you are spying from."

As Nebit led her out of the manor, Kasmut said, "I thought you'd like to know about what's going on with that snake Sakakwi. I have some good news."

For the first time in a long time, Nebit's heart leapt for joy. She nodded emphatically.

"While Sakakwi has many friends in the temple and among Pharaoh's court, he also has many enemies." Kasmut began. "Having told your story to a number of interested persons, I think I've almost garnered enough support to start a movement against that wicked man. The favor of Ptah shall not rest on him much longer."

"Thank you," Nebit said. "I appreciate all the work you're doing on account of me."

"Not at all!" Kasmut exclaimed. "I want justice to be done just as much as you for what he's done. It'll be better for my husband if Sakakwi falls too, though he'd never admit it. The man's purposeless plans drain away resources and cause more problems than they solve."

Finally, they arrived at street of Aaron's home and Nebit pointed to it saying, "This is where Moses is staying. We are borrowing a room in that house." She pointed at the window where they saw Tau's shadowy face.

"Good," Kasmut nodded in approval. "Now walk back with me."

"That's it?" Nebit asked, "You don't want anything else here?"

"Silly girl, how else can we talk privately?" Kasmut laughed. "Now escort me back and tell me about Yalu and Tau."

So Nebit escorted her back to Rashidi's manor and told her everything about Yalu and Tau. The set, casting its last light over the walls of the city. The blue sky grew darker and darker until pinpricks of twinkling light sparkled from it.

As they approached Rashidi's manor Kasmut told Nebit, "You may go back now. And I trust you shall keep everything we talked about to yourself."

Nebit nodded and Kasmut smiled her a smile of complete sincerity. Then she walked back in through the gate and Nebit returned to the Hebrew district.

When she returned to the room Tau was watching at the windows, Yalu was snoozing, and Badru was busy mixing his powders. He looked up at her and greeted her but she ignored him and climbed into her bed. Thoughts of Sakakwi finally getting what he deserved filled her mind as she drifted off to sleep.

Tau yawned as he gazed at the twinkling lights above. His legs felt stiff from sitting down at the window, but watching the night sky always filled him with wonder. His eyes traced the constellations, each god bringing stories his father told him. All of them living around the great celestial Nile. He watched as Pharaoh's star came into view, becoming the brightest

star in the sky, heralding that morning should come
soon.

*I wonder what the Pharaohs of old think of what's
happening with this new god.* Tau thought.

Suddenly, movement in Aaron's manor caught
his eye. A figure left the manor house and walked over
to a place in the courtyard near the wall. By the light of
the lamp he carried, Tau was able to tell that he was
Moses.

At first he wanted to tell everyone that Moses
was going somewhere, but he noticed Moses wasn't
going toward the gate. Instead, he laid out a reed matt
on the ground near the wall, knelt down on it, and
prostrated himself on the ground.

What is he doing? Praying to his god?

About half of an hour went by and then Moses
took up his matt and went back inside. The rest of the
night went by without event. As Tau was about ready
to awaken Yalu he heard him stirring.

"Anything happen last night?" Yalu stood up
and walked over to the window.

Tau told him what happened and lumbered
over to his reed bed where he collapsed. Yalu nodded
and began his watch.

At about noon-time the next day, Tau and
Badru went to buy food. Nebit watched while Yalu
tried to get some sleep. After Nebit noticed him tossing
about a few times she said, "You told me that Tau saw
Moses on a matt last night?" She asked and Yalu
grunted in confirmation.

"If he were praying to his god then it may be
good to know what he was saying. We should tell Tau
to wake me up if they go out and talk again. I might be
able to sneak up to them and listen in."

"Clever idea." Yalu sat up. "The more we tell Rashidi the better they can handle the problem."

"The problem." Nebit repeated. Then she gasped in realization, "I don't know why I didn't see it before. Of course, it only makes sense they'll do it."

"What do you mean? Do what?"

"Don't you see? They want all this information to use against him. They're going to give it to someone to kill him in the shadows. We can't let them do this. We have to protect him." She said with determination.

"Protect him? We don't know what they have planned. Are you suggesting we cross Rashidi?"

Nebit took a breath to respond, but let it go instead. She thought about what Kasmut's been doing to help her. "Maybe you're right."

Yalu laid back onto his matt. "I know it may seem right. My father used to say 'Say what is right and do what is right'. But it's not always that easy. What is right?"

Nebit hesitantly nodded and wished him a good sleep. However, as his mind became more peaceful in slumber, hers became more agitated in thought. She was sure the signs of an assassination were there. She's seen them hundreds of times. She breathed a breath desperate to become a protector but wasn't sure what to do.

Not long after, Tau and Badru returned to restock their dwindling food supply. Nebit didn't even look to saw who had entered; she kept her eyes on the home across the way. After everyone laid down to sleep for a while she spotted Moses and Aaron leaving the manor again. She woke the others and they quickly ran out to follow. They were led to Pharaoh's palace again where they saw Moses and Aaron enter the gate to the palace.

Nebit saw Yalu look at the guards and hesitated for a moment. Badru seized the opportunity. He ran ahead and motioned for the others to follow him, which they did.

He approached the gate and when one of the guards approached him he took out his gold token and said "I am Badru, apprentice to Haji and these are my servants. I am here on official business, let me pass."

After the guard examined the token he nodded and allowed them inside.

Tau smiled at Badru and patted him on the back after they enter.

Nebit looked around and said in a whisper, pointing, "There they are! Let's be quick or we'll lose them." She pointed at Moses and Aaron right before they turned a corner around to the side of the palace.

Yalu looked and ran up with Nebit and the others following as the pair turned a corner. Nebit peeked around to the other side. A large circular stone track dominated this area and on the inside were many chariots, too many for him to count. Moses and Aaron approached Pharaoh, who was standing on his personal chariot. The gold overlay on the wooden vehicle sparkled brightly in the sunlight. Servants prepared a couple horses to be harnessed to it so Pharaoh could ride. Nebit looked around for something they could hide behind that would get them closer and saw a large statue with a base tall enough to reach his chest.

After a short conversation between the two men and Pharaoh, Moses turned to Aaron and spoke to him. Aaron lifted his wooden staff above his head with both hands. Pharaoh's guards scrambled to get to Pharaoh and protect him as they had done earlier in Pharaoh's audience chamber. Pharaoh had that curious look on his face again, but more fearful this time.

Aaron thrust the staff downward and hit the ground with the bottom end of it. The force of his strike made the earth quake for a brief second and the dust on the ground jumped up to everyone's waist. But, the dust didn't settle. It appeared to stay where it was: to float in the air. As they looked closer, they could saw that it wasn't dust at all, but gnats.

Suddenly, the gnats started flying in every direction. They covered everything and everyone. No matter how much they wiped the gnats off, the things returned. Nebit felt disgusted by the frogs, but these gnats absolutely repulsed her. She climbed up onto the statue's stone base to escape them.

"Come up here." She urged the other three. They also climbed up for a little relief.

When she looked back at Pharaoh, his officials, and the servants, she saw the gnats climbing all over them too. The gnats covered Moses and Aaron. One servant handed Pharaoh a cloth which he tied over his nose and mouth. The horses for Pharaoh's chariot started bucking wildly and proved difficult for their handlers, who were already having a difficult time because of the gnats.

After a few minutes, Haji and a three other magicians arrived. Pharaoh reached his hand out to them. At first, the magicians had perplexed expressions. Then Haji started talking to them, and they began performing some incantations. Badru paid close attention.

Then he started nodding and said, "As I suspected, they are calling upon the power of Geb."

"Why call on Geb?" Yalu asked, "He imprisons those unworthy of the Field of Reeds. How can that help?"

"Where do those imprisoned dead stay?" Badru asked Yalu.

He shook his head.

Badru answered his own question, "In the earth, of course. Appeasing Geb means they have a better chance to go to the Fields of Reeds when they die."

"What do you think Geb will do to fight against this attack? Do you think he'll win?" Tau asked.

Badru just sighed and shook his head. As Nebit looked onward, Haji and the magicians finished their incantations. But nothing happened. Pharaoh yelled at them furiously. Haji attempted to appease Pharaoh, and they tried performing their incantations again. Still, nothing happened.

Tau asked in a high voice: "Is Geb hiding in his shell like a scared little turtle?"

"You may not be far from the truth," Badru replied gravely. "After witnessing what happened to the other three gods, I would be surprised if Geb actually came and risked a battle with this Hebrew god."

"Look!" Nebit pointed, "Pharaoh is going back to the palace."

The others watched the scene as Pharaoh angrily stormed into the palace, the magicians and servants following after him. Moses and Aaron were left alone once again. Covering their mouths and noses, they looked at each other, sighed, and headed back. Looking at them now, Nebit felt sorry for them. It seemed like they've been trying so hard and wanted to protect them even more.

The four scouts used the statue to hide from Moses and Aaron as they passed by.

Nebit gestured for them to follow and she leapt down to the ground, into the churning sea of gnats. The others did likewise, and they continue their pursuit. Badru handed her a strip of cloth to cover her nose and mouth. She quickly tied it behind her head and nodded in thanks. He did the same for the others.

As they left through the main gate one man shouted at the guard, "Let us see Phar. . .," He stopped to cough up the little flying menaces. A crowd behind him shouted as well. Some of them had put cloths to their mouths while others had draped cloths over their entire bodies.

Moses and Aaron slipped by all of them unnoticed. The scouts followed them back to Aaron's estate, and hid behind a wool cart, pretending to browse the wares. They saw the Hebrew woman from before approach Moses and Aaron. The three of them talked for a little while and then went inside the house.

"So do we go back to our room and continue our watch?" Tau scratched the side of his face and stared at the dead gnat paste on his fingers.

"Uh… No we don't. We're going to go wash up in the Nile first," Nebit looked at herself with disgust, "I feel so dirty! I'm not going to sleep like this, and neither are any of you!" She pointed accusingly at the others.

Badru nodded his head in agreement. They walked down to the Nile but found the riverbank packed with people washing themselves. They heard a shout and saw Hoshea waving to them with Lior at his side. They walked down and joined them.

As the water flowed over Nebit's skin to wash away the disgusting little creatures, she felt relief.

Hoshea asked, "Any more adventures?"

Yalu glanced at the others and said, "No. Just ordinary guard work today."

Hoshea nodded, revealing a little disappointment. Then his gaze turned toward Badru and he said, "You don't look like a soldier."

Badru replied, "Perhaps not, but I know my way in a fight well enough."

Looking at Lior, Yalu asked, "More guard work for you too?"

Lior glanced at Hoshea, who looked a little embarrassed, and chuckled. He said, "With what happened to Yadid, Nun wants to take no chances with his son."

Hoshea and Lior finished washing themselves, waved goodbye, and left.

"Badru, does this count as another victory for the Hebrew god?" Tau asked as he threw water on himself and rubbed with his hands to dislodge the gnats.

"It would seem," Badru said in a resigned tone as he scrubbed at his feet and the gnats between his toes.

"We can't spend too much time here," Yalu warned as everyone continued splashing water on their arms and faces. "We don't want to miss anything about Moses. Is everyone done?"

Nebit looked at him, and then redoubled her scrubbing efforts. Soon she felt that she'd rid herself of as many of those things as she could. It was not to her satisfaction, but she felt better. They headed back to their room and began their watch again.

Badru awoke with a start the next morning amid muffled shouts of "Moses" among other things. He roused quickly, grabbed his pack, and followed the others out. To his dismay, the gnats remained.

Tau whispered, "Where are they going? The way to the palace is down the other road."

"This way goes to the Nile," Badru replied "Perhaps they intend to catch Pharaoh during his morning bath."

"Not a moment's peace, eh?" Tau laughed and then coughed up some of the bugs that had gotten in his mouth. Badru tossed him another piece of linen.

"That reminds me, we'll need to bathe again," Nebit put cloth over her face.

Sure enough, Pharaoh, accompanied by his guards, stood knee-deep in the water while servants bathed him. They saw Moses and Aaron wade through the gnats to get to him. When Pharaoh spotted them he put his hands on his hips and shook his head to show his annoyance. This time, they found a storage building to hide behind. Moses and Aaron talked with Pharaoh for a little while, and then they left.

"What just happened?" Nebit asked. "Aren't they going to do something else? Or do you suppose that Pharaoh decided to let them go worship?"

"If Pharaoh gave in, I would expect Moses to look much happier." Badru replied. "But neither of them looks very happy to me."

Moses and Aaron walked by the place where they were hiding and Pharaoh continued to bathe while his servants continued scrubbing the gnats off of his body. After a moment of perplexity, Badru and the others chased after Moses and Aaron.

On the way, Badru heard Nebit's voice speak up, "I think we're being followed."

He turned and saw Yalu's concerned expression. They casually turned, glancing behind them but didn't see anybody.

Nebit continued, "They're staying hidden. But I can spot them when they move. I started seeing them after we left Pharaoh."

Then Badru stopped walking, turned around, and scanned the area. Everyone else stopped too. The collective buzzing from the gnats became annoyingly obvious. The black cloud moved about the whole area, making it hard to see if anyone was peeking out at them.

Badru took a deep breath through his cloth and shouted, "The eye of Ptah sees all!" The other three looked around and waited for something to happen.

After a few moments, five Egyptian men emerged from hiding and approached him. One of them, who had several scars on his face and a couple daggers strapped to his legs, pointed at him and demanded in a raspy voice, "Who are you?"

"I am Badru, an apprentice of Haji. We are on a task authorized by Ptah and given to us by pharaoh himself," Badru said confidently. Then he accused them, "Are you hindering us?"

The same man responded, "We also serve Ptah. We were to track and kill four murderers. The description matches your three companions, but not you."

"Well," Badru thought for a moment. He tried to recall the man's face but could not. "The description doesn't match entirely then. Does it make sense that Ptah would send one group on a task and then send another group to kill that first group?"

"What proof do you have?"

Badru searched the pockets on the inside of his robe and produced a bronze seal. He showed it to them.

The man whistled and walked over to the other four he was with, and they huddled in a circle and whispered to each other. After a few moments the man turned to them and said "We will ask Ptah. If you are honest, I wish you success on your task. The great eye watches over us all."

Badru smiled, "Indeed."

They turned and walked away. The soldiers stood in silence watching them disappear quickly into the fog of gnats. Badru turned to Yalu with a concerned look on his face.

"Well done!" Tau cheered and clapped his hands, "although it's a pity they didn't attack. After all that sitting down I could use a fight."

"Do not congratulate me yet," Badru turned back toward them and saw Tau's puzzled expression. "They may yet decide to come after us. I think my words have only delayed them for a time. In order to resolve the situation, we need to go to the source of the problem directly: the priests of Ptah."

"Flesh and fire! Confronting a priest isn't something I woke up this morning wanting to do," Yalu sighed. "It looks like we lost Moses and Aaron too. I guess we should wait for them again."

They left the street and walked back. After washing themselves in the Nile again, they headed back to their room, where Badru settled down for his watch while the others slept. He thought about the men they encountered and wondered if they reported to Sakakwi.

Had Sakakwi lost trust in me? Did he send these men to keep an eye on us? Or perhaps they really are hunting the other three as traitors to Egypt and the gods. Badru wondered as he watched the cloud of gnats as a treacherous sea in the helpless neighborhood below.

Chapter 10

Nebit stirred and woke to gentle rubbing on her shoulder. She opened her eyes and blinked a few times. A lumbering figure towered over her.

"He's here." Tau whispered, pointing toward the window.

Realizing that this was her chance, she and jumped up and rushed to the window. She looked out to see Moses laying his matt out on the ground near the wall. Then she bolted out the door. Tau sat down at the window again to start watching.

She stared at the man at the gate and waited until his back was turned to slip by. As she moved in between the wall of their target and the neighboring home, she heard the whispering of a voice. Once she was sure that he was right on the other side, she quietly scaled the stone wall with her fingers and toes. When she reached the top, about one and a half times taller than she was, she peered over and saw him laying prostrate on his matt.

"I have indeed found favor in your eyes, my God. For was it not yesterday when I asked the Egyptian magicians not be able do the same signs as you? And look how foolish you made them to Pharaoh! They are as children playing in the dust of the ground. But you, as you watch me in my sleepless nights, are wise beyond any of them."

Suddenly, she felt her foot slip, and she fell a short distance. She quickly regained her footing on the stone, but could already hear suspicious tones in the voice on the other side of the wall. She crawled back down the wall as Moses called for a soldier to investigate the noise. He saw nothing and moved on to another area. Nebit took and released a silent breath of relief, and slipped back to the borrowed room.

When she lifted up the canvas and slipped inside, she heard a whistle. Looking up she saw Tau's grinning face. Her eye twitched as he said "I always knew you liked making a scene. Next time we'll kick down the front gate."

Her face scrunched at the barb. Then she lifted her eyebrows and her expression softened, "With you hiding in the dark, somebody needs to go where the excitement is."

Tau growled. A small smile escaped Nebit's lips as she sat down in her reed bed near Yalu.

Yalu slowly regained his senses. His eyes stung from lack of sleep, so he tried to keep them closed. As he consciously began controlling his breathing, he took extra care to keep it unchanged. Since he knew he needed to wake up soon, he cherished these last few moments of rest. As he heard footsteps approaching he forced himself to open his eyes and relieve Tau.

Before he could fall asleep, however, Yalu asked, "Did you see Moses again last night?" Tau grunted incoherently, but after some cajoling he told Yalu what had happened.

"Do you think he'll be there every night from now on?" Yalu pressed but the only response was a light snore. He thought to himself to tell Kasmut about it. Then he settled down at the window, scanning the manor for anything out of the ordinary. He rubbed his face with his hands and then rubbed his eyes with his fingers to fight against his drowsiness.

Before the sun rose people were up and about their business as usual. Yalu saw the sun's first ray of light appearing above horizon. Looking toward the edge of the sprawling mud-brick houses, a darkness grabbed Yalu's attention. He rubbed his eyes, at first blaming it on morning grogginess. But when he looked again it was definitely there, and definitely getting closer.

Yalu felt like he wanted to shout and warn the people in the estate and alleyways below him, but the only words he could think of would make him sound like a fool. He turned toward his sleeping companions and saw Nebit stir. He called her name and she startled awake, staring at him. He pointed out the window and said, "Come look at this."

She left her bed and Yalu moved out of the way to let her see. He could tell she saw the encroaching darkness from her wide eyes and gaping mouth. She turned to him and asked, "What is it?" But he shook his head with a fearful expression.

The people in the alleyways below them could see it now. Whoever saw it coming stared at it for a few moments in unbelief and ran the opposite way in a panic. The people who were surprised by it dropped whatever they were carrying and desperately rubbed their hands on their face and ears.

Finally, the darkness flowed underneath the alleyway of their room as a flood and Yalu knew what it was. He whispered, "Flies."

He turned toward the other two and shouted, "Wake up!"

Tau instantly opened his eyes and sat up but Badru merely stirred and mumbled incoherently.

Tau asked, "What is it? And what is that sound?"

Yalu and Nebit hadn't realized until Tau asked, but now that they listened they could hear a distinct buzzing sound coming from everywhere like conversations of many people in a large chamber. At about that time the flies came in through the window accompanied by random shrieks from the people outside.

Thinking quickly, Nebit dashed over to a burlap sack void of the barley the purchased in it and started cutting long strips. She gave the first one to Yalu, who figured out what she was doing, and put it over her nose, mouth, and ears, tying it behind her head. The next one he gave to Tau and then he put one on himself.

Finally, Badru awoke screaming as flies landed on his face and body. Yalu tossed him the last burlap strip that Nebit cut and he figured out what to do with it.

"Flesh and Fire! What's going on here?"

"You were on watch!" Badru reminded him. "Can't you tell us?"

Remembering his duty, Yalu quickly went over to the window again. Then he recounted what happened for everyone, giving a frequent glance toward Aaron's estate. Then he asked, "But why? It is as though the gnats were mere babies which grew up overnight."

"It's a shame all those frogs died," Tau grunted.

"I hate flies," Nebit said. "I hate flies. I hate flies. I hate flies."

"It must be the Hebrew god again," Badru replied. "Flies accompany the dirty and dying aspects of the flow of life, which is Geb's realm. Because he refused to reveal himself and fight the Hebrew god, this double display of power must be a sign of complete defeat for him."

"Impressive." Tau stated and nodded his head. Badru and Nebit looked at him with more surprise than the flies. Then he added, "Just think of the power of the god which can do all of this. I feel ashamed that

Geb numbers as one of the gods if he behaves so cowardly as to run and hide from a fight twice now."

Yalu turned and shouted at everyone through the burlap, "Kasmut and a palace messenger are already at the gate."

The others looked at him and waited. Yalu saw Moses and Aaron emerge from the house and leave with her and the official without delay. They grabbed their weapons and ran after in pursuit, but it didn't take long to catch up to them.

Walking along, Yalu noticed Nebit shake her head and her face contorted in disgust. She fanned her face with a hand to keep the flies from her eyes. "They swarm on animal dung and will track it onto you if they land on you."

"There's plenty of grazing land along the Nile," Yalu reasoned. "Why don't they swarm over there? We're not a bunch of animal dung!"

"Unless the Hebrew god disagrees." Tau laughed. The others cringed and looked at him nervously. Nebit was the first to turn away and fanned herself more vigorously. Then Tau coughed, "I think I swallowed a fly."

Once again they arrived at the palace gates where Moses, Aaron, and the messenger entered unobstructed. Kasmut left after walking with them to the gate. Tau leaned over to Yalu and asked, "Should we follow them inside?"

"I think we can wait here," Yalu answered. "I'm guessing that Pharaoh summoned Moses to get rid of the flies like he did with the frogs."

"I just hope that the Hebrew god takes these flies away soon. And I mean 'take away' this time. I don't want to have to step on them all the way back," said Nebit with tense breaths.

"It is obvious that Geb will not do anything about it." Badru added. "Pharaoh must ask the god of

the Hebrew slaves who brought this about to bring it
to an end. It makes me wonder what godly power
Pharaoh really has."

"He commands the people who can get favor
from the gods, perhaps. That's a lot of power," Yalu
reasoned and hoped. But he felt now that it was a blind
hope.

"Over there!" Nebit shouted and pointed down
the road toward the palace. They saw the armed
emissaries of Ptah from before. Like most others, they
had covered their bodies with cloth to block the flies.
Nebit hissed, "What do you think they want now?"

"I suppose we should find out," Yalu stared at
them as they approached. They saw the one with the
scar on his face leading the others. Yalu instinctively
put his hand behind his head to the hilt of his khopesh
as he thought they looked more serious this time.

When they met, Badru advanced to meet them.
"Were my proofs not sufficient? Why do you continue
to hound us?"

"You must follow."

"What?" Badru exclaimed in astonishment.
"We have our mission from the priesthood. You
cannot interfere with us."

"You may be carrying out their orders, but so
are we," the man with the scars scowled. He and his
men started reaching for their weapons.

"Come now, let us be reasonable," Badru raised
his hands to attempt a calming gesture but Yalu knew it
wasn't going to work anymore. "We both serve the
same god. Why must you insist to trouble us?"

In reply, they drew their weapons. Badru turned
to Yalu and they stared at each other for a moment. In
that stare Yalu saw Badru ask whether to go or fight.
Yalu took a deep breath, and after a brief internal
weighing of the consequences, shook his head.

Nebit stepped toward Yalu and touched his shoulder. He turned and looked into her frightened eyes with surprise. But his expression was one of confidence and optimism. She felt secure under his comforting gaze.

Without changing the expression on his face, Badru turned back to the man. After a short breath he said "Very well, we will go with you. But it had better be quick"

"Let's go now," he said in a mocking tone, "The sooner we go, the sooner you can get back to your mission."

The five armed men surrounded the four soldiers and took them to the grounds of the temple of Ptah. They entered a small mud brick building that had a large mat in the center and two armed men sitting on reed mats near the door. While one of them lit torches, the scarred man removed the mat and revealed a tunnel with a ladder going underground. He and another man led the way, while the other three took the ladder after the four. After everyone had climbed down the ladder, one of the men covered the opening again with the mat and darkness settled in.

Nebit had always felt comfortable in the darkness, but this time was different. She felt nervous, very nervous. By the torchlight, she saw the packed dirt that closed her in as she marched with the others through, single-file. The flies had even invaded this secret passage. She heard a myriad of crackles as flies that buzzed too close to the flames fell dead and landed in the growing heaps on the dirt. The cool air gave her goosebumps and the musty smell made her nauseous.

Eventually the tunnel changed to stone. Nebit looked upon the stones with familiarity. With every step she took she could feel herself getting closer and closer to him. She felt the pain in her chest return. She took slow and deep breaths, hoping nobody would notice her vulnerability.

Yalu leaned toward her and said, "I don't know if I can find my way back. I lost track after the first five turns or so. I wonder if we could find our way back by ourselves."

"Of course we can," Badru scoffed defiantly. "We simply need to keep careful record of which passages we take. It would take some time, but we should find the way out before we starved."

Nebit wanted to say that she knew the way, but was too scared that whatever she said might give herself away to the scarred man.

The scarred man finally interrupted them, "Every one of these tunnels leads to some part of the city. You would find your way somewhere, soon enough." Silence and the buzzing of flies accompanied them after that.

Finally, they reached a wooden door reinforced with bronze bands and on the right-hand side they saw a hole three times as tall as it was wide. The scarred man searched a pouch on his belt and pulled out a small bronze rod with a bronze pennant on it. He inserted it into the hole and turned. After a few clicking noises, the door opened. A rush of fresh warm air came out that cheered them up, except for Nebit. The others took deep satisfying breaths. After all passed through the door, the scarred man closed it and used the rod on it again and it disappeared back into his pouch.

Torches attached to the wall lit their path as the scarred man led them into a huge chamber. They saw a large statue of Ptah covered with black lacquer and overlaid with gold clothing. Around the statue blazed bonfires and priests who prostrated themselves in worship of the god. Nebit could see the others were impressed by all of it.

Badru leaned toward the others and whispered, "This is the heart of the temple. Not many besides priests enter this illustrious and sacred place."

Tau grunted, "Sounds like a great honor."

"An honor I could do without right now." Yalu muttered.

Nebit almost found herself voicing her agreement but remained silent. She wished she could tell Yalu about this place and all the happened and about her master, but in the safety in their rented room while Tau and Badru were off bartering.

The scarred man took them into a side-room, and then into another, smaller chamber. Inside waited a man wearing a black kalasiris robe and with a cleanly shaven head, standing behind a bronze table. His eyes burned with unquenchable fire, like the bonfires near the statue. On his head sat a golden circlet that depicted the eye of Ptah and an arm with a hammer. Nebit recognized Sakakwi instantly and hid as best she could behind the others, praying to whatever god who came into her mind that he wouldn't notice her.

Badru and Tau stood mouth gaping open, looking at the priest before them.

"Master, these are the ones we told you about," the scarred man said and bowed humbly. "They claim to be on a special assignment from Pharaoh."

"You imbeciles! Were the descriptions given to you not sufficient? Or has the great god Ptah cursed your eyes?"

The scarred man and the others with him were taken aback with surprise and fear.

Tau spoke up, "My father is working the bronze you gave me from before. He tells me it is indeed high quality as you said and is making something very special."

"Good." Sakakwi contorted his face in a half-smile.

The sound of his voice instantly brought painful memories back to Nebit's mind. The pain in her chest continued to grow.

Badru stepped forward, gave his customary bow and said, "But what is not good is your pack of mongrels interfering."

"Indeed," Sakakwi gave the scarred man a menacing look. "I shall have to find other dogs more competent."

His eyes looked over Tau and Badru. Then he sized up Yalu. Finally, his gaze rested on a small shadow behind them and his face instantly brightened. He turned to the scarred man again. "Perhaps not. What is this you've brought me?"

Badru, Tau, and Yalu turned and looked at Nebit. She stood as though frozen, staring at floor. Her body trembled.

Yalu turned toward Sakakwi and said, "She is one of the soldiers working with us for Rashidi. She has proven herself to us in our mission for Pharaoh."

"I'm sure she has," Sakakwi said slowly. The smile remaining on his face. "Yes. This is the perfect place for her now. With her talents, I'm sure the problem will be taken care of. Isn't that right, Nebit?"

She didn't reply.

"At any rate," Sakakwi said to the scarred man, "because you've found something precious that I lost, though unwittingly, I will have mercy on you and give you one more chance." Then he turned toward Badru. "As for you four, these men will hinder your mission no longer. You may go."

Badru bowed courteously to him again and they turned to leave. However, before Nebit exited Sakakwi called out her name. She stopped and something compelled her to bring her face up to look at his.

"Would you be so kind as to show your companions the way through the tunnels?" Sakakwi curled his lips back to show his teeth. "And once this mission for Pharaoh is done, I shall have you back."

Nebit felt cold and started to sweat under his oppressive gaze. Her heart beat fast in her chest. She just stood there, gaping at him, not knowing what to do or say.

She felt hand grasp her arm and she was pulled out of the room. She felt herself off balance and falling, but then arms caught her. She looked up into Yalu's concerned eyes. "Are you alright?"

She took a breath and steadied herself. When she looked at the others she saw that they were looking back at her. "Let's go," she said and led them silently back through the labyrinth of stone and dirt.

"I hope Moses and Aaron have not done anything important during this little diversion," Badru complained.
Tau put his arm around Badru, "It is good we already knew Sakakwi. If only I'd known earlier those men were from him, we could have told them."

"At least we have less to worry about," Yalu gave a sigh of relief.

Nebit eyed Badru, Tau, and Yalu suspiciously as they talked. She remembered how they talked with Sakakwi like friends. She thought about Sakakwi's words to her. Although there was a hope she could escape Sakakwi's grasp she could see it was a false hope now. Then she glanced despairing at Yalu and sighed. He was surely in league with Sakakwi like the others.

They emerged through the same house from which they had entered the tunnels, feeling the eyes of the armed priests on their backs as they went. When they arrived back at their borrowed room, Badru took up position at the window and began his watch. Yalu and Tau laid down to sleep.

Sitting on her matt, Nebit hugged her knees to her aching chest. Once again, she felt alone and in the dark. But looking up, she saw a beam of moonlight sneak through their door and was reminded of Kasmut's words. And with that single ray of hope, she fell asleep.

The next day, Tau woke Yalu up who relieved him at the window. Gazing out into the sunrise he realized the flies were gone. He turned to ask Tau what happened but saw him snoring away on his bed.

Not too long after sunrise, Yalu saw another messenger from Pharaoh, accompanied by an escort of four guards armed with spears approach the gate of Aaron's estate. After a brief exchange of words, the messenger from Pharaoh waited at the gate in silence.

Yalu quickly turned to his sleeping friends and whispered intensely, "Get up everyone! Moses will be on the move soon!" He turned back to the window while the others woke.

Nebit yawned and stretched her arms over her head. "Is he going to the Palace again?"

"I think so," Yalu replied. "Let's get close enough so we can follow them."

The four ran out of the room with Yalu leading them. When they arrived in the busy street they saw Moses and Aaron talking with the messenger. As they neared, they could hear the conversation.

Moses demanded, "He already agreed that when the Lord my god took the flies away that he would let my people go to worship. He's already done this before."

"I dare not claim to understand the mind of Pharaoh," the messenger replied. "The words of Pharaoh are wise. Do not question a god."

"The Wise words of Pharaoh," Moses spat out angrily. "We'll see how wise they are when the next calamity befalls Egypt."

"Indeed," the messenger smiled smugly and then turned to leave. His guards followed him. The brick-makers along the road muttered in fear and contempt as they hurried out of the way. The four watched as Moses and Aaron stared at the messenger with discouraged looks on their faces until he left their sight. Then they turned to each other and spoke in Hebrew.

Tau turned to Badru and asked, "What is he talking about?"

"Pharaoh probably agreed to let them go worship if the flies were taken away," Badru guessed. "Like the other times, it seems that Pharaoh has rescinded his agreement."

Yalu scoffed, "I always hated the parts in the old stories when the gods broke their word!"

"Yalu!" A voice called. The four turned and saw Moses looking directly at them. Yalu flushed red for giving up their stealth. He cursed himself under his breath. Both Moses and Aaron approached the group.

Moses greeted them with a wave of his hand, "I couldn't help overhearing your outburst."

"There was another question I wanted to ask you," Badru capitalized on Yalu's gaffe. "May we speak in private?"

Moses looked at his brother who spoke to him in Hebrew. After a short back and forth Aaron looked to them and offered, "If you want to accompany us back inside my home we can talk there."

They nodded and Aaron led them through the gate and inside the home with Moses following behind. He took them to a large room with reed mats to sit on. After they entered the room, they noticed a few armed servants following after them.

When Aaron saw the confusion on their faces, he tried to calm them by saying, "Do not be troubled. We mean you no harm. Since you have weapons this is just a precaution." He sat down on one of the mats in the middle of the room.

Yalu cautiously sat down as well, and so did the other three. He hoped that so much interaction with Moses and Aaron would not make them suspicious.

Then Badru began, "I have heard some rumors about you. I do not know if they are true, but being an Egyptian it is something that weighs heavily upon me." As he spoke they saw the same expression of pain on Moses' face that they had seen when they escorted him to the palace, as though Moses already knew what Badru was going to say.

"Is it true that you murdered an Egyptian and then fled to escape the wrath of Pharaoh?" Badru asked frankly.

Yalu noticed Tau staring with his mouth open at Badru in surprise. Nebit seemed to be looking at Moses curiously. As Yalu looked and waited for the answer, he thought of the time he killed the thief.

Moses' gaze drifted down toward his hands. Through his eyes they saw anger, fear, and then shame as though reliving the experience. He took a deep breath and then, closing his eyes, he released it. Then he opened them again, except this time with a quiet sort of confidence. He looked at them and said "Yes. I was defending a slave against a master who was beating him. I killed him. Afterwards, my Egyptian mother was able to warn me that Pharaoh ordered the city guards to arrest me where he would see my public execution. So I escaped the city by night and fled."

Yalu kept glancing at Badru as Moses answered. He seemed surprised at such a quick confession. But he felt his own guilt start to well up.

Then Yalu took and released a deep breath saying, "I have killed. Not long ago I kept watch over the market and a thief came and took a wood plank. I caught him in the act. I chased him down and trapped him in a dead end. We fought, and I killed him."

Moses looked at him with an empathetic look and asked, "Do you feel shame or guilt from your actions?"

Yalu averted his eyes and looked around the room as he thought how to answer. Finally he said, "The man deserved it! He committed a crime and I was at hand to catch him. But thinking back on it, I would rather he choose to live and spend time in the prison pit over death."

Yalu looked into Moses' eyes. In them he recognized the same feelings that there were in his own. Moses nodded to him and he nodded back.

"I too have killed," Nebit confessed. She didn't look up. Her face seemed sad. "Though I'm sure most did not deserve it."

Yalu looked at her. Her thin black braids hung still. Then they rustled and she looked up at him and gazed into his eyes. She made a pained smile and he returned with one of his own.

"One thing confuses me," Badru said after a moment's pause, "Even though your people have lived in Egypt as long as I can remember, your ways are still your own. Other slaves that come learn to accept the Egyptian way of life and our gods because ours is the culture of the civilized world. Even the cursed Hyksos, who were not slaves, took up the god Set as their patron, which is of course why the old Pharaoh Ahmose spared their priests."

"I don't know how my people were able to retain their identity," said Moses, "But I do know that the Lord my god chose my ancestor out of all the people of the whole world and set him and his descendants apart to be his people and He their god."

"What did he do that your god showed him such favor?" Badru shifted his legs on the reed mat.

Moses shrugged his shoulders and said "Nothing, really."

When Badru gave him a quizzical look, Aaron clarified, "All he did was listen when he was called. The Lord, our god, told him to leave his family and his city to a place he did not know and he obeyed. And he was told of what would happen in the future and he believed it."

"That seems too simple: listening, obeying, and believing," Badru grunted in disbelief. "In all the stories, a mortal must do something incredible or provide critical help to the god in order to be worthy of such favor. The great Imhotep was granted favor by the gods because of his amazing work in the medicinal art. I saw him painted next to the gods Nut and Geb, and even Ammon-Ra's wife Hathor!"

"Well, I won't make you agree with my words." Aaron took a breath. "But do consider: Pharaoh is listening, but not obeying. What has been the result so far?"

Yalu shook his head, "Gods often change their minds, but you are right: his decisions are bringing on your god's wrath." Everyone else in the room nodded or grunted in agreement. Some of the men with swords did so emphatically.

Moses agreed, "Letting us go would diminish Pharaoh's glory. For that, he tries the strength of our god, and we all suffer."

Badru leaned forward and asked, "Pharaoh and many other officials say that a Kushite god is the one who is giving you power to perform this magic. Is that true?"

"They think the Lord is one of the Kushite gods?" Moses exclaimed.

Suddenly a man burst into the room and called Moses by his name. They spoke in Hebrew for a while.

"There is some business I need to attend to," Moses told them. "It was a good talk." At that, everyone stood up. Moses walked out of the room while Yalu and the others stretched their legs. Then they were escorted out of the manor and out of the estate.

The four returned to their room and resumed their watch. Tau, Yalu, and Badru readied for sleep as Nebit sat by the window.

But before Badru lay down, he told the others, "I do not know what the rest of you think, but I feel uneasy about all of this. The future is plunged into deep fog in the dead of night and I very much dislike being kept in the dark."

"I too feel it. A weight on my chest heavier than the mightiest water cow." Yalu confessed. He gave a belabored breath as he shared his anxiety. "Pharaoh seems to want to cause the Hebrew slaves to suffer, no matter the cost. And I fear it may cost greatly."

Nebit continued to watch the manor as she said, "Before you start soaring like hawks on the high winds, perhaps you should go and buy more food." Tau immediately perked up at the thought of food and grunted a couple times before he lay back down.

Yalu replied, "Right. Shall we continue talking in the market?" Then he got up and started walking to the door.

Badru stood up and said, "Yes. Sometimes I find my best thinking happens when talking with others."

They both left Nebit alone to listening to Tau's comforting snores.

As they walked the now-familiar labyrinth of streets and alleys, Yalu noted, "It is good to hear the normal dull roar of conversation in the city again."

Badru nodded as he glanced at some garlic and onions in a grocer's baskets. Then he said, "Something is amiss in the palace. The god of the Hebrews has proven himself powerful. Why would they continue to ignore him? And why would they think he is from Kush?"

Yalu thought as they bartered for a small basket of figs and dates. Badru picked one of the choice figs and tossed it into his mouth. Then he offered one to Yalu who took and ate it eagerly. They chewed on fruit as their minds chewed on the questions.

"The coming war with Kush?" Yalu offered.

"War with Kush," Badru repeated as he stopped and looked intently at some salted meat in front of another tradesman. "Could this be a confusion of a war in the realm of men instead of in the realm of the gods?"

"Pharaoh is preparing for war and might think these events were related. If the Hebrew slaves leave, then Pharaoh's ability to raise an army will be considerably hindered. The God of the Hebrews has already wrecked so much devastation. Perhaps…" Yalu stopped short.

He saw the scarred man was glaring at him. Yalu felt the anger and resentment emanating from his eyes in his scarred and scowling face. The man's face twitched so oddly that it put Yalu off-guard. Badru followed Yalu's eyes and saw him too. Then the man suddenly vanished in the crowd.

Yalu put a hand on Badru's shoulder and said, "We should go now."

"The scarred servant of Sakakwi? Pay him no mind." Badru replied. "He is a toothless dog and should not be any more trouble to us."

Gazing into the people walking back and forth, Yalu wanted to believe Badru. But something in his gut told him that man hadn't caused them trouble for the last time. He decided to keep it to himself for now.

When they traded for a few more baskets of food they walked back to their room without any incident. But all the while the depth of Moses' words weighed heavily on Yalu. The day went by, and then evening came with stars sparkling and the moon looking down on them. The night passed slowly as each of them found difficulty sleeping.

Chapter 11

Again, in the morning, Yalu saw Moses and Aaron leave the manor early to go to the palace. Yalu roused the others and they followed the men. Moses and Aaron entered the palace and after a short time they exited again and headed back.

Tau leaned toward the others as they walked and whispered, "That was quick. Did something happen my eyes didn't see? Or maybe Pharaoh agreed to Moses' terms."

"I doubt Pharaoh would alter his pattern of behavior," Badru disagreed. "We should ask Moses what happened."

"Let's keep following them. Perhaps we'll find out," Yalu said and the others nodded.

While passing through the market, Nebit noticed the scarred man who worked for Sakakwi. But when she tried to point him out to the others he was gone.

"It must have been your imagination," Badru dismissed her.

"Certainly not!" She scowled at him. "I think he's following us."

"Perhaps, Nebit is right." Yalu said, trying to get a better look at where she saw him. "We did see him before."

"Ridiculous." Badru responded. "There is no reason Sakakwi would send men to follow us."

She wasn't able to think of anything to say to him, so she gave him a look instead. Something inside her knew that the man was up to no good.

They went back to their room and continued their watch. The next day, during Yalu's early morning watch, he heard footsteps approaching his room. His thoughts instantly turned to the scarred man. He quietly readied his khopesh as he crept toward the doorway.

"Hello? Yalu? Nebit?" said a familiar voice.

Yalu breathed a sigh of relief and lifted the canvas to reveal Kasmut behind it. He asked, "Please come in. How can we serve?"

"Rashidi has a task of great importance for you," She said as she entered. Upon seeing the other three fast asleep she added, "Wake up the others and follow me. I'll wait outside." Then she left.

Yalu quietly roused the other three and explained what happened. They got their weapons and grabbed some food to eat while they exited. Kasmut was staring out toward's Aaron's manor and only looked at them when they got close.

"What is this task?" Badru asked, "It must be more important than our spying."

"It is," Kasmut turned to lead them away. "Rashidi will explain. Follow me."

As they neared Rashidi's estate, they noticed a commotion around the neighborhoods and the markets they passed. Eventually they arrived and entered Rashidi's house. Kasmut led them to the meeting room where Rashidi sat, awaiting them. Another man wearing leather pants and gloves stood at the side of the room.

As soon as they entered, Rashidi burst out, "The livestock… they're dying. Some disease has infected our herds. Pharaoh gave me the task to investigate this matter, because it relates to Moses and the Hebrews. Moses came to the palace yesterday and warned Pharaoh that a terrible plague would come upon our livestock. As a precaution, last night the herders gathered their animals together South of the city along the Nile and guards were hired to ensure nothing happened. Nobody reported any activity, but in the morning they started to see… sickness."

Rashidi continued, "Let me explain the way I think it happened. There are records of animals in the South that continuously carry a disease. It is highly likely that some Hebrews working with the Kushites sneaked some of these animals, or their own livestock that were infected, into our herds. Since they follow one of the Kushite gods, this explanation fits perfectly together."

"Mahud will show you how to identify the disease from our herds," Rashidi pointed to the man at the side of the room, who took a couple steps forward. Then Rashidi said "Once you are able to identify the disease, you are to go to the Hebrew herds and find the livestock that have it. If my guess is right, and I'm sure it is, then you'll find the evidence we need to prove the Kushites are behind this. Do you understand?"

"Yes master Rashidi," Yalu replied. "I just want to remind you that we've been following Moses, and this task will take us from that for a while."

Rashidi shook his head, "I know, but that is precisely why I need you. You've been watching him and better know what to expect." Rashidi paused and added emphasis on his next statement, "All of our livestock have succumbed to this disease and are dead or dying. Every cow, goat, and sheep is affected. Even now though, we're making arrangements to acquire livestock from our allies and trade partners to rebuild our flocks. Rebuilding our flocks will take a lot of time. Moses has inflicted great loss this time, and we need to prove his guilt so he can be punished. Go and report when you have the evidence I need."

"Come with me," Mahud walked to the exit. "I'll tell you all I know about what has happened." The four of them followed Mahud south toward the herds.

"We were first told about this yesterday afternoon. We decided to protect the herds by isolating them from the Hebrew herds as Rashidi said. So we took them to the south and posted guards to keep watch. We first noticed the disease spreading among the herds at daybreak."

"What manner of disease is this?" asked Badru. "It must be terrible if the livestock are dying in a matter of hours."

"It is terrible," Mahud confirmed. "The animals shake uncontrollably and have trouble breathing. As the disease progresses, their legs give out from underneath them. Right before they die, they struggle violently on the ground. After it subsides, we notice blood streaming from the nose and mouth. As well you know, after the Nile floods, eventually it stops, but this blood floods continuously and doesn't stop."

"Have any of the herders been infected with the disease?" Yalu asked. "Or is it only the livestock?"

"We're not taking any chances," Mahud answers. "As you can see from my clothing, we're not even touching them. When I left, some of the herders were trying to find unaffected animals and keep them away from the diseased ones. Hopefully we can save some of them."

"Didn't you say none of the watchers saw anything?" Tau asked. "If so, then how could Moses get the disease to your herd?"

"Someone trained in stealth can find ways of not being seen," Nebit shot a well-pleased grin at Tau, who just grunted and lifted up his crooked nose.

They left the city and walked out along the Nile river bank. The palm trees growing fairly thick here provided some protection from the heat of the day. In the distance they could see the livestock grouped by their kind.

"Look at all of them!" Yalu exclaimed. "I've never seen so many cattle and sheep before. Is this all the livestock in the city?"

"This is all the livestock belonging to Pharaoh and his officials," Mahud clarified. "There are much smaller herds owned by some others. But yes, this is most of them."

As they came closer, the smell of the animals grew. Soon, they could see devastation of the disease. A quarter of them already lay motionless on the ground. Another quarter of the livestock had already collapsed and were in varying stages of dying. The rest seem to be struggling to stay on their feet. The cries and whimpers of dying animals, the wailing of their keepers, and the crowing of carrion birds filled the air.

The other herders wore leather clothing like Mahud. Most were busy with some kind of work. One tried to coax a sheep to drink some water. Another man chopped grass into small pieces and attempted to feed them to a goat. Still more ran about carrying baskets and jugs.

One of them saw Mahud and the soldiers approach and ran to meet them. Mahud called to one of the other herders and shouted, "Did you take the well livestock by themselves like I asked?"

The herder covered the rest of the distance quickly and replied, "We were able to group some of them together, but whenever we started moving them away from the big group at least one of the animals would fall to the ground. Then when we inspected other animals near it we found traces of the disease as well. Some of the men think they just need to eat or drink more. But most of us don't know what to do."

"I see," Mahud said. "I don't know what more we can do either. We can't eat the meat, we can't make leather from their hides or risk spreading the disease, and we completely lose our breeding stock!"

Badru stepped forward and said, "Rashidi sent us to investigate. Show us one of the animals with the disease."

"Yes," said Mahud. He led the four over to the nearest dead animal. The goat had grey fur and its head lay in a pool of its own blood which still dripped from its nose and mouth. Badru crouched down nearby and examined it.

"What a horrible sight!" Mahud shook his head. "I don't know what we're going to do with all the carcasses. We'll have to burn them downwind so we don't risk infecting the rest of the livestock. Assuming there's any left!"

"I've never seen such an awful sight in all my life!" Nebit exclaimed. "Just look at all this death."

"Something is wrong with the flow of blood," Badru observed. "This is swift-flowing like the flooding of the Nile. Can you slice open its belly so I can examine the organs?"

"I will do no such thing!" Mahud stated loudly. "Whatever disease this is, I've never seen anything like it. If we touch the dead animal then we might get infected with it."

Badru paused and then stood, "Very well, I don't want to expose anybody to this disease. It is causing enough damage among the livestock. Imagine if this were to spread to the people!"

"Is there anything else I can help you with?" Mahud asked. "I need to start making preparations for disposing of the carcasses."

"No," Badru replied. Mahud walked away, talking with Nakuku. Then Badru addressed the other three, "We ought to walk around and see what the earlier stages of this disease look like. Then we need to find some way examine the Hebrew flocks."

"Maybe Moses will help us," Tau wondered aloud.

"Why would he?" Nebit asked. "Though he does tolerate our nagging questions." She shot Badru a dirty look.

Yalu rubbed his chin with his fingers and grinned. "I have a feeling he may. Badru, have we seen enough of the disease?"

Badru answered, "The animals will behave restlessly. When their strength gives out they will collapse to the ground following a period of stillness. After they die, blood flows from their noses and mouths like water. Yes, we can go."

"I've definitely seen enough," Nebit stopped. "Let's leave. I hope I never have to see such an awful sight as long as I live."

They trudged around the groups of livestock, trying to keep a safe distance. Chaos enveloped the whole scene. Some animals still on their feet seemed to wander aimlessly and bump into one another. Other animals just stood where they were with their heads low to the ground. Every once in a while, one of the animals left standing collapsed to the ground in a heap.

"Do any of you believe Moses and some other Hebrews snuck some diseased animals past the herders without them noticing?" Tau asked the others. "I think only a god can cause death like this. Even if I started slaughtering these animals myself I wouldn't be able to finish them so quickly."

"If they did sneak diseased animals here, then how did they manage to keep their animals alive during the journey?" Yalu said. "Considering how fast this disease works, I don't think that would be possible."

The four left the fields of dead and dying animals and walked back to the city. Once there, they went straight to Aaron's gate and asked to speak to Moses.

When Moses got to the gate he greeted them with a raised hand, "Am I summoned to the palace again?"

"No, not this time," Yalu answered. "Pharaoh wants us to inspect the Hebrew flocks and livestock. Can you take us to your grazing land?"

Moses grimaced and answered, "I see Pharaoh doesn't believe that the Lord would not allow any of our livestock to die. I will be glad to show them to you. When do you want to go?"

"Now, if it is acceptable to you," Yalu responded. Then he asked, "Where are they?"

"The land of Goshen is a three-day journey on foot to the North-East," Moses answered. "You will need supplies."

"Hmm… Goshen. That is farther away than I thought," Yalu glanced at the other three.

Badru shook his head, "That may be too late to see signs of the disease."

"Could we travel down the Nile? It should be faster than walking." Nebit said. Her dark brown eyes widened and danced with excitement at the thought.

Moses nodded and thought aloud, "If you have a boat then that would be a more preferable means to travel."

Badru eyes lit up, "As a matter of fact, my household owns a boat we can use. However, I do not think we have any slaves to spare to take us there."

"I can help row or punt!" Nebit said enthusiastically. "Maybe we can each take turns."

"The boat needs five punters," Badru explained. "We can try with three, but won't have as much speed. During the night we would still need one or two at the rudder."

"That sounds fine," Yalu said. They all agreed to take the boat. Moses went inside to get his supplies ready. Badru went to the dock to get the boat ready. And Yalu, Nebit, and Tau went to Rashidi's manor to see what supplies they could get from his stores. Everyone would meet at the dock where the boat was when they were prepared.

When the three got to Rashidi's manor, they were pleasantly surprised to find the man at the store had already been given instructions to give them whatever they required. As they finished filling their sacks with food and supplies, Kasmut approached them.

"I have some news for you Nebit, come with me." She said.

Nebit told the others that she'd meet them up at the dock and went to follow her. Kasmut asked Nebit about their plans to investigate the livestock and Nebit told her about using Badru's boat to go to Goshen. She nodded in approval.

Once they arrived at a secluded corner of the manor Kasmut turned to Nebit and said, "Things are getting complicated and I may need your help. But first, I need to tell you what is going on."

"Through my network of informants I've been using various reports I've heard, including your story, to give the impression among Pharaoh's court that Sakakwi is being too reckless and ambitious. At first, my influencing was going well. I received reports that officials were asking more questions when Sakakwi requested their assistance. Some even outright refused."

"That is good news," Nebit said. "But can't you bring some charge against him? I want to see him at the bottom of Pharaoh's prison pit."

Releasing a frustrated breath, Kasmut replied, "My influence among the officials is great but Sakakwi has a very established position. Just bringing charges against him would fail. He is very resourceful and would bounce out of the way like a nimble gazelle escaping the jaws of the crocodile. No, like the crocodile, we must be patient and cunning. We slowly gain the advantage and only when we are sure of our victory do we strike."

"Yes I understand," Nebit nodded. She felt disappointed at having to wait for her satisfaction.

Kasmut continued, "My hopes by using people loyal to me to give out information that I design is to slowly turn the tide of opinion against him. Every single thing that happens around him I determine how to use it against him. When his name becomes distasteful in the mouths of Pharaoh's officials I shall then strike the killing blow."

"So where is the complication?" Nebit asked.

Holding her face with a hand, Kasmut answered, "Sakakwi must have seen what I was doing. There are now others who are reporting events that cast question into the way I want the officials to interpret them. With your story, for instance, there are now two other rumors about what happened to your master. One was that a Kushite assassin took her while another that she died by accident."

"Both of those are completely untrue." Nebit said, allowing some of her anger to show through. "I saw Sakakwi strike her down with my own two eyes. Her blood is on his hands and nobody else's."

"Are you willing to stake your life on that claim?" Kasmut asked, her eyes stared into Nebit's.

At first, Nebit hesitated as she grasped the meaning of her answer. She realized Kasmut's gaze was intended to ascertain the truth. Then her anger of Sakakwi overwhelmed her. She answered, "Absolutely."

"Perfect." Kasmut smiled. "I will get rumors started that there is a witness to her murder. That should build up interest. Then, when the time is right, I will have you speak out publicly against Sakakwi. But right now I need more allies. Are your companions trustworthy?"

Nebit drew an uneasy breath. She replied, "I fear not. They seem on friendly terms with Sakakwi."

She shuddered as she remembered her last encounter with him. Kasmut put a comforting hand on Nebit's shoulder and Nebit told her everything. The two women stood together in silence for a moment.

Then Kasmut looked into Nebit's eyes again, but this time so that Nebit would know the truth, and said, "As real as you see me living and breathing, you will see Sakakwi brought to justice. Keep up your hope. He shall not have you. And keep our words a secret between you and me."

With that, Kasmut left to attend to other business. For a little while, Nebit stayed there in thought. She thought about what Kasmut might have her say and to whom she would say it. She thought about finally delivering to Sakakwi what he deserved. She thought about Yalu and sighed. Then she left.

Nebit arrived at the dock to see Badru, Yalu, and Tau preparing the boat. It spanned about four times the length of a man and about as wide as one is tall, with long poles positioned along each side at the front and a rudder at the back. Designs and images of the gods adorned the wooden planks on the hull. A small reed house stood in front of the rear steering oar. The boat sat along a wooden pier and bobbed up and down in the water.

Yalu noticed her approaching, smiled, and waved. She faked a smile and waved back. Then the

wind gently touched her face and she felt refreshed.
She looked out over the river and this time gave an
honest smile. The morning's death could do little to
dampen the excitement of river travel.

Nebit ran over to them and asked, "How are
the preparations? Do you need any help?"

Badru answered, "We are almost done. I need
to rearrange some of the cargo so that we can be sure
to have enough room for our supplies. Moses sent a
messenger to tell us that two others will be joining our
expedition. Can you stay in the front and watch for
sandbanks?"

Nebit nodded as she carefully boarded the boat.
She felt the boat give under her foot as she stepped on.
Bobbing back up came as a surprise to her and she
used her arms to regain her balance. Yalu grabbed onto
her hand and she used him to finally stabilize herself.
She rewarded him with a smile, which he quickly
returned. Then she closed her eyes and took a deep
breath. Releasing it she opened her eyes to gaze
downstream. The water glistened in the sunlight.

"Badru, was this latest act by the Hebrew god a
defeat of Apis?" Yalu asked. "On the way over here
Tau and I passed by the temple and heard that the
current Apis bull had died of the disease. So we went in
to take a look. It had the same disease as the rest of the
livestock."

"Yes, you are right!" Badru stopped moving a
sack of figs as he spoke. "This is also a defeat for Ptah
because the Apis bull is a manifestation of himself
following the laws of nature of the world he created."

"The Hebrew god seems to be more than
willing to give our gods lessons in the laws of nature,"
Tau grimaced, feeling a bit defeated himself. Their
thoughts turned toward the death they visited earlier.

Just then Moses, Aaron, and a Hebrew woman arrived. Both Moses and Aaron carried large sacks on their shoulders with one hand and walked with a staff in the other. She wore a robe similar to that of Moses and Aaron, but of a redder hue. A white cloth was draped over head to cover her hair.

Badru motioned with his hand for them to board as they approach, "Welcome to our boat. I have room for your belongings in the shelter. Be careful stepping on."

"Thank you," Aaron motioned to the woman with his staff. "This is our sister Miriam. She wanted to come with us and see our flocks of sheep as well."

"It has been too long since I've seen them. I hope it is alright. I brought my own supplies," She said, gesturing to a small sack slung over her shoulder.

"As long as you don't interfere with our mission, I see no reason to prevent you," Badru said.

Yalu extended his hand to help her board. She took it and stepped onto the boat carefully. As soon as she did she felt the shifting balance she wobbled a little. Moses and Aaron tried to grab her arm and help but she refused them.

She spoke some Hebrew words with an imperious tone. She nodded in thanks to Yalu and walked carefully to the shelter and sat down.

Then Moses boarded with Badru and Yalu assisting them followed by Aaron.

Moses looked around at the boat and asked, "Where shall we sit?"

"You two take the water-poles here," Badru pointed at the benches nearest to the shelter. Poles about one and a half the length of a person lay nearby. He waited for them to sit down and take up the poles. Nebit sat herself down at the front and watched everyone else.

"Tau and Yalu, you two take up the water-poles in the rear."

Once everyone was settled and ready, Badru loosened the rope tying the boat to the pier and took his position at the back to man the steering oar. Then he shouted at them to push away from the dock.

Tau and Aaron pushed their poles against the dock and the boat moved onto the river. Miriam moaned queasily inside the house, but the others focused on their punting and took no notice. Badru heaved his oar to the river side and the boat steered away.

When they had cleared the shallows with Nebit's help, they began punting in earnest. The men used the poles to push along the bottom of the river bed. It was slow-going at first, but then the boat moved faster as they cleared the other city boats.

Once again, Nebit felt the wind in her face as she looked from side to side, searching for waters ahead for dangers. She breathed in deeply of the refreshing river air. Off to the Eastern shore of the river quite a few men stood or sat on boats to fish. Most of the boats were nothing more than reeds clumped together to make a floating island onto which the fishermen could store their catch in pottery, sacks, and whatever else they had made. Several large boats moved quickly across the river to ferry people from one bank to another and connect the two sides of the river.

They quickly passed by the boat of a nobleman and Nebit turned to look at it. The man waved toward them and Badru waved in reply. She shifted her gaze to Yalu. From the front she needed to move her head to the side so she could see his back past Moses. When he pulled back against the water, his muscles swelled from his back.

The boat rocked suddenly, causing Nebit to lose her balance. She toppled, her head over the side of the boat, and yelped in surprise. Tau shouted up to her, "Hey, is my punting too strong for you?"

She pulled herself upright again, and scowled at him. "Overwhelming," she replied sarcastically, "a little more and I could have gone for a swim."

Tau redoubled his efforts. The boat began curving toward the bank and Badru had to work the rudder oar to correct their orientation.

"Tau, stop that!" Badru shouted commandingly, "Punt like everyone else."

Tau slowed down, but turned his head to smirk at her.

Nebit laughed at him and saw Yalu laughing too, before he turned back to focus on his own punting. Every once in a while Yalu would look out at the bank on his side of the boat. She saw beads of sweat appear on his head and then one fell down his neck, down his back, over his muscles and into his belt.

After they lost sight of the great white-walled city, Badru called up to them, "You can stop punting for now." Then he carefully walked up to the others who wiped the sweat from their brows and relaxed.

"Now that we are in the current, we should be able to have two people punt and one at the rudder, so two people get to rest."

Everyone got some water and bread from the shelter to eat while they rested. Badru proposed the punting groups and schedule. Nobody objected, even when Moses and Aaron were selected for the first shift when Badru cast his pouch of bones on the deck.

When it was relayed to Miriam, she showed a hint of dissatisfaction on her face and spoke up, "Already? I was hoping you would be able to sit with

me and watch the bank pass by for a while." She spoke
to the Moses and Aaron in Hebrew.

After a little discussion Aaron concluded so
they could understand, "This is how it was decided, so
we'll abide by these rules. It's only a couple hours of
work for us, you can wait that long." Miriam responded
with silence and by turning her head away from him as
he stood up and left her.

And so Moses and Aaron took up the first
punting positions on either side of the boat while
Badru continued to steer. Every once in a while the
boat started drifting to Moses' side. Badru corrected it
and smiled.

Eventually, Badru laughed and commented,
"Even though you are brothers, Aaron punts stronger!"

Once the allotted time was up, Moses' arms
were very sore but Aaron showed little sign of
tiredness.

Moses asked him, "Are you not even a little bit
tired, brother? How is it that I can barely lift a water
skin and you're ready to punt another shift?!"

"While you were shepherding in Midian, I was
slaving away under the Egyptian taskmasters in the
city," Aaron pointed out with a laugh.

"Well, after the Lord convinces Pharaoh you'll
have the chance to get just as weak as me!" Moses
retorted and they both laughed together. They went
into the shelter with their sister and talked with her in
their language.

The late afternoon sun moved toward the
horizon, causing brilliant orange and yellow to mingle
with the blue of the sky. The river reflected it in waves
and shimmers. All the way the eye could see, from one
end of the river to the other, was a second sunset just
as brilliant as the one in the sky. Soon, the stars began
to show themselves in the sky above, and the sunset

faded into purples and blues. The black of the night sky set in with all the stars within it shining in the darkness. A gibbous moon crept up behind the star-filled sky. All that was left of the sun was a memory of the colors it created.

A few hours after sunset, Nebit found herself with her hands behind her head staring up at the stars. She lay down on the deck near the bow. Tau and Badru gently punted the boat down the river. She heard the sound of the water as their punters did their work. Every once in a while, Badru walked to the rear of the boat to adjust the oar in the back.

Then the sound stopped. She moved her head to her chest in time for Tau to point to the poles with his thumb. Then moving her head up as far as she can, she saw Yalu gently snoozing right at the bow.

She looked at him with mixed feelings. After a moment she tapped him on the shoulder. He gently shook himself out of slumber and joined her at the middle punting positions as Badru and Tau took their turns on the deck for some sleep.

They began to punt. On either side of the river they heard bands of crickets making a little night music for them. She took a deep breath and released all of her anxieties into the soft night air. She felt better and smiled a bit.

Yalu whispered, "I feel at home, here on the river."

Nebit glanced at him as he gazed over the water. Then he looked up to see the starry night that covered them both. She did the same.

"I've always enjoyed looking at Nut's evening dress all adorned with stars. Even with all her power, will she too fall to this Hebrew god?" Yalu shook his head and sighed.

"I suppose everyone falls eventually," Nebit said. She thought about her master and Kasmut's oath what will happen to Sakakwi. Then her thoughts turned toward the battles between the Egyptian gods and the Hebrew god. "I wouldn't be surprised if she did. I feel a sense of duty to rally behind Pharaoh, Anuket, Ptah, and the rest of our gods. But on the other hand, I think Pharaoh is treating the Hebrews unjustly. Then again, putting a disease on the Egyptian livestock hurts everybody, not just Pharaoh. It isn't fair! If their god is trying to punish Pharaoh, then why not make only him suffer?"

"If Pharaoh is making this god's people suffer, then I suppose a response in kind makes sense." Yalu stopped punting as well to look at her, "I too feel loyalty to Pharaoh and the gods. But Moses said that his god keeps his promises. And I'm feeling discontent with how Pharaoh isn't."

"But I suppose the only thing you can do is report back to your masters, Rashidi and Sakakwi." Nebit said.

Yalu was taken aback. He replied, "We do serve Rashidi, but not Sakakwi. I wouldn't have anything to do with him if I could choose. A man who resorts to hiring even bandits to achieve his aims."

"But the way you were talking with Badru and Tau," Nebit whispered with surprise.

"Perhaps he is their master or at least on friendly terms, but not me." Yalu replied.

Nebit took a breath as his words sunk in. Suddenly she felt her heart leap into her chest.

"What about you?" Yalu asked. "When we met with him he seemed to know you. He isn't your master either?"

"He... was." Nebit said. She felt the urge to shed tears, but resisted. "I worked for someone who was underneath him. She was my master. Someone who raised me and taught me how to be... who I am."

"What did you do for them?"

"I was an assassin," Nebit answered reluctantly and quietly. Yalu's face showed how surprised he really was. "They told me who they wanted killed and I would do it until…"

"Until what?" Yalu pressed.

She thought about what to tell him, wondering if she should talk about the baby she saw, the feelings stirred up within her, and what her master told her to do. But she said, "Sakakwi killed her. Somehow I escaped and came to Kasmut. She took me in and gave me work."

Yalu gave an understanding nod as he looked at her.

A few moments passed by, and they noticed the boat start to turn towards Nebit's side. She punted a couple stronger strokes and when they straightened, Yalu started punting again. They looked up at the stars again, gazing at the wondrous sight. Then one fell near a rope of stars.

"Ah, I saw Nut let one of the stars go," Nebit turned around and looked at Yalu. "It must have slipped through her fingers."

"Indeed," Yalu smiled at Nebit and she smiled in return. He looked away to focus on his pole gliding through the water.

"He told me that he will get me back. I would rather die."

"No," Yalu told her. "I won't let that happen."

Nebit looked at him and stopped her punting. She searched his features for something to give her security. He glanced at her and then continued watching his punting. But she continued to stare at him with wide eyes. When he realized she was still looking at him, he turned his head and looked back to her.

For a moment, they gazed into each other's eyes. They heard each other's breathing as their chests

rose and fell. The sounds the crickets made begin to
fade into the background. Yalu put his hand on the
deck and leaned towards Nebit. He opened his mouth
as though to say something, but to his surprise, no
words escaped. A lump hotter than mid-day heat
burned deep in his chest.

Nebit saw his difficulty and raised her
eyebrows. She leaned toward him, unconsciously
mirroring him as though to draw the words from his
mouth. Her dark hair, shining in the moonlight, waved
in the gentle breeze. Her dark brown features were
silhouetted against the reflection of the stars in the
river.

As he took a deep breath to speak, he heard her
voice instead, "Field of dreams."

She went on as he looked at her, "That's what
your name means, right? I like it. It's a good name."

He nodded and smiled warmly. Then he asked
her, "What about you? Were you really named after a
leopard? Or did you change it when you became a
soldier. You sure fight like one."

She grinned mischievously as she leaned closer
toward him. With her face almost brushing up against
his, she gently pinched his lower lip between her teeth.
Then she looked into his eyes with desire.

Suddenly, he pulled back and gazed with a
pained look into his hands. Nebit sighed feeling a little
hurt. She asked, "I remember what Lior said. Your wife
died?"

Yalu nodded, feeling the hot lump even more.
He put a hand to his chest and breathed deeply several
times.

"What happened?"

Yalu sighed and looked at her again.

"My wife was from one of the small towns to
the north-west of the great city. We would often take

our daughter and barter passage with caravans so she could see her family and I would scout ahead to make sure the way was safe. One trip, I found some ruins. While looking around I discovered secret passages underneath.

"Unfortunately, I only realized it was a bandit hideout all too late. There were a lot of provisions and very few people guarding them. Of course, most of the bandits were out raiding a nearby caravan, my, nearby caravan. I hurried to return but found I was too late. Nobody was left alive. After that I volunteered with other soldiers to go and wipe them out. I met Lior there. We spent about a year fighting alongside each other."

She nodded as she looked at him and listened. When he was done she said, "I'm sure they found their way to the reeds of paradise."

He looked into her sympathetic eyes and sighed. She moved to sit right next to him and put a reassuring arm around his waist. They both looked down the river and then up at the stars above as the crickets played on.

The sun peeked over the hills during Moses' and Aaron's shift in the morning just a little south of the Nile's route. As everyone woke up they saw the dry and barren desert replaced by grasslands and even the occasional tree.

Soon, houses and tents dotted the hillside near the water on either side of the river. They saw women collecting water in jars. They also saw men watching them pass by as flocks of sheep grazed on the grass. Those who saw them waved, most with smiling faces.

Moses, Aaron, and Miriam lined up on the shore side of the boat and looked out over the water at their brethren. Miriam smiled, "I never tire of seeing this land and our flocks and shepherds. I can't wait to see what land the Lord will bring us to." She breathed deeply and looked rejuvenated.

Aaron frowned, "There are so few people since the last time I came here. Pharaoh's overseers have moved more of our people into the cities to slave away making bricks. It's one thing to look at the numbers on papyrus, but quite another when I actually see the people."

"Look at all those sheep!" Nebit exclaimed as she stood closely by Yalu's side. "Are we really going to examine all of them? There must be hundreds!"

"No, thousands," Aaron corrected her with a lofty tone, "Our people have grazed sheep on these slopes for hundreds of years. Part of me will miss this land when we go."

A few moments passed until Badru shouted from the back, "Upriver I see a docking post." He pointed it out for everybody. "Should we moor here?"

"Yes, that should do fine," Moses called back to him. "There is another downriver on the other side when you're ready to ferry across."

"I don't mean to seem ungrateful," Yalu hesitated to say. "But you've been very helpful even though we're agents of Pharaoh, who is keeping your people enslaved. Why are you doing this?"

Aaron frowned, "Why should we hide from Pharaoh? We hope that when he understands what is happening, he will make the better choice."

"This is an important place to us," Miriam said as she looked over the land. Then she turned her head towards Yalu and told him, "This place connects us to our ancestor Jacob. Every mother and father tells their children stories about him. Coming back here makes the past feel so much more alive." She looked back out toward the flocks of sheep on the hills.

"Take your stations!" Badru shouted. Yalu, Tau, Aaron, and Moses sat down on the benches and grabbed their poles. Miriam sat down with her hands on the deck and Nebit leaned up against the bow to savor the last moments on the boat as she grabbed the docking rope. A couple nearby men rushed to the dock and helped steady the boat.

Once the boat had almost stopped, Nebit leapt over the side with the rope. The punters put their poles down inside the boat and eagerly made their way to the house in order to get their belongings. The men on the dock helped Miriam out of the boat. She breathed a sigh of relief once she felt the solid timbers of the pier underneath her and ran to dry ground. After that, Tau, Aaron, Moses, and Yalu quickly disembarked.

As everyone else followed Miriam, Badru stated, "We have quite a job that Pharaoh has given us." He looked around and marveled at the amount of livestock in sight. "We know what to look for, so at least it will be easy to determine if any of them have the disease."

Moses and Aaron went to Miriam and started talking to her in Hebrew.

"Tau and I should search east while you and Nebit search the west. Then once we're done with this side we cross the river and examine the sheep on the other," Badru suggested.

Yalu and Nebit agreed. Then they looked over at the other group embroiled in their conversation. Yalu spoke loudly to get their attention, "Moses and Aaron, We are splitting up into two groups to search through the livestock. Do you want to accompany us?"

They stopped talking to listen to him. Miriam looked disappointed and said "I was going to visit some friends while we were here. Do you really need us?"

"It will be much easier if we have someone who knows the area to show us where the flocks are," Yalu reasoned, "to be thorough."

"Yalu is right." Moses said as she waited for their conclusion. Then he said "But Aaron and I should be able to do it" Then he spoke to her in Hebrew again and another conversation between the three of them erupted.

After it subsided, Aaron turned to them, "First we must take Miriam. Then we can escort you through the flocks. Acceptable?" And so Moses, Aaron and Miriam walked up the hill and left their sight when they crested the top.

"Do you really think they'll let us see all of the flocks?" Tau turned to the others and asked. "Won't he steer us away from the infected livestock?"

Yalu raised his eyebrows, but Badru answered first, "I think I believe him when he says he has nothing to hide. Changing the staff to a snake was no deception. Changing water from the Nile to blood was no deception. The frogs, gnats, and flies were not deceptions either. But we should be cautious nonetheless."

Nebit gave a sideways glance to Yalu, "If I were him I'd do whatever it took to protect my family and friends."

Yalu acknowledged her with a nod and said, "Agreed. We would be punished severely if it was found we were negligent."

Before they could discuss their plans any further they heard Moses shouting from over the hill. The four walked over to meet them.

Once they got close Moses said "Are we ready?"

"Moses, you can go with Badru and Tau along the South side," Yalu said pointing that direction.

"Aaron can come with Nebit and me down North. Agreed?"

They did agree and split up. Badru and Tau followed Moses up the nearby hill. As they came to the top, the rest of the land unfolded before them and all the livestock as well. Badru and Tau looked at each other as they realized the enormity of their task.

"Shall we begin our work?" Badru sighed.

They started looking at a nearby sheep. Then he turned around and pointed, "You take the sheep over there Tau." And he did as his friend requested.

After they looked through a few sheep they heard someone shouting. When they looked up they saw a robed man with a staff running up to them. He called out to them in Hebrew when he neared.

Moses immediately answered him and they talked for a while. Then the man nodded his head, gave them one more searching look, and left.

"You handled that quicker than I expected," Badru commented.

"It's quite simple really," Moses explained with a laugh. "I told him the truth: that the Lord afflicted the Egyptian livestock with disease but not our livestock and that you are here to see."

Tau tilted his head and laughed, "When you put it that way, we sound pretty harmless."

Towards the end of the day, Moses found Tau staring at a particularly large sheep grazing near the top of a hill that overlooked the massive river below. Moses asked, "What is the matter? Do you see a trace of the disease?"

Tau licked his lips and answers, "I don't know. This particular animal might need a closer inspection." He continued to stare at it as he talked.

Moses smiled, "What sort of inspection do you think is necessary?"

"Well, the animal looks good on the outside. It looks really good." Tau's eyes widened as he stooped down to get a better look. "But I wonder what it looks like on the inside."

Then Moses laughed and called to the nearby shepherd. "Very well, tonight we all will inspect this sheep to see if it has any disease." He spoke with the shepherd briefly, and then patted his shoulder, smiling. Tau stepped up alongside the sheep and grabbed it by the legs. Other than making a few noises it offered little resistance as Tau lifted it up and over his shoulders. He followed Moses back carrying it.

Moses led Tau and Badru up a well-worn trail. Clouds dotted the northern horizon and the sun slowly set behind them. Tau wiped the sweat from his forehead with the back of his hand and then wiped that on the wool of the sheep. Looking up ahead, he saw a large tent at the top of the hill. Glancing back at the sheep, he smiled at it hungrily and then trudged up the hill with renewed strength.

Lifting up the door made of sheep-skins, Moses entered the tent followed by Tau and then Badru. Yalu, Nebit, and Aaron sat on leather mats. Miriam and another Hebrew woman stood in another corner and stopped talking as they arrived. Both of them stood and Miriam started, "You're finally done! I was wondering if you were coming back." Then she continued in Hebrew.

At that moment everyone noticed the sheep on Tau's shoulders. Miriam stopped talking again. Her mouth hung open as she took a step back.

"Did you," she stuttered. "Did… did you find one?"

Badru laughed, "My friend does not believe that the outward appearance of this sheep is telling of the truth. So we shall examine this animal by taste."

All the worried faces changed to smiles as he explained. Miriam and her friend showed Tau out of the tent.

"If this is the best luck you've had at finding animals with the disease then you fared better than we did," Yalu confessed with a laugh. "To tell you the truth, I wish we'd thought of that. Tau is a very wise man indeed."

Miriam took Tau over to a nearby canopy where they slaughtered and prepared the animal for their evening meal.

As they ate, Yalu observed, raising his wine, "It's been a long time since we've had meat like this. I might even say this is the best meal I've ever had. I give my compliments to ones who cooked this." He looked at the woman and she nodded. Then he turned to Miriam and she waved dismissively as she smiled.

"Hear hear!" Badru declared and joined his raised wine-skin, "This food is very good. The sheep here in Goshen surpass the ones in the Pharaoh's white walled city. I am sorry for them."

Moses raised his wine and said "Praise be to the Lord our god who gave us the sheep; because of him we are able to enjoy this meal in the land of our ancestors."

Everyone else raised their wine in agreement. They had their fill of meat and wine and then slept. The tent sown together of mostly sheep hide provided good protection from the cool night wind.

Yalu awakened to something cold on his face. He opened his eyes to see the flap of the tent waving in the wind. Sitting up, he whispered, "The wind." He sat there for a moment, staring at it. Then he looked up at the night sky. He got up and wrapped the fur blankets around himself and walked to the door. He moved the rock holding the flap in place and looked through the door into the night. He stepped through.

Looking up he saw the moon shine brightly on the grassy hills. In a few days' time it would be full. He looked out over the rolling pastures of green and white. Scattered shrubs and trees dotted the landscape. In the distance he the dark blue of the sea before him. He drew a breath as beheld the beautiful sight.

Upon hearing a rustling behind him he saw Nebit exit the tent. She went and stood next to him. Movement drew their attention to one of the many groups of scattered sheep. Some of them were behind walls of piled rocks and others just huddled together to stave off the cold.

One such group, unprotected by rocks, was approach by a lone wolf. Lucky for the shepherd was vigilant and sent a rock to wolf from his sling. With a yelp of pain the wolf went limping away. A few of the sheep raised their heads in curiosity but only saw the comforting hands of the shepherd as they went back to sleep.

"These people. These Hebrews. The slaves," Yalu began. "They don't belong in Egypt."

Nebit turned to him and asked, "Where do they belong?"

He turned to her and they looked at one another for a long moment. Then he looked down and said, "I don't know."

After another moment of watching the sheep, they reentered the tent and covered the door again with the rock. With the draft gone, the tent felt warmer. They went back to sleep on their separate beds of sheep skins.

Badru's enthusiasm to continue the inspection woke everyone up early the next day. After eating a breakfast which included a large portion of barley and some figs, they crossed the river to examine the other flocks.

At mid-day, Nebit looked around and concluded, "I guess that is all of them. Should we head back now?"

Before Yalu could reply, Aaron answered, "Not quite, I was told there is another herd that is grazing about an hour to the West. It is only a small flock of about fifty goats. Do you want to go see them?"

"An hour's walk?" Yalu asked with surprise.

Aaron replied with a nod.

Yalu looked westward and didn't see anything but hills. Then he looked back at the river. Turning to them he sighed, "Let's go see them."

About early evening they returned to the tent after finishing their inspection of the rest of the sheep. As soon as Miriam saw them, she stood up, "Are you done already? We can have the evening meal prepared right away."

"That won't be necessary," Yalu interrupts. "We need to report to Pharaoh."

"Yalu is right," Moses sighed. "They must go back and report that the Lord has kept this disease from our flocks and herds."

With a resigned expression, Miriam nodded. She, Moses, and Aaron gathered their packs for the return trip. Meanwhile, Badru, Yalu, Tau, and Nebit prepared the boat.

Rowing upstream proved expectedly more difficult. It took them nearly two full days to punt all the way to the city. After Badru docked the boat, Moses, Aaron, and Miriam departed to their residence. Then Yalu led the four scouts back to Rashidi's manor. They told Kasmut they were ready to report. She sent a servant to notify Rashidi.

A few minutes went by before Rashidi burst out of the manor. His face anticipated their report with excitement. He approached and ordered, "Well out with it! Tell me your report. How many animals of the Hebrew flock had this disease?"

"None of them has this disease, Rashidi," Yalu stated bluntly. "We traveled all the land of Goshen where the Hebrew slaves keep their flocks, and spent the better part of two days searching through their sheep for traces of this disease."

The news crushed Rashidi's excited mood. He rubbed his hands together nervously. He looked at them disbelievingly and asked, "Are you sure you went through all of their livestock? Perhaps they hid some from you."

"It is true," Badru insisted, "We searched all of them."

Rashidi's eyes darted this way and that, searching for other option. Then he scrunched his face up in resignation and said "Come, we report this to Pharaoh."

Upon arriving at the palace, they were met by one of Pharaoh's officials at the door to Pharaoh's audience chamber. After Rashidi explained their message, the man said "Rashidi may relay your words to Pharaoh." The official turned around, and entered the chamber with Rashidi. The guards closed the door behind them.

A few minutes later, the official returned and whispered to them, "Come with me, Pharaoh wants to question you personally." He led them into the chamber where Pharaoh sat behind an elegant wooden table with scraps of papyrus resting on it. Two servants stood by him on each side. He wore gold jewelry polished to a high sheen. Rashidi stood to the left side of the room with his head bowed enough to be respectful but not enough to obscure his view of the room. The official bowed before Pharaoh as did the three soldiers and Badru.

Pharaoh turned his head to them and looked sternly. He said in a clear tone, "According to your report there were no traces of the disease. Tell me, is that really the truth?"

Continuing to bow his head, Badru answered, "Great Pharaoh, it is the truth." A bead of sweat traveled down his cheek and dropped from his chin onto the cold stone floor.

Pharaoh frowned and then leaned forward demanding, "Are you sure you searched all of their livestock? Did you go through every animal they had." Badru nodded and said so. Pharaoh sighed and leaned back in his chair. His golden earrings jingled as he rested his head against the cushion. Then he turned his head to Rashidi, "What do you make of this?"

"Obviously the Hebrews are good at covering their tracks." Rashidi concluded. "So, we don't have the proof that we need from this to expose their treachery. But there are still other paths. I still have. . ."

Pharaoh raised his hand to stop Rashidi from continuing. Then Pharaoh looked at Badru and waved for them to leave. Before they knew it, guards had shuffled them out of the room.

They waited for Rashidi to finish talking with Pharaoh, and about an hour later Rashidi emerged from Pharaoh's chamber.

A sly look covered his face and he told them, "Keep your watch on Moses and continue reporting everything to Kasmut." All five left the palace together and they escorted Rashidi back to his manor.

The four spies returned to their perch across from Aaron's home and resumed their old task.

Chapter 12

The next day, Nebit awoke to Yalu's gentle hand on her shoulder saying that Moses and Aaron left the manor again. She left with the others and they took the same road to Pharaoh's palace.

As Moses and Aaron reached the palace, she heard the sound of someone clearing his throat behind them. She whirled around to see the scarred man and his associates. The scarred man stood with his arms folded and a grave expression on his face. He told them bluntly, "You need to come with us."

Nebit's heart jumped in her throat. But Yalu stepped forward and she felt some measure of relief. He said, "Why? Your master has talked with us. We have our task."

"You have your task and we have ours. He wants to see you again." The scarred man drew one of his daggers and started flipping it in his hand.

"What for?" Yalu asked.

"You'll have to ask him that." The man watched them oddly. Every once in a while his face twitched.

"We are presently on the trail of our target." Badru stepped forward. "Sakakwi can wait until we are ready."

"No!" The scarred man threw his dagger into the ground. It stuck into the sand so far the blade was no longer visible. The man looked up, the hatred and resentment now visible. "You will see him now."

The rest of his gang drew their weapons and grimaced. Nebit cast an anxious glance at Yalu. Yalu looked around at the approaching aggressors. Then he looked back toward the palace at the guards there.

"It's best we don't cause a disturbance near the palace. Alright, we'll go with you." Yalu said. He glanced at Nebit and saw her fearful eyes. Then he added, "But be quick about it. I expect to be on our way quickly."

The scarred man gave a maniacal smile, "You'll be on your way quickly, sure enough." His cohorts put away their weapons and the man grabbed his dagger out of the ground.

They marched them to the same house and through the underground tunnels. The scarred man and his gang each took a torch. Nebit felt the pain in her chest again. But then noticed something was wrong about the way they were going. After a few turns more, they found themselves face to face with a stone wall.

"What is this? I thought you knew these tunnels well," Badru said.

"I do," He placed his torch in a sconce and drew his daggers. The other four drew weapons with their free hands and held the torches still. Standing between them and the way out.

"What are you doing?" Badru asked in confusion.

"Do you know what happened after you left Sakakwi's chambers? Of course you know, he holds you in such high regard and tells you everything." The scarred man said, his face twitched again.

Nebit got her daggers ready. She could see that this was going to end in bloodshed. She noticed Yalu preparing his shield as well.

"I have not talked with Sakakwi since then!" Badru shouted. "How should I know? If something happened then it has nothing to do with us."

"Enough! To the afterlife with you." The scarred man contorted his face in the most terrible expression of anger and hatred as he stabbed with a dagger.

Surprised, Badru stepped backward. But instead of feeling the sting of the blade, they all heard the clang of metal and a blur as Yalu's shield took the blows that were meant for him. In a second, battle was fully joined on both sides.

Yalu covered Badru, and Tau found himself facing two opponents, both wielding khopeshes. One of them slashed at him rather shallowly to test his defenses. The other one took a step forward and slashed with the intent to draw blood. In a bold move, Tau stepped forward to meet him and caught the attacker arm while he slugged the man across his cheek, causing him to drop his torch to the ground. But the other attacker sliced a small wound along his arm.

Nebit found herself at the end of a spear. She tried to draw her daggers, but quick thrusts forced her to tumble and dodge, making it impossible to get close enough to attack. When she tried to retreat, the attacker advanced, closing the distance and keeping the pressure on her. The frustration showed on her face.

The fourth attacker leapt forward with his bronze shield and khopesh to pierce Badru's heart. Badru saw him coming and grabbed a handful of his specially prepared powder. The attacker protected his chest with the shield leaving his face open. Just what Badru wanted. At just the right time, Badru flung the powder toward his attacker's face, he instantly cried out in pain and dropped his khopesh. Badru seized the moment to draw his mace and strike at the man's skull, but failed to get past the shield. The man scowled as he knelt down to pick up his khopesh. Badru made another ineffective attack. When the man grabbed his khopesh he swung and cut Badru's robe, putting a deep wound in his right leg. The pain dropped him to one knee as he watched his attacker stand back up.

The scarred man, frustrated by Yalu's interference, growled angrily. Yalu struck with his khopesh, but it was easily deflected with a dagger, and the attack was returned. Yalu tried to block with his shield but was too slow. He took a small wound on his sword arm.

Suddenly, a gust of wind entered the tunnel and everyone felt it as they breathed deeply from the excitement of combat. The air was uplifting and refreshing. However, no sooner had they felt refreshed than they all started blistering. White bubbles appeared on their skin with an itchy redness.

Nebit felt the sores on her chest, but she noticed that her attacker also had sores on his arms. Reasoning that the sores would slow his thrusts, and in a gamble for her life, she grabbed the shaft of a spear with her hand. Her attacker realized what she was trying to do but was unable to focus on a counter. She leapt forward with a dagger in her hand and a victorious smile.

The pain of the sores overcame Badru's legs, and he forgot the other pain. He looked up at his attacker and saw him brush a hand against his blistering face. Badru took the opportunity to break the attacker's left knee with his mace.

Tau felt the sores on his body and roared in rage and desperation. He picked up his closest enemy and tossed him at the other. They both lay on the ground in the agony of their sores and wounds.

The scarred man screamed in pain as he saw the sores growing on his forearms. Yalu felt the sores on his legs, but noticed his only chance to gain the advantage. He leaned forward with his shield tucked close to himself. Just when he was nearest, he thrust his shield and bashed it against the scarred man's chest, causing him to lose his breath. It also hit his enemy's arms which burst some of the sores. The scarred man screamed at the pain. Then Yalu made a single thrust with his khopesh at his opponent's chest.

As they finished the last attacker, Nebit gave a sigh which turned to a whimper of pain. She looked at her sores, and, caressing around the sensitive areas, she cried, "What happened to us? Badru! Did your accursed powder land on us too?"

Badru shook his head, "It wasn't me!"

Just as alarmed, Yalu replied, "Then who? That was the most ill-advised battle tactic I've ever seen."

Grunting between words, Tau added, "This hurts more than ointment. I saw you use some powder. You're sure some of it didn't get on us?" He also rubbed around the reddish areas of his sores.

Sitting on the ground to rest his hurting legs, Badru answered, "Quite sure. My powder will not cause sores like these."

Badru took the torch from his fallen attacker and closely examined his wounds. He poked at one blister with one hand while holding the torch with the other. The others gathered around him and looked at his sores as a welcome distraction from their own. Then he looked up at them and said "These look like the sores one gets after a wound that has not been properly anointed or prayed over. It can grow and corrupt a limb or even lead to death."

"Death!" Yalu pled with wide eyes, "What is the treatment?"

Badru opened up his sack and began to browse through it. "We must lance the sore, cleanse it, and cover it with these herbs. The physicians also use prayer."

The other three stared at him in disbelief. Nebit protested, "The white part is what hurts the most. Is that really the only way to treat this?"

"I assure you," Badru nodded grimly. "If there were an easier way I would have told you." They all sighed in reluctant resignation. Finally, Badru found his jar of ointment. Then he requested, "I will need a dagger." Yalu took one belonging to Scarface and handed it to him. Badru held the dagger over the flame of the torch. When he finished he looked up again and asked, "Who is first?"

"I'll go first. But I want some of that powder that numbs pain!" Yalu demanded.

Badru nodded and gestured for him to lie down on the floor. Tau held him down and Nebit held the torch so Badru could see. Badru closed his eyes, recited a prayer, and then got ready to work with the dagger.

Badru got to work with the dagger on Yalu's shin and released the fluids in the sore while Yalu yelped. He applied ointment to the wound and Yalu grimaced as the pain continued. Then Badru wrapped the wound and moved on to the next sore. As Badru finished treating the last sore, Yalu took a moment to express his pain and exhaustion.

Badru repeated the process for both Nebit and Tau. Finally it was Badru's turn to undergo the treatment. He looked around, "Which one of you will treat me?"

Tau stepped forward and grinned. He said in his best attempt to mimic Badru's voice, "Any friend of mine must get the best treatment I can offer."

Badru pursed his lips into a pout but didn't resist as Yalu held him down and Nebit held the torch. Badru gave instructions, and Tau followed them exactly. Badru groaned with every cut and scrape.

When done, Tau helped Badru sit up, "Isn't it Sekhemet who inflicts and cures these diseases? Is this her doing?"

"I cannot think of any better explanation," Badru groaned between words. "It did happen at just the right time. The most reasonable conclusion is divine intervention."

"We can talk about that later," Yalu changed the topic. "We need to get out of here. Nebit, do you know the way out?"

She nodded. Yalu grabbed the torch from the sconce and handed it to her who started down the tunnels.

"Should we do anything about these bodies?" Tau wondered, "Will they hunt us with renewed fervor once they find out what happened?"

"Maybe you have the strength to carry them but I don't," Yalu confessed, "and I wouldn't know where to put them anyway. Perhaps this is out of the way enough so that nobody will notice."

Tau shrugged and looked over his shoulder at the bodies one more time. Nebit led them through the tunnels while Yalu limped to follow. Tau helped Badru limp along as well. After a few turns and hallways, they came to a ladder that looked similar to the one they had climbed down. Yalu climbed up first and pushed up the mat. Two pairs of suspicious eyes looked down at them.

As Yalu climbed up, one of them asked, "Where are the priest's men?"

"Uh. . ." Yalu searched for an acceptable excuse. Then he noticed that the two men keeping watch were also afflicted by the sores.

"They remained to treat their sores, begging Sekhemet to remove this curse." He stifled a laugh, hoping they wouldn't press the issue.

"Sekhemet?!" they said in surprise. "Moses and that god of the Hebrew slaves are responsible for this."

"Is that right?" Yalu asked as the other three climbed out, He moved to exit the house and then hesitated. Thinking of something else to say to make sure they aren't suspicious he turned back to them and said, "Be sure to keep your guard up."

They both instantly stiffened. Yalu left and the other three followed him out.

As Nebit returned with the others to their room overlooking Aaron's manor, she heard the wailing of many in pain. Some of the people they passed had bandages from treatment, but those who couldn't afford it had to endure their sores.

One man lay on the side of the road. Several of his sores oozed and his body shook from the pain.

He cried out, "Sekhemet, heal me!"

Badru stopped several paces from him and looked on him with pity. He pulled his ointment from a sack, and approached the man.

"Sekhemet may not have power to help you, but this may," he put the salve into the suffering man's hand. "Use what you need, and then help others."

When he returned to his friends, Tau stared at him with a question in his face. Badru stared back stubbornly.

"I can make more," he insisted.

When they neared the city's outskirts they stood in amazement.

"What... What is this?" Yalu looked around, "How can this be?"

Badru dropped his jaw and then his sack, causing the wooden cases inside to crack against each other. He ignored it.

"Do none of the slaves have these cursed sores on their bodies?!" Nebit demanded, feeling treated unfairly, "What makes them different?"

"It's their god," Tau answered. "It must be."

Badru nodded and hypothesized, "The stories of Sekhemet tell of plagues she inflicted on the whole of mankind. To prove herself as the mightiest warrior of any battle she inflicts the wounded with ailments. But by inflicting all of us with these sores, the Hebrew god could be proving that he is the more powerful warrior. If she is unable to cure us, then that would mean. . ." He trailed off as he considered the implications.

"But why is the Hebrew god punishing common Egyptians like us?" Nebit argued, "The fight is between the gods. Why should he bring us into it?"

Badru folded his arms (carefully) and speculated, "One way to attack a god is through his worshippers, or her worshippers in this case. When Pharaoh spared the Hyksos priests of Set it was because he knew doing them harm would anger the god himself."

Nebit watched the unaffected Hebrew slaves for a moment longer and then continued walking back to their borrowed room with the others. They received strange, pitying looks from the healthy people who stared at their bandages, and it seemed somehow backwards to be pitied by the lowest of them. They saw Moses and Aaron talking with Nun. Hoshea and his escort, Lior, was also there.

Hoshea and Lior saw the four and approached them saying, "It is good to see you again, friends. But I would have hoped for better circumstances. Were you just in a battle?"

"A big one!" Tau bellowed. "They said they wanted to take us somewhere, but that was just a pretense. They trapped us in a dead end and surprised us. And the battle was raging like…" He grabbed Hoshea's wrist to demonstrate and swung him hard enough to knock him into Yalu who shouted in pain.

"But in the end we stood victorious."

"But in the end," Yalu clarified, "we didn't win because we were better at fighting. They had the upper hand because of the advantage of surprise. But then these sores came on us all and we were able to wrest the advantage from them."

"Oh, that must have been when Moses tossed the ash into the air. He just finished telling us," Hoshea said.

"What do you mean? He tossed ash into the air?" Badru stepped forward and asked.

Hoshea started at the beginning, "The Lord spoke with Moses and sent him to Pharaoh. Before he went, though, he took a sack full of ash which he scooped from the cooking furnace in the kitchen in Aaron's house. Without saying a word in response to Pharaoh's accusations, he took the ash out and tossed it into the air. Then a wind came that picked up the ash to spread it all throughout the city and caused sores over all the Egyptians. The nobles and even Pharaoh himself could not stand up to Moses!"

• "They're so painful!" Nebit exclaimed. She described the process to treat them in gruesome detail. Hoshea and Lior cringed as she did. Then she said, "Surely that kind of pain would change Pharaoh's mind."

"Sounds more painful than battle wounds," Lior grimaced. "Unfortunately, Pharaoh still has his mind set against us."

"Well, Pharaoh is preparing for war in Kush," Yalu suggested, "Perhaps he thinks that all of these things have been set loose by the Kushite gods in their defiance."

"If he thinks that, then he's a fool!" Hoshea scoffed and shook his head. "No, Moses must have made it clear who sent him."

Nebit asked, "Does that mean these plagues will continue?" The weariness showed on her face.

Hoshea opened his mouth to speak, but, deciding against it, sighed instead. He took a breath to collect his thoughts.

"You could be safer among us," he suggested, but couldn't finish the thought.

"Hoshea, come here boy!" Nun shouted from where he spoke with Moses. Hoshea ran a little way toward him and turned back to wave goodbye.

Lior smiled but before he left he turned to Yalu and said, "It would be grand to fight alongside you and your comrades again." They returned the smile and Lior ran to follow Hoshea. Moses and Nun parted ways.

Nebit arrived with the others and returned to their surveillance, attempting to avoid any further attention. They walked up the stairs and Yalu was first to enter the room, flinging the cloth door open. Without a word, they all sat around the small table in the center of the room except for Tau who sat watching over Aaron's manor.

Nebit, while hurting from her wounds, felt relieved that they weren't taken to Sakakwi. At the same time, Badru eyes darted back and forth as he rubbed his temples.

Finally, Yalu took a breath and broke the silence with a grim chuckle, "So much has happened. I feel like an egret caught flying in a sandstorm. But it's good that we don't have to worry about that scarred man again."

Tau leaned toward them and asked, "Do you think those men were following orders from Sakakwi when they attacked us?"

"No. They likely received some sort of punishment from Sakakwi after they first brought us to him," Badru said. "If Sakakwi wanted us dead then we would not be sitting here."

"Then they acted on their own." Tau grunted to himself and continued watching the manor house.

"But it makes me wonder what sort of company Sakakwi is keeping," Badru said.

"Bandits," Yalu spat out and scowled. Nebit and Badru looked at him. Even Tau spared a moment to glance his way.

"Come now," Badru replied. "They may be questionable, but Sakakwi isn't all that bad a judge of character. He wouldn't get where he was otherwise."

"He's a good judge of competence." Yalu retorted. Then he gave a knowing glance to Nebit and she looked down with regret. When Badru asked what he meant, Yalu told him about Gahiji.

"Come now," Badru dismissed with his hand. "Not everyone who is hard to deal with is an evil person. Just because they rub you the wrong way does not mean they are a bandit."

Yalu grunted beneath his breath with discontent. He looked away toward the window. Then he posed the question, "What about what Hoshea said? That it may be safer with his household?"

"I feel safe enough with Rashidi and Kasmut," Nebit replied. She thought to herself to tell Yalu about what Kasmut was doing, but knew that in front of Badru and Tau was the wrong place. She could see Yalu getting a bit red in the face talking about bandits and decided it wasn't the time either.

"If he means safety from the Hebrew god… then perhaps." Badru rubbed his temples in thought. "However, with a war between the gods there is no telling who will become a casualty and on which side.

Who is to say that next time an Egyptian god curses the Hebrew God and his people and those allied with them."

"There's a war going on, a war between the gods." Tau spoke up. "I don't like the idea of switching sides in the middle."

Yalu nodded. But then he said gravely, "I'm not sure this is a war we're winning. I was taught to say what is right and do what is right. But I don't think we're doing the right thing."

"We owe Rashidi loyalty. Besides, one of our gods would surely prove victorious," Tau reasoned.

Badru said, "If we stop worshipping our gods for this Hebrew god we would lose the advantages they give us like success in battle or medicine. As for me personally, I fear I would lose my power and position."

"Moses gave up his," Yalu reminded him.

Badru gave no reply.

After a small pause, Yalu said, "I'm getting tired from the events of today. I just want to let me wounds heal."

The others agreed. Yalu and Badru laid down on the mats while Nebit took her station at the window.

Tau grunted with dissatisfaction and said, "I need to make a visit home and check on my family."

He waved goodbye to them and left the room.

Arriving at his home, Tau lifted the burlap door and entered. He saw Kesi cradling little Ebo with extra care. Their bodies still had the sores.

She looked up at him with weary eyes but didn't say anything. He could tell she had been crying.

After dropping off some bags of food he bartered for, he went over to them and looked over the sores. He asked, "How many do you each have?"

Kesi shook her head, "I've counted on his poor little body. I'm not sure about myself, maybe five or seven. If only there was something we can do. But none of the physicians I know have any time."

"My friend, Badru, successfully treated my wounds," He offered to peel a bandage to show her, but she declined in disgust. Then he asked, "I watched him closely and he even told me how to perform the treatment, though it will hurt quite a lot. I removed the sores from him. Do you want me to try?"

"I don't think I want to try some treatment one of your friends came up with," Kesi shook her head.

"No, no, Badru isn't one of those friends." Tau said. "He's a very learned man. His family has standing in Pharaoh's court. He's even an apprentice to Pharaoh's chief magician!"

She looked at him skeptically. But he nodded to her with a serious expression and looked into her eyes.

Then she sighed and shook her head, "These sores are killing us. You don't know how long he was crying until he fell asleep. If there's something you can do without making it worse, then please help."

"You won't regret it!" Tau encouraged her and then dashed to the kitchen to grab a knife. After washing it the best he could, he came back to her.

She laid the baby in a nearby bed and looked relieved to see he hadn't woken up. Meanwhile, Tau found some scrap cloth and cut them into strips to use as bandages. Then she laid down and Tau got to work, just as he remembered from Badru's instructions. At first, Kesi cried out in pain, but cut it short to try not to wake the baby. Tau noticed tears dripping down her face as she restrained more cries.

When he finished, Kesi had bandages around all of her arms, legs, chest, and even one on her neck. He sat by her side as she breathed and recovered.

"I'm surprised," She finally spoke. Tau looked at her face. She was looking up at him with a soft smile. "Even though it hurts, it feels as though things are flowing in the right direction now."

Tau smiled back and felt glad.

"Can you treat little Ebo?" She asked. She tried to get up but cringed in pain. "Give me a moment and I'll help."

"Isn't he kind of young for this?" Tau pointed out.

She sat up and looked over at the baby. Tau could see the pained look in her eyes. Then she turned to him and said, "Yes, he is. But he's also kind of young for sores such as that. I don't know what kind of beast that Hebrew god is to afflict such a small child. He's only a baby!"

She went over to her baby. She unwrapped the cloths around his sores while Tau washed the blade with some fresh water. Tau stood over the baby boy with knife in hand. He looked at Kesi. She nodded and then closed her eyes and looked away as she held him down.

The baby instantly awoke and started crying the moment the knife touched his skin. Tau tried to work as quick as he could. He felt like he was really getting good at it. When he finished, he looked up to see the pained expression on Kesi's face with tears running down her cheeks.

"It's done." He said. When she looked down, she saw the cloth bandages where the sores had been.

She gave a sigh of relief and wrapped him up in blankets. Then she looked at Tau and said, "You hold him."

Even though a little surprised, Tau obliged and cradled the baby in his arms. Ebo was still crying. But they both felt things would improve.

Then he looked up at Kesi and said, "I've been thinking, Pharaoh seems to be treating the Hebrews unfairly. We may have an opportunity to join them."

Kesi's face and tone instantly soured, "You're not serious! After all we've been though there's no way you could do that."

Tau grunted in response. Then Kesi continued, "All those people and their god have ever done was cause us trouble. Do your duty to Rashidi and increase the prestige of our family. That's the what you should do."

Tau nodded to her hesitantly. He stayed with her a little while longer. She told him about how they managed to live through the various catastrophes brought by the Hebrew god as well some of her family gossip. After Ebo stopped crying and fell asleep again, he handed him to Kesi, said goodbye, and left.

Next, he headed to his father's house. He was surprised to see his father working in his condition. There were several sores on his body, including his arms which he used frequently.

"Have you tried getting those treated?" Tau asked, "If not, I can help."

His father shook his head, "No time. I've got orders to fill. Including yours."

"How is it coming?" Tau asked.

He motioned over his shoulder with his head, "See for yourself."

Tau walked over to the lineup of incomplete metalworks. Among swords, pots, lamps, and others, he saw a blade larger than the rest. The curve intrigued him. It did not have the sickle shape.

"What is this khopesh used for?" Tau studied it.

"It's not a khopesh, this is a Northern sword. The kind they use across the sea." His father answered.

"I've been thinking, father." Tau said. He felt awkward but said the words he rehearsed regardless, "Working for Rashidi has been good but I think there is something more for me out there-"

His father interrupted, "You've been doing your duty?"

"What?" Tau asked, thrown off guard. "Yes, I have."

"Good, do your duty to your family. Listen to the wife I got you, she has a good head on her shoulders as I've told you before."

"Yes, but…"

"I have a lot of work to do son. Can we talk later?"

Tau stood with his mouth gaping while his father worked some red-hot metal. Feeling frustrated and not knowing what to say, he left.

At the start of the next day, during Yalu's watch again, Moses and Aaron left for the palace. And Yalu led the other three in following them.

To his relief, there were no surprises for them on the way. Badru showed his gold token to the guards, and they let him enter. He took them to the secret viewing place in the audience chamber of Pharaoh, and they saw and heard the exchange.

Pharaoh sat on his throne with his back straight against it. A somber and serious expression painted his face. He wore golden rings on his fingers; golden earrings hung from his ears, and bracelets of gold adorned his wrists. They all glittered and flashed in the brightly lit room. Sekhemti crowned his head, and his gold-embroidered clothes showed the utmost of his regality.

"What is it that you've come for now?" Pharaoh spit out as he looked over the two men he had come to despise. A few other men wearing less gaudy jewelry surrounded him on either side.

Aaron stepped forward. His dark and earthen robe lightly brushed on the cold hard stone. He lifted up his staff in his right hand and pulled it straight down, striking the floor and making a loud thud.

He raised his left hand toward the heavens and declared, "Our Lord, the god of the Hebrews, says this:"

Pharaoh raised his hand to his chin and rested his elbow on the arm of his chair. He stroked his smoothly shaven chin and listened intently.

Aaron lowered his hand and bellowed, "Let my people go so they may worship me." Then he raised a pointed finger at Pharaoh, "If you do not then I will strike you, your servants, and your whole people with the entire might of all my plagues. This is so that you have no doubt there is no one on Earth like me. I could have wiped you off the face of the Earth." He waved his arm horizontally, as if to sweep Egypt off a table as one would clear off the dust.

Speaking softly, Aaron continued, "But I didn't. I allowed you to remain so you could see my full power. And my name will be proclaimed throughout all the Earth." Then he pointed at Pharaoh again as though to accuse him. "But you still exalt yourself and oppress my people. You still will not let them go." He raised his hand heaven-ward again. "Because of that, tomorrow at this time, I will send such a storm of hail that has not ever been seen in this land. Bring everyone and every beast in the field to safety. Anyone caught in this storm will surely die."

Some of the men standing near Pharaoh showed concerned faces, while others looked skeptical. They whispered amongst themselves. Pharaoh's face showed a hint of anger. Then a wry smile appeared on his lips and he raised a finger toward the sky, "Do not think that I cannot see through you, Moses. The snakes, the blood, the diseases, yes, those were within your power. But you have no dominion over the sky. And behold!" He raised his hands together in the shape of a pyramid. When his arms reached their peak, they arced open as though he held the whole sky in them. "There is not a cloud to be seen! Your acts of treason and aggression against me, our gods, and our people will end. Your weather prediction will not come to pass."

Awakening from his quietude, Moses took a step forward. Aaron turned his head in curiosity. All conversation in the chamber stopped as Moses spoke. "This is no prediction. It comes from the Lord my god. You don't need to grant his request now; you can wait until your land is ruined and your people are destitute." Then he turned his back to Pharaoh, and walked out of the audience chamber followed closely by his brother.

A dull roar of concerned voices immediately sprang up and filled the chamber. Pharaoh sat stubbornly on his throne and continued to nurture his angry look. The jewelry glittered in the sunlight. A few officials bowed down to Pharaoh to show their obeisance. They left as quickly as they could.

Yalu glanced behind him and looked at Nebit, who shrugged her shoulders. Then he looked ahead of him at Badru, who nodded and pointed toward the exit. After quietly making Tau aware of their intentions, they exited the small secret passage. Trying to avoid bumping into people, they hurriedly raced down the hall to catch up with Moses and Aaron before they left the palace.

Finally, they spotted Moses and Aaron as they made their exit from the main palace door. Filled with relief, the four soldiers walked casually some distance behind to avoid drawing attention.

When they reached the main road from the palace gate, Yalu turned to the other three and whispered, "You follow Moses and Aaron back. I will go and report to Kasmut."

"If you leave from here you'll pass by the market," Nebit touches his shoulder. "Can I come with you? I need to trade for a few things."

Yalu agreed. They turned down the road leading to Rashidi's estate.

The other two continued following Moses and Aaron not back to their home, but to a different one. Pretending to browse the wares of a street peddler, Tau leaned over to Badru and whispered, "What do you suppose they're doing?"

"Well, they did say that a hail storm will come tomorrow," Badru recalled. "Perhaps they are informing the other slaves so they can be under the safety of a roof. But Pharaoh did observe that there aren't even any clouds." Badru looked up at the sky. "I wonder if this god of the Hebrews is powerful enough to defeat Nut."

Tau gazed heavenward too. "Whatever happens I'm sure we'll be dragged into watching it first-hand, right?" He gave a hearty laugh and slapped Badru's back.

Badru released a muffled breath as he felt the sting. Then he warned, "Keep your antics to yourself."

Tau, unphased by Badru's gruff response, responded only with a grin.

Badru said, "But you may be right. I wonder how long we can withstand the ripples of this war between the gods. Given big enough waves, even the sturdiest of ships will sink."

"Do you think Yalu may be right? That it'll be safer on the Hebrew side?" Tau asked.

Badru's only reply was a short grunt as then continued to go after Moses and Aaron.

"Hail, you say?" Rashidi continued his skepticism. "They already held the festival of Anuket and are awaiting the harvest. You can already see barley almost ready to pluck from the stock, and the wheat will be following soon after it. You must have heard wrong."

"I'm afraid not," Yalu replied, "He declared to Pharaoh that any person or animal caught in the hail storm will die; it will be that severe."

"And this will happen at mid-morning tomorrow?" Rashidi asked.

Yalu nodded and looked at Nebit to corroborate his words. She nodded as well. Rashidi took a deep breath and then released it with a sigh.

"Thank you for your reports, they has been most helpful. I believe it's time to take stronger action."

Yalu tilted his head curiously, "Stronger action? What do you mean?"

Caught off guard by the question, Rashidi stumbled over his words, but recovered quickly: "It's nothing to concern yourself with. Be sure to keep me updated of Moses' comings and goings. This is more important now than ever."

Yalu continued nodding as Rashidi spoke and finally said "I understand, master. We shall continue watching him and report back as we have been doing."

Rashidi nodded in return, and attended to other business.

After they walked out of the manor, Yalu whispered to Nebit, "I'm not sure why, but I feel compelled to know what this other action he's talking about is. Something bad is about to happen."

"What concern is it of ours?" Nebit asked. "Whatever Rashidi is planning is his own business, right?"

"You asked me show you how to be a protector, right?" Yalu reminded her.

She said, "Yes I do. I want that more than anything." As she said that she realized it might not be true.

"If they're planning something against Moses then it's our job to protect him." Yalu told her. "He's just an old man!"

Then Nebit knew that now was the right time to tell him. "Yalu, I'm not going to argue with you. I think you're right. But I need to tell you something that may change your mind."

Yalu looked on curiously while Nebit told him about Kasmut's plan to deal with Sakakwi.

"So you see," Nebit concluded, "we can't make enemies out of them. I can't afford to lose my only opportunity to see justice done for my master's death."

"I see what you mean," Yalu said feeling deflated. "You're right. I spoke too hasty."

"But," Nebit folded her arms and rubbed her cheek with a finger. A wry little smile adorned her face. "Learning more about what's going to happen would help us to make the wisest choices."

Yalu looked at her and grinned: "Then perhaps we should look to Rashidi for some wisdom. What are you plotting? He won't tell us that much is plain."

"He doesn't need to tell us. I'll sneak inside his manor without being observed. I can hide and listen."

"You do know the consequences of getting caught inside their house without permission are very serious. It could be time in the prison pit. Or worse, execution. You think they won't catch you?"

"I'm confident," Nebit glanced back at the manor. Her mind began thinking of how to get inside the house without attracting attention.

Yalu sighed and shook his head, "And I'll be nearby to help if you need any. I hope Badru and Tau can handle watching Moses and Aaron without us."

"How hard can that be?" Nebit waved her hand in dismissal. "They're only following them. Between the four of us, those two got the easy job. They'll probably just be waiting for us back at the room and wondering what took us so long. What could possibly happen?"

"This is disastrous!" Badru shouted. He and Tau walked along a market road. Various craftsmen and traders lined the side of the road. Men and women bustled passed them. He accused, "How is it possible that you lost both Moses and Aaron? I only left you for a moment to release the flood in private."

"Oh Badru, don't exaggerate."

Badru punched his arm. Tau looked at him with amusement.

Tau thought of an excuse: "They must have slipped out a back exit or something. How do we know they even left? Maybe they're still in there."

"We waited at the manor for more than two hours, by that shadow," Badru pointed at the dial in the courtyard. "At the other places they went to, we only waited less than half so long. Can I not trust you to even keep your eyes open for such a short time?"

At just that moment, Tau stopped walking and swung his arm out. It caught Badru square in the stomach. He wheezed out air in a short breath and squealed in pain.

Tau whispered excitedly, "Quiet or you'll give us away. I see them up ahead there." He pointed at the road ahead.

Badru followed his finger and saw them too, still trying to muffle his groans. "Looks like you made up for your failure," Badru smiled at Tau, who frowned in return.

They continued their pursuit of Moses and Aaron, who walked with two other men: one an elder and the other quite a bit younger. Suddenly, they split up. Moses and the elder made a right turn down another road while Aaron and the younger man kept going straight. Tau turned and looked at Badru with a confused expression.

Thinking quickly, Badru told Tau to follow Aaron while he followed Moses. The two parted ways and chased after their respective targets.

Hiding in the shadows of the manor cast by the hot overhead sun, Nebit snuck along the wall. She came up to a small window with a burlap curtain just high enough so she could see inside if she stepped on her toes. She pulled up a tiny corner of the curtain and saw the sacks of wheat, barley and other supplies: she had found a storeroom. Most importantly it was empty of people.

She looked back at Yalu. He was leaning against the outer wall underneath a palm tree next to the pool. She recalled not that long ago, she saw a man-servant whipped and left in the sun for being caught trying to cool himself in it. She reasoned that's why Yalu kept a healthy distance from the water and merely gazed at its enticing beauty.

Putting a hand on the sill she jumped up and through it, landing quietly on the brick floor inside. A closed door ahead of her, made of thin planks bound by copper bars, muffled the sounds of people.

She touched the cool wood and suddenly heard someone approach the door. Instinctively, Nebit pushed herself against the left side of the door where the copper hinges were. A woman opened the door and entered the room. She went to one of the sacks of grain lying on the floor and filled a basket. Then she left and closed the door behind her. Scrunching her nose in frustration she realized she was next to the kitchen.

She carefully crawled out the window and continued to creep along the side of the house, looking into windows. The next curtain-covered window she came to was a bustling kitchen. At least four maidservants prepared the afternoon meal. Luckily everyone was too afraid of a scolding to look up from their work.

She glanced back one more time at Yalu. He looked down at the pool and then back out over the courtyard again. A few servants went about various tasks. Everyone seemed oblivious to her plans, just what she wanted. She rounded the corner.

The wall surrounding the manor was several arms' length away from where Nebit stood underneath another curtained window. When she peaked inside, she saw another storeroom. This one looked more like an armory, with torches and blankets as well.

"This has got to be the right one," Nebit thought to herself as she put her hand in one corner of the window and raised her foot to the other corner. Then she gracefully lifted herself up to crouch inside the window frame and lowered herself onto the brick floor just as gracefully. Looking around, she noticed two more doors.

She walked to the door ahead of her. Becoming very still, she listened to the other side and heard nothing. So she slowly and steadily opened it and saw a passage on the other side. There were doors on either end, and another door across from her.

Curious about the other door in the room she closed the one she had opened and snuck over to it.

She pressed her ear against the door and raised her eyebrows as she heard Rashidi's voice. Noticing some light from the bottom of the door, Nebit crouched down and laid the side of her head against the floor. She was able to see part of Rashidi's audience chamber from underneath. From the feet in her view, she could see that he was speaking with two women.

"Look, just find some anywhere; I don't care what it takes," Kasmut barked. "I expect meat for every meal. Do you understand?"

"Yes, mistress Kasmut," The maid replied in a shaky voice. "But I tried talking to every butcher in the city. They tell me that the shepherds and herders won't trade any animals to slaughter until the new herds have grown."

Kasmut sighed angrily. Then she conceded, "I suppose we must suffer in the name of Pharaoh. Get back to work!" The kitchen worker's feet left the room. Nebit quietly took a breath and waited.

In another part of the city, Tau stood near a baker. He periodically glanced at the door of the house Aaron had entered. The baker finally noticed Tau seemingly examining his loaves.

He said in a somewhat annoyed tone, "Do you want a loaf? Or are you just standing around?"

"Uh, I'm just standing around," Tau admitted.

The baker raised his eyebrows and gave Tau a curious eye. After a moment he said, "Can you stand around somewhere else?"

"Actually, I want to trade for some bread. What do you have?"

"Wheat and barley. What do you have to trade?"

Tau glanced at the door again and saw Aaron walking the other way down the street. He started running to follow but quickly turned to the trader and shouted, "I changed my mind."

"Go curse someone else with your presence!" He shouted back.

Aaron's pace surprised Tau as he struggled to keep up. After a few minutes, Aaron stopped at an intersection where his brother awaited and they started speaking with each other.

Tau tried to hide behind a rack of drying leather-tanning. Then out of the corner of his eye, he spied Badru. Tau made some hand gestures toward him, and Badru finally spotted him. First checking to make sure Moses and Aaron didn't see him, Badru walked casually over to Tau.

Badru ducked behind the same tanning racks, and Tau leaned over and whispered, "You'd be proud of me. Other than when he went inside of a house I didn't let Aaron out of my sight once."

Badru chuckled, "That is well. Although I must admit that there was one time when I lost Moses."

"Aha!" Tau poked Badru and grinned at him.

Badru explained, "You see, he wasn't even inside a house yet. He was standing at the door and talking with the resident. Then some Hebrew servant bumped into me and I got distracted. After I got done scolding her for her inattention to where she was going Moses was gone and the door was shut. I wandered around the market for a good hour trying to find him."

"Look! There they go again," Tau pointed and they chased off after them.

Gahiji folded his arms inside a room at Rashidi's manor and scowled. He commented in a low raspy voice, "How long is he going to make us wait here? We do have better things to do besides sit."

The man he spoke to, adjusted his spear next to where he sat on the mat and shook his head. "Hear hear! Are there no more slave riots to quell?"

"I don't blame him," another soldier gazed down the edge of his axe. "I don't like to be disturbed when I'm eating either. Give me a huge slab of grilled gazelle and then leave me alone while I enjoy getting to work." He gave a good belly laugh.

"Don't be such a locust!" accused another as he cleaned his bow.

"Maybe if you ate some savory meat you wouldn't be thin as a reed! I'll wager my axe would slice you right in half. I won't eat it unless I can kill it!"

"You don't have to keep flaunting your stupidity; your axe can just as easily be used to harvest barley for baking bread. It can cut up some old and dead tree branches for a fire to bake with. And then we'll use your precious axe to slice the bread when it is finished."

"You speak blasphemy, oh tall and thin one! That's not how you treat a weapon of war. Do I need to teach proper manners for a warrior?" Spittle sprayed from his mouth.

A few moments of awkward silence passed by as the two stared intently at each other.

Then the silence was broken, "Quit your bickering or I'll skewer you both and roast you over a fire," he laughed loudly. "Because of that cursed Moses it'd be the only meat to eat for a while."

Suddenly Kasmut entered the room and declared, "We are finished with our afternoon meal. Please accompany me into his audience chamber."

They followed him around the kitchen, through a hallway, and into the chamber. Rashidi sat with a few scraps of papyrus on the table and his fingers playing with the strands of hair on his wig.

Without looking up, Rashidi motioned for them to come up to the table across from him and they sat down as he bid them.

Finally, Rashidi spoke, "The time for which you've been preparing is almost at hand." He looked up at them and excitement grew on their faces. "It will be tomorrow night and the hour will be when the moon is at its highest. According to our informants, he will be praying in the courtyard at this time. It is a manor house on the other side of town. Kasmut will provide directions."

"I also want you to remember," Rashidi stopped abruptly as everyone heard a noise coming from a door to the side of them.

"It came from behind that door over there! Where does that door lead?" Gahiji asked.

"That is only a storage room," Rashidi answered.

A soldier reached the door and swung it wide. Light filled the darkened room revealing miscellaneous supplies. A single brown and white feather lay on the floor. They noticed the curtain of the window on the right wall swinging, allowing specks of light to dance on the floor.

"Someone was listening!"

"Go after him!" Gahiji yelled.

With a running start, he jumped onto the window ledge while crouching low so the top of his bow didn't catch on the top of the window. He heard footsteps to his left and caught sight of a dark leg running around the corner. He gracefully landed on the ground and ran in pursuit.

As soon as he turned the corner, he saw one of the other crew of soldiers hired by Rashidi leaning against the wall near the pool. "Hey!" One of the men shouted and ran up to him. "Did you see someone come around the corner here?"

"Pardon? Someone running over here?" Yalu broke his stare on the pool and looked up. "What did he look like?"

"I only saw a dark leg. Maybe he was a Kushite. Perhaps he vaulted over the wall."

"No, I can't say that I noticed anybody," Yalu shrugged his shoulders. At about this time, the spear wielder and axe man came around from the front door. Rashidi arrived a few seconds behind them.

"What are you doing here?" The man with the spear asked suspiciously. "You weren't spying on us? I assume you know the punishment for doing that is severe."

Yalu raised his open palm to them to show he wasn't threatening as he replied, "No! He said the man was likely to be a Kushite."

The soldier with the bow corroborated. Rashidi looked among them and rubbed his hands together nervously as they waited for him to say something.

"You let him get away. Yalu, you need to pay more attention. I will not suffer fools in my employ. Do you understand?" They both nodded and apologized. "Now come, we still need to finish our business. And as for you, Yalu, don't just stand around cooling yourself in the shade. I pay you to work. Now get to it!"

"Yes, Rashidi," Yalu stopped leaning against the wall. "I will get to work at once, as you command."

"Let's go back inside," Rashidi said. Then he looked around and demanded, "Where is Gahiji?"

Nebit breathed a sigh of relief as she leaned against a mud-brick building while enjoying its shade. Suddenly, she saw movement from the corner of her eye. Before she could move to a better hiding place, Gahiji spoke.

"You are skilled indeed, as I have heard." Gahiji approached her and stopped a few paces away. "I've not seen an escape like for a long time. But I wonder where the sound came from."

Nebit froze and looked at him cautiously, ready for fight or flight. She said nothing.

"Fear not, I won't reveal what you did. I hear there are big plans for you."

She looked at for a moment, trying to decide what to say or do. She knew he was an enemy, but he didn't seem like an enemy right now. She said, "A bird flew in and bumped into one of the wooden crates."

Gahiji chuckled and folded his arms. Then he looked serious and asked, "Who's that man in your group? The one who threatened me before. Do you know why he seems to hate me so?"

"You were a bandit?" Nebit asked. Gahiji nodded his head. "That's it. His family was killed by bandits and he's been protecting caravans ever since."

"Ah yes," Gahiji smiled a devious little smile. "I thought he looked familiar. Where did it happen?"

"I don't know, around some ruins with underground passages."

"Hmm…" Gahiji thought for a moment. Then an expression of realization passed through his face. But he looked at her and said, "Time for me to go now."

As she was wondering what he meant, she heard footsteps coming from behind her. She turned and saw Yalu walking toward her. When she looked back Gahiji was gone.

"What did you hear?" he asked her.

She shook her head, "We shouldn't talk here. Let's wait until we get back." Yalu nodded in agreement and started off toward their borrowed room.

"We're back and have…" He began when they arrived, but didn't see anyone at the window. Looking around they saw neither of their companions.

Standing around for a moment, they wondered what to do.

Then Yalu pointed toward the window, "You can watch while I barter for some food."

She complied.

About an hour later, Nebit saw Aaron and Moses return. A few minutes later, they heard footsteps coming towards their room, and the two missing spies passed through the burlap door.

"Where have you two been?" Yalu asked. "I thought we would get back long after you, but here you are now."

"We have been chasing those two men all day!" Badru said with a frustrated tone between breaths. "We hardly had a moment's rest. They went from house to house all the way to the other side of the city and back. I am exhausted." He sat heavily on his mat and lay with the back of his hand over his eyes.

"And we've barely had anything to eat either," Tau said as he noticed the food on the table. "I could eat a whole water cow right now!"

Nebit turned toward them and said, "Now that we're all here, I have something to talk about. Rashidi met with Gahiji and his group."

"Rashidi invited you to such a meeting?" Badru asked with disbelief as he sat up and turned toward her.

"Well," Nebit looked up trying to find the right words, "invited isn't exactly what happened. I, uh, was in the area, um, coincidentally. And I heard some things. . ."

"You were snooping," Badru said.

"Look, do you want to hear it or not?" Nebit asked with frustration. She took a deep breath and released it. Then she started, "As all of you know, we've been watching Moses and Aaron and reporting back everything to Rashidi. But we didn't know what he was going to do with that information until now."

Badru ripped a chunk of bread from Tau, who sat down next to him and had already grabbed a loaf.

Then Badru replied, "I assumed that Pharaoh wants to keep watch on him to make sure he does not start a rebellion or something similar."

"Rashidi plans to kill Moses," Nebit said bluntly. "Gahiji and his men will complete that mission tomorrow night, when the moon is in the middle of the sky."

"Kill him? I knew they were up to something. We should stop them." Yalu said.

"Why should we interfere?" Badru swallowed. "If the Hebrew god is really as powerful as we have seen, then let him defend Moses. We should not have to get involved."

"But we already are involved, aren't we?" Yalu pointed out. "We've been following Moses for a while now and we know he hasn't done anything to deserve death. Shall we sit by and watch?"

"I don't like sitting and watching," Tau declared folding his arms. "I'd prefer we choose a side and fight."

"I agree." Yalu nodded. "If you really are itching for a fight then we warn Moses about this attack and defend him."

"We can also choose not to fight," Badru pointed out. "We simply stay here and do nothing."

"If we do nothing then Moses will die," Yalu reasoned.

"Would you take his place?" Badru asked gravely.

Yalu remained silent.

"What is in our best interest? I don't see why we should risk our lives for Moses." Badru said. He looked around the room but no one met his eyes.

Yalu looked out the window and thought. His mind wandered and he remembered the words of his father. Then he asked the group, "What is the right thing to do?"

Badru met his eyes but words failed him.

"Defend the defenseless," Tau answered soberly.

Nebit shook her head, "I don't know about this. What are we about to do?"

Yalu looked around and nodded his head. He said, "Well we do have a day and a half to think about this. I suppose there is wisdom in thinking before acting. I propose we sleep on it and see how we feel in the morning."

Badru nodded. He took another bite of bread, "Hail? That would be the realm of Nut. If it happens then the Hebrew god will be showing dominance over her as well. Though we owe the Hebrew god a debt from sores we got while fighting the men from the priests. We did win the battle because of it."

With that, they settled into their room with their supplies in hopes to wait out the coming storm.

In the dark of night, Kasmut heard a knock on her wooden door. A maidservant told her that a man from the temple was waiting for her downstairs. Kasmut already had an idea who this was as he was meeting late with Rashidi. She went down to go meet him.

"Good evening to you Sakakwi," she said politely. "I trust I haven't made you wait long."

"Ah, no indeed." He smiled at her. It was an odd smile and she wasn't sure what to make of it. "I've been thinking about all the help you and your husband have done for me and wanted to thank you personally."

"There is no need. It is an honor to serve," Kasmut replied. She felt his attitude was most unusual.

"It is good to hear you say that," Sakakwi told her. "In fact, I have another service you can render to me."

"Oh, and what is that?" Kasmut knew he was being too nice to her. Her mind raced to think of what he would want before he even said it.

"You are always so good with people. Very well-connected. I've arranged some business early tomorrow morning in the fields that I want you to oversee. You would do that for me, wouldn't you?" Sakakwi said.

His unusually smooth and elegant tone put Kasmut off-guard. She asked, "I heard that a storm is coming. Perhaps you should reschedule this business."

"No!" Sakakwi growled. In that single word she saw the true man emerge. She knew he was up to something and was determined to find out what it was. He continued, "It needs to happen tomorrow morning. This business is very important to the temple."

"Very well," Kasmut answered. "I shall have one of my servants go first thing."

"I only trust you," Sakakwi said.

Kasmut looked at him fearfully. She thought of all sorts of possibilities and rightly felt this to be a trap. But try as she might, she couldn't figure out his scheme.

"Alright, I'll go. It is an honor to be trusted by the temple." She replied.

Sakakwi smiled his devious smile again. He told her, "Very good. And give my regards to your husband." Then he stood up and left.

She watched him go. Somehow she felt that he knew what she'd been doing. And that even though she couldn't see it, somehow she fell right into his hands.

Chapter 13

The morning did not greet them with the usual Egyptian sunrise. Dark clouds covered the sky. A somber chill awakened the citizens of the city of the great white walls. Yalu woke and rubbed his hands against his arms as he yawned. He looked up and saw Badru staring out the window. He got up and stood beside him.

"My mother always told me this was a blessing," Badru recounted. "That when clouds fill the sky Nut shields us from the harsh sun Ammon-Ra brings. These are not the clouds of blessing but cursing. The Hebrew god is showing dominance over Nut and Ra by bringing these clouds. This is only the beginning of the true battle to come. The hail will strike the Earth and in doing so, attack the realm of Geb."

"The true battle…" Yalu repeated, thinking on those words. "I've never seen hail. I've never even seen ice. My father told me stories of it, from his father. Some of the traders from Kush told me stories about frost from the high mountains."

Nebit leaned up from her bed and added, "I heard stories from traders. They told me about snow. Very small flakes of ice would fall slowly from the sky and cover the land in a white blanket."

They started eating their meal, and as the morning lingered, the anger built up in the clouds. Loud rumblings emanated from them. People looked up at the sky in fear and amazement and wondered what would happen next. Surprisingly, onlookers were wetted with a gentle rain, teasing them of what was yet to come. Without warning, a brilliant flash of royal purple lit up the clouds overhead. A terrifying crash echoed and sent men, women and animals alike into a panic, running for the nearest shelter.

And then, amid the silence left by crashing of the clouds, the first wave of hail fell to the ground. Some of the stones were as big as a man's fist and no smaller than the rolling ball of a scarab. It pounded into the ground, shattered on stone, and slowly wore away at the protection of the mud buildings.

About mid-day, when the sun would be shining at its brightest and the cool of his home would provide him comfort from the heat, Rashidi felt cold. Even wrapping himself in his ornamented cow-skin blanket didn't ease all his discomfort. Gahiji entered the room and Rashidi immediately looked up and asked:

"Have you seen her? Is there any word?"

Gahiji frowned and shook his head in reply, and Rashidi sulked back in his chair in disappointment. Then Gahiji rested a hand on the handle of one of his khopeshes and said in his low raspy voice, "A messenger from Pharaoh is here."

"What?!" Rashidi shouted with alarm, "a messenger from Pharaoh, in this weather? What does he want?"

Gahiji looked behind him and motioned for someone to come forward. The messenger, wearing the traditional gold trimmed skirt, came forward and read aloud from his papyrus, "I, Pharaoh, summon you, Rashidi, overseer of my Hebrew slaves, to an audience. Come now and without delay."

Reluctantly, Rashidi stood up, leaving his blanket behind, and walked over to the messenger. As they start out the door he asked, "My wife was out on a task when the storm came and hasn't returned yet.

How did you manage to get here without showing a single welt from those hail stones?"

The answer waited just outside his front door. He saw what looked like a wooden house on wheels. The walls and roof attached that were attached to the chariot on the yokes provided cover for riders and horses alike.

"Very well, I will go with you at once. Gahiji, come and attend me."

They hurried into the covered chariot to avoid being hit by falling hailstones, and the messenger took up the reigns and rode out the gate. They heard the knocking on the wood above them, and on either side. The top extended forward about the five forearm lengths in front. The back, however, was wide open and every once in a while, a piece of hail landed inside and ricocheted off the walls before plummeting out the back.

Here and there, peppered with hailstones, Rashidi saw the body of someone who didn't make it to shelter in time. He looked out among them and wondered if he would see the body of his wife. Then he shouted to the messenger, "Can't we go any faster?"

"I wish we could, sir," The messenger replied, "but the chariot would fall apart if I went any faster. The wheels may break. The roof also isn't very sturdy. Pulling a heavier load also puts more strain on the horses."

They spend the rest of the bumpy ride listening to hailstones knocking on the makeshift wooden ceiling. But just as the messenger said, they arrived at the palace gate where a handful of servants awaited with a movable roof on four wooden poles. Once the chariot pulled inside the gate, the servants picked the movable roof up by handles and set it down next to back of the chariot so Rashidi and Gahiji could exit without fearing the hail. Then they picked it up again

and everyone walked to the palace entrance in relative
safety together.

They walked through the hallways of the palace
hearing echoes of ice crashing on stone. Guards,
nobles, and a large number of commoners sat against
the walls to wait out the storm. Arriving in Pharaoh's
audience chamber, Rashidi left Gahiji behind to wait.
The door opened, revealing an angry and frustrated
Pharaoh arguing with the man Rashidi recognized as
the chief of agriculture. Rashidi approached slowly and
then bowed down to show obeisance.

"Are you really telling me that we won't be able
to bake bread or weave cloth for a half-year?!" Pharaoh
shouted angrily. "What about our storehouses? We can
produce from them, can't we?"

"Yes, Pharaoh; for a while."

The man knelt before the throne. Rashidi
noticed the man displaying a large bruise on his right
cheek the same size and shape as the royal scepter in
Pharaoh's hand. He cringed.

"But those storehouses will not last. We will
need to acquire grain from somewhere else."

"By all the curses of Set!" Pharaoh shouted, "I
just traded surplus grain to buy more treasure for my
burial chamber. I could rend it back with my armies."

Then Pharaoh shifted his gaze to Rashidi. "And
what about you? How are the plans coming?"

"Very well Pharaoh," Rashidi bowed low. "But
if this weather continues then it will be delayed."

"Yes, I shall summon Moses immediately.
Perhaps we can have him appeal to his god and bring
an end to this disaster. We need to preserve what little
we have left. Wait," Pharaoh said before the servant
could leave, a vengeful expression slipped onto his face.
"Have the messenger deliver the summons with an
outfitted chariot, but not offer protection to the man

responsible for all this. And if he should be struck
down by the hail then we'll be better off," He laughed
heartily at his own suggestion.

The servant bowed to the ground in obeisance
to Pharaoh's order and then left.

Nebit waited with the other three in their room
as hailstones pounded the bricks of mud. The ice piled
up near the window almost up to the sill. They gave up
watching long ago. The repeated drumming of the hail
dulled her ears. So when the sound diminished and
eventually stopped, it took a few minutes before she
realized it. At first she just looked out the window.
Then she saw people start to fill the streets again.

Jumping up, Nebit told the others, "I need to
stretch my legs. Can you continue watching without me
for a time?"

"I'll join you," Yalu stood up. "I need some
walking as well."

"Seems Badru and I are stuck here, then." Tau
laughed. Then he looked out the window and heaved a
heavy sigh. "Come back soon so we can take a turn."

Badru also agreed and so Yalu and Nebit left.
The clouds turned summersaults in the sky and the
wind gave a cold chill. But Nebit felt good being
outside, hearing relative silence. The dull roar of
people's conversations was welcome in their ears. She
glanced at Yalu and from his expression, he also
seemed to be glad the hailstorm was over.

Just then, a woman approached Nebit. She
begged, "Oh please, can you help me? I think I've seen
you talk with her. But she hasn't come back yet. Please
help."

"Slow down woman," Yalu said. "Who are you
and what help do you need?"

"It's Kasmut! I'm her maidservant. I fear she
was out in this terrible storm," she said. Both of them

gasped. The pain in Nebit's chest flared up again. She hoped nothing happened to her. "My master left early this morning and hasn't come back."

"Where did she go?" Nebit asked, trying to restrain her emotions.

The maidservant took them out to the field where Kasmut told her she was going. They searched there for the better part of an hour. Then they found a group bodies together underneath balls of melting ice. As the three of them pulled the bruised and battered bodies off each other, they saw Kasmut's body lying at the bottom.

The maidservant burst into tears and knelt down beside her mistress. Nebit wept bitterly. A tear escaped Yalu's eye, and he put a hand on Nebit's shoulder. She grasped it desperately.

"We should take her back to Rashidi," Yalu said.

Nebit and the maidservant agreed. They found a cart in the field that somehow managed to escape destruction from the hail. Yalu hoisted Kasmut's body into it, took up the yoke upon himself, and pulled it back into the city as the two women trudged behind.

Rashidi stood outside his manor gate, receiving reports. Normally, the heat of the day would already be bearing down, but it was cold and he wore an animal skin draped over his shoulders. Still, he wasn't able to fully concentrate on the task at hand.

That's when the conversations around him died down and he looked around to see Yalu pulling a cart. His heart sank as he realized what it carried.

He approached and his servants made a path for him. He saw Kasmut laying lifeless in the cold wooden planks. Her body was filled with bruises and indentations. Her skull was cracked but her face was still recognizable. He dropped to his knees as he beheld her before him.

The maidservant knelt by his side. She looked at Rashidi and said, "She was a good woman. I'm sure she's waiting for you at the reeds of paradise."

"Reeds of paradise," Rashidi muttered.

Then he asked, "If they are a paradise then why must I remain here while she is there?"

She looked at him with a puzzled expression but said nothing. Rashidi leaned forward and caressed Kasmut's cold face.

"The slaves work tirelessly for Pharaoh. The foreman and servants give me reports. And I give Pharaoh the news about how much they've produced for him. What is it all for? Will we be better off once we cross over? For all Kasmut's work for Pharaoh, will she be rewarded for it? Or is it all for nothing? She lived, toiled, and now she's dead. What does she have to show for herself except a body void of life?"

Rashidi sighed. A tear escaped his eyes and slid down his cheek.

Then he looked at the maidservant and said, "She is to have a good send-off. Tell my servants to collect jewels, oils, and unguents for her. Take her and prepare her for burial."

"As you command," she replied. "I'll see that my mistress is given the honor she's due."

Rashidi stood up and gazed down at her one more time. He remembered when she told him about the early morning business. She casually left the estate and went to her death. Then he turned to his foreman and continued to hear their reports as Kasmut's body was taken.

When Rashidi noticed Yalu and Nebit standing around he told them abruptly, "You still have a job to do. No go off and do it!"

Nebit drearily walked the familiar roads back toward their room. Yalu walked beside her. More than a few people searched the dead on the streets for family and friends. Nebit felt a building up as though someone were trying to block the Nile. A hard lump formed in the back of her throat. The waters rose. The lump grew harder. Feeling she could not contain herself any longer, she burst into tears.

Feeling Yalu embrace her she said, "Do you know what she meant to me?"

"What did she mean?" He answered.

"She was my friend and family. She was the escape from my former life. My life apart from him. That monster! I don't know how, but I know he was behind this." She could feel her hope being torn asunder.

Yalu nodded reluctantly but said nothing. When she got herself under control, they continued back.

When they entered Tau admonished them: "Where did you go? Walk around the entire city while we're cramped in here?"

Then Tau noticed the tears. Nebit sat down quietly on her mat.

"Sorry to make you wait. We were delayed." Yalu told them what happened.

When he was done, there was a moment of silence.

"I want to protect Moses," Nebit burst out surprising everyone, including herself. "I've had enough of this disaster after disaster. It needs to stop!"

"But couldn't it also stop with the death of Moses?" Tau asked.

Badru shook his head and explained, "Even if Moses was killed, who's to say that his god wouldn't send another emissary to Pharaoh bringing calamities even worse than before? It's not the man Pharaoh is contending with, but his god."

"If that happens, then protecting Moses would be a gesture of good-will to his god," Yalu said. "Then perhaps we would be spared from the coming calamities."

Badru breathed out a heavy sigh. He looked at Tau and asked, "What do you say, my friend?"

Tau grunted. Then he looked back out the window toward Aaron's manor. He said, "Moses seems like a decent man to me. He just got caught up in all this business with the gods. He has brought all sorts of plagues with him. But he is only the messenger. Whether he deserves to live or die is not something I can say."

"There are many ways to look at this situation," Badru said and shook his head. "Who's to say which way is the right way?"

Yalu leaned toward the others with a glimmer in his eye. He said, "Let's just look at it from our way. We're close to Moses and we know about a plot against his life. What's the right thing to do?"

Badru breathed out another heavy sigh. He and Tau looked at one other again. Badru didn't answer.

But Tau did: "Protect him."

Then everyone looked at Badru. After a moment he nodded in agreement.

"Then it's settled. And I already have a plan," Yalu said and told them exactly what he intended to do.

As he spoke, Nebit felt the pain in her chest lesson. Hope of her new life grew again. She took a breath and listened intently.

Gahiji looked up at the moonlit sky as he crouched next to the building. He guessed that the moon was about nearly at its apex.

Seeing the face of Thoth in the nearly full moon, he grinned and recited, "Oh great Thoth, arbiter of justice, let it be done tonight on those whose deeds warrant it." Then he looked back at his fellows who crouched behind him and said in his low and raspy voice, "The moon is full. Thoth is with us and assures our success."

"It never hurts to have a god on your side," his companion said as he tightened his grip on his axe. "But we don't need the help. I could do it by myself."

"True words. Sending all four of us to do this job is a waste of sleeping hours," said another.

"We could kill the whole household, to be thorough."

"This is why Rashidi made me the leader," Gahiji scowled at them. "He didn't send all four of us because it's difficult, but to make it smooth. Once Moses is gone then the Hebrew slaves will be broken and docile."

They moved up close to the wall of Aaron's home. Around the corner they saw the gate and a servant posted there.

Gahiji turned around and whispered, "Go to the middle of the wall where Moses lays down to pray. Once you hear him, give me the signal. I'll signal our bowman to shoot that slave, and you two jump over the wall and kill him. Do you understand?"

"I don't see him," the soldier scanned the building top where Gahiji had sent his associate.

"Yes? Good. He's not meant to be seen," Gahiji answered, "He will not reveal himself until after he has struck."

They both nodded and took their positions around the middle of the wall.

In the moonlight, one shadow studied another shadow. His right shoulder leaned up against the building as he stared across the street. An arrow, knocked in his bow, waited for him to pull the string.

"I must be careful," Nebit thought to herself. "If I alert him to my presence then he'll be turning that bow on me and his friends below will know." She looked on the floor ahead of her to be certain her step would not make noise. She took a step closer. Nothing happened. She took another step closer.

A few more steps and she found herself directly behind him. The dagger in her right hand shone in the moonlight as she raised it. She struck with both hands. Her left hand covered his mouth as her right hand placed the dagger on his throat.

Gahiji stared overhead at the moon in the silence of the night. He glanced at his subordinates who both leaned against the wall. They shook their heads, indicating they didn't hear anything. Gahiji watched for his bow across the street from his hiding place at the corner of the wall. He had felt so confident in his ability to hide that he boasted none of them could spot him when he made his shot.

Suddenly, movement on the second floor of a building caught his eye. He started scanning that area with his eyes. A few seconds later he saw a shadow moved there again. He grinned and whispered, "Not too good for my falcon eyes." He glanced back at the other two and saw both of them emphatically gesturing. He turned back toward the building and gave the signal to attack.

He waited for what felt like an eternity, but nothing happened. The servant at the gate simply covered his mouth to cough. Gahiji turned and gestured again but still nothing happened. A moment of panic washed over him as he frantically signaled toward the building. Then he remembered the servant at the gate and looked over at him, hoping that he hadn't noticed. He remained oblivious as ever. He finally gave up and snuck over to his companions.

As Gahiji neared them, he heard the man praying in a language he didn't understand on the other side of the wall.

When he reached his men, Gahiji whispered, "You and I will scale the wall. Then he will kill the guard at the gate."

He nodded in agreement and wove his fingers together to provide a step for Gahiji's foot to propel him up the wall.

Gahiji quickly swung his legs over the wall and jumped down onto the dirt below with a thump. The man looked over at him when he heard it. The man got up and drew a sword and grabbed a shield. Gahiji pressed forward with two khopeshes in hand as the second man landed behind him.

"Who are you?" The man shouted, "What do you want?"

"I want you to die," Gahiji replied and continued to advance. Cold confidence filled each stride.

"What have I done to deserve death?" the man asked.

Gahiji walked forward, "Shall I recount your crimes? Traitor to Egypt, rebel against Pharaoh and our gods, you'll get what you deserve after I send you to Osiris. Then the god of the underworld himself will judge you." At this point they heard the sounds of fighting at the gate. Gahiji laughed again, "You will not escape!" The sword met the khopesh and Gahiji's other khopesh banged against the man's shield.

As the other attacker tried to flank the Hebrew man, two other men leapt out of the shadows to intercept him.

He stopped short of them and stuttered, "I… I know you. You work for master Rashidi! What are you doing here, Yalu?"

Yalu grimaced, drawing his khopesh and shield as he advanced with a Hebrew soldier. The axe-wielder swung at Yalu who deflected it with his shield. The Hebrew solider flanked him but the man brought his axe around just in time to block the attacks from him. Yalu tried to bash the man's head with his shield, but he saw it coming and used the handle of his axe to block it. Then Lior struck low and cut deeply into his knees, drawing a shout of pain.

Gahiji watched from the corner of his eye as Yalu dispatched a comrade with a thrust of his sword to the chest. But Gahiji was too busy with his own fight. The robed man in front of him attacked with his sword, but Gahiji easily knocked it aside with a khopesh. With the other khopesh, he swung upward from the back, gaining momentum, and landed a hard blow against the man's shield.

The shield held steady, but the man was forced to put a knee on the ground from the strength of the attack. Gahiji grinned as he executed a neat trick. He feinted close by his opponent's head, and as expected, the defender raised his shield to block it. But the other khopesh came around from the other side and hit the inside of the shield, knocking it out of the defender's hand.

There was shouting toward the gate of the estate. When Gahiji looked in that direction he saw Yalu running up to attack him but also noted that the Hebrew soldier was running to the gate.

Stepping back with his right foot into a defensive stance with a weapon guarding the front, he

waited with the other khopesh to strike. The attack
came as a windstorm; strong and vibrant, but lacking
the strength required to do any real damage to a
prepared opponent. The robed man took this
opportunity to stand up and rejoin the fight.

Gahiji was now defending himself against two
attackers. He backed up, being careful to line them up
and avoid fighting them both at the same time. But
then he saw their next mistake. Instead of backing up
with each on either side of him, they both moved in
front of him. With another grin, he crouched down and
folded his arms like Osiris. Leaning forward he pushed
with his back foot and started to roll forward. As soon
as his head came up he mustered all of his might.
Unfolding his arms, he sliced his khopeshes outward at
his opponent's thighs.

Yalu saw Gahiji's tactic and moved his shield
into place to block it. But the Hebrew man wasn't as
observant. He placed his sword defensively but was no
match for the slicing khopesh. It easily brushed the
sword aside and left a deep wound on his thigh where
the leg met the torso. The robed man fell over and
shouted in pain as Yalu stood in front to defend him.

Gahiji stood and faced them sideways with
both weapons out in front of him in his accustomed
attacking stance. He chuckled to himself at having the
upper-hand.

"You're much better with a sword than I
thought, Moses. But my next attack will finish you for
sure. You are a lucky one. If your sword wasn't there, I
might have cut your leg off," he taunted, taking a step
back to prepare his next attack.

"My name is Hoshea," his wounded opponent
gasped between groans of pain.

Gahiji halted his attack in bewilderment. His
mind raced to think of what it could mean. He

wondered if they came to the wrong house. That was impossible, Yalu and the other scouts were here.

"The man you seek is safe inside the manor. But I doubt you will get so far." Hoshea smiled, showing his teeth.

Gahiji hissed as he saw his enemies took this time to circle around him. Only had he lost the upper hand, but his escape route was closed off. Sakakwi's associate, Badru, had even showed up and was bandaging Hoshea's wounds.

"What. . . What is going on here?" Gahiji demanded. He pointed his khopesh at Yalu and accused, "You were supposed to tell us where Moses would be. You've betrayed us! You're traitors to Egypt, Pharaoh, and our gods!"

Yalu had no answers for him.

Gahiji saw his hesitation and struck, "Or do you want to give up, like you gave up on your family?"

Yalu felt his face get red hot. He stepped forward, "What? You know nothing of my family!"

Gahiji smiled when he saw that his barbed arrow hit true. He replied, "I know them more than you could guess. If you pay attention, you may be surprised how much you can learn about who someone really is, when they're dying."

Yalu's face turned red and Gahiji could feel the anger welling up inside him. Yalu made no reply but tightened the grip on his khopesh

"Oh, it's true!" Gahiji smiled wickedly. "I remember watching a man die in a caravan my fellows raided a couple years ago. Mentioned the woman I was taking with me was the wife of his son, that I should have mercy on her, for the sake of the dying. Only made it so much more satisfying when I killed her in front of him."

"Lies!" Yalu shouted.

"Truth. Lies. What's the difference? If you weren't there you don't know what really happened." Gahiji chuckled to himself. He saw Yalu breathing heavily between his clenched teeth. "And I suppose if you become like the Hebrews slaves then you'll be making their deaths meaningless. What a pitiful sight that would be. A promising young soldier in the mud. Like a pig."

His taunting worked beautifully. Yalu struck hard and swift, but blind with anger. Gahiji was ready, the provocation having done its job, he relied upon his khopeshes to do theirs. He knocked Yalu's khopesh and shield aside with slight difficulty and managed to kick him in the stomach. Yalu fell backward and Hoshea came to his aid.

He heard footsteps and whirled around to see Nebit step forward. He recognized her and said, "You again? I must thank you for telling me about why our hot-headed acquaintance hates me so. I remembered that it was I who killed his dear loved ones."

"What?" Yalu gathered himself together and stood up. "I'll kill you!"

Gahiji realized he pushed Yalu a little too far. He needed a gimmick and fast. The thought came to him. He dropped his two khopeshes to the ground. They clanged against each other. Gahiji held out his open hands and asked, "You'll kill a defenseless unarmed man?"

"Like you would have murdered Moses?" Yalu raised his khopesh. Gahiji could see the uncontrolled rage in Yalu's eyes who stepped closer.

"Hold Yalu!" Hoshea quickly stood between him and Yalu, prompting a shout of anxious disapproval from Lior. Gahiji raised an eyebrow in surprise.

"Out of the way, Hoshea," Yalu yelled at him.

Hoshea groaned from the pain and grasped his side. He said, "If you kill him now then then it would make you a murderer like him. I've seen you, you're the better man. Let justice take its course."

Yalu's sword arm wavered. Gahiaji saw him struggle with Hoshea's words.

At that moment, Gahiji took advantage of the opportunity and slid a small knife from his belt, put it against Hoshea's throat, and braced his forearm against the back of Hoshea's neck. The others ceased speaking.

"Treacherous wolf!" Lior exclaimed.

Hoshea groaned again as Badru's half-applied bandage fell to the ground. "What are you doing? Was I wrong to try and save your life?"

"Everyone get away from me!" Gahiji spat out as he started dragging Hoshea towards the gate. He cocked his head toward Hoshea, "You were wrong to turn your back on me."

Then he shouted, "Let me pass or he dies!" Tau and the Hebrew servant, with weapons drawn, reluctantly complied.

Once his path to the gate had cleared, Gahiji kicked Hoshea toward them and fled toward the shadowy gate. He felt relieved to make it out of there alive, an accomplishment his comrades could not claim. But felt angry at Yalu's betrayal.

Yalu silently looked at Gahiji fade into the darkness, hot with his own anger. Then he turned to Nebit and asked, "Why did you tell him?"

"Tell him what?" She asked.

Feeling even hotter with anger, Yalu began shouting, "Did you tell him my family was killed by bandits?"

Nebit paused to think.

"Did you?" Yalu demanded.

"He seemed to already know so much. I didn't think it would cause any harm."

"Do you know what you've done?" Yalu demanded.

She didn't reply.

"You've given information to my enemy and he used it against me. You betrayed my trust!"

"You never told me it was to be kept secret."

"I shouldn't have to! Didn't you try using good judgment?"

"He caught me off guard! I didn't think this would happen. I was-"

"You didn't think," Yalu interrupted.

"What's said is said" Lior walked between them. "There's nothing to be done about that now. But you've more urgent things to talk about. Gahiji will tell your boss all about what happened tonight. What are you going to do?"

"I don't know," Yalu took a breath to calm himself. "I guess we'll have to go into hiding."

"That's not my favorite place to go," Tau shook his head.

"Why not speak to my father about joining our household?" Hoshea asked. "You've proven yourselves to me. He trusts Lior who speaks very highly of you. I can't see any reason why he would refuse."

"That is a very thoughtful gesture and I am honored at your offer." Badru told him, "But I do not know if I can take advantage of it. Even now I am positioned to take over for Pharaoh's chief magician. Joining you would put me at odds with many of the people and I would likely lose my power and position. I do not know if I can give all of that up."

Hoshea sighed. Then he looked at Badru and said, "At the very least I can persuade my father to let you stay with us for a little while as guests."

"I like your hospitality," Tau smiled, "especially if we could soak in your pool again. Then we could recount our glorious victory to your father." He laughed and clenched his fist.

"Ah right, my father," Hoshea cringed and groaned as Badru leaned him up and wrapped the bandage around him. "How about we keep our adventures here a secret between us?"

"How would you explain your injury if we did?" Tau laughed. "You were taking a walk in the moonlight and accidentally slipped and stabbed yourself?"

"Hmm," Hoshea tried to think of a more believable excuse, but shook his head in surrender. "I may have to tell him the truth. He'll want his physician to look at me." He gave a forced laugh and the others laughed encouragingly.

Badru tied off the bandage and helped him to his feet. Hoshea pointed toward the gate, "Shall we depart?"

"Do we need to inform Moses and Aaron?" Yalu asked as he helped Hoshea up to his feet. Hoshea put his arm around Yalu's shoulder to steady himself.

Lior answered, "I'll inform them in the morning. Don't worry about anything else tonight. You've done right by us. I suspect Moses may want to thank you personally as well. I'll take care of these bodies. Rest well."

Yalu and Lior embraced. Tau helped Hoshea walk toward the gate as Lior began dragging the corpses. Nebit and Badru walked behind Yalu on either side of him. Tau grabbed Hoshea's arm to try and help, but Hoshea pulled away and waved him off.

After they passed through the gate, Hoshea pushed away from Tau, "Let me walk on my own now. When we get there I don't want my father thinking the injury is bad." Tau let him go and Hoshea held out his hands to steady himself. He took a step forward and almost buckled. But after a few more, he found decent walking pace.

A few more steps and Yalu noticed the window of the room they had been using and remembered their food and supplies were still in there. He looked over his shoulder at Badru and Tau gestured toward the building with his head. Tau replied with a puzzled look but Badru tapped him on the shoulder and they discreetly make their way back to the room.

Nebit sighed and said to herself, "It will be good to finally get out of that room."

"What room?" Hoshea turned to her. "Are you staying nearby?"

Nebit's eyes widened with alarm, and her face flushed as she tried to think of something to say. Before she could, Hoshea's eyes spotted Badru and Tau going up the steps to the room overlooking Aaron's estate.

He glared at Yalu and said, "You never told me how you knew they would attack. Or about how they knew Moses' habits." He waited for Yalu's reply even though he already knew the answer.

Yalu glanced uncomfortably at Nebit who just stared at the ground in shame. Then he glanced up at the room where Badru and Tau collected their things. He confessed, "We were the ones watching Moses. We followed him wherever he went and reported everything to Rashidi."

"So all of this is your fault!"

Nebit looked up and said, "We were just doing the task assigned to us. If Rashidi didn't send us he would have sent someone else. They may not have warned you like we did."

"That may be true but it doesn't excuse your guilt. Were you going to keep this from us?"

"You're right Hoshea," Yalu admitted. "We are the ones responsible for the trouble caused this night. But what did you expect? Egyptians coming by to help you Hebrew slaves just when you need it? We didn't just decide to start helping at our own expense. This was our task. But we've seen the wonders your god has brought, trying to convince Pharaoh to relieve the suffering of your people. I hope that our actions tonight prove our loyalty."

Hoshea looked at Yalu as he spoke and nodded when he finished. Nebit and Yalu quickly exchanged glances as they walked down the dusty, moonlit road.

Tau and Badru met up with them at the gate to Nun's home. Hoshea took them through the house to an empty room with six raised reed beds with wooden frames.

He said, "Tomorrow I'll talk to Yadid about getting you something in our servant houses, but you can stay here tonight. The morning meal will be ready a couple hours after sunrise. I'll come by and take you there. For now, I should head to my bedroom before my…"

"Well, well, well…" A voice called from the hallway, and Hoshea froze as though paralyzed. Then Nun casually entered the room and put an arm around his son. "It seems you all were out late." Nun gasped as he saw the bandage.

"I'm sorry?" Hoshea stirred as though waking up.

Nun pointed an accusing finger at him. "Is that a bandage around your waist? And is that your blood?"

Hoshea looked down and said, "It could be."

"It could be!?" Nun raised an eyebrow. "You'd better explain."

"Can we talk tomorrow? It's been a long night." Hoshea requested.

Nun looked at him sternly. Then he looked at the other four and his expression softened. Then he sighed and shook his head, "You promised them lodging?"

Hoshea nodded. Then he added, "I think we should offer them a place in our household."

"A place our household?" Nun repeated, and gave each an assessing look. "I'll need some time to consider it. Rest in our guest room tonight and I'll have a good long talk with you tomorrow. But now, you my son, must see our physician."

He gave his son another stern look who nodded in obedience. They said their good nights and then Nun pushed Hoshea out of the room. Harsh whisperings faded down the hallway.

Yalu and his tired companions each choose beds and lay down on them. The victory he felt from the fight with Gahiji was by his feeling of betrayal from Nebit. He glanced at her and saw her looking at him. He shifted and turned away from her. Then he thought of Kasmut. Nebit had a lot of hope in that woman. Thus he struggled with his conflicted feelings as he drifted off to sleep.

Chapter 14

Nebit woke to warmth on her face. As she opened her eyes, the sunlight coming down almost blinded her. She quickly covered her eyes with her hand and rolled on her bed to escape the light. After she blinked a few times and yawned to recover, she sat up and stared at the glow coming through the window to welcome her into the day.

Looking around, she saw Tau, Badru, and Yalu sleeping on reed beds nearby. When she looked at Yalu, she remembered feeling hurt when he accused her of betraying him.

Just then, a tapping on the other side of the tightly bound reed door interrupted her. The others began to stir.

"Is everyone awake? The morning meal is ready and being served." Hoshea popped his head inside the room. "We have tender grilled lamb."

"Tender grilled lamb!" Tau instantly awoke. "Let's go eat."

Hoshea led them down a flight of stairs and outside the house where a fire pit roared and about thirty people sat on reed mats. Everyone instantly recognized them, and people started murmuring. Nebit could see Nun sitting at a wooden table talking with some other people. Yadid took a few seconds from arguing with the cooks to wave at his rescuers.

Hoshea stood proud and announced, "Listen up my family, friends and servants. You certainly know of the valiant heroes who saved Yadid. Last night we fought against our enemies. As a reward they'll be staying in our household for a time. I, for one, am honored to live among such strong and courageous adventurers. I ask that you make them welcome." A warm cheer erupted from the small crowd.

As the four helped themselves to a piece of the grilled lamb from near the fire, people frequently looked or pointed at them. Afterwards, Hoshea led them to the table to sit with his family. On the tables are baskets of bread, figs, garlic, onions, and other vegetables.

"Both times you have eaten with us we have had a very prodigal meal." Nun leaned toward them as he picked meat off a leg bone. "This is another feast we are celebrating in your honor. We do not always eat like this. And once again I thank you for saving one of my own, even though he disobeyed me by going with you without my consent." He gave a stern look toward Hoshea, who rubbed his wound lightly and tried to ignore him by breaking open a fig.

"You could have been killed, my son! Praise be to the god of our ancestor Abraham who sent these guardian angels to watch over you. Now, tell me all about what happened."

"The story begins further back than you think," Tau began.

And so Tau told about how they were first hired to keep the brick slaves working and how they first saw Moses and Aaron where the staff changed to a snake. Nun nodded as he recalled seeing Moses perform that miracle in front of the other Hebrew elders. Then he explained the plot against Moses' life and their plan to keep him safe. Badru interjected every so often with his own theories about how the disasters were battles between the Hebrew god and the Egyptian gods.

After they concluded telling the full story, Nun lifted up his wooden cup half-filled with wine, "This is so much more complicated than I thought. And we've just been sitting around waiting for Pharaoh to release us. All this talk makes these old bones want to get up and do something. But what would that be? Perhaps waiting is all we can do."

"Yadid seems to be finding things to do," Hoshea observed and they all laughed as they watched Yadid running by, trying to hold more than he can carry while giving instructions to other servants. Upon hearing his name, Yadid stopped and looked at them for a moment with a puzzled expression but continued his work.

A strong eastern wind blew, cooling Nebit's face. The heat of the day would soon set in and she would do well to remember that feeling. After breaking off a piece of bread she looked up at the sky in that general direction. Movement on the ground caught her attention. She saw one of the green desert grasshoppers crawling on the ground. "Osiris curse you," she said and shooed it away with her hand.

It fled, jumping into the air to fly where the wind swept across the courtyard and into the stone wall, bouncing off onto the ground. Satisfied at her successful attempt to rid herself of the pest, Nebit started eating her morning meal. The sun behind her cast her shadow towards Yalu, who was eating across from her.

For a moment her eyes met Yalu's, but he broke his gaze away. He turned to Nun and asked, "I, and I'm sure we all, appreciate your hospitality. Is there any way we can be of help?"

Before the Hebrew elder could answer, Yadid, who happened to be walking by carrying two clay jars, told them what he wanted help with: "I want to go to the market to buy some things. You can accompany me."

Nebit tore a piece off her loaf and opened up a fig, "Are you afraid of being taken again? When do you want to go?"

"In about an hour when we finish repairs from the hail storm," Yadid answered the second question but ignored the first.

Badru leaned toward Nun and asked him, "Has Pharaoh decided to let you people go and worship your god yet?"

Nun shook his head with a frown. At that point, Yadid called over to him. Nun got up, bringing Hoshea with him and left the four alone at the table.

"What will the Hebrew god do next?" Tau asked after swallowing. "Each attack has been worse than the one before. But I don't know what can be worse than that storm."

"Perhaps we can escape it, if Nun accepts us into his household. Helping protect them would be doing what was right." Nebit said, glancing at Yalu who still didn't look at her. She winced and tried to think of something else that would get him to talk.

"I must say," Tau licked his fingers, "after this meal I would gladly join them. However, I still have my family here. I don't know if they would allow me such freedom."

"Not just that, but we would be abandoning our position here." Badru added. "We would make enemies of Pharaoh, our people, and our gods. We may be shunned by our families. The shame would be too much to bear."

"Too much to bear?" Nebit argued. "You should know most of all! You've been telling us about these battles and which gods have been defeated. Pharaoh is leading us all down a path of destruction."

"That is true," Badru admitted. "I have extensive education in the religious arts and have insight into these battles. Perhaps that is the very reason my decision is so much more difficult. Shall I turn my back on all of that? Would all of that work have been a waste?"

"I wouldn't say it was wasted," Yalu spoke up. "Without your wisdom we would still be stuck in that room."

Their conversation ended when one of the servant girls came up to them with a clay jug as long as her arm. They looked at her and she looked down shyly.

"Excuse me, I don't mean to interrupt... I just wanted to know if your water skins were empty. I could fill them up for you if you want."

Yalu answered, "Mine is empty. Here, fill it up." He held it open for her. As she poured from her jug, the others held theirs out as well.

She filled up Nebit's and then Badru's water skins. As she started pouring the last one she asked, "You're called Tau, are you not?"

He nodded and grunted.

She continued, "I heard that you're responsible for single-handedly fighting off twenty armed men when you rescued Yadid."

"Twenty!" Nebit scoffed, "I don't think the building could even..."

"Twenty is about right," Tau interrupted. "I'm not sure the exact number, of course. When you're in the heat of battle and enemies are all around you, you focus on staying alive. As I recall, the fight wasn't too difficult. Not that any soldier could pull through a fight like that, just not too difficult for me."

"Ah, I see," she smiled at him as she topped off his water skin.

Tau replied with a confident half-smile of his own. "The others heard the rumor and wondered if it were true. But I will be sure to set them straight."

After they finished the morning meal, they waited near the gate until Yadid arrived. He came with his arms full of Hebrew clothing and started distributing it.

"I have a robe for each of you!" he announced. "These are made of the finest wool from the sheep in Goshen, the land of our ancestors."

They put their gifts on as they received them.

"Will they get very hot in the afternoon sun?" Badru complained.

"I think these will slow my movements down," Nebit said skeptically as she put her robe on, "What happens if we get in a fight? Do I ask my opponent to wait while I take it off?"

"Mine's too tight, don't you have a bigger one?" Tau asked.

"Ha! Well, I think you all look more Hebrew already." Yadid laughed again and motioned for them to follow.

They followed him into a market and watched him barter for a while. After a short time, Yadid turned to them with a disagreeable look, "Let's go."

As they left Tau asked, "Why? I thought you needed barley."

"He is asking too much," Yadid said as he walked to the next grain trader. This one didn't agree to Yadid's offer either. Finally, at the fourth trader, he looked at them with a winning smile, "We've agreed. Can stay here and watch these sacks for me while I get some servants to help move them?"

"Aren't you afraid of something happening to you on the way back?" Tau asked with a mischievous smile. He crossed his arms and the way he held his head accentuated his crooked nose.

"I'll be alright. It's just a short walk." He waved his hand dismissively and laughed as he went back to the manor.

After he was out of sight, Nebit gasped: "Gahiji."

She pointed and everyone looked. There he was with an arrogant smile on his face. He stared right back at them.

"What is he doing here?" She asked.

Then he waved his arms behind him. A few moments later, a handful of Pharaoh's royal guards ran toward them. Hebrew men and women fled from the guard's path.

"We should run away, right?" Nebit asked frantically.

"If we run they will kill us for sure," Badru answered. "Our best chance is to comply and use well worded arguments."

The large spears surrounding them threatened to skewer anyone who tried to escape. Through the encircling spears, Gahiji casually walked forward with his smile. Then he folded his arms and said in his low and raspy voice, "I thought you'd be here among your slave friends. All this time I thought we were allies. But it feels good to bring criminals to justice."

Yalu growled, "You're the only criminal here! If justice is to be done it should be on you."

"Is that so? Then what should we call one who ambushes and murders fellow Egyptians out of revenge?" Gahiji looked Yalu straight in the eyes.

But Yalu could not answer. Nebit saw anger fill his eyes and his face. Then he looked down with a pained look of guilt. At this moment Nebit looked on Yalu with sympathy. She realized the full impact of what she did, despite all her reasons. She felt that she shared in his guilt.

"As I recall, you and your band entered property that does not belong to you with weapons drawn breathing threats of violence." Badru said.

Gahiji tilted his head to look at Badru. He carefully sized him up. Then he said, "We shall see how you are judged. Take their weapons."

Gahiji took the rolled-up flax rope from his shoulder and approached Yalu first. He looked at his face and smiled gleefully, but he ignored him and looked over his shoulder into the distance. He bound them all on their legs and tied them together with another length of rope.

Yadid finally returned with servants to carry the barley, and ran up to the soldiers shouting, "What is going on here? What have these poor people done to be arrested?"

"What do you care, Hebrew?" Gahiji retorted. "They are murderers and traitors. Let everyone here see and know that Pharaoh reigns everywhere in Egypt and that criminals will be punished." Then Gahiji led the guards and his prisoners away.

He took them to Pharaoh's palace. At the door to the main audience chamber, they saw a few nobles walk out and waited their turn to stand before Pharaoh. Gahiji led the guards and prisoners through the ornate double doors. Pharaoh sat on his throne wearing the red and white crown and frowned as he watched the parade.

Gahiji bowed and showed obeisance to Pharaoh. The guards poked the prisoners with spears, prompting them to bow as well. Then Gahiji stood up and introduced them: "Oh great Pharaoh! I bring before you traitors to Egypt. These lawbreakers have interfered with your plans and murdered my comrades."

"I remember these faces." Pharaoh looked at them with resentment. "Rashidi brought them to me to report on the Hebrew livestock. No doubt you lied to me. The consequences for your treachery are great indeed. Are there any words to be said in your defense?"

Before any of them could say anything a voice came from the back of the room: "I have some words to say, if it pleases you my Pharaoh."

They turned and looked. There was Sakakwi walking up to them. He looked over them with a smile of satisfaction. Then he gave a knowing nod to Gahiji, who returned it. Nebit felt the pain in her chest come back stronger than ever.

Pharaoh replied, "It does. Speak your words, priest of Ptah."

"Thank you, Pharaoh. There has been a great treachery inflicted upon you. But it was not by your servants bound before you." Sakakwi began with a tone of concern. "They were merely pawns under the thumb of the real Hebrew sympathizer. I feel compelled to bring this to your attention because I know the Kushite man, Badru who kneels before you. He is apprenticed to your chief magician! Few could be called a more loyal subject than he. Badru, and the others, have been unwittingly taken orders that contradict your own."

"Who is this sympathizer you speak of?" Pharaoh asked.

"None other than the wife of the overseer of your Hebrew slaves, Kasmut." Sakakwi said with a sly grin.

"You have evidence?" Pharaoh asked.

From within his dark robes Sakakwi produced a scrap of papyrus and held it high. Pharaoh gestured with his hand and Sakakwi brought it to him with a low and elegant bow. Pharaoh studied it carefully.

Nebit tried to hold back tears as she realized the utter defeat of all her hopes and aspirations. He killed her master. He killed and ruined Kasmut. Her eyes moved to Yalu, the last person left alive with whom she's confided in.

"Yes, I see." Pharaoh looked up. "Where is this woman now?"

"She was caught in the hailstorm yesterday and perished."

"Good. At least some measure of justice was given. A shame she could not stand trial before me." Pharaoh handed the papyrus back. "Now what do you suggest happen to them?"

"Obviously, they cannot go back to Rashidi." Sakakwi replied. "I would give them to a master who can ensure none of Kasmut's treachery remains in them."

"I agree. And I can think of no one better than you. If you'll accept them."

Glancing over to Nebit, Sakakwi grinned and said, "I do accept them."

Pharaoh gestured with his hand and the guards lowered their spears. Gahiji untied them. Then Badru and Tau walked over to Sakakwi with relief. Nebit, her head down and hand clutching her chest walked with sullen resignation.

But Yalu stood where he was. Then he looked up at Pharaoh. He said, "May I ask a question."

Pharaoh nodded, giving him permission. The others turned back to look at him, surprised.

"I have always believed that you were a god worthy to be worshipped like all the other gods of our land. However, Moses has come to you with a request that the Hebrew slaves go to worship their god and you eventually agreed to it. But why do you rescind your agreement and break your word?" Yalu said, shifting his weight nervously under Pharaoh's regal gaze.

Pharaoh rolled his eyes and heaved sigh.

"How foolish you are. Do you think that your understanding is greater than Pharaoh's? You are an insignificant foot-soldier. You know nothing of why I make my decisions. The Hebrews have been stuck in their old ways ever since they came here. They refuse to acknowledge my rightful place and deserve to be treated like the slaves they are. They are mine and will worship me like everyone else. ."

"What about the power of their god?!" Yalu insisted, "How long can we stand against such a powerful god?"

Pharaoh stood up from his throne and walked toward Yalu. His gold jewelry clinked together at each step. When he stood directly in front of Yalu, he raised his golden scepter and struck Yalu across the face. The blow sent Yalu sprawling on the floor. "Be silent!" Pharaoh commanded.

Yalu touched his hand at the round imprint the scepter had left on his cheek. One of his teeth knocked loose from the blow and he spat it onto the ground with his own blood. He looked up at Pharaoh, who looked down upon him fiercely.

Pharaoh continued, "We are at war! I will not be manipulated and defeated by this foreign god. But I can see Kasmut's treachery has not died with her. You will await public execution tomorrow when Ammon-Ra reaches the center of Nut so all my enemies can witness the fate of those who come against me. For a crime of your magnitude, I would consider throwing you to a pit of wooden spikes and let you die slowly as the crows and vultures pick at your flesh. However, if you renounce your evil deeds, pledge loyalty to me and worship me like good citizens of Egypt, then in mercy I will offer you beheading. But any claims you might have had to the reeds of paradise are now gone."

Unable to contain her tears or herself, Nebit ran back to Yalu and held him in her arms. She looked up at Pharaoh defiantly and said, "How could you do such a thing? He only asked a question?"

Pharaoh laughed, "Today must be cursed among days that I am questioned like this." Then he looked at her and said, "Because of your actions you'll share his fate."

"But," Sakakwi interjected. "Great Pharaoh I-"

Pharaoh cut him off, "I shall not tolerate such behavior in my presence. These two shall be punished for their crimes and that is my final word."

He flicked his wrist and turned back to them as he sat on his throne. The guards grabbed Yalu and Nebit and tied them up again. Badru and Tau stood dumb-founded. They wanted to speak out, but fear of losing the rescue stopped them.

As the guards took them, Nebit looked back at Sakakwi. He glared at her with an anger she knew all too well. There was nothing he could do to get her back now, and he knew it. All of his scheming to get her back had failed. She smiled at him which made him so angry he trembled.

Gahiji took the prisoners out of the palace, but while they were still inside the palace walls they arrived at a large pit dug at about two lengths of a man deep and five lengths wide and at least three times that long. Guards stationed at each corner watched the prisoners inside.

As they arrived, the closest guard lowered a rope down to the bottom. Some of the prisoners gathered around and asked if they were going to be released. The guard ignored their pleas. They stood on the edge as the guards untied them.

"Such a kind gesture of solidarity you showed should get a kind gesture in return," Gahiji said, looking at Nebit.

She turned to look at him with a puzzled expression.

"Why don't you go first?" He suddenly struck her lower back with his hand so forcefully that she lost her balance and fell over the edge. As Yalu watched her fall, with horror, he felt Gahiji's strike and soon came falling after her.

They looked up and saw Gahiji grinning down at them. Then he turned away and left them, laughing. When the ladder was raised the other prisoners went back to sitting down in the wedge of shade left by the lip of the pit. Nebit groaned and touched where Gahiji had hit her. Yalu nursed his aching mouth. And they sat there together, at the bottom of the pit.

Hoshea sat down at a wooden table inside his private room in his father's house. Sarah entered with a copper plate carrying some figs, dates, and a leftover leg of lamb preserved with salt. Eagerly anticipating his meal, he picked up the leg almost before she placed the plate on the table.

But just before he took his first bite, Yadid burst into the room followed closely by Lior. "They've been taken! The palace guards took them away!" Yadid shouted desperately.

Hoshea took his attention from his food to reply, "Look, just because the city guards arrested the men you drink and gamble with again doesn't mean you can come here and interrupt my meal."

Sarah rolled her eyes and started to leave.

"Not them. . . this time. Yalu, Nebit, Badru, and Tau!"

Yadid leaned his palms on the table next to Hoshea's food. Sarah stopped in the doorway when she heard Tau's name.

He continued, "Guards from the palace came while we were bartering for supplies at the market and took them. We have to do something!"

Lior interjected: "They could be executed by now. And if they're not, rescuing prisoners from Pharaoh's palace is too dangerous."

Hoshea thought for a moment, looking at Yadid and Rashidi's officer in turn. "Here is the way I understand the situation. When Yadid was kidnapped and we lost hope of mounting a rescue ourselves, they came to his rescue. Then, when Moses was under threat of violence, they came to his rescue as well. The Lord our god is using these people to help us. Do we not owe them?"

"That is all true. And I want to rescue Yalu and them just as much as Yadid," Lior said. "But is our debt to them so great that we must attempt such a risky venture?"

"Risky, yes," Hoshea put his meat down, "Because of me one of the attackers got away, the one that caused this wound. The responsibility is partly mine."

"I see you've already made up your mind," Lior gave a smile, "Alright, what do we do?"

"We gather the servants who know how to fight and ask for volunteers," Hoshea explained, "And then tonight we will breach the palace gate and go to the prison pit. If they are still alive, Pharaoh will likely keep them there. What do you say, are you with me?"

"No." Yadid said plainly and folded his arms.

Hoshea scowled. "What do you mean, 'no'? They rescued you. How can you say no?"

"I mean, if that ill-conceived notion you spoke of is your plan, then I want no part of it," Yadid said bluntly. "Storm the gate at night-time! Folly!"

"When do you suggest, then?" Hoshea picked up the leg of lamb again. "Night is the best time because have both surprise and concealment on our side. If we are to have any hope of success then we will need them both."

"Surprise is good and concealment is good, but having them will not give us victory." Yadid explained. "The palace wall is designed to withstand armies of attackers both in the day and in the night."

"Very well; I am a fool! The situation is hopeless," Hoshea admitted.

However, the corner of Yadid's mouth showed a wry smile. Hoshea stared at him and blurted out with a twitch on his eyebrow, "You haven't changed a bit since you were my teacher! Do you have a plan?"

"Indeed I do," Yadid replied. "I am delighted there are still a few things I have left to teach you. The number of guards in the palace is too many, if they know we're attacking then they will sound the alarm and tear us apart in moments."

"So we need a distraction?" Hoshea asked, and put down his food. "But we don't have anything that can distract an army of guards."

"You are very correct," Yadid replied. "But, as I have always taught you we must trust the Lord our god to provide the things we lack. Do you believe that Moses is truly the man sent to free us from Pharaoh?"

"You know I believe," Hoshea picked up his meat again. Then he thought for a moment and said, "Something that will distract an army of guards. . . locusts?"

"Yes, of course!" Yadid shouted. "While the guards are busy with the locusts, we have a chance to mount our rescue."

"Yes, I see," Hoshea dropped the leg of lamb on his plate and stood up with excitement. "An army of locusts brought by the Lord will battle the army of guards in the palace for us. That's brilliant!"

"What are you waiting for?" Yadid took a step toward the door, "We have preparations to make."

Yalu lay on the ground and groaned in pain. The agony in his mouth equaling the agony in his spirit.

Then a deep voice called to him, "Yalu."

It called again, "Yalu."

A ghostly man appeared before him.

"Father?" He lifted his head and asked in surprise, "Am I dead?"

"Yalu, my son."

"I... I... I'm sorry." Yalu started. Tears flowed down his face. "I'm sorry I wasn't there when you needed me. Because of me, you and mother and... my wife..."

"Remember what I always told you. Say what is right and-"

"Do what is right. I know. But I did what I thought was right and you still died!" Yalu said, feeling all mushed up inside. "And now it's happening again. I tried to do what I thought was right and now we're going to die for it."

"You mean Nebit?"

"I mean," Yalu said but hesitated. "Yes, Nebit. Maybe if I say the Hebrew God forced me against me will I can save her. Say that it wasn't my-"

"Not your fault?" The spirit asked with an irritated tone. "Doing the right thing was not your fault? You're my son. And you must face the world."

"But the world is full of those who wish evil on me," Yalu protested.

"Evil people do evil things. You can't change that. You will always be my beloved son. Say what is right and do what is right. Now get up and face them."

Yalu shook himself and opened his eyes. He was lying in the dirt, his head propped up on Nebit's lap. He looked up and saw that she was sitting down, leaning against the dirt wall of the prison pit, quietly sleeping.

He stared at her face for a moment and was surprised how peaceful she looked. After all that had happened to them she could sleep peacefully. He reached up with a dirty hand and stroked her cheek. She stirred and grasped his hand in hers and looked into his eyes and they held each other in their gazes.

Then Yalu's eyes filled with shame and he looked away. "I'm sorry," he said.

"Sorry? For what?"

"You're condemned! Both of us are. All because of me." Yalu sat up.

She looked indignantly at him. "Don't think you're so important, Yalu." She said.

He looked at her confused, not knowing how to respond.

She continued, "I made my own choices. What happens to me is my own doing. I'd rather face death with you than spend my life killing for that wretched man."

He looked up into her eyes and she looked down into his.

Then she told him, "I'm sorry."

"You? What for?"

"I shouldn't have told that bandit about you. I'm sorry for betraying your trust."

"I was angry and reacted too strongly. I was wrong to say betrayal," Yalu shook his head. Then he smiled, "Maybe just, learning to protect my trust."

Nebit's face softened and she gave a laugh. They smiled at each other.

Then they heard an odd noise in the air. Nebit sat up so she could listen to the sound better. The wind blew strongly and a great commotion among the guards stirred outside the pit. The sound, slowly but surely, grew louder and louder.

She asked, "What is that I hear in the wind? I've never heard anything like it before."

"You don't recognize that sound?" Yalu asked, an odd mix of bitterness and hope in his voice as he gazed skyward. "It is from an animal similar to one we see often, the desert grasshopper. My mother told me stories of them. How they bring entire kingdoms down to its knees."

"You don't mean. . ." A chill ran down her spine as she realized what he is talking about.

High overhead, they saw a dark cloud moving fast. Other prisoners noticed too, and began to panic. Cries and screams fill the air. Even some of the guards dropped their weapons and ran indoors for fear of this new plague. And then the swarm, a cloud of yellow and black, descended onto the city.

The locusts collected in the pit around Yalu and Nebit. They tried to brush them off their arms and heads, but for each one they moved another took its place. The locusts ate everything, even the clothes of the other prisoners, which only fueled their panic.

"These must have been brought by the Hebrew god," Yalu said. He observed, "But why are they eating their clothes, and not ours?"

Nebit looked down at herself and saw the woeful creatures walking on their gifts from Yadid, but making no attempt to eat them.

"Is it some blessing from their god?" Yalu wondered.

"I'll take any blessing we can get," Nebit said grimly. "I've heard of the voracious appetite of the locust. They won't eat us, will they?"

"No, I don't think-Ouch!" Yalu shouted. He hastily brushed off a locust and raised an arm showing a tender piece of skin where it bit him. Nebit and Yalu looked at each other fearfully.

Outside of the palace wall, Hoshea's stomach grumbled and he winced as he put a hand on it. He looked up and asked, "What do you see?"

No one answered.

He repeated himself more loudly.

Lior who was standing on his shoulders, peered over the top of the wall, looked down and asked Hoshea to repeat himself.

"What do you see?!" Hoshea demanded, almost yelling.

Finally understanding, Lior said "The prison pit is about fifty arm-lengths away from the wall. There are twelve guards and most are cowering."

"Perfect!" Hoshea grinned and looked at his right to an armed servant, then nodded.

Lior jumped down from Hoshea's shoulders. Then he took the rope and metal hook slung over his shoulder and tossed it over the wall. He pulled it tightly, but the hook didn't catch. After two more attempts, it finally could hold his weight as he pulled himself up. He looked at the three other men trying to attach their ropes to the wall as he did. When Lior had climbed to the top of the wall, two of the others had already started climbing their ropes. He waited for a few more seconds and then hurled himself over to the other side.

When he landed he crunched on a few locusts underneath his sandals, but once he recovered his balance, he drew his sling and a few stones. On his right, he saw a couple comrades join him on the other side. Luckily, the guards were all still busy with the locusts. Lior slung a rock at the closest guard and hit him square on the side of the head, laying him out flat.

By the time Hoshea landed on the other side of the wall, there were eleven other Hebrew fighters waiting for his command. He drew his sword and led the way to the prison pit. A group of six guards saw them approach and rushed to attack with their spears. More stones flew. Lior's stone hit one of the guards in the chest, causing him to stop and grasp his wound in pain. Another hit a guard, but the other rocks missed their mark. The four remaining guards charged into the line of sword-wielding Hebrews.

Each guard faced two Hebrew swordsmen in addition to the four slingers keeping their distance and looking for opportunities. Hoshea faced his guard and used his shield to deflect the thrusts from the spear. The guard used the back end of the spear as a staff to try and hit the opponent behind him. Then Hoshea bashed the tip of the spear with his shield causing the guard to lose his balance. The Hebrew behind him saw the opening and attacked the weapon itself, lodging his blade into the wooden shaft. With the weapon immobilized, Hoshea went in for the kill.

When Hoshea looked around at the other three guards, he was pleased to see them already on the ground. He motioned for them to follow him and they continued to the prison pit.

Before they arrived at the edge of the pit, the other eight guards came rushing at them. One of them wielded a strange and menacing weapon that looked like a khopesh, only bigger. He charged forward and held it in both hands.

Hoshea looked around at the prison pit and ordered his squad to run along its edge. The guards

followed about fifty arm-lengths away. As soon as they
turned the corner, Hoshea ordered his slingers to
attack. Lior instantly launched a rocks and one hit the
guard in front, causing him to stumble, lose his balance,
and fall into the pit. A few other guards were knocked
off the wall before the first guard met the Hebrew
swordsmen. Hoshea ordered them to form a line, and
the swordsmen rushed up to meet the spear-wielding
guards to protect their slingers.

Hoshea stood behind the slingers and watched
from there. Suddenly he felt something on his
shoulder. Startled, he whirled his head around with his
sword at the attack. But the enemy he saw was just a
locust. Breathing a sigh of relief, he brushed it off and
it flew away.

Then out of the corner of his eye he saw
movement. When he turned around, he saw the man
with the giant khopesh rushing toward his squad from
behind. He nudged Lior with his elbow and shouted,
"The rear!" Lior whirled around and saw the leader
who had flanked them. In a second, he hurled another
stone from his sling. But Lior frowned when a flying
locust took the rock, so Hoshea readied his sword and
shield.

The downward slash was so forceful that it left
a deep incision down the length of Hoshea's shield and
nearly threw him off-balance. But Hoshea steadied
himself for the second attack. The leader slashed
sideways with just as much force as before, but Hoshea
managed to deflect it. Hoshea leaned forward and
slashed at his opponent's open arm, causing a sharp cry
of pain. When he finally brought his weapon around
again, Hoshea had backed away and he hit only air.

All the prisoners in the pit noticed the battle
now. Many of them were cheering. Hoshea took a
moment to look at them before he re-engaged the
leader, and saw Yalu and Nebit, who easily stood with

their Hebrew robes. With renewed vigor, he focused back on the fight in time to see his attacker preparing another sideways slash.

Hoshea came in again after the attack and widened the wound he had inflicted earlier. The man cried in pain again, but this time realized his mistake. Hoshea frowned slightly as he changed battle stance. He held his weapon straight up with the handle level with his chest on the right side, and stepped back with his right foot. Hoshea raised an eyebrow and prepared a defensive stance with his shield in front of him. The leader stepped back again, but with his left foot this time and brought his weapon backwards. Hoshea saw the man's gut contort and stretch to its limit.

Then the leader released a furious cry and leapt forward, swinging his weapon in a sideways motion again. Hoshea brought up his shield, expecting to deflect the blow as before. But this time the attack knocked Hoshea back with surprising force. He tried to recover quickly to riposte, but saw that the leader had turned completely and was preparing to come around again. Without enough time to counter, Hoshea took a deep breath and prepared for the next blow.

It landed, and forced him back another step. The leader kept spinning and forced Hoshea to keep retreating. On the fourth attack, the weapon finally sliced through the shield, breaking the straps, and it fell to the ground, useless. The shock hurled Hoshea back even further, and he fell to the ground next to the broken shield, and looked up toward his attacker.

The impact reminded Hoshea instantly of the wound he had gotten at Aaron's estate. Locusts squirmed and hopped around him. The leader made another spin before he realized that Hoshea had fallen. He grinned and readied a downward slice meant to end his helpless foe.

As the leader brought his blade down, Lior stood over Hoshea and intercepted it with his own. Lior roared as he pushed the leader's large sword away. The leader stepped back to catch his balance. He stepped back again to block a flurry of slashes from Lior. Advancing, Lior saw the great effort it took to move that large blade around. He swung his sword at him from every side.

Finally, the leader was too slow to block from one side and was punished with a large cut on his right arm. Then he got a matching cut on his left arm. The leader tried a desperate attempt to strike Lior with a sideways slash. Lior, seeing it coming, ducked underneath the strike. Then he stood up as the man tried to bring the sword back to block but not in time. Lior stabbed him through the chest and he fell to the ground.

Lior turned to Hoshea to offer a hand but he was already standing.

Turning his attention next to his squad, Hoshea saw about half of the guards still fighting. He turned to the pit and called, "Yalu, Nebit, Badru, Tau are you here?"

Yalu and Nebit stepped forward among the crowd of fifty or so prisoners and stood near the corner. He lowered a rope. Nebit pushed Yalu to go up first and followed after him. About then the Hebrew fighters finished the last of the prison guards.

"Glad to see that you're still all alive!" Hoshea shouted so they could hear him over the buzzing of the locusts. "Where is Badru and Tau?"

"They were let go," Yalu yelled back.

"Let go?" Hoshea shouted with surprise. "Why them and not you?"

Before Yalu could answer Lior grabbed Hoshea's shoulder, "We're running out of time! Look, the other prisoners are trying to escape too. What should we do?"

Hoshea looked down at the prisoners desperately clinging to the rope for their freedom. He turned to Lior and said, "Let them go. They'll be less likely to talk about our rescue."

He led the Hebrew fighters with Yalu and Nebit to the high palace wall. Locusts piled up against it like sand in a windstorm.

Yalu climbed up after Lior while Nebit climbed on another rope right next to it. Once Yalu got up he straddled the wall and looked out over the city. It was a terrifying sight. The entire city was engulfed in the plague as far as his eye could see.

Coming up to the top next, Nebit straddled wall behind him. He turned and looked at her. Dirt from the pit was on her face. She gazed into his eyes. And with locusts flying about them, they embraced on the wall. They felt warmth as they pressed their cheeks against one another for a moment that felt like eternity. When they pulled back they looked into each other's eyes and truly smiled.

"Flesh and fire," Yalu mumbled as he landed on the other side to meet the architect of their rescue.

"Good to see you alive," Yadid greeted them with a smile. Then he asked, "Where are Badru and Tau? They weren't..."

"They're fine. I'll explain later." Yalu answered the unfinished question.

Yadid nodded and before the former prisoners could give their rescuers proper thanks, he said, "Let's hurry. It is best to be gone when more of the palace guards come."

Hoshea led them through the winding streets of the locust-infested city. Many people walked around naked except for leather or fur because the locusts had already eaten the clothes. In fact, they were the only people on the streets with clothes on.

"It's amazing that the locusts aren't eating these robes you gave us," Nebit shouted and rubbed the woolen fabric between her fingers. "Is this some divine protection?"

"Divine protection?" Yadid looked back toward her as he ran. "Egyptian clothes are made from flax. These are wool. Maybe these locusts don't have a taste for it."

They finally arrived at the outskirts of the city again. As they did, they felt a shift in the winds. Stopping to wonder what was happening, they saw the direction of the locust swarm change back to where they had come from, the East. The wind grew stronger, and soon the bulk of the locusts were caught up in it. The terrible sound they made started to dissipate and everyone breathed a sigh of relief.

"Where are they all going?" Yalu asked as he looked about as they slow to a walk. "Do they obey the command of the wind?"

"They obey the command of our god," Yadid answered as he tried to catch his breath. "Moses prayed to our god to bring them here and persuade Pharaoh to grant his request. I guess Pharaoh agreed, so our god sends them away."

"Who is this god who can command all manner of things?" Yalu demanded. "During the festival to Anuket, we already heard from the head priest of Osiris that the harvest this season will be bountiful. Yet, your god has usurped the will of Osiris and brought them anyway."

Hoshea replied as they neared the home of Nun, "I'm sure my father would be glad to tell you the stories of our god. I've heard them since I was a child, so he hasn't told anyone in a long time."

When they arrived at the gate, Hoshea stopped and turned to them with a concerned look. He whispered, "That reminds me… May I ask you all for a favor?"

Everyone nodded in agreement.

"Please do not tell my father what we did. He doesn't even know that you were gone, so if he asks about anything, just say we were out escorting Yadid to trade for supplies."

From the other side of the gate they heard a voice:

"Yes, just tell that gullible old fool anything." Hoshea winced as Nun came into view from around the corner. "You don't really think you can keep secrets from me, do you? And Yadid, I am disappointed to see that you're involved in this as well. I trust you with the lives and wealth of my family. However, it is good to see that your rescuers have returned."

He gave Yalu and Nebit a second look when he saw them. Shaking his head he said, "Except for the first time you came to me, you've always been battered and bruised. You've sure kept my physician busy lately."

"I thank you for your hospitality," Yalu said and bowed to him.

Nebit bowed as well.

"It is the least I can do with how much you have helped my servants. But we must take care of your wounds. Sarah will take you," he motioned with his hand and she emerged from behind the wall.

"Traitor!" Hoshea pointed an accusing finger at her.

She looked at him with a knowing smile, but said "Come with me. I'm sure you're also very hungry. Since Moses gave us warning about the locusts we locked all our food away and it is very safe."

They started towards the manor, but Nun grabbed Hoshea by the shoulder.

"You and Lior will help peel onions for tonight's meal."

"Me too?" Lior asked.

Nun glared at Lior, "I tasked you to keep my son out of harm's way."

"And here he is unharmed!"

Nun continued his glare and Lior backed down.

Hoshea cringed as he watched the others head off to eat, "I should have finished my salted leg of lamb this morning."

Chapter 15

Fire danced in the stone pit, creating shadows on the stone wall and across Badru's face. He stared intently at it, deep in thought. The flames of thought in his mind flickered from one idea to another but all the time burned from a single ember. The words from Yalu haunted him: "Say what is right and do what is right."

He shook his head in repulsion. But what choice did he have now? The fate of the Hebrews had already been sealed by the plans of Pharaoh and Sakakwi. All that waited was the toil of bringing them about.

"Can we do something?" Tau asked from behind him. He sounded conflicted.

"Their destiny has already been sealed, my friend." Badru said with resignation. Tau lowered his head in discouragement.

Footsteps echoed from the passage entering the room and Badru turned his head to see the man he had been expecting. He sat on the couch of water-cow leather next to Badru and stared at the fire with him for a while. Tau looked at him for a good long while where he leaned against the cold stone wall. Finally, Sakakwi broke the silence.

"We shall continue with the plan. Although I'm grieved at the loss of Nebit. Did you know who she really was?"

Badru turned his head and gave an inquisitive look: "She was one of your servants once, yes?"

"Not just one of my servants. She was one of the best assassins in Egypt. She could get into anywhere and kill anybody. I thought I could somehow get her out of the prison pit, but there was nothing left of her."

"What do you mean? Did not the locusts have their fill of our former companions?" Badru asked.

"I went there myself to look for her," Sakakwi clenched his fists. "Not even a strap of leather or a dagger was left behind. I know not how, but she escaped. Seems both you and I are tangled in this web of betrayals."

Upon receiving a confused look from Badru he explained: "It all started with that Hebrew traitor Mutmose, the one they call Moses. It was I who hired the small band of men loyal to Pharaoh to discourage the antics of the Hebrew slaves. But I discovered the slaughter of these innocent Egyptians at the hand of those traitors. Gahiji proved a valuable tool to capture them and bring her back to me. But now I'm robbed of that, too!"

Badru looked back at the fire as it swerved from left to right and back again. He tried to mask the hope for his friends that lifted his spirit.

"I'll replenish my men. We will go door to door in the Hebrew district to find them if we must. I will not be defeated!" Sakakwi spoke with a determination that unnerved the two of them.

One of the logs cracked and fell, causing an explosion of ash in the pit.

Badru objected, "But do you not realize that the real battle is a heavenly one and not an earthly one? This Hebrew god has engaged our gods in battle and is winning!"

Sakakwi turned to him and put a hand around his shoulder, "This time the priesthoods of Ammon-Ra and Apis are joining the effort. We will unite to ensure the elimination of this Hebrew god and force the Hebrew slaves to worship Pharaoh. You know how

important an event like this is? The three great
priesthoods of our city have never embarked on a joint
venture in the history of Egypt, until now. With the
combined power of Ptah and Apis with Ammon-Ra
leading us, the Hebrew god will fall like dried up tree in
the sand."

Badru pressed, "How can you be so sure?"

Sakakwi tilted his head back and laughed,
"Badru, have more faith in our gods! Take my word for
it. Even if this Hebrew god defeats a few of our minor
gods, what defeat is that? All of that is meant to test
your faith. As followers of Ptah, we must be resolved
and steadfast in our dedication. Know for certain that
our gods will prevail."

Badru took a breath intending to speak, but
released it in a sigh instead. The dancing fire played
with shadows along his face as he studied the man
sitting beside him. Finally he said "I wish had your
faith. Perhaps you are right and I have faltered. What is
it that you want us to do?"

"You have seen their neighborhoods and their
land. You know their culture and their ways more than
any of us." He looked at Badru in the eye and they
locked stares. "But best of all, you are trusted among
them. You can infiltrate and influence them in a way
that nobody else can. In fact, this is the method that
the three head priests agreed upon. Yes Badru, your
name was on the lips of the head priests! Does that not
excite you?"

"I… I do not know what to say." Badru broke
the stare and looked back at the fire. He truly did not
know how to feel about that either. "So many things
have happened. My emotions are like a sandstorm,
scratching and tearing at my heart. It is hard to reason
right now."

"I understand. We will give you some time to
recover your mind. You will need it for the work to

come." He rose and started to leave. "Do not lose heart nor lose hope in our gods. You will see their victory in the end." Then he disappeared through the hallway.

After he left, Tau said, "Maybe Yalu and Nebit escaped the pit then."

"I do not see how," Badru replied. "The prison has high walls and many guards. But enough of this. I ought to go home. I am sure there are things that need handling."

Tau decided to join him, and they left the temple of Ptah together. As they walked, he asked, "How well did your daughters make it through those sores from the Hebrew god?"

"As best as can be expected," Badru grimaced. "Behati told me there was a lot of crying and it was hard to handle the two girls. But she seemed to manage. How about your son?"

Tau told him about how he performed the treatment on Kesi and Ebo. Badru looked impressed. Afterwards, Tau said, "I think they both recovered well too. Are things going better with Behati?"

Badru heaved a sigh, "No. In fact, things are worse. She accused me that I don't care about the family! How can she say something like that? Of course, I care about the family. Despite explaining everything clearly, she still holds that view. I do not understand."

"Have you asked her why she thinks that way?"

"Every time!" Badru replies. "Then I tell her why she is wrong. But she does not seem to follow logic."

"What about if you said something to make her laugh?" He offered.

"Behati is always so serious," Badru answered. "I do not think any such thing would help."

"Does she laugh with the girls?"

"Well," Badru looked up in thought. "Yes, she does. Hmm…"

They reached the point where the parted to go back to their homes, and they said their goodbyes.

The next day, Badru sat across from Behati eating breakfast with their two daughters. The early morning sunlight eagerly rushed into the room from the open windows. Servants walked about bringing food and doing their business. Badru felt completely frustrated.

"How could you waste all of those slaves, sending them to the temple?" She asked.

Badru raised his lip, feeling hot in anger. He replied, "The temple asked for help and I gave it! And moving things around in our storehouses is not a waste? It defies logic!"

"The place is a mess!" Behati defended. "How can we find anything if it is not reorganized?"

Just then a servant came and told Badru someone was calling at the front door. Badru left Behati's question unanswered and went to the waiting room where Sekakwi stood.

"Come," he beckoned. "Today we attend a meeting between Pharaoh and the head priests. Get yourself ready, Badru."

Badru nodded and left to gather his things. As he passed by, Amahl called to him, "Daddy, are you leaving now?"

He stopped and walked over to her. Crouching down between Amahl and Omphil, he put his hands on their shoulders and said, "Today I attend a meeting between Pharaoh and the head priests of Ptah, Apis, and Ammon-ra."

Amahl told him enthusiastically, "I finished studying those words you wrote down for me. Creator Ptah."

"You did?" He asked.

Bahati added with crossed arms, "She saw them written down at the temple this morning. She pointed them out and said what they meant."

"Very good! I'll have to write down some more for you to learn."

He kissed her on the cheek. Then he turned and kissed his other daughter on the check. Suddenly, while looking at his daughters, he was reminded of Tau and his offered advice. At first, he dismissed it. But then he thought to give it a try.

He looked over at Bahati and said, "If she keeps learning like this she'll soon be reading and writing better than me."

From within her serious expression and folded arms, a small and solitary laugh came out. A little smile appeared on her lips. He smiled back. Then he stood up, waved goodbye to them, and left the house with Sakakwi.

En route to the palace, Sakakwi briefed Badru: "I need not remind you how important this meeting is. They will discuss their plans and may have questions for us. I assume you know the proper etiquette when in the presence of Pharaoh, yes?"

Badru nodded. Then his face flashed with concern, "There will not be any complication due to my recent presence in front of Pharaoh, will there?"

"Do not fear. Pharaoh has been informed of your involvement and understands your reasons."

"I see," Badru's concern diminished only slightly.

They passed through the familiar gates to the palace and traversed the halls until they reached the waiting chamber. About thirty men and women lounged in the chamber and talked amongst themselves discreetly in three distinct groups.

Sakakwi took Badru to the group with the eye of Ptah embroidered on their robes. As they walked, Badru saw that some from the other groups looked at him and murmured. One group had the Apis bull embroidered on their robes, and the third group, the sunrise.

Badru recognized a high priest he had faced so long ago, a withered old man, who watched him approach, pleased with the attention from the other priesthoods. Sakakwi presented Badru, and they both bowed respectfully. The high priest declared, "So this is the young man I've heard about. So wise and cunning at his age. You shall serve us well in the days ahead."

Glancing toward the Apis priests, Badru saw them scowling. He looked back with a pleased expression on his face. Then he looked at everyone, "It is time."

The three high priests who led their respective temples approached the guards to Pharaoh's audience chamber and they opened the doors. Badru proceeded into the chamber near the back with Sakakwi. The guards shut the doors behind them. All of them bowed to the ground to offer obeisance to Pharaoh, who sat tall and regal on his throne.

While still lying prostrate, the highest priest announced, "Oh great Pharaoh, head priest of the goddess Mayet, ruler of upper and lower Egypt, we come to you at your call. What do you wish of us?"

Pharaoh stated in a loud clear voice, "The problem facing our great nation of Egypt is the Hebrew god, and Moses, his messenger. He must be dealt with. I ask for your council on how to proceed. The three high priests may stand and answer."

The three at the head of each group stood at Pharaoh's command. The high priest of Apis was the first to respond. She stood tall and slender with a grim expression on her face. Next was the head priest of

Ammon-ra. He flipped back the hood of his robes and moved a lock of wig hair from his face. Finally, a couple assistants help the ancient high priest of Ptah to stand. His staff hit the floor a few times as he steadied himself, and then took a step forward.

The head priests said, "My god Pharaoh, we three have discussed this at length. There were several options open to us."

"They have done us the most serious insult. The Apis bull lies dead ahead of his appointed sacrificial time. We could round up that Moses and his entire family for a public execution. This man Moses is a murderer and we want to see justice done."

"Very dramatic. We do not recommend that approach as it may kindle a riot among your slaves."

"But I recommended a more subtle and devious method. We poison the Hebrews from the inside. A god's power resides in the worship he receives, and this Hebrew god has a lot of worshippers. Because of their worship, the god tries to take them out of our land so he can have them for himself. He knows if they start worshipping you and our other gods that his power will diminish.

"So we spread discontent among the worshippers. We plant discord that creates a yearning for them to leave this foreign god and worship the gods of civilized people. The more people fall away from this god, the weaker he becomes and the easier it will be to defeat him."

Pharaoh leaned forward and said, "So we will demoralize the Hebrew slaves and dissuade them from their folly of following their uncultured and uncivilized god by infiltrating them and influencing them from within. Once they start to worship the truly powerful gods Apis, Ptah, and Ammon-Ra, they shall be troublesome no longer."

"My god, Pharaoh, is wise indeed," the head priest of Ammon-Ra stated pompously. "Does he have any questions or additional commands for his servants?"

After thinking for a moment he commanded, "Tell me about the infiltration."

He lifted up his head and answered, "One of our own has been immersed in the Hebrew people for some time and has learned their ways and customs. In fact, this is the same man who recently appeared before Pharaoh as a criminal."

Badru panicked a moment and hissed in a breath when he heard this. But when his Sakakwi's hand rested at his back, he relaxed.

"Bring this man forward," Pharaoh commanded. The high priest turned his head to the back of the room and looked for Badru. Everyone else looked back at him as well, and Badru felt his face flush.

Steeling his nerves, he stood up and approached Pharaoh. When he reached the row of high priests he stopped and bowed down low to the ground and said "Here I am, my god Pharaoh."

"I must admit that I was almost fooled by your actions," Pharaoh confessed with candor. "I can see why the priesthood would choose a devious man such as you for this critical task. May you go with the blessings of the gods."

"Thank you, my god Pharaoh," Badru answered. Pharaoh motioned for Badru to leave, and continued to talk with the high priests about the plan. Sakakwi welcomed Badru back with a smile and nod of approval. Pharaoh and the high priests discussed the plans until the sun reached the middle of the sky, at which point they finally took a recess.

After they exited the chamber, Sakakwi said to Badru, "Tell me, friend, what is it like? One day you appear before Pharaoh as a criminal and the next you are praised by him. You are surely in good favor with the great Ptah!"

"Favor, is it? But if something goes wrong then Pharaoh and the head priests will lay the blame on my shoulders." Badru told him.

"If you keep saying things like that, something is bound to go wrong. I do not understand why you have been asking such questions of late. You truly have been given a unique opportunity to show yourself to our god Pharaoh. If I could kill enough of the Hebrew slaves to wear your robes..." he sighed jealously.

"It is just. . ." Badru shook his head, "my mind has been terribly restless. I could not sleep until very late last night. Perhaps you are right."

"Of course, I am right" he laughed and put his arm around Badru. "Come, let us have our mid-day meal."

They walked through the stone hallways and entered a large chamber with three long tables made of wood. Food sat on the tables, being eaten by the various priests and religious figures.

"As expected," Badru commented. "Each temple is isolated to itself."

When they entered, one of Ptah's priests waved for them to approach. She wore a sleeveless robe embroidered with the eye.

"Hello Sakakwi. It is good to see you again," she said dryly. "The eye commands you to begin preparations immediately. You know what must be done?"

"Yes I do mistress of the eye," Sakakwi bowed to her, "We will do as the eye wills."

As they left he chuckled to himself and whispered to Badru, "So much for eating palace food today."

"I wasn't hungry anyway," Badru mused, "so what of the preparations we need to make?"

"I have a contingent of young priests in my charge," he explained as they left the palace and walked to the temple of Ptah. "You are to teach them everything you've learned about the Hebrews. What are their customs? What do they like to eat? How do they worship their god? Tau is already with them."

"I see," Badru nodded his head. "So they learn how to be Hebrew."

"Precisely!" Sakakwi raised a finger. "Then we assign roles and tasks to everyone. We will train them to subvert the heathen Hebrews."

He took Badru into the now familiar underground passageways of the temple. Coming from the hot and bright city into the cold dark of the tunnels took some small adjustment. They wound through the tunnels as if it were a maze and ended up in a huge stone room. Badru guessed the ceiling to be about the height of three men standing on each other's shoulders.

A dull roar came from the multitude of men and women kneeling before a statue of Ptah on the other end. They chanted and worshipped. Tau was talking with a handful of priests near the back.

Sakakwi led Badru down a worn path on the right side of the room onto a stone platform where the statue stood. The multitude stopped their worship as they noticed the two, and watched. Torches on the walls and pillars flickered with a devious delight as they held back the darkness.

Sakakwi stepped to the middle of the platform with Badru behind his right shoulder. Raising his arms high in the air, he shouted with a loud echo, "My brothers, the time of our revenge against the Hebrew god is drawing near. With our blessing from Pharaoh, we will crush their rebellious spirit and put an end to their schemes." Cheers erupted in their vindictive passion.

"I am pleased to show you one of us has been among the Hebrews and studied their ways. He is none other than the foremost apprentice to the great magician Haji. His name is Badru," Sakakwi stepped aside and raised his arm to introduce Badru. "With his help, all of you will be as a vexing curse from Sekhemet to plague the Hebrews. By the combined power of Apis the Bull, Ptah the Creator, and Ammon-Ra the ruler of all and lord of the sun, we shall be victorious against this barbarian god who dares to threaten our way of life."

The crowd cheered again and Sakakwi held his hands high up into the air and looked around at everyone. He glanced back at Badru, who forced a smile at him and applauded like the others.

He continued to speak to the crowd but Badru didn't pay attention. He instead studied the crowd and their enthusiastic responses to Sakakwi's statements. People raised their clenched fists high into the air and shouted passionate agreement whenever he paused.

Then he noticed something strange. At first he thought it was just a trick of the light. But then he realized that the entire room was getting darker. He stared at one of the torches and the flame looked half the size it was when he had entered. The flame slowly diminished as he continued to stare at it. As it started to die, he felt a chill come over him. The feeling entered into the center of his body, and he felt anxious, his heart in his throat.

Others began to notice too. Sakakwi ceased his talking, and no sound could be heard. Badru backed away from the edge of the platform slowly. A cold and hard object touched his back and he felt chills run down his spine. He whirled around to see the statue of

Ptah looking down at him with an oblivious smile. Ptah's beard protruded toward him arrogantly.

With deadly silence, the last light from the torches finally snuffed out. The room was completely dark; nobody could see anything. Badru felt the coldness of the underground become ice to his skin. The deafening silence lasted for a few seconds, and then a startling scream broke it. Then other screams joined it, and the room filled with the terrible, dreadful, and unbearable sound. Badru stood paralyzed as he gazed into the cold darkness, and shivered.

Nebit sat in the shade staring blankly at the stone board. It was carved with holes arranged in four rows by eight columns, about two knuckles deep, which contained various kernels of grain. Hoshea sat on the other side. He yawned out of boredom. The sounds of people going about their business filled the air. A hot breeze hit her face and she sighed hopelessly.

"There is no move I can make!" she protested as she tugged stray hair into place.

"There are at least three!" Yadid shouted from inside a nearby storage room. He continued to stack the sacks of grain on the shelves without interruption.

"Try looking at your house," Yalu offered as he peeked over her shoulder.

"Don't give her any hints!" Yadid scolded. "She needs to learn by herself. Otherwise she won't ever be able to play on her own."

Yalu held up his hands in surrender and chuckled.

Taking Yalu's advice, out of defiance of Yadid's warning, she looked to the fifth hole from the left in the front row. At least half of her holes were empty. The other half contained one or two kernels of grain, but the fifth hole had seven. Most of her kernels had been captured by Hoshea and lay in obscenely large piles in his holes.

As she continued studying the board, Yadid exited the storeroom and glanced at the game again.

"You still haven't figured it out?"

She glanced up with a look to slit his throat but he paid it no mind.

"It's not that hard. I told you about this move almost right before we started playing."

"Well I don't see it!" She blurted out with frustration, "There are so many rules! And I don't even know what I'm supposed to be doing. Should I move the grain from this hole to that hole?"

"It is very simple," Yadid calmly explained. "Take the kernels from your house over here…" He pointed to the fifth hole on her left. "Then you sow them like this." He pointed to each hole in sequence starting on the right. "And then you can capture my kernels here. See, it isn't difficult."

She shook her head as he made the moves for her.

"I'm done!" Nebit stood up. She suppressed an urge to kick the board figuring it would probably hurt her foot more than it. Then she pointed an accusing finger at Yalu, "It's all your fault for tangling me into this Bao mess. It has no purpose or value. Games like this are just a waste of time."

"Bao is an intellectual game and stimulates the mind," Yadid said as he replaced the kernels into the holes.

Nebit rolled her eyes and stomped to look out the window with her arms folded.

Yadid gestured for Yalu to sit down opposite Hoshea.

Sitting down on the mat he said "I was surprised to learn you have a Bao board here. And you seem to be quite good at it, for a foreigner."

Hoshea laid his head in a hand as he decided how he would open the game. He said, "At the behest of my father, Yadid makes me play. I suppose I've got a decent skill at it."

"Are you sure we can't leave the manor?" Nebit asked as she gazed skyward and longed for freedom. "It's so boring here; there is nothing to do. I'm sure it is safe to go out by now. It's already been two days since you rescued us."

"ALREADY two days?! You mean ONLY two days. I have no doubt every soldier loyal to Pharaoh is still looking for you three." Yadid said as he scooped up the grain from one of the holes and distributed them in others.

"How about we train with our blades in the courtyard?" Nebit offered.

Hoshea lit up and looked at her. He replied, "That sounds like a great idea. Let's go!"

"But!" Yalu looked up with shock, "But we just started a game. He beat me last time, so I need to get revenge."

"Good idea. Hoshea and I can use the Bao board as our practice dummy." Nebit laughed.

Hoshea took a step forward as Yadid let loose a cry and cradled the board as a mother would her child.

The three left a disappointed Yadid and exited the animal-hide covering. Hoshea stood in the middle of the main courtyard holding his bronze sword. He looked at Yalu and said, "Show me how I could defend that strike the Egyptian attacker made in Aaron's manor."

Yalu told him how he watched Gahiji's movements and predicted what he was going to do. Then Nebit explained the basics of how to fight with a weapon in each hand. But Hoshea wanted to see it in action, so they put Nebit in Gahiji's place and replaced her daggers with some wooden practice swords.

Lior laughed first at Nebit and then Yalu fell down on the ground while trying to recreate the fight. From where he stood guard at the gate he could see everything. Yalu gave him a dirty look but said nothing.

After a few minutes, Nun entered the yard by the main gate straight ahead of them. Once they saw him, they stopped practicing and approached him.

Hoshea asked, "How was the meeting? What is the news from Moses?"

Nun looked at them casually, "Moses said that the darkness over the Egyptians will be lifted after tomorrow when the sun comes out in the morning. Some of the other elders were discussing the logistics to move all the food we stored if Pharaoh does decide to let us go, but I won't bore you with those details."

Then he looked at Hoshea harshly, "And don't waste all your time sparring. When you become head of the household you will need to use your head more than your sword. One more thing, Moses did inquire about the wound inflicted on your thigh. I told him that you've been mending quickly from the adept hands of our physician."

"Come now, the wound wasn't that bad." Hoshea folded his arms. "But I'd give most of the credit to the Lord our God."

"How odd, Moses said the same thing." Nun contorted his face as though in thought, "Your similarities must be why he asked me to bring you to the next meeting."

"Moses wants me at the next meeting?!" Hoshea exclaimed with pleasant surprise.

"Why, yes. Didn't I mention that before? My old age must be catching up to me."

Nun started back to the house but Yalu spoke up, "Sir. There's something I've been meaning to ask you. It's a decision that's been stalking us for a while now. Hoshea mentioned we might be able to join your household and what you'd ask of us. With all the trouble we seem to be in, I wanted to know if you would allow it and if you require anything of us."

Nun gave him a thoughtful look. He glanced at Nebit who seemed interested in the answer too.

"I will allow it. Ever since I first laid eyes on you I had a good feeling about you. As for what I would ask of you, I assume you are already circumcised as is the custom here. Yes?"

Yalu nodded.

"Then nothing else is required. If you make that decision then I'm sure we will find a good use for you."

"The way you ate the food and slept here I thought you were a part of the household already," Lior quipped.

Nun walked back to the house, but before he entered he shouted back, "Hoshea, go to Yadid for more teaching."

"He will probably just make me play another game of Bao with him." Hoshea shook his head. "It seems that is all we've been doing lately."

Nun turned back to him, "Yes play some Bao with Yadid. It's good for your mind and will do you better than swinging your sword around." He turned to Yalu and said, "Every year we hold a Bao tournament and Yadid usually does very well."

Then he entered the house and shut the solid wooden door behind him.

Hoshea looked at the sword in his right hand and sighed loudly. Looking at Nebit, he shrugged, and nodded with disappointment. Then he walked over to the storehouse and sat down on the reed mat in front of a beaming Yadid.

Badru lay on his reed mat gazing wearily into the darkness. Thirst parched his dry throat. He reached out on the left-hand side of his mat with a shaky hand. He couldn't see it, but he knew he left a water skin there. After a couple tries, he found it and brought it to his lips for a sip. To his dismay, it was empty and he remembered he had drank the last drops of it some time ago. He heard another scream echo from the tunnels, a common occurrence now.

"Badru! Badru, are you there?" A scared voice called out in the darkness.

"Yes, Sakakwi, I am here," Badru answered, "Did you dream again?"

He caught his breath and answered. "I keep seeing myself walking through tunnels with no light. Even though I couldn't see, I knew the corpses of my fellow priests were under my feet. I tried to find my way out, but could not. I felt lost and hopeless. Oh, how long will this cursed darkness last?"

"I envy you," Badru put down his water skin. "I cannot even sleep to dream. I am so tired and weary, yet this cold darkness gives me no rest. I have prayed to Ammon-Ra for light as you suggested, but I receive nothing. Is this really his punishment?"

"Only Ammon-Ra has the power over light and darkness to do something as great as this. But why is he punishing us? We were doing his will by planning against the Hebrew slaves when the punishment came upon us." He paused and thought for a moment.

"Perhaps he aims to test our resolve. Yes. . ." For the first time since the darkness had begun, he sounded hopeful. "Ammon-Ra wants to know how dedicated we are to his purpose. I see now: we must endure this test and so be declared worthy for his task."

"I cannot even set off a spark using my flint and steel," Badru recalled. "Why would Ammon-Ra test us in such a harsh way when faced with a hard battle against the Hebrew god? Should he not provide us a blessing of favor so we can be better able to carry out this task?"

"But does a warrior not test his weapon rigorously before going into battle?" Sakakwi leaned up on his elbows. "He must know that his weapon will not break when the heat of battle roars like an inferno."

"Are we not already in battle?" Badru wondered aloud, "How does testing your weapon while you are in the middle of fighting your opponent help?"

"This is why you are so easily deceived," Sakakwi snapped as he sat up. "We are in a respite before the final battle. Ammon-Ra, Ptah, and Apis gather their strength and this must be part of it. If it is not a test then what do you say it is?" Sakakwi asked, to no reply. "I know what you're thinking. But the foreign god can't influence the temple of Ptah. He would not allow such desecration to occur. The only possibility is the gods are inflicting this themselves and the only reason is to test us."

"As you say," Badru resigned the argument. He took a breath and released it.

"Badru? Sakakwi?" They heard Tau's voice call out.

Both of them eagerly called and Tau was able to stumble over to where they lay. He crouched down nearby them. They offered him their empty water skins. He used his hand to comb through the blackness until he found someone's and filled it up with water from the jug he carried. Then he filled up the other water skin.

"Could you not come earlier? We're dying of thirst!" Sakakwi said after he drank deeply.

"Everyone's dying of thirst!" Tau quipped with a laugh.

"Hold your tongue! I do not tolerate disrespect." Sakakwi warned.

Tau cringed and drew back at the harsh words. He replied, "My apologies, master Sakakwi."

Not long after, they heard a commotion outside of the room where they lay. The voices sound excited, but too muffled to make out any words. Suddenly, they saw the desolate blackness turn to blinding whiteness.

Badru sat up and they all stared at the torch the man in front of them held. Then they turned and looked at each other, shouting for joy that they could finally see again. They stood up as the man quickly walked over to the torches on the wall and lit them. Soon the entire room was lit, and the man left as fast as he entered, to give light to the other people who still resided in blackness.

"Do you see now?" Sakakwi laughed, "Perhaps Ammon-Ra would have lifted the darkness sooner if you had only agreed with me sooner."

"Don't be a fool," Badru shook his head. "Do you still not think it is odd that as we are supposed to be blessed by the god of the sun, we lose all light?"

"When all this is done you will see the wisdom of this fool. Come, let us go and report all of this." Badru followed Sakakwi through the newly lit stone tunnels to the chamber of the head priest.

There, that priest had already gathered several other officials who were heatedly discussing something as they entered. They stood next to the wall, out of the way, and patiently waited for their turn.

"So you're telling me that because of the darkness you have a three-day delay in your plans?" He snarled at one of the officials on the other side of the wooden table.

"At least." The man tried to explain himself, "We could get no work at all done during the darkness and my priests are in disarray! It will take at least another day to fully organize them."

He sighed on his wooden chair. The purple cushion on the seat provided little comfort. "I suppose there isn't anything to do about it." Then he glanced towards the wall and Badru stiffened from the attention, "And what about you Sakakwi? I suppose you also are going to tell me about the delay in your task."

"Not at all!" Sakakwi stepped forward with excitement in every word. "In fact I wanted to tell you that we are very spirited after passing the test."

"Passing the test? What test?" he spat out and folded his hands on his chest as he tried to discern what Sakakwi meant.

"We passed the test that Ammon-Ra set before us," Sakakwi explained. "The test of three days without light. We are stronger than ever and ready to be wielded as his weapon against his opponent, the Hebrew god."

"The three days without light," he replied slowly, "was credited to Moses and his god. Pharaoh summoned him as soon as Ammon-Ra rolled his disk over the Eastern sand dunes and light came back to us. I hear Pharaoh chastised him severely."

Sakakwi stood speechless. Then the head priest raised his eyebrows, "If the men under you believe that it was a test from Ammon-Ra I see no reason to tell them differently. Be quick about making up the lost time. We have much to do and much less time to do it in." He dismissed them with a wave of his hand and the next official began talking.

Badru and Sakakwi bowed reverently and left his office.

Badru looked at Sakakwi, swallowing a smug smile.

"He told us that he sees no reason not to tell everyone it was a test from Ammon-Ra. So that is what we will say."

Badru drew a breath for a rebuttal, but Sakakwi interrupted.

"I know, he didn't exactly say that. But we can imply it. Just follow my lead and everything will work out."

"As you say…" Badru replied with some anxiety.

They walked back to the area of the underground section assigned to Sakakwi's men. He quickly mustered them to the large meeting hall again and stood to address them on the platform. They looked at him with suspicion and fear. Some grumbled about the ordeal of darkness and others wondered if the light would leave them again. Badru noted that their number was noticeably smaller but Tau was among them.

Sakakwi addressed them, "My brothers, I am pleased to see every one of you who has passed the test. Yes, I tell you we have been tested by Ammon-Ra himself! I declare to you that we are now deemed worthy to be his weapon for the battle to come."

They mumbled to each-other in confused tones. Sakakwi heard them and realized their dissention. After thinking for a moment, he shouted, "Our brethren have seen all these things. Would you defy them?" The subtle threat of punishment quickly silenced the dissenters.

"Today we learn the parts each of us will play for tomorrow we take vengeance on all the injustices done to us."

Some in the crowd cheered when Sakakwi said this, and he breathed it in as air. He smiled and turned to Badru, the one on whom all his plans relied.

Chapter 16

Yalu pulled the hood of his robe over his head even tighter, hoping to stay hidden from any prying eyes. He heard the footsteps and clinking of metal approach the alley he knelt in. Patiently, he waited in the shadow of the mud brick building as the guard passed. Yalu studied the man's face for any indication of suspicion but found none.

When the guard turned a corner, Yalu leapt from hiding and quickly crossed the dirt road. A few houses down, he lifted up the burlap door and slipped inside. He walked over to the far wall and looked down at his mother sleeping soundly. Crouching down, he rubbed her shoulder to gently rouse her.

"Hello mother," he whispered to her. She groaned, turning toward him and mumbled something under her breath. Then she quickly turned her head and looked into his eyes. In them she saw a glimmer she hadn't seen in a long time.

"Sorry to wake you. But this is the first chance I have had to come back home."

"I'm just glad to see you," she said, putting her hand on his cheek with a warm smile. "My son doesn't come home often lately. I keep telling the women that you are on a special assignment for a wealthy man. But there are rumors that you were a condemned criminal. I knew it wasn't true."

"They are," Yalu sat down beside her.

She sat up with a surprised look on her face. Yalu told her about the plot to kill Moses and how they had stopped it. She gripped his arm tightly when he told her about his arrest, sentencing by Pharaoh, and being thrown in the prison pit. Then her face was elated when he described the rescue from the Hebrews.

"A lot has happened since you left home," she whispered as she stared blankly at the wall in front of her. "My friends talk about the Hebrew slaves lately. The women think they should be allowed to worship their god as we worship ours. They tell stories about how they are mistreated by Pharaoh and the overseers and we feel sorry for them. But there isn't anything we can do."

"There is something I can do," He said. "I will join the Hebrews. I'm in good standing with one of their elders. This god of theirs keeps defeating our gods. Even if he gets defeated in upcoming battles, what he's done already is more than worthy of worship."

"And perhaps he would spare you from anymore of his curses", she said. Then a look of concern flashed across her face and she asked, "But if Pharaoh's soldiers catch you, what will you do?"

Yalu looked at her, in thought for a moment. Then he said, "I just need to make sure that doesn't happen."

"I hope it doesn't. You've already endured more than your share." She said and sighed.

Yalu shook his head. "The worst part is that Pharaoh keeps going back on his word with the Hebrews."

"Yes, I remember what your father kept telling you." She rolled her eyes. "That was just something he told you boys to keep you from trouble. Especially with… what happened… I don't know if it's really something to hold on to."

"Not something to hold onto? If I can't hold on to what is right then what can I hold on to?" Yalu asked. He looked at her with firm determination.

"What is right?" She probed.

"I don't know," Yalu blurted out. "But I do know that the Hebrews and their god have done right by me."

"You really are your father's son," She said with a small smile and Yalu gave a quiet laugh. Shen she asked, "What about that girl you were talking about? You know, the Kushite? What was her name again?"

"Nebit?" he answered, then face flushed in slight embarrassment.

"That's right. Can you tell me more about her?"

"Well," He began as he recovered. He told her about Nebit's violent past and that she wanted him to teach her how to be a protector. He also mentioned her history with Sakakwi, Kasmut's plan to get justice on him, and what happened to her in the end.

"I see. Are you going to offer for her? Or do you need my help?" She said, more as a prompt for him to act than genuinely asking.

Yalu looked toward her with a penetrating gaze, but quickly averted his eyes. "I want her. I like watching the way her braids move when she walks. I enjoy spending my time around her and listening to her voice. Even though we've suffered much together I wouldn't give any of it up if it meant parting from her."

His mother raised her hand to his cheek again with a smile, "It sounds like you love her. Whatever happens, don't let her go."

Yalu looked at her and nodded. Then he took a deep breath and handed her a small brown sack. She heard clinking as she opened it up. He explained, "Fifteen deben worth of copper. Use it wisely. I don't know the next time I can slip away. Until then, goodbye."

"Goodbye Yalu," she said, and watched him duck under the burlap door, leaving her alone in the darkness.

Tau walked the cold stone of the underground passages he had become much more familiar with now. After teaching the priests everything he learned about the Hebrews and their ways he set out to find what sort of work they put Badru to. He heard from one of the priests that they saw Badru walking with Sakakwi nearby the kitchen. He also hoped to get a quick bite of food while he was there. He was disappointed that they only had stale bread and old vegetables. But he took and ate them nonetheless. Recalling the feast laid out before him at Nun's house, he sighed deeply. Then he went on to look for Badru.

The training room was buzzing as priests and warriors trained. He thought to himself that his father would be proud of their dedication. But Badru wasn't there. He looked around the main audience chamber where priests worshipped but he wasn't there either. Out of sheer luck, Badru and Sakakwi came walking down the tunnel toward him, talking to each other.

Tau called out Badru's name and they stopped. When he approached them, he gave a sideways glance to Sakakwi, and then said, "There is a matter I need to discuss with you. If you have time."

"Sakakwi and I have just finished our rounds inspecting how the training is going," Badru said. "I think I can spare some time."

"You do that. I have other business that needs attending. Badru, I leave these operations in your charge until I return." Sakakwi told them and left down the tunnel.

"So, what did you want to talk about?" Badru asked.

Tau had a couple things he wanted to talk about, but seeing that Sakakwi was still within earshot, he asked, "Are things still going rough with Behati?"

Badru nodded, "They are. But I must give you some credit. I made a joke and her stonewall face cracked a little."

Tau laughed and nudged him, "See, I told you."

"But that is only foam on the surface. The current underneath is still turbulent." Badru added. "It seems that whatever I decide to do she sets herself against. It is maddening!"

Tau grunted in acknowledgement and nodded his head. Just then, an idea came to him. He said, "I wonder if she gets made when you make the decision without her."

Looking up in confusion, Badru asked, "What do you mean?"

"Have you tried asking her what she thinks? Then making the decision with her instead of just making the decision yourself?"

Badru folded his arms and thought. By this time, Tau noticed that Sakakwi was gone and sure to be out of earshot. They were alone.

Tau said, "There's something else I wanted to talk about. That darkness was a curse from the Hebrew god. You know this is true, right Badru?"

"Well, yes of course I do." Badru admitted. "But Sakakwi wants to use that information to keep morale high among the priests and soldiers. It's pretty effective as I observe."

"It's a lie," Tau hissed. "He's deceiving all these people. They think Ammon-Ra is blessing us and giving him the credit due the Hebrew god. If the Hebrew god curses us with something more dangerous he could be leading all these people to their deaths!"

"Let us not jump in the river without checking for crocodiles first," Badru said. "The outcome of the next battle has not yet been revealed to us. With the might of the priesthoods and the gods at our backs we are sure to prevail."

"But look at all the battles that have happened already. Every single one has ended the same. The Hebrew god always ended up the victor."

Badru looked at him with anger and said, "You do not have enough faith in our gods. Soon enough you shall see what our combined power will do."

"Listen to yourself!" Tau shouted at him. "You sound just like Sakakwi. Here I thought you were the wiser between us."

Badru was taken aback. He first thought of a response to him, but before he said it he realized that it was what Sakakwi would say. Tau was right. He couldn't think of what to say in response. A frustrated breath escaped his lips.

"I may have great prowess of might, but you have such incredible prowess of the mind. Shall you use it for what is right or what is not?" Tau held out a hand to Badru.

Releasing another frustrated breath, Badru stared at Tau's outstretched hand. He thought again of the defeats of the Egyptian gods. Sakakwi's words seemed so hollow compared to the harsh reality of the curses he'd been forced to endure on behalf of his Pharaoh.

"Perhaps you were wrong," Badru said solemnly. "I seem to be the one being a fool right now."

"Any day I am wiser than the great Badru is a good day for me," Tau chuckled.

Badru rolled his eyes and folded his arms. He said, "Yes, yes, have your laughs now. Tomorrow I shall have mine. So do you know what to do now?"

"Um... no."

"I thought so," Badru gave his own chuckle. "Come with me."

"Why, where are we going?"

"I shall leverage my contacts and find out where they are."

"Who? Why?"

"Yalu and Nebit, of course. We're going to join them again."

"What about Sakakwi?"

"Do not worry, my friend. I know how to deal with him."

In the morning, Hoshea followed closely behind Moses. Hoshea wondered how this old man, who was probably as old as his grandfather would be if he were still alive, moved with surprising speed. Hoshea took a couple of breaths before he repeated back:

"Slaughter the perfect lamb at twilight, put its blood on the top and side door posts using hyssop, roast it, and eat it with bread without yeast."

"Burn whatever that remains in the morning. We don't want to leave anything behind," Moses added with his stride unyielding, "And horseradish! Not with other food but by itself. The Lord our god also commanded us to eat horseradish, so don't forget it…"

"Horseradish!" Hoshea exclaimed and stopped in his tracks. Then he sprinted to catch up.

Hoshea then repeated back the list told to him by Moses. After Moses nodded assent he said, "That is everything then. I will make sure we prepare everything as the Lord our god has commanded."

"Be sure you forget nothing. Your life is in your hands," Moses turned back to him and warned. "But I must go to the other households now. Farewell Hoshea."

"Farewell Moses," Hoshea stopped and watched Moses continue his hustling pace until he turned a corner and passed out of view. He reviewed

the list once again in his head, and when he was
satisfied, he ran back to his father's house.

The manor bustled. A sea of people ran back
and forth as if in a tide. One servant walked briskly,
carrying an armful of silver cups. Another servant had a
large burlap sack slung over his shoulder.

Hoshea found his father among them and
repeated Moses's instructions.

Nun nodded his head after each item in the list.
When Hoshea had finished he looked back with a face
scrunched with bewilderment.

"Yet another odd request from Moses. So we
kill a sheep and put its blood on our door to protect
our sons from death?"

Hoshea shrugged his shoulders, "There have
been so many odd things happening lately, this one
doesn't seem out of place to me at all now."

Nun smiled and laughed, "Yes I suppose you're
right. Go tell Yadid so he can make the necessary
preparations."

"I will," Hoshea looked around. "But where is
he?"

"He's not here?" Nun turned to look as well,
"He's been coordinating the gifts from the Egyptians.
I'm sure some of the servants running around can tell
you where he is. Go ask them."

Hoshea left his father as other servants came to
him with their questions. At first he looked for
someone idle. When he failed, he stopped a man
carrying an armful of random silver objects to ask,
"Can you tell me where Yadid is?"

The man shook his head, "Sorry Hoshea." He
continued with his task.

After asking three more servants, he stopped
and leaned up against the wall of the manor as he
thought of a new strategy. Then he spotted Nebit and

Yalu on the other side of the manor, helping move bags. He went to them

"Have either of you seen Yadid?" He asked when he was within a couple strides from them.

Yalu looked up after putting down a heavy sack and wiping the sweat from his brow.

"I haven't. As soon as we woke up all the servants were out. It seems something important is happening so we wanted to help. Do you know what's going on? Everyone else is too busy to say."

"Oh they didn't tell you?" Hoshea folded his arms. "The Lord is planning one more catastrophe to befall Egypt. He will come tonight through all the land and kill the firstborn son of each household."

"But Hoshea," Nebit asked, "Aren't you the firstborn son of Nun?"

"We received a ritual that will spare the Hebrew households. So I'll be perfectly unharmed... as long I can find Yadid so we can make the proper preparations." He took a moment to look around before he ran off.

The sun passed overhead almost unnoticed as the people below it busied themselves. If it weren't for the intense heat of the day, people might have forgotten it was there altogether. Inside his father's estate, Badru sat next to his wife. But his attention was on Sakakwi.

"This part is vital to my plans," Sakakwi began. "I need your family to integrate with the Hebrews without suspicion."

Behati replied, "You mean moving house? That is outrageous! It's too disruptive. Badru, how could you agree to something like this."

"I have not agreed to it yet," Badru said. Behati looked at him curiously. He continued, "I wanted to talk to you about it first. Then we can make a decision about it together."

She looked passed him for a moment. Badru could tell she did not expect to hear his response.

Finally, she asked Sakakwi, "Why us? Why not go integrate with your own family?"

"Badru is in a very special position. He is trusted by an influential Hebrew elder. Among all of us in the priesthood, he can move about freely. The rest of us must limit ourselves to the Hebrews as much as possible or risk being found out."

"What's in it for us?" Behati crossed her arms.

Sekakwi handed her a papyrus scroll. She began reading as he spoke, "You will receive these lands, a portion of the Hebrew slaves, and honorary titles bestowed from Pharaoh."

"And how long will we have to live among those Hebrew slaves?"

"If things go as planned then you'll be back in your house as soon as three weeks from now."

Behati sat there and thought for a moment. Then she turned to Badru and said, "I think that it's still too disruptive. But I realize that this is important to the priesthood. How about just you go to the Hebrews?"

"The chances of integration without suspicion will increase," Sakakwi replied. "If his entire family comes with him then they will trust him more."

Behati sat there silent, looking at Badru. He looked at her and then looked down. He knew Sakakwi was right. But remembered Tau's words. Would he side with Behati and risk Sakakwi's plan or side with Sakakwi and anger her? He felt the beads of sweat slide down his face.

Then Badru looked up and said, "I will go alone then. If Behati thinks it is too disruptive to the family, then I will trust her."

Both Sakakwi and Behati looked surprised. Then Sakakwi leaned forward and asked, "Are you sure?"

Badru nodded. Sakakwi let out a tense breath and said, "So be it."

Afternoon faded into dusk and the setting sun cast gold and red into the sky. And the Hebrews began their next task.

Yalu and Nebit stood with the other servants of Nun's household in the courtyard, and watched the ceremony closely. Hoshea held the rope tied around the lamb's neck while Nun knelt before the lamb with a knife in his hands. He rubbed the lamb's skin, examining it for spots. The chief shepherd who tended Nun's flock held the lamb's head in his arms. Yadid stood behind him carrying a small bronze basin.

Finally Nun declared, "I find no blemishes on this lamb. This shall be the one we will use." Several of the servants started cheering and the rest of the crowd joined in. Nun nodded to Yadid, who placed the basin on the ground underneath the lamb's head. The crowd hushed and all was quiet.

The lamb remained eerily silent. The shepherd pulled close to the lamb with his head next to its ear. He whispered into the lamb's ear as Nun readied the blade.

Just then, the lamb felt a sharp pain on the bottom of his neck. He tried to make noise, but could not. He heard his shepherd whispering comforting words. Never before had he known this kind of pain. Never before had he felt this weakness and panic. But the shepherd's voice he had known all his life.

Inside the shepherd's embrace, he did not struggle. By this time, he felt lifted off the ground and disoriented. But he also felt the warm hand of the shepherd on his nose before he slipped away and all went black.

Hoshea and a servant held the hindquarters of the lamb up in the air as blood poured from the slit on its neck, streaked down the lamb's nose, and splashed into the basin. It took a few minutes for the basin to fill up with the blood. When it was full, Hoshea lowered the lamb, and the servants took it away to finish preparations.

Yadid moved the basin of blood to the open entrance of the house. Nun handed another servant his knife and took some of the long hyssop which had been bound together. He dipped the tip of the plant into blood in the basin. Then he lifted the plant above his head and painted the lintel with the blood. Then he bent down to dip the plant into the blood again. Reaching first to his left, he painted the side doorpost and then again on his right. Yadid nimbly moved the basin from side to side to prevent any blood dripping on the ground.

Turning around, Nun announced, "I have now put the blood of the unblemished lamb on the doorposts of my house. Everyone who eats the lamb under my roof is now protected from the wrath of the Lord our god."

The crowd of Nun's servants cheered again. Soon afterwards, Yadid brought them under control and gave tasks to people while they waited for the lamb to finish cooking. Once finished, the cooks prepared it and the meal was distributed to everyone in the household.

The evening wore on and the sky darkened. Strange clouds hid the sunset from view making the night darken faster than usual. Tau could feel an ominous mood in the air. Despite the warmth left over from the day it chilled his bones.

A cry sang out from behind him in the city. It was a long and mournful cry. He whirled around to look at it, even though it was too far off to see. Then another cry joined it. And another. And another. Soon, there was a whole chorus of them singing out from the city behind him. But what really frightened him was that the chorus seemed to get closer and closer to him.

Then he started to hear words, "My baby, my poor baby, my poor son." The word "son" sent a pang of fear through him, though he didn't know what he was afraid of. He started running. Down the streets he ran as fast as he could. He kept running until he arrived at the front of his home.

Before he entered, he listened carefully inside, but he heard no crying or mourning. So he slipped through the burlap door of his house. His wife sat on a reed mat with their son nursing at her breast. A concerned expression worn her face as she listened to the screams coming from elsewhere in the city.

She looked at him shocked and asked, "What are you doing here?"

"I live here!" Tau replied with a forced laugh. "Am I not welcome in my own home?"

"Of course, welcome. But I thought you were dead! Some friends in the palace say the saw you dragged to Pharaoh bound and headed for the executioner."

"I was taken to Pharaoh, but I was saved by Sakakwi at the last minute. But how many women can claim their husband was taken to Pharaoh himself as a criminal?" Tau gave a broad smile.

Kesi laughed. Then she looked up with a serious expression and asked, "What's going on out there? I'm too frightened to leave our doorstep."

"I'm not sure," Tau admitted between breaths. "Perhaps it's another curse from this Hebrew god. How do you fare?"

"Well enough, I think." Kesi answered, she looked down at Ebo in her arms. He wasn't crying but making short cooing sounds. "The darkness was absolutely miserable! I don't know how we would've survived if I didn't have the house in my memory."

Tau dropped sack of supplies down next to her. She browsed through the grain, fruit, and vegetables contained within, he supposed she was guessing their value.

"There was something I wanted to ask you," Tau said. He felt uncomfortable because he wasn't sure how she would respond. "From my work, with Pharaoh's overseer, I've seen a lot of the Hebrew people and their god. It seems no matter which one of our gods go up against this new god has been defeated. For this reason, I think allying ourselves with the Hebrews and their god is best. Would you consider coming with me to join the Hebrew slaves?"

"Allying ourselves with the Hebrews?" Kesi asked. "Weren't we just talking about how they've made our lives so horrible?"

"Horrible as enemies," Tau said. "But if we were allies then wouldn't things be much better?"

Tau could see from her face that she was starting to understand what he was saying as the flow of thoughts meandered through her mind. She replied, "Yes, I see. All these things happened because Pharaoh opposed their god. How can this alliance be done?"

Tau held her shoulders, "I know one of the Hebrew elders. They offered to let me join their house before… well… before I got dragged away."

Just then, an odd expression came over his son's face and he started crying. Both of them looked at Ebo with concerned faces.

Kesi began to panic, "The warmth! It's leaving him!"

Tau reached out and touched Ebo. His skin felt unusually cool. Tau went over to grab another blanket and, together with Kesi, wrapped him up in it. But it was no good, he didn't seem to get warmer.

The baby stretched out his hand and Tau gently took hold of it. Tau thought about how small the baby's hand looked in his. But even that wasn't enough to keep the hand warm. The crying grew fainter and fainter. Then it stopped. His hand went limp and he exhaled his final breath.

Kesi looked up at Tau shocked. She began crying, "What is this? Is this the Hebrew god?"

Tau's mouth gaped open, but he didn't speak. He could not believe what just happened. They both sat down on the ground together. The baby, eerily still, lay in Kesi's lap.

Suddenly, Kesi began screaming. It startled Tau so much he almost jumped up with his weapon at the ready. They he realized she'd given in to panic.

He stepped in front of her, crouched down, and said, "Kesi. Kesi. Kesi."

At first she didn't respond to him. She looked passed him as though we weren't even there. Then she saw him and her face grew angry, "It's your fault! You've been with those Hebrews. You brought this down upon my poor little Ebo."

Tau shook his head, "No. Listen."

She took a breath and stopped talking. She gave him a look that told him, "Listen to what?" Then she

heard it again. The wailing and crying from the
neighborhood all around them.

Kesi gasped, "Have children died in every
house?"

Tau didn't answer but cringed to think of it. His
heart broke, not only for Kesi, but the other
households who lost this night. It felt as a heavy lump
in his chest.

"Let's go," Kesi said with resignation.

"Go? Where?" Tau asked.

"To the Hebrew elder. Let's go ally ourselves
with this Hebrew god. What else can we do?"

Tau had no other answer. They found a place
to bury little Ebo. Kesi cried and Tau embraced her.
Then they left. But Tau had one more home he wanted
to go. One more time, he found himself at the
doorstep to his father's house. Kesi told him that she
didn't want to talk to anyone right now and would wait
outside.

As Tau stood, he recalled all the things his
father had taught him. Surely, his father would see his
decision as a slap in the face, and be angered. Tau
repeated what he planned to say in his mind. Then he
threw open the burlap sack attached to the top of the
doorframe and saw his father inside their house
sharpening the large blade Tau had seen before.

Tau's father nodded haughtily to his son as he
rubbed a smooth stone along the edge of the blade.

"My boy," he looked up from his work and
wiped some sweat from his brow. An emotionless
mask covered his face. "Surprised to see you out this
late at night. But, then again, it does seem to be a night
for it."

Tau stood in front of him and said, "I know
you've always looked out for me. But there is
something I must do. The Hebrew god has defeated

our Egyptian gods in battle. I plan to live with the Hebrews with Kesi and worship their god."

"You're going to run from your duty?" His father didn't look up.

"No," Tau stepped closer. "There are some things I need to do for myself. This duty for Rashidi was handed to me. Now it's done and I choose a duty on my own. Now my duty lies with the Hebrews and their god."

He stopped working and looked at Tau with a slight frown. Setting the blade down, he walked up to him and looked him over. Tau felt uncomfortable in his gaze. But he made up his mind and showed his determination as he looked his father in the eyes.

Keeping the same frown, he put his hands on Tau's shoulders, "If that is your new duty, then you must do it."

"But father, I think it is. . . what?" Tau stuttered, shocked.

His father stopped and looked up at him, "You're a grown man now. I've taught you to fight well. But now you've learned one thing that cannot be taught, and I've been too late realizing it. There are many ways to forge a blade, though some are better than others. Every man must forge the blade of his own destiny."

Tau took a deep breath, unprepared for his father's encouraging response. His father patted him on the back roughly. Then he roared like a lion and Tau responded with his own roar.

Then Tau said somberly, "I was just at home with... my wife's son is... dead."

"You never know when death might take you. During my hellish days on the battlefield I earned my glory and saw my fair share of death. But still I've seen nothing like this. The old live to see the young perish." Tau's father lifted up the blade to examine it for imperfections and then continued sharpening it. He sniffled and let a tear escape. He wiped it with the back of his hand and then put that hand on Tau's shoulder.

"Many sons of Egypt won't get the chance to tell their sons of the glories they won in battle to inspire them to even greater feats of glory as I have told you mine. Now it is up to you. I see now that I've tried too hard to fit you into mold not meant for you. Go and make your own mold."

"I will." Tau nodded. Then he turned to leave. "Badru is leaving soon and I need to get back. I wish you well, father."

"Wait!" His father called out to him, "Where do you think you're going?"

Tau turned around, confused.

"Huh? What have we been talking about all this time?"

He walked up to Tau, "I'm not letting you leave here. Not with that piece of garbage hanging on your waist." Raising his arm, he displayed the weapon he had been sharpening. The curved metal blade shone brightly in the torchlight. "The finest quality metal I have ever worked with. The handle is made be wielded by large hands, by you. Think of your old father when you take it into battle."

Tau stared at the weapon with wonder. "I... don't know what to tell you," he said as he took up. He gave a few swings to get the feel of it and smiled with delight.

"Tell me that you will win glory in triumph on the battlefield. Tell me that you will face whatever foe stands before you with courage. Tell me that one day your children will tell stories of your valor and the valor of their grandfather."

Then they shared an embrace. Tau could feel a tear escape his eye. He suddenly felt embarrassed that this should happen in front of his father. But when they ended Tau could see a similar tear on his father's cheek. They chuckled.

"I shall," Tau patted his father on the back one last time. He rested the sword on his shoulder looked upon him one last time and left.

The screams and cries echoed through the night as Tau and Kesi walked down the road. He felt leaving his home was a bittersweet parting. He knew he would miss his father's insistence on duty. But at the same time, he felt free; a heavy burden was lifted from his shoulders. He took a breath of the brisk night air and imagined what adventures the morning would bring for them.

Yalu turned the corner, and when he saw the house he quickened his pace. Whirling his head around, he spotted none of the city guards. Despite being the dead of night, the city was hardly silent at this hour. The wailing seemed to come from every household in the city.

He entered through the burlap door and his mother gasped.

"A ghost?" she asked with wide eyes.

"No mother," Yalu answered.

She approached him cautiously. Then she touched his shoulder and when she was finally confident he was not an apparition come to torment her, she embraced him.

"I was afraid you died. All night long I heard how the sons of the neighbors died. I'm so glad you're alright." She shed tears of joy.

"Mother," Yalu started, "Pharaoh finally gave permission for the Hebrew slaves to leave Egypt. I'm going with them."

"Give me a few minutes and I'll collect our things," she said, and started going about the house.

She picked up a bag filled with garlic, poured the bulbs out on the ground, and started filling it with her possessions.

"You don't need to come with me," Yalu tried to reason with her. "There may be dangers. It would be best if you stayed behind these city walls."

"Don't contradict me!" She scolded him while continuing to put things in the bag. "I am coming with you. Will you abandon your mother as she faces old age without a husband? I can't survive in this city by myself. And besides, you need me. You never were any good at taking care of a home. And only the gods know if you're going to settle down with that Nebit."

Yalu shook his head and accused, "You always change things to mean something that it doesn't! I know you've been keeping the house while I work. I mean that if something happened to me out in the desert, I don't want the same thing to happen to you. And don't bring Nebit into this conversation. It's not fair!"

"Sure it is," She fired back as she grabbed another sack to fill. "Is she not coming with us?"

"Well, yes she is." Yalu admitted.

Before he could say any more, she continued, "Then you definitely need my help. You're my only son and I love you. You're all I have left in this world. If I lose you out in the desert then what hope for the future do I have? I don't care what kind of work they have me do, but if I can help you in any way then I would consider it a fair bargain. Do you understand?"

"I. . ." Yalu hoped that words come to him, but they did not. He shook his head in disgust. After all these years, he was still under his mother's influence. Then he raised his hands in surrender, "Very well. You can come."

"Good," she handed him another empty bag. "Now help me fill these bags."

He complied and soon they had filled three large burlap sacks.

As they left, his mother took one last look at her longtime home. She reminisced, "I remember when you were born and your father and I took you home to this house. I remember when you got hurt playing soldier with your brother out front here. There are so many memories I have with this house."

Yalu grasped her arm, "It's time to go."

She gave the house one last look to make sure she remembered what it looked like, and then yielded to Yalu's pull.

They arrived at Nun's home, awaited by Nebit, Hoshea, Lior, and Yadid. The dark and empty house was eerily quiet in the moonlight.

"Everyone else already left? You didn't have to wait for me." Yalu asked.

"Actually, we did." Lior told him.

Hoshea explained, "There is one matter that needs to be attended to. A matter of great importance and honor. There is little time, we will tell you later."

"But who is she?" Yadid asked, pointing at her.

"My mother," Yalu shook his head at her. She just smiled. "I could not persuade her to stay."

"We can't bring her with us," Lior told them.

"Why not? I don't eat much food. I won't be a burden to you." She pleaded.

"That's not what I mean," Lior shook his head. "We're going down into the underground tombs. I'm afraid you would be a burden there."

She gasped and touched her hand to her mouth. She stepped forward, "You don't mean the ones with all the stories and legends, do you?"

"We do indeed," Hoshea nodded. "I don't think we're likely to run into any half-god half-animals or other sorts. But if we do, I'm sure the Lord our god will save us."

Yalu's mother folded her arms and looked at him skeptically. Then she glanced at Yalu and concern flashed over her face. Seeing this he stepped up to her.

"Meeting random gods in the tombs are the least of my worries right now. With Lior, and me we should be able to handle anything else." Yalu put a hand on her shoulder to comfort her.

"Don't fret. I'll look after your son." Nebit walked up and comforted her with a smile. She smiled back.

"In the meantime, I can accompany you to Sukkoth. I wasn't very keen on joining these adventurers down into the tombs anyway." Yadid admitted.

"Looks like you have your excuse to stay out of harm's way again!" Lior quipped.

"As usual." Yadid smiled and they all laughed.

So Yadid and his mother left the city by the North gate while the others travelled west of the city to the tombs. The Medjey who guarded the entrance received word from Pharaoh to let them pass and they did without incident after telling them where to go and where not to go.

With a torch in hand they passed through the cold darkness of the tunnels and arrived at room they were told about. As per the Medjeys' instructions, they stood on the appropriate floor tile and pushed a stone of the wall. They felt their stomachs turn and a brief panic as the floor gave way and the slid down a chute and landed in a heap.

Lior groaned, "Even with their warnings I wasn't quite ready for that."

"If I didn't know you better I'd mistake you for a weak man," Hoshea grinned at him. But Lior just gave him a dirty look and dusted himself off.

They continued on. The tunnels became very stuffy and they noticed growth on the walls and much dust and debris on the ground. They guessed that nobody travelled these passages for over a hundred years.

At one area in the tunnel, they noticed much more dirt and debris than normal. They saw fallen rocks and stones. A number of wooden beams held large rocks up on the ceiling.

"I'll go first," Nebit offered. Yalu took hold of her arm and they looked at one another. She saw the concern in his face but smiled a confident smile at him and he let her go.

Arriving at the first beam, she surveyed the floor. Nothing looks sensitive to her eyes in the torchlight. Nevertheless, she crouched and began creeping across. She was careful not to touch anything and ready to bolt at the slightest movement or sound.

When she passed over to solid stone above her she looked back to see if anything changed. It hadn't. She breathed a sigh of relief and gestured for the others to follow.

The next person was Yalu. He carefully creeped along as she had and made it across. Hoshea went next. While he was about half-way through, they heard the noise of some small rocks hit the floor. Hoshea froze as a small cloud of dust appeared nearby him. But nothing else happened so he continued across. Lior came last.

"I hope nothing happens while we're on this side of it," Hoshea said, looking back.

"We just need to be quick," Lior said pointing down the passage. There was a fork in the road ahead of them. "I believe the medjey said we take the right-most passage at this time."

They nodded their heads and continued on. As they passed, Hoshea stopped and gazed curiously at the darkness of the tunnel to the left.

Yalu stopped and went to him. "You remember what they told us; the dangers if we took the wrong passage."

"I must admit, part of me would like to see those dangers. I wonder what rumors were true and which ones were not," Hoshea mused.

"If you're going to go that way then you'll be on your own," Nebit warned. "Lairs of half-god lions and hidden traps and who knows what else. I won't go with you."

"Come all," Lior said from up ahead in the passage to the right. "We'd best hurry while the multitude is still gathered at Sukkoth."

Hoshea finally conceded and they followed Lior to a hall of small bronze doors. Ornate carvings and symbols decorated each one. After counting off the number told to them, they opened a door. Inside lay bones and a skull carefully placed on a green silk cloth. Embroidered on the cloth were letters of gold.

"What is this? Did we make that perilous trip for some bones?" Nebit scoffed.

"Long ago, one of our ancestors was made a promise." Hoshea told her as he and Lior carefully took and packed the bones and skull. "When we Hebrews finally leave Egypt we take him up with us to the land promised to us. There shall be his final place of resting, with the rest of people."

They finished packing it up and Hoshea carried it over his shoulder. Then they closed the bronze door and left. When they came to the fork in the road,

Hoshea once again stopped to gaze down the other direction.

"Come, let's be quick." Lior nudged him.

Just as soon as Hoshea turned around they heard footsteps. Turning around they saw twinkles in the darkness. Then they heard a guttural sound echoing through the tunnel. The twinkles advanced until they saw the dark brown heads and rounded ears of three hyenas.

One of the hyenas gave a series of high-pitched calls that made the four feel as it was laughing at their misfortune. At the end of the torchlight, the three of them halted. Nobody moved.

"What do we do?" Hoshea whispered.

"You run back down the way we came," Lior told him. "We shall hold them off and meet up with you. The promise must be honored."

"I'll fight too!" Hoshea protested.

"I promised your father to keep you safe. Now get going!" Lior pushed Hoshea back toward the exit.

Then they attacked. The hyenas sprinted toward them as Hoshea ran with the bones. Yalu and Nebit engaged two of the hyenas but the third was bigger and stronger and knocked Lior aside to chase after the one who was running away.

Lior recovered quickly and ran after it. Luckily, Hoshea saw what happened and had his sword out in time to slash at the beast before it could pounce on his back. Then Lior attacked from the side, stabbing it in through the belly.

It jumped back in pain right into one of the wooden posts, knocking it down. The big rock it held up smashed down upon the beast. Then another rock fell and another. Soon, the other wooden supports snapped and whole ceiling came down.

A deafening roar echoed through the tunnels. The two engaged with Yalu and Nebit ran away in fright allowing them to hold their hands over their ears from the noise which lasted about a minute. Then the tunnels filled with dust leaving the two coughing.

After the dust settled and the echoes subsided, Yalu went over to the rocks where the tunnel caved in. He shouted Lior's and Hoshea's names. After a short while they heard an answer but the voices were faint.

"We are fine," Lior said. "The bones are intact as well. How are you?"

"We aren't hurt either," Yalu answered. "We're on the other side."

"Can we dig to the other side," Hoshea asked.

Lior replied, "That's a bad idea. Who knows how long it would take. And it may cause more rocks to fall. It's too dangerous."

"What are we going to do?" Nebit asked quietly.

Yalu grunted as he thought. Then he lifted up his eyes to the darkness of the tunnel from which the hyenas came. Nebit followed his eyes and gasped as she realized what he was thinking. But should could think of no better option so she said nothing.

Yalu said, "You two go back. There's no point in you staying when there's nothing you can do. Nebit and I will find our way through the tunnel."

Lior asked if Yalu was sure and he affirmed it. So they said goodbyes to each other, promising a warm reception when they reunited at Sukkoth. Then Lior and Hoshea went back through the passage while Yalu and Nebit braved the unknown darkness from where the beasts came.

Walking down the tunnel, Nebit and Yalu only heard the sound of their footsteps. The kept going on and on. Sometimes the torchlight played tricks on their eyes and they thought they caught a glimpse of the hyenas again. But it turned out to be some piece of debris instead.

After a good long while they came to a four-way intersection. Each passage looked the same as the others. However, just when they were going to choose a direction from their intuition, they saw a light flicker down the passage on their left.

They tightened their grips on their weapons, ready for the beasts to charge at them. But then they noticed that it was torchlight. After a little waiting they could see two figures coming toward them. They both watched on in curious amazement.

As they got closer and closer, Yalu finally recognized them. He smiled with delight and shouted, "Badru and Tau! It is good to see you. We were caught on the wrong end of a cave-in. But what are you doing here?"

Tau held a torch in one hand and the biggest axe they'd ever seen in the other. Badru walked beside him with a content smile on his face. But Yalu wore the biggest smile.

"We were looking for you. After we heard the cave-in, I had a good guess where you might be." Badru answered.

"But what brought you here?" Yalu asked.

"We talked it over and want to join the Hebrews with you," Tau answered.

"No!" Nebit yelled at them. Everyone turned to her in bewilderment. She looked at them with enmity. Before they could speak she continued, "You two are allied with Sakakwi. I'll have nothing to do with you. I'd rather die in these passages torn apart by wild beasts or crushed by giant slabs of stone than go back to him."

Yalu spoke gently to her: "But Nebit. If they know the way out then it may be our only chance."

"I don't care!" She pleaded to Yalu. "Sakakwi rescued them. Why should they leave him now? They'll take us to him and I'll be killing whoever he says until my days end. I want to have a family and be someone who protects other people. Please, don't do this."

"You do not have the right of it," Badru argued. "We are not allied with Sakakwi and we will not bring you to him. We aim to join the Hebrews, as do you I presume."

"But her reasons stand," Yalu looked at them suspiciously. "Why give up the friendship you've gained with Sakakwi to follow the Hebrew slaves and us? Nebit and I are even condemned by Pharaoh. If it was found out you helped with us then you'd have severe punishment."

"There's no going back for me," Tau said. His expression became grim. He told them about what happened with his wife's son. Then he lifted up his blade. "I've made peace with my father and he gave me this, his best work, as a gift for my departure."

A tear escaped Nebit's eye as she listened. Yalu put a comforting hand on Tau's shoulder. Nebit still looked at them suspiciously. Yalu sighed as he glanced between them, deep in thought. Then they looked into each other's eyes.

"I'd like to trust them," Yalu said.

"I know," Nebit responded and broke off her gaze. Then she pointed a dagger at Badru: "If we find Sakakwi or any of his other men at the exit waiting for us then I will personally slice you up into as many pieces as I can."

Badru gasped, being caught off-guard by the threat. Then he raised a hand and forced a laugh, "I assure you that he will be nowhere to be found."

Nebit softened and lowered her dagger. Badru and Tau turned back. Somewhat reluctantly, Yalu and

Nebit followed them down the dark passageways with the hope seeing the light of day once more.

Tau was the first one out. He saw the light up ahead and started running. The others followed him. He saw Kesi there waiting for him and shouted to her, she waved back.

"Unky Tau!" Amahl yelled at the top of her lungs. Tau was surprised to see her, her Omphil, and Behati waiting for them too. He looked at Badru who told him they weren't coming to ask why but noticed Badru was even more shocked than he was.

Amahl ran to Tau and started climbing on him. Omphil ran too so she wouldn't be left out of the fun.

Badru approached Behati and said, "I thought you weren't coming? You said it was too disruptive."

"Yeah, I did." She said with a smile. "But after talking with the girls I realized that it would be even more disruptive for you to leave the family for three weeks."

Badru smiled back at her and leaned over to kiss her on the cheek. But before he could, Nebit gave a loud gasp. Everyone turned to her. Tau saw she was staring straight at Kesi, who looked even more confused than everyone else.

"What's wrong?" Tau asked.

"I can't believe it." Nebit said with horror in her eyes.

"What is it?" Yalu put a hand on her shoulders.

Kesi now started to look anxious. "I know I didn't prepare myself well, but I don't think I look that bad."

"No," Nebit buried her face in her hands. Then she tightened them to fists and pulled them down, looking Kesi in the eyes. In a fearful tone she asked, "Did you have a husband who was killed?"

Kesi looked at her with a curious eye and released a short breath. She answered, "Yes, that's right. A man came into my house and killed my husband. And soon after, Tau's father arranged our marriage."

Nebit glanced at Tau and then looked down at her feet. A look of pained guilt covered her face.

"Don't feel ashamed for asking, the past is in the past." Kesi tried to cheer her up.

"No," Nebit looked up and told her. "You don't understand. The man who killed your husband wasn't a man. The man was a woman. And the woman was me."

Kesi looked confused as she tried to make sense of this new information. Slowly by slowly, both realization and anger filled her face. Finally, pulling up a trembling and accusing finger she angrily said, "You! It was you! You did this to me! All of my suffering is your fault!"

Stumbling backward, Kesi locked her stare onto Nebit. Tau came to Kesi's side and helped steady her. He said in a calming tone, "Remember what you said. The past is in the past, right? We can move forward as we-"

"No. No!" Kesi shouted. "I won't go anywhere with that woman. Come Tau, we stay in Egypt."

"I can't stay in Egypt." Tau told her. "Don't you remember all of the things the Hebrew god has done? We're allying ourselves with him now."

"No. Not me." Kesi backed away from him. "No. Curse you. Curse all of you. This is just a cruel trick of the gods."

Then she turned and ran off. Tau looked at her, a hand outstretched. He wondered what he could say. He could not think of anything. No joke or light-hearted jest. No words to make light of the situation and make her laugh. Then she rounded a corner and was gone.

Nobody spoke. Even Amahl and Omphil didn't say a word. Tau turned around and saw everyone looking at him. They looked at him with pity.

Finally, he said, "Let's go."

Chapter 17

Rashidi awoke with a start. He took a few short, quick breaths as he peered around his dark room. From underneath his silken sheets he saw nothing move and nothing out of the ordinary. The silence broke with a sudden knock at the door.

"What is it? Who's there?" Rashidi demanded.

"Sorry to bother you, master Rashidi." Gahiji spoke from the other side of the wooden door. "But Pharaoh sent a messenger."

Rashidi groaned. Then he muttered under his breath, "I should be used to these meetings at all times of the night by now."

Then he said louder for Gahiji to hear, "Tell him I will make myself presentable and go with him at once."

Gahiji walked back down the hall and into the room where the messenger awaited. "He is getting ready now and will go with you soon."

"He had better!" The man warned.

An uneasy silence preceded Rashidi's entrance into the room. His embroidered blue and red robe glistened in the lamplight. The messenger got up without a word and exited with Rashidi following and Gahiji close behind. They quickly got on the chariot and the messenger grabbed the reigns of the horses and took them to the palace.

The messenger escorted Rashidi and Gahiji directly to Pharaoh's audience chamber. Five generals of Pharaoh's chariot armies stood around a table with Pharaoh at the head. Pharaoh gave Rashidi his full attention as soon as he entered, and Rashidi quickly bowed down to the ground, as did Gahiji. Sakakwi was also there.

"I have not the words to express my anger and hatred for my Hebrew slaves and their god." Pharaoh spat out. "The god of your. . . slaves has killed my son, my only son! In my grief I sent orders to let them out of the city to worship their god. But they have broken and betrayed my trust. They weren't planning to go worship their god at all, they are fleeing! Even now, my spies report they are running to Sukkoth. What say you?"

"My god and king Pharaoh," Rashidi kept his face to the ground. "This news has not found its way to my ears until now. I humbly beg that you give your servant a moment to think on this." He looked up at Pharaoh intently.

Pharaoh folded his arms and gazed at him with a most stern expression.

Rashidi glanced around at the men in attendance, who all looked back at him. Then he grabbed a piece of cloth stashed in his robe to wipe the sweat from his brow. He looked up and asked, "How does it come to pass that Pharaoh, in his wisdom, lets his slaves go free without the knowledge of his devoted overseer to ensure they don't escape?"

Pharaoh straightened his back uncomfortably, "What are you saying? Do I need your permission to do what I wish with my own possessions?"

"No my Pharaoh," Rashidi replied, "I'm saying that it must be the meddling of their god! He is trying to trick you into letting them escape. Don't you see?"

"Tricking me?" Pharaoh scowled. "Not Moses or his god, nor any man alive."

"So then what does Pharaoh intend to do?" Rashidi asked.

"I shall take my best chariots and chase after them," Pharaoh stood up. "You will go, lead my chariots and reclaim my slaves."

Rashidi's jaw dropped with shock. He started to mouth the question, "Why?" but decided against questioning Pharaoh, especially when he was so angry.

Upon seeing Rashidi's expression, Pharaoh explained, "These are the slaves you oversaw and they are your responsibility. If you don't bring them back to me, then I will have your head."

Rashidi cringed, which gave Pharaoh some pleasure.

"I understand my Pharaoh," Rashidi replied. "I shall not fail you."

"You had better not," Pharaoh warned. "My advisors tell me that without the support they provide I will have logistical issues with my campaign in the South. We already have a plan. My chief advisor will explain it to you."

Badru wiped the sweat off his forehead with the back of his hand and then wiped his hand on his robe. It didn't help that much since it was already soaked, but it did provide a small amount of relief. The tops of his legs ached as he climbed yet another sand dune. He looked down at one of his daughters who held his hand tightly. Then he looked over at his other daughter who held his wife's hand.

With renewed strength, Badru continued to climb to the top with everyone else. He bent over, put his hands on his knees, and tried to catch his breath. After a short time, Tau thrust a water skin towards his chest and Badru gladly took it. As he straightened up to drink it, he noticed the lakes that bordered Egypt ahead of him. Before it, lay a multitude of sheepskin tents.

Sitting on his sack, Yalu emptied the sand from his sandals. "Look how close we are! We should be able to make it before nightfall. It's good they haven't left without us."

"What do you mean, left without us?" Badru's wife asked, approaching Yalu. "They're not planning to stay at Sukkoth? Where are they going?"

"I don't know," Yalu answered as he scanned the horizon of tents. "I suppose that the Hebrew god is taking them to a better place."

"If you don't know where their god is taking us, then how do you know that it's better?" She folded her arms as she asked.

"Any place where the slave masters weren't whipping them would be better, I think." Nebit answered.

"Not necessarily." She said. "At least they were given food and water. What life is there out of the city? They'd be living like nomads, not knowing where their next will come from! Or if it will come at all."

As they argued back and forth, Badru spotted a small dust cloud to the West. His eyes widened as he realized it was the tell-tale sign of a chariot squad. He looked over at the others. They didn't notice it. He glanced back at the cloud again and then quickly down at his hands.

Then he saw one of his daughters talking with Tau. She held the small papyrus scrap he wrote for her with the words 'barley bread' written on it. She was teaching him to read it and telling him all of the different places she saw the words.

Badru glanced at the cloud again. Then he took a deep breath and sighed.

"Look! Does anyone else see that cloud over there?" Badru asked with a finger pointing westward.

"Cloud?" Yalu repeated. He looked to where Badru pointed. When he found it he asked, "What could that be?"

"I am not sure," Badru tried his best to fake ignorance. "Could it be a squad of chariots?"

"What are chariots doing out here?" Nebit asked. "Do they normally patrol this far away from the city?"

"They must be from Pharaoh," Yalu concluded. "I'll wager he changed his mind about letting the Hebrew slaves go free again and wants to take them back. We need to move fast."

"But why would they send a small squad of chariots to bring back a multitude such as the Hebrew slaves?" Tau asked. "Sure, they are slaves but there are enough people to overwhelm them."

"Unless…" Badru rubbed his temple with two fingers. "Unless the chariot squad is only the advance scout. The real army must be assembling or may already assembled."

"If this is the advance scout then it would be to their disadvantage if it never returned." Tau turned his head and looked at Yalu, Nebit, and Badru.

"What are you saying?" Nebit shook her head, "Can the four of us take on a squad of chariots by ourselves? We will be dead after the first attack!"

"There is a chance we can win," Yalu started slinking down the other side of the dune and gestured for everyone else to follow him. "During the war with the Hyksos, my father told me of a trick his infantry unit used against the enemy chariots. And if the Hebrew god is on our side it will work for us too. Let me explain how it works."

Both the hot afternoon sun and the desert rocks jolting the chariot as well as the constant squeaking of the wheels contributed to Gahiji's irritable mood. The anger of from master Rashidi didn't help either. He looked up at the harsh sun and thought of

him and then Pharaoh above him making him feel like
a kernel of grain on their Bao board.

He looked at the chariot next to him and then
at Sakakwi's chariot behind him. That one had a leather
roof to keep the sun out. He thought how nice it must
be to be an influential priest. He started thinking of
how he might be able to get some of that power.

Suddenly he heard his name shouted by the
chariot driver. "Gahiji, I see more of them. They are up
ahead and a little to the South." The driver pointed
towards a dune. As Gahiji followed his finger he saw
the silhouettes of two figures on top of it.

"No doubt more of the Hebrew stragglers. Do
you think they've seen us yet?" Gahiji asked as he tried
to make out the figures.

"They'd have to be blind to miss us!" his
second exclaimed, "But they look more Kushite than
Hebrew. Should we kill them like the others?"

"Yes, we can't let them alert the Hebrew
multitude to our presence." Gahiji signaled the rest of
the squad to change course towards that dune. "How
are we going to get to them? The chariots cannot climb
the dune of sand, can they?"

"The ground seems to be level in between that
dune and the adjacent one. If we fire a few arrows then
we can scare them to run down the other side and then
snatch them up."

"Can't we just shoot them down with arrows?"
Gahiji suggested with annoyance.

"The bows can't be aimed properly in a moving
chariot, especially at the longest range," he explained,
"The best we can hope for is to shoot near them."

"Alright, you're the captain of your squad. Do
what you deem best." Gahiji agreed. Then he thought
to himself, "Rashidi did say these were the best scouts
in Pharaoh's army."

The second signaled the other four chariots and they prepared for the maneuver. The squad closed in on the figures on top of the sand dune. Once in arrow range, three squad members fired a volley. The arrows missed their targets widely but the figures ran down the other side of the dune. The charioteers drove the horses faster and faster to intercept them.

When they finally made it around the dune they saw that the two figures they had been chasing were Kushite women. As soon as the women saw the chariots, they turned and tried to make their way up the sand dune, but arrows fired from the chariot archers landed above of them and they stopped in their tracks.

"What are you doing?" Gahiji whirled around and glared at the archers. "Aren't they within range for accurate shots now?"

"Do you really aim to kill them?" his second in command asked with a roguish smile.

Then Gahiji's face flashed in understanding. "There are other things we can do with women besides kill them. Perhaps we kill them when we're done."

Gahiji called up to the frightened women, "You two come here! Try to run and you'll be shot to death."

The women approached until they were nearly ten strides from the chariots. They wore large Hebrew robes. Gahiji noticed youthful skin in the sunlight, but a hood obscured her face so he couldn't see if it was pleasant-looking. As Sakakwi's chariot pulled up he felt something oddly familiar about these women but was at a loss for what it was.

The men dismounted from the chariots with lurid grins. An air of fear surrounded the women that only fed the men's lust. Gahiji said as they approached, "If you run or fight back then your deaths will be assured. Now step forward so we can see you."

One woman looked to the other, not knowing what to do. But the other woman stood her ground.

Gahiji raised his voice, "I said step forward."

He stomped over to them, struggling through the sand and lifted the hood of one of them. He took a step back and gasped at who she was. Sakakwi took a step forward, a small smile growing on his face.

"You! I thought you were dead."

The captain approached and said, "Don't worry, after we're done she will be."

Before Gahiji could warn them, three new figures appeared from beneath the sand in the dune behind her. Catching them unaware, three of the men fell immediately. One of the archers tried to nock an arrow to fire, but the large assailant sliced the bow in half with his axe and then used another slash to finish off the archer. The other woman ran out of the way as soon as the fight erupted.

Gahiji found himself defending his skin from a whirlwind of strikes and backed away to escape the daggers. He snarled, "You were supposed to die by the executioner's blade! I'll just have to use mine."

"I'm more than a match for your blades," Nebit retorted and unleashed another attack, meeting stiff resistance and a counter attack.

While Gahiji fought her, the rest of the chariot squad rallied against the other three. They formed ranks with spears at the ready. The captain examined the Egyptian with the khopesh and shield in front of him, the one with a large sword his right, and the stout Kushite man with a mace to his left.

He made a guttural shout and his squad moved to the left with him. They disengaged from the axe-wielder and tried to surround the Kushite. The captain and his comrade on the left made a whirl of attacks against the Kushite, causing superficial wounds, while his other comrade kept the shield-bearing Egyptian locked down with heavy strikes.

The captain took a step back and swung forward, launching himself with his legs in thrust the speed of which not many could match. But before his blade tasted flesh and before he knew what had happened, something hit him in the face and his eyes burned with a fire he had never known before. He felt a strong blow to his head which dropped him to his knees. Unable to see, he flailed around wildly with his khopesh in a desperate attempt to defend any possible incoming attacks, hoping that his comrades would defend him.

Another comrade was also hit by the flying poison dust, though he had missed the bulk of the attack. And so, with burning eyes, he desperately tried to fend off the Kushite's punishing blows.

The two Egyptians punished the other, who frantically tried to defend against both of them, expecting his comrade to support him. The Egyptian with the sword and shield took a step back from the fight, prompting the Egyptian with the axe to do the same.

The charioteer at first breathed a sigh of relief at this respite, but then he realized it must be a ploy and readied himself for the next attack. The one with the khopesh took a step to the side, away from the other one, and the captain knew exactly what they are trying to do.

The first attack came from the sword-bearing attacker on his left. He defended himself and turned his head to see the attack from the other, as expected. After defending, he turned his head, expecting an attack from the first. But it didn't come. Moreover, the Egyptian disappeared.

Knowing he didn't have time to see where the Egyptian had gone, he turned back to the other attacker. As he turned, he saw the attack, but not as he had expected. Instead of attacking with his khopesh, the attacker threw his body forward to push him.

"A risky move," he thought to himself. "As long as I don't fall, he will be open, and I can easily kill him." So he bent his knees into a sturdy stance, expecting only to slide a short distance along the sand.

The impact was harder than he expected, but he was able to keep his balance. He felt himself sliding. However, he felt something behind him preventing his legs from moving. He felt the cold metal on his skin and then realized that he had fallen into their trap, but there was nothing he could do about it.

Tau pushed the captain's waist flush against Yalu's shield. As soon Yalu saw the top half of the captain pushed over him, he braced himself and pushed up. The man's legs left the ground and he started flipping so his head was now pointed at the ground. He managed to keep hold of his khopesh even as he landed head first into the sand and rolled onto his stomach.

Tau dashed toward his prone foe. A quick swipe at the charioteer's defenses sent the khopesh flying. Then Tau delivered the killing blow, securing the first tale of glory requested by his father.

Scanning the battlefield, Yalu saw two more charioteers, but Badru and Tau were keeping them at bay. He remembered there was another man by the chariots, but didn't see him now. He looked over his shoulder and saw Nebit backing away from Gahiji's attacks up the sand dune.

He moved around to be directly behind Gahiji as he approached. Walking up carefully and slowly, he tried not to alert him. Finally, he was within three arms lengths, and he prepared to strike.

Gahiji glanced suddenly over his shoulder and blocked his attack with a khopesh. Nebit took her moment of opportunity to slash at him with her daggers, but Gahiji's other khopesh parried. Gahiji looked frantically to either side to dodge and defend their attacks.

They could see Gahiji was getting tired. He tried to side-step them, but they followed and kept up the pressure with attacks. One mistake on his part and either of them would take advantage of it.

He moved faster, and they advanced faster to keep up with him. Then he firmly planted his right foot into the sand and crouched to the ground. Almost instantly, he launched forward and threw some distracting slashes with his khopeshes. Nebit and Yalu easily defended against his attacks. With the added speed, he tumbled and stood up to turn around.

Gahiji smiled at them, having broken their pincer attack. But the two continued approaching steadily, Yalu on his right and Nebit on his left. Gahiji pointed at them with one of his khopeshes and taunted them with a laugh. At the same time he sidestepped towards Nebit.

At that moment, Nebit's name was called out. They all stopped to look and saw Sakakwi on the top of the sand dune above them. She felt the pain in her chest flare up again. Sakakwi saw her pained look and smiled.

"I knew I was right to come with them," Sakakwi laughed. "The gods sure favor me to lay you right in my lap again. I know not why you threw in your lot with that trash over there, but quit your fighting and come back with me. I promise good living and good pay in return for your services."

As he spoke, her breathing became difficult. She felt a weakness and fell down to her knees as she grasped her chest with a hand. She looked down and the sand became blurry. Then next moment she looked up and Sakakwi was almost right above her.

"You shall not have her!" Yalu shouted. He launched an attack towards Sakakwi. Sakakwi defended with his own khopesh and looked down haughtily upon him.

Sakakwi's eyes lifted up for a second, giving tell of Gahiji's blade aimed for Yalu's back. He blocked with his shield and while the two became embroiled in their own fight, Sakakwi stepped closer to Nebit.

"You know you can't escape. This is the only path you know. Now come along like a good servant." Sakakwi carefully came even closer.

Still clutching her throbbing chest, she glanced over at Yalu. As he fought, she remembered what he told her. She remembered the images of Kasmut's bruised and battered body from the hail. She remembered the words of her late and former master. And she remembered her vow to find a husband and be a protector.

Despite the pain, she stood up and looked Sakakwi in the eye. Hers shown with a determination and fire Sakakwi had not seen before. Then she said, "I choose a different path."

Infuriated at her defiance, Sakakwi shouted, "Then your path ends here!" Then he slashed, summoning all his rage against her.

She took the power of his attack and redirected it upwards with her daggers. Then it was her turn to attack. She went for his face. He dodged but she managed to draw blood on his cheek. This only fueled his rage. After a few more clashes he landed a kick that sent her tumbling down to the bottom of the dune.

As soon as she recovered she saw him bearing down upon her. But she slipped aside and landed a strike of her own against his shin.

Sakakwi howled and lifted his leg instinctively. He looked around and saw Badru not far off. He called and Badru turned to see him. Sakakwi commanded him, "This woman is a traitor. Help me defeat her!"

Badru took a step toward his old friend and then saw Nebit. She stared right into his eyes. Then he looked back to Sakakwi and said, "I have learned there is a lot that you need to account for. And I think the one to whom you need to pay that account to is that woman."

"Worthless excuse for a sorcerer! I'll see you never become chief magician!"

Then he felt a sharp pain in his chest. He looked down to see a dagger sticking out of it. As he fell he looked at Nebit who threw it at him and then skyward. There was a thud as his back hit the sand. His vision started to fade and then darken.

Not far off, Yalu jumped forward and slashed at Gahiji's head. Gahiji defended and swiftly counter-attacked with two blows that Yalu took with his shield. Then he thrust at Gahiji's chest, but was blocked again and countered.

They exchanged a few more blows, and Gahiji realized that none of them had much of an advantage right now: neither could penetrate the other's defense. While delivering the next few blows, Gahiji tried to think of a maneuver that would get him the advantage he needed. Then it came to him. He smirked as he achieved the proper stance and launched himself forward.

Yalu clenched his fist as his shield rang from the latest round of attacks. At first, Gahiji's flurry of attacks surprised him. He could not attack at all because Gahiji forced him to constantly defend with his shield.

Just then, after a particularly hard blow, Yalu noticed a chip at the edge of his shield, and at that moment he realized Gahiji's plan. If this kept up, then Gahiji would slice through his shield and probably take his arm off. Yalu switched to a more balanced defense and tried to favor his khopesh.

Then Yalu's heart jumped up into his throat as he saw Gahiji's perfectly aimed right-handed strike slice into the shield. Relief filled him when it stopped nearly the width of three fingers above his arm. He saw Gahiji ready his other khopesh to use as a hammer to punch through it.

Yalu pushed his shield arm forward. Gahiji lost his balance and his grip on the khopesh. Yalu advanced and attacked as Gahiji defended with his single remaining khopesh.

As Gahiji tossed his khopesh from his left to his right hand, Yalu released the straps on his shield and let it fall to the ground. Then they stood ready, waiting for the other to move. Gahiji engaged and the two exchanged blows.

Gahiji tried a quick stab at Yalu's head but Yalu dodged it and threw a kick at Gahiji's loins. Gahiji saw it coming and brought his foot up to check Yalu's leg in time. Then Yalu grabbed the blade of Gahiji's khopesh with his hand, ignoring a sharp pain from the cut, and lunged forward. With Gahiji out of position because of Yalu's kick he was thrown backward and the packed sand gave little cushion to his fall. They both dropped their remaining weapons.

Yalu tried to pull his hand free from Gahiji's grip in order to strike a killing blow as his other hand bled on the hot desert sand. While Yalu struggled Gahiji moved his leg out and managed to give himself enough leverage to roll, coming out on top of Yalu. Then he smiled maniacally as he pulled himself downward with all of his might, to crush Yalu's face with his forehead.

But Yalu moved his head just in time, and Gahiji got only a face full of sand. But then Yalu felt Gahiji's teeth sinking deep into the base of his neck. Yalu let out a terrifying scream as he writhed in pain, unable to escape.

Gahiji pulled his head up and looked Yalu in the eyes. He smiled showing his bloody teeth as though to gloat. Gahiji spat Yalu's own blood and flesh on his face. In response, Yalu hit Gahiji in the side of his head with the pommel of his khopesh, knocking him over.

Yalu grabbed his khopesh and before Gahiji had the wits to grab his he saw Yalu's pointing toward his face. He backed away from it. But then cursed himself as he realized he was no longer in reach of his khopeshes. Then his back hit a rock and he could no longer escape. He stared down the sharp end of Yalu's khopesh.

"Well, what are you waiting for?" Gahiji hissed. "Haven't I killed enough people to die many times over by now, including your family?"

"He's right," Tau spoke from behind Yalu. "We let him go last time and it ended badly for us. We shouldn't make that same mistake again."

Yalu inched forward with his khopesh. The point of it almost touching Gahiji's nose. He thought about his family. Ever since he came back he wanted nothing else than to see those bandits die. Now he had the one who killed them and thought of what satisfaction it would be to kill him now.

He glanced around. All the charioteers had been killed. The horses were rather restless from the fighting but unharmed. Then he saw Nebit and he took a second look at her. He turned back to Gahiji and lowered his khopesh.

"Ha!" Gahiji snarled. "I knew you were a weak man. Or are you trying to give me some kind of mercy?

I spit on your feeble pity. You should just kill me." And he spat down at Yalu's feet.

But Yalu took no notice and continued looking at him sternly. He said, "You'd like that, wouldn't you? I'm sure that somewhere deep down in your black soul you think that you can make up for all the evil deeds you've committed in your miserable little life. Maybe you think your death will make up for it, somehow. But that's not what I'm going to give you. No! Today, I curse you with life. You must live in the anguish of all the misery you've caused."

Then there was silence. Gahiji's mouth gaped wide open. He looked down as though in thought, but made no move. Yalu backed away slowly, all the while keeping his eyes on his foe.

Nebit ran over to Yalu and smiled with relief. Then she noticed the wound oozing blood on his neck, "Oh Yalu! It looks like a crocodile bit you. And what happened to your hand?!"

Badru called out and his wife uncovered herself with his two daughters from where they hid underneath a large piece of cloth on the sand dune. Then he ran over and examined him. In no position to argue, Yalu submitted to Badru's prodding.

"This is a bad wound," Badru said grimly. "I can see the bone and muscle underneath. I will do my best but you need much rest to recover. If we had an easy way to take him to the multitude it would help."

"What about those?" Tau asked pointing toward the chariots. Two horses attached to each of the three chariots moved restlessly in the hot sun. "Could we just bandage him up here and then ride the rest of the way?"

Suddenly, they heard movement from where Gahiji was sitting. They all whirled around to look at him. Gahiji stood up and was dusting himself off.

Badru looked at the chariots and then looked at Yalu. Then he looked up at Tau and nodded. Yalu rode with Nebit, Badru with his family, and Tau by himself.

Gahiji found himself left all alone. He walked over to the chariot they left behind and grabbed the reigns. He turned and gazed toward the city. He turned and looked forward at the three chariots his enemies' drove. Then he looked down and wondered what he should do now.

Chapter 18

"What do you mean, 'He's not back yet.'?!" Rashidi demanded. The young servant cowered and shook at his master's angry tone. "I sent him with Pharaoh's fastest scouts three days ago. Sakakwi even went with him. He should have returned and reported back by now!"

"I am sorry, Rashidi," he apologized with a deep bow. "I wish I could bring you good news. But this is the truth of it."

"He wouldn't turn to the Hebrews. He's been almost as loyal as. . ." Rashidi trailed off as he momentarily glanced at the empty chair next to him. He almost saw Kasmut's figure sitting in that chair. He'd felt incomplete without her. "He must be unable to come back for some reason." Sitting in silence, he pondered the possibilities.

Then the clean-shaven man sitting on the opposite side of the wooden table broke the silence. "Other advance scouts report that the Hebrew slaves are at Sukkoth right now."

"If we can find out where they are going, then we can send our chariots to meet them and take them back to the city." Rashidi attempted to defend his plan, but realized his words were not persuasive. "If we just march to where they are right now then they will likely be gone by the time we get there."

"And if we wait too long then the slaves will escape our grasp entirely," the man pointed out. He twirled some hair on his wig around his finger. "I know it is not my place to question Pharaoh's chosen servant. If your plan fails, it won't be my execution."

Rashidi scowled with annoyance at the man's remarks. He knew very well the consequences of the decisions. But he also knew it to be unwise to anger the general of Pharaoh's charioteers.

"So what is your decision?" He asked, "Do we march? Or do we wait?"

Feeling cornered, Rashidi swelled with anger. He imagined that the general enjoyed watching him wriggle in his chair. But he could only think of one proper response.

So he took a deep breath and said, "You are the highest ranking military official. I suppose it would be unwise not to take your recommendation. Let us march to Sukkoth and if the Hebrew slaves have moved we will need to rely on our scouts to determine where to march next. With luck we won't waste too much time mobilizing them."

Watching the frown appear on the general's face replenished Rashidi's spirit. This political Bao had many possible moves. He hoped this move would allow him to share blame with the general if things didn't go as planned. He might even escape Pharaoh's capital punishment.

"Then I shall give word to muster the chariots. Shall I assume you will tell Pharaoh personally?" he asked.

Rashidi agreed with a nod, and the general left his manor and rode his chariot to the barracks. Rashidi gathered his personal bodyguards and the rest of the soldiers he employed. As they all marched to the palace, they saw some odd clouds forming in the distance to the East.

The morning sun shone gently on the tents below. The clouds forming above them allowed the sunlight through every once in a while, although briefly.

A sudden gust of wind blew, tossing Badru's robes back and forth as he gazed out at the Hebrew encampment.

Suddenly he heard his name called. He looked and saw Tau who ran up to him.

"Your wife is looking for you. They say we'll be going soon."

Badru nodded. He took a deep breath and released it. Then he said, "Just look at all those tents! No wonder Pharaoh didn't want to let them go. There are so many people."

Tau beheld the sight with Badru for a moment.

"And there is the Lake of Timsah just beyond the town of Etham. Do you know why this place is so special?"

"Because it's a small town nearby a lake?" Tau guessed.

"Besides that, they have a very important export to the city."

Badru continued on and pointed to the men and women at the banks of the lake. "Here they gather all the salt we use in the city. Haji told me that the goddess Sekhemet fought a great battle for Pharaoh long ago on these very grounds. She cursed the land with salt so that nothing would grow."

Tau grunted in response. Then he said, "Look, I don't want your wife to be mad at me again. Let's go."

Badru nodded again and followed Tau back to the encampment.

They passed the small wooden palisade that surrounded the town. Ahead of them, the Hebrew encampment stretched far out among the plains. As they entered camp they saw everyone taking down their animal-hide tents and packing their belongings.

Entering Nun's area, they saw Yalu and Nebit leaning against packed wagons. Lior was there speaking with them. Yadid gave instructions to other servants but Nun and Hoshea were not around. Badru's wife was fussing with his daughters.

"What luck the both of you have!" Yalu shouted to them. "We've already finished most of the work under taskmaster Yadid's whip."

Yadid stopped talking long enough to give Yalu a dirty look and the other servants tried to muffle their laughter.

Nebit cocked her head and grinned roguishly, "Except weren't you the one making excuses to avoid all his work?"

Yalu turned red and touched the bandage around the base of his neck, "They're not excuses! I still need to recover from my wounds."

Nebit smiled with arms folded under her chest and shook her head at him. Lior shook his head and laughed.

Suddenly, a thunderclap surprised them from above. A furious movement of the clouds captured the attention of everyone in the camp. The clouds coalesced into one single and giant cloud. It reached up before them as a pillar for holding up the sky, and more clouds stretched out to cover them as a roof.

Whispers arose from the Southern end of the camp. Then they heard a shout:

"It is the Lord!"

They all looked up at the cloud in amazement with everyone else.

Looking up at the huge column, Yalu's mouth gaped open and he muttered, "Flesh and fire."

"So where is he?" Tau asked loudly, putting his hand over his eyes to help him see better. "I don't see Him."

"What?" Yadid exclaimed and broke his heavenward gaze. Then he answered, "In the cloud up there."

"Where in the cloud? I don't see him." Tau squinted his eyes, hoping to get a glimpse.

"He's not in the cloud, he is the cloud," said one of the other servants.

Tau stared at the cloud with his mouth gaping open. Then he turned to the man and shouted, "Go jump in the Nile! Do you take me for a dull blade? Are you saying that this Hebrew god is a cloud?"

"No, our god isn't a cloud," Yadid admonished Tau and shook his head. "But he is within the cloud, all the same."

"I'm looking in it and I don't see him!"

"Perhaps this cloud was sent directly by the Hebrew god," Badru suggested. Then he looked up at the cloud again. "Never before in all my life have I seen clouds forming like this." Everyone else looked up with him.

A call rang out and was carried by the multitude of people: "Time to move." Eventually they saw the people far ahead of them start to move. Slowly at first, but almost before they knew it, they were at a full walking pace.

Badru looked over to the salty lakes as he passed.

"In all my years I never questioned. Should I have?" He wondered. On a whim, Badru gazed out to the West and saw a familiar dust cloud in the distance. He muttered under his breath, "Chariots."

The cloud above continued to lead them south. The wilderness passed by on the left as the desert passed by on the right. A warm breeze flowed from behind them and gently urged them forward. At the same time, the cloud above shielded the people from the harsh, overhead sun.

Rashidi wiped the sweat from his brow with a small white cloth. He could feel the heat radiating from the top of the pavilion. Pharaoh sat on a large wooden throne in the middle, like a boat floating above his sprawling sea of chariots. At each corner of Pharaoh's throne, a servant boy waved a large fan of ostrich feathers to keep him in a pleasant coolness, although one would have thought they pumped a bellows, from the way he complained.

The sun had already passed the midpoint of the sky, and now journeyed back toward the Earth. Rashidi spotted a chariot squad approaching the encampment from the South. He smiled to himself as he glanced over at Pharaoh, who was too busy fussing with the servant boys to notice. So Rashidi casually walked to the Southern end of the pavilion and waited for the charioteers to arrive.

The chariot squad stopped a respectable distance from the tent. The men dismounted, and made their approach. To Rashidi's dismay, the general of Pharaoh's chariots left the comfort of the pavilion to meet them. This kind of competitiveness was infuriating and petty. Nevertheless, he kept smiling.

The general returned to the pavilion and approached Pharaoh, with Rashidi following behind. They both knelt and prostrated themselves before Pharaoh, who gestured to them to speak.

"My Pharaoh, the scouts have reported the Hebrew multitude on the edge of the wilderness heading south," the general said.

"South," Pharaoh repeated with curiosity. "Why in the name of the gods would they go there? Nothing but desert and sea awaits them. If they truly wanted to escape they would head north. They are either lost, or Moses intends to lead them to death in this heat."

The general waited until Pharaoh took a breath, and then interjected, "That is not all; they seem to be traveling underneath a strange cloud. The cloud moves south as well. They may just be trying to follow the cloud to avoid the hot sun."

"Whatever the reason, they shall feel the heat of our spears and arrows soon enough. Make ready our chariots!" Pharoah commanded. "Where and when will we intercept them?"

"We should overtake them tomorrow at dusk near the tip of the Sea of Reeds nearby the town of Migdol," he answered.

Then Pharaoh gave the order, and the general relayed it to the troops. Pharoah's servants took down the pavilion as the charioteers made their horses and weapons ready. Pharaoh left the pavilion and stepped onto his golden chariot, and Rashidi stepped into another one nearby. Then the sea of chariots parted in the middle as Pharaoh, Rashidi, the general, and Pharaoh's personal guard made their way through.

Finally arriving at the southern end, Pharaoh gave the order to continue their pursuit as the sun continued its descent towards the Earth. At the head of the company around Pharaoh, they rode eight chariots side-by-side, and then it changed to four chariots wide further back. Looking backward, Rashidi was reminded of a serpent. Swiftly slithering along the ground, the Egyptian snake stalked its Hebrew prey.

The sun finally touched the Earth, and rays of red and gold shone forth. The clouds above changed color to royal shades of purple. Suddenly, the wind died down and the cloud stopped moving. The Hebrew multitude stopped and looked skyward in confusion. As the sun set, its last ray of light touched the cloud as if it were flint and tinder to an oil-soaked torch. The cloud lit up and glowed as though all the campfires in Egypt were gathered together.

"It's warm," Nebit reached a hand toward the cloud. The others felt it too, as they all stood staring up into the glow with dumbfounded expressions.

The Northern wind picked up again, and more murmuring from the multitude arose. The cloud started moving southward again, and once again the call to move spread among the people.

"Such a display of power. Simply amazing!" Badru exclaimed, a hand raised. He looked down at his wife, who nodded. His daughters just stood with mouths gaping open.

"I'm amazed too," Tau said as they saw people in the distance start walking. "But why change from a cloud of. . . clouds, to a cloud of fire? Won't it make sleeping more difficult?"

"Yes, that would, unless. . ." Yalu rubbed his chin with his fingers. "Unless the Hebrew god plans for us to walk day and night."

"Day and night?" Nebit exclaimed in disbelief. "We'll wear ourselves out! Doesn't that Hebrew god know we need sleep at night? Even the taskmasters don't work the slaves this hard."

"That is true," Yadid said as they started to walk. "But tell me, what is the hour? Are you tired or sleepy yet?"

"Well...." Nebit started, "Now that you mention it, this is strange. With all the walking we've done so far I don't feel tired at all."

"Even with my injury I'm not really tired either," Yalu added. "Is the Hebrew God giving us strength?"

Nebit released a sigh and shook her head as she gazed toward the bright burning cloud above them.

The cloud lit up the night sky as a beacon. A red glow came slowly into view along the southeastern horizon: the Egyptian snake.

Pharaoh turned to Rashidi and asked with a pointed finger, "What is that? Not campfires, is it?" For a long moment, everyone stared at the southern sky in silence. Men murmured under their breath, asking what god must have caused such a thing.

Taking advantage of Rashidi's hesitation, the general answered, "No amount of campfires could make a light such as that. But it looks to be in the same location as the Hebrew slaves."

"Perhaps it is another boon from their god," Rashidi finally said. He gave the general a sharp eye, "He provides light to them in the dark of night to aid their escape. He plans to march them through the night."

"Through the night?" The general exclaimed, "but then by morning we will be have much ground to make up."

"Not if we ride through the night as well." Rashidi replied with grin.

"But," he tried to defend himself, "the horses will be too exhausted if we do that! If we recover our strength we can follow them with renewed vigor."

"We cannot lose them after the work spent mustering the chariots to pursue them." Pharaoh announced, "If they march through the night, then so shall we. It will take more than tricks with fire to escape me."

Pharaoh gave the order, and chariots began riding again toward the Sea of Reeds and closer to the Hebrew assembly with the burning clouds above it. Halfway through the night, they were finally close enough to see the cloud of fire itself.

The people of the town west of them assembled to look as well. They also watched the royal procession of chariots. The town sat on a hill that sloped down to the sea. The Hebrew multitude stood near the water's edge.

"There they are, Rashidi," Pharaoh pointed toward them. "Go round up my slaves and bring them back. Try not to kill too many of them."

"Yes, my Pharaoh. It is as good as done."

Rashidi clenched his hand to a fist and raised it high in the air. The chariot squad leaders organized the troops and built a line stretching out on either side of him as far as he could see.

While the troops still organized themselves, the general spoke to Rashidi.

"This is good. We have them pinned against the sea of Reeds. There is no escape for them."

Rashidi smiled from ear to ear as he realized his task was nearly complete. He waited patiently for the line to form again. By now, the Hebrew slaves had noticed them and Rashidi could see them running about in panic.

"Look at them! They are like rats on a sinking ship. Now they realize Moses led them into a trap and soon they will be swallowed up by the water snake."

Once the line of chariots had formed, Rashidi glanced back one last time to Pharaoh, who stood in his chariot with his arms folded. Fifteen of his personal guards surrounded him. Then he nodded to Rashidi: the gesture for him to begin. Rashidi raised his fist high into the air and shouted for the chariots to charge. The squad leaders took up the call, and soon all of the chariots rose forward against the throng of Hebrews below.

They rode hard down the hill. The hard-packed sand made for excellent terrain to maneuver the chariots. Small shrubs were trampled under horse and wheel. As they reached the bottom of the hill, Rashidi didn't even notice the clouds above move toward them.

"What in the name of the gods. . .?" He mouthed, as the cloud descended in front of them. The light that had been as bright as day moments ago, vanished, leaving only darkness in its wake. The line of chariots wavered and eventually stopped before the cloud.

"What is this sorcery? Did Moses command the cloud to shield them?" The general asked. He looked at one of the charioteers nearby and ordered him, "Go into the cloud to see if it is safe."

The man's face showed his terror. He shook his head and replied,

"You can whip me for disobedience later, sir. But I'm not getting close to that thing. It was like fire before, and I don't want to enter an inferno."

"What about a horse?" Rashidi tried again with a hint of annoyance, "Send in a horse and see what happens. Sure, it was like fire before but now it looks like an ordinary cloud."

The charioteer reluctantly complied. As he hopped down from the chariot, all the others nearby watched to see what would happen. He unburdened one of the horses from the yoke of the chariot. Leading it toward the cloud, he whacked its hind quarters with the blunt end of his spear to send it galloping forward.

But as the horse neared the cloud, it stopped quickly, throwing its head back and forth. Then it dashed to the right, in between the cloud and the line of chariots. The other charioteers gasped in surprise.

The general only laughed.

Rashidi turned to him.

"Why are you laughing? Do you have a better plan to get through the cloud?!"

The general grunted. He didn't even look at Rashidi, which only infuriated him more. The anger burned hotter than anything he had ever felt before.

Then they heard Pharaoh's voice from behind them, "What is it? What is going on? What happened to the cloud of fire?"

They turned and saw Pharaoh with his guards.

"The cloud protects them," Rashidi answered.

Pharaoh raised eyebrow and folded his arms. "That wispy cloud keeps you from reclaiming my slaves?"

Rashidi's face flushed red as he realized his foolishness. "The cloud was filled with fire not long ago. We dare not enter the cloud for fear of burning up. Even the horses won't go near it!"

"I see..." Pharaoh replied. "General, what is your assessment?"

"I agree with your servant Rashidi," the general replied. "It's too dangerous to ride through the cloud, even if the horses would allow it."

"And what course of action would you recommend, general?" Pharaoh asked.

The general answered bluntly, "If this task were assigned to me then I would send riders down each side of the cloud and see if it goes all the way around to the water. If not, we should go around the cloud there."

Pharaoh looked back at Rashidi, who silently stared at the ground, clenching his fists. Then he looked back at the general.

"Do it, and report to me immediately if you find passage beyond the cloud."

The general gave the order, and chariots rode out on either side of the cloud. As they rode, Rashidi desperately tried to think of what to do next. Finally, they returned with a report.

"My Pharaoh," the charioteer began, "There is no passage. It even extends some distance over the water."

"There is another way we can get to them. With the town so close, we can force the villagers to make rafts from the reeds near the water. We could ferry our army across," Rashidi proposed.

"We couldn't make enough rafts for everyone. And if we only make a few rafts then our men would be overwhelmed as soon as they walk ashore."

"If circumstances were normal, you would be right." Rashidi grinned as he saw his advantage over the general. "But we have a latent poison within the body of the Hebrew slaves. The priests of Ptah have sown seeds: men able to help us. Once they see us they would surely come to our aid."

"Yes, wise Rashidi has spoken again," Pharaoh smiled. "Go to the town and rouse them. Have every able-bodied man making reed rafts for my army. When the sun rises we shall attack."

"Let us also separate the charioteers and have some of them help make rafts," Rashidi continued. "The best warriors we let rest while the others make rafts."

"Very good," Pharaoh signaled for his chariots to go. "I will rest now and leave this matter in your capable hands."

Rashidi bowed low to Pharaoh as he took leave to his pavilion. Then Rashidi sat up and sighed. He started thinking about how to organize the town even while he felt fatigued from lack of rest himself. His confidence slowly returned as the plan solidified in his mind.

As soon as the plan came together Rashidi started giving orders. He found out which charioteers had boating experience, and allowed them to rest. As they rode to the town, they saw that the crowd had already mostly dispersed. Rashidi ordered the charioteers to enter the homes and bring out all potential laborers.

Carrying torches, the soldiers went house to house. Some of the houses were made of mud-bricks, and others were made from reeds bound tightly together. Distractedly, Rashidi noticed one of the huts' lit ablaze from a charioteer who had waved his torch rather carelessly.

In a little less than half of an hour later, the townsfolk were all assembled, and Rashidi marched everyone to the nearest patch of reeds near the sea. They started clearing it, and then Rashidi directed half of the townsfolk to carry the reeds back to an area of flat and dry ground where they were to start binding the reeds together.

Couriers constantly brought reeds back from the gatherers. Hours went by, and rafts filled the shoreline. Soon, Rashidi could see the light of dawn approaching. In the twilight, he directed the rest of the gatherers to help the builders finish. Walking to Pharaoh's pavilion, he counted fifty rafts.

The guards allowed him to whisper through the fabric of Pharaoh's tent. "Pharaoh, it is time." Convinced he hadn't spoken loud enough, he repeated himself. Without warning the entrance flap was thrown open and Pharaoh stood there.

"I heard you the first time," Pharaoh adjusted his wig and walked out. "I could not sleep. A thorn in my mind would not let me rest. But I am sure once the slaves are back in my possession, then rest will return to me."

They both met the general, who had already roused the charioteers chosen for the attack. The first ray of sunlight shone upon the land, and the cloud lifted.

Pharaoh, Rashidi, the general, all of the charioteers, and the townsfolk stared, half in disbelief and half in wonder. Beyond, lay the Hebrew congregation, rapidly diminishing.

The general broke the trance, "Gear up! Prepare the horses and the chariots! Make ready to ride!" The squad leaders relayed the general's orders and the charioteers did as he said. In a matter of moments, the chariots were ready and the general stood on his chariot to lead them.

Then Pharaoh raised his hand, and everyone stopped what they were doing. He lowered it and pointed toward Rashidi. "My good servant Rashidi shall be the one to retake my slaves. They are his responsibility and he deserves to lead the chariots."

Rashidi raised his voice so he could be heard. "I gladly accept this responsibility you bestow upon me. I shall return with your slaves!" His chariot driver maneuvered the chariot next to the general's.

The general leaned over and asked quietly, "I suppose you'll want me to stand out of this charge? You don't want me to share any of your glory do you?"

"Not at all. I appreciate your presence at my side as I lead Pharaoh's chariots," Rashidi replied smugly as the general frowned and grunted in response.

Rashidi looked at the newly-formed line of chariots on either side of him. A knot tied itself in his stomach. He wiped the sweat from his forehead with his white cloth and took a couple of deep breaths. Then he raised his hand and looked around. All eyes looked to him, awaiting his command. He took one more breath, and waved his hand forward. The charioteers moved forward with him as though they were an extension of his own body.

They rode hard to close the distance, but the closer they got, the farther away the Hebrew host was.

What is going on? Are they escaping into the sea? Rashidi wondered. *If so, then we can take their possessions and their. . . Oh no!* Rashidi gasped. *They aren't swimming to boats are they? We may have underestimated Moses.*

The chariots neared. Finally, the method of escape came into view. At this close distance, all the charioteers could feel the wind on their faces. And then, one by one, they slowed and stopped. Everyone's mouth gaped as wide as it could in amazement.

Ahead of them, lay dry earth in the place where the sea of Reeds should have been. The soil stretched for half the length of the line of chariots. The path extended onward with walls of water on either side, shallow near the beach, but taller farther into the sea. The clouds above moved about furiously as the wind threw itself down to the ground.

"What... is this?" Rashidi muttered, "What are we to do when the water throws itself out of the way for the Hebrews to escape?"

"Well, the ground looks dry enough," the general observed. "Perhaps we should follow them."

"Follow?!" Rashidi exclaimed, "How can we follow them through that?! I don't think Pharaoh himself would follow them through. . . through. . . that!" He pointed at the giant walls of water to prove his point.

"Then shall I retreat back to Pharaoh and inform him that you are going to let his slaves escape?" The general asked with a grin.

Rashidi pursed his lips and scrunched his nose as he looked back toward the dirt path through the sea. It was this moment when the general made him the angriest. Not because the general was wrong, but because he was right and Rashidi knew it.

"No, we follow them." Rashidi said defiantly.

The general continued, "Are you sure it safe enough to. . ."

"You," Rashidi interrupted. "You, General, will go first. Didn't you say that the ground looks dry enough for a chariot to ride through?" Rashidi turned his head and fixed his gaze on the general's eyes: the eyes of a true warrior, hardened by the cruel realities of battle.

Even in the face of such terrible wonders, his courage didn't waver. Without a word, the general assumed his role, and with a wave of his hand, he led the chariots forward. Rashidi followed behind, and the army of chariots cautiously rode forward. The general's chariot entered the riverbed first. The wind from above had completely dried the ground, and the chariot rolled over it with ease. Then he forced his horses to gallop forward, and the other chariots followed him.

The Hebrew throng had a large lead ahead of them, but the chariots gained on them quickly. Rashidi's chariot hit a rock embedded in the ground, and the force of it knocked his wig loose. The wind picked it up and blew it away. He tried to grab it, but it slipped through his fingers, and the chariots behind him trampled it into the ground.

"No time to mourn my loss now," Rashidi said to himself, as the wind whipped around his bald head. "I can buy myself a new one with the reward Pharaoh will give me." He looked forward, just as the last Hebrew exited the riverbed. "Another minute and they will be ours!"

At that moment, something happened which he had dreaded in his heart from the moment he had seen the wondrous parting of the waves. He no longer felt the wind blowing down on him. Then he heard a roar, a roar as he had never heard before nor ever would again. He felt like a tiny little ant at the whim of beings larger than he could possibly imagine.

He knew this was the end and he thought of his dear wife, Kasmut. How did she feel when she was caught in storm of hail? Was it anything like this? Would he be able to see her in the afterlife? The walls of water on either side of him crashed down with all the might of an intemperate sea.

Pharaoh stood in his chariot. The tassels of his wig rested limply, with the absence of the wind. The golden rod in his hand and crowns on his head made him appear as a god. Without a hint of expression, he watched as the walls of water crashed down onto his army of chariots. He stood like an Egyptian god, taught his own divinity from his youth, watching the mortals far beneath him bob up and down in the water.

And so, he watched in horror as all the plans he set in motion lay ruined before him. The men around him cried out with misery. But he remained silent, calm, and defeated. Then he gave the order to pack up his royal pavilion and to leave.

The congregation of his Hebrew slaves cheered and danced and sang joyously in triumph on the other side, but Pharaoh could not hear them over the crashing of the sea. The side of his lip twitched. He looked upon the unused rafts on the beach and then the horrified townsfolk nearby. In minutes, bodies of men and horses began washing up on the shore. Wreckage of wooden chariots floated on the surface of the water. They moved with the rising and falling of the waves.

The handful of royal guards at his side gathered around him.

He turned to them and commanded, "Take me back to my white walls."

At first they just stared at him. He repeated his words more earnestly, and they begin tearing down his pavilion. He looked one last time at the people he once called slaves, and heaved a long and forlorn sigh.

As Yalu stood on the Eastern shore of the Sea of Reeds, he watched the water cover Pharoah's army. Loud cheers and cries of joy erupted from the people all around them. Nebit threw her arms around him as she joined the celebration.

"I just had a thought," Yalu told her. "Things could have happened differently and we could have been part of Pharaoh's army pursuing the Hebrew slaves. And we would be buried underneath all that water too."

"It's a good thing that didn't happen," Nebit smiled at him warmly. "We are sure better off here. We may not have the comforts we're used to but at least we have a god who protects us."

"When I saw Pharaoh's chariots behind us, I was sure they were going to catch us!" Yalu returned her smile. "With all we've been through, I should have realized that the Hebrew god wouldn't lead us out here just to be captured by Pharaoh again."

Nebit shuddered, "I can only imagine what they'd to do us if that happened."

"Yes, I'm also glad." Yalu's mother smiled and put her hands on each of their shoulders. "Now, perhaps there is time for more important matters as we discuss your future." Both faces of Nebit and Yalu flushed red.

Then Lior approached them. He smiled as saw the two of them together.

"The future. I won't pretend to know the future. But I think that whatever happens you two will be better for the decision you made."

Yalu and Nebit turned and looked into each
other's eyes.

Tau gazed at them feeling forlorn with a sharp
pain in the bottom of his chest. Just then, he felt a tug
on his arm. He looked down into Sarah's deep brown
eyes. "Come with me," she urged him.

"Why?" Tau protested, "Where?"

"Moses' sister is organizing the women to sing
and dance," she answered while pulling on him with all
her strength. He did not budge.

"So what," Tau replied.

"So I want you to watch me!" she shouted at
him with exasperation. Finally, he gave in and followed
her through the crowd. Badru and the others watched
him leave, and laughed to themselves.

Badru shifted his gaze to look into the deep
brown eyes of his own wife. She looked at him with
confusion and uncertainty. He wanted to quiet her
fears and give her the security she longed for. But he
knew that this was neither the time nor the place.

Just then, someone bumped into Nebit, causing
her to stumble to the ground. "Watch yourself! Can't
you see where you're going?" She shouted at him as
Yalu helped her up.

The man apologized, "I was carried away by all
the excitement."

"Wait a minute," Yalu walked over to him.
"You look familiar. Do I know you from somewhere?"

The man looked at them and thought for a
moment. Suddenly a look of remembrance flashed
across his face, followed closely by dismissal. "No, I
don't think we've met before." Just then, one of the
folds of his turban came loose and he took a moment
to tighten it back up.

"Are you sure?" Yalu pressed, "I'm almost
certain I've seen your face before."

"Yes, I'm quite sure. We've never bumped into. . . I mean met before. Now if you'll excuse me, I need to be going. . . somewhere. . . else."

The man faded into the crowd as though escaping, while the group stood there and shook their heads.

At about that time, Hoshea grabbed Badru's shoulder. "What are you doing out here near the water? Come and join the celebration! We have food and drink. Where's Tau?"

"He's. . ." Badru paused to choose the right words. "That is, the servant girl Sarah already pulled him into the celebration."

"I see," he replied. "Well now it's your turn!"

Before he followed Hoshea with the others, Yalu gazed out once more over the waters still roaring and tumultuous. He gasped with his mouth gaping open. A tear escaped his eye as he beheld the sight. Hovering above the waters, shimmering in pale blue and wearing the dress he liked so much, was his wife. Her face was soft and looked upon him with a smile. Beside her, his father stood, tall and proud. Next to him was his older brother, the same arrogant look adorning his face that Yalu always remembered.

They raised a hand to him. He nodded to them in reply. Then they turned and walked back, across the waters, toward Egypt, where they belonged. Soon they disappeared from his sight. Yalu wiped his face with a hand and brushed the wetness on the shenti covering his waist.

Giving in to Nebit's tugging, he came alongside her, behind Hoshea and joined the celebration. As they did, a pair of spiteful and menacing eyes peered out from beneath a dark hood. He watched the festivity around him, completely immune to its contagious effect. When he felt a hand on his shoulder, he turned and recognized his comrade. "What do we do now? This wasn't supposed to happen."

"We make the best of it," Gahiji answered. "There is no chance that this many people can survive wandering in the desert on their own. It is only a matter of time before these wretched slaves run out of food and water. Eventually, they will come crawling back to Egypt, begging to be our slaves again because that will be better than dying of hunger and thirst. Come, we have work to do."

And as they went, they found the other priests and soldiers loyal to them. The oblivious multitude continued to celebrate joyously. Moses and his sister led the Hebrew people, as well as the Egyptians who followed them, in song, describing the victory of their God over the Egyptian taskmasters. Pharaoh returned back to his palace in defeat, and the children of Israel ventured victoriously in exodus of Egypt to the wilderness, with just a glimpse of the future wrought by the God of the Slaves.

About the Author

Kris Murray is a Software professional currently residing in Northern California. He regularly attends weekly worship services at a church where he helps out with music. He is also a member of Bible Study Fellowship where he's volunteered teaching the Bible in the children's program.

About the Publisher

Philip Conrod is the President & Publisher of BibleByte Books which is a publishing imprint of Kidware Software LLC. BibleByte Books publishes academic textbooks for Christian schools, homeschools and lay leaders. BibleByte Books also publishes a video game design, development and computer programming tutorial textbooks which teaches students how to design, develop and publish their own Bible inspired video games. BibleByte Books & Games is based in Maple Valley, Washington

http://www.BibleByteBooks.com.

BibleByte Games also publishes a video game inspired by the characters and events found in Exodus: God of the Slaves. The video game, Exodus Vigil, is available for purchase on the publisher's website:

http://www.BibleByteGames.com.